Matthew Reilly was born in Sydney in 1974 and studied Law at the University of New South Wales. He has written both screenplays and magazine articles and has also directed three short films. He lives in Sydney. *Ice Station* is his second novel.

MATTHEW REILLY

ICE
STATION

PAN BOOKS

Originally published in 1998 by Pan Macmillan Australia
First published in Great Britain 2000 by Pan Books

an imprint of Macmillan Publishers Ltd
25 Eccleston Place, London SW1W 9NF
Basingstoke and Oxford
Associated companies throughout the world
www.macmillan.co.uk

ISBN 0 330 37399 4

15 17 19 18 16 14

A CIP catalogue record for this book is available from
the British Library.

Typeset by SetSystems Ltd, Saffron Walden, Essex
Printed and bound in Great Britain by
Mackays of Chatham plc, Chatham, Kent

For Natalie

ACKNOWLEDGEMENTS

Special thanks to Natalie Freer – the most genuine and giving person I know. To Stephen Reilly, my brother and my good friend, and my loyal supporter, even from thousands of miles away. To Mum for her comments on the text and to Dad for his woeful title suggestions and to both of them for their love and support. And, lastly, thanks to everyone at Pan (in particular, my editors, Cate Paterson and Madonna Duffy, first, for 'discovering' me and second, for enduring all of my crazy ideas). To all of you, never underestimate the power of your encouragement.

SOUTH-EASTERN ANTARCTICA

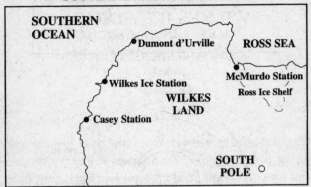

SOUTHERN OCEAN

Dumont d'Urville

ROSS SEA

Wilkes Ice Station

McMurdo Station

WILKES LAND

Ross Ice Shelf

Casey Station

SOUTH POLE

THE ANTARCTIC ICE SHELF

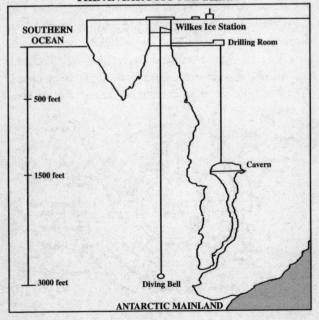

SOUTHERN OCEAN

Wilkes Ice Station

Drilling Room

500 feet

1500 feet

Cavern

3000 feet

Diving Bell

ANTARCTIC MAINLAND

WILKES ICE STATION
WILKES LAND, ANTARCTICA

A-deck

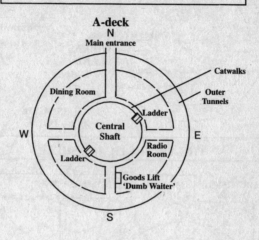

B-deck

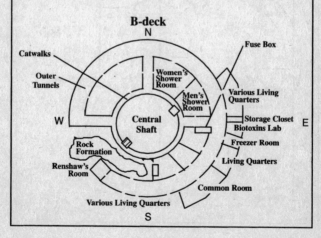

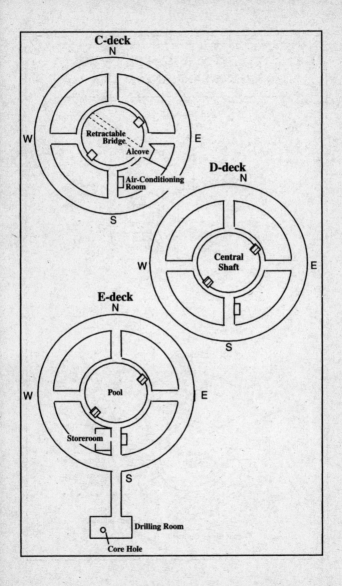

INTRODUCTION

From: **Kendrick, Jonathan**
The Cambridge Lectures: Antarctica –
The Living Continent
(Lecture delivered at Trinity College,
17 March, 1995)

'Imagine, if you can, a continent that for one quarter of the year, doubles in size. A continent in a constant state of motion, motion that is *undetectable* to the human eye, but that is devastating nonetheless.

Imagine if you were to look down from the heavens at this vast, snow-covered mass. You would see the signatures of motion: the sweeping waves of the glaciers, bending in curves around mountains, falling down slopes like cascading waterfalls captured on film.

This is the "awesome inertia" that Eugene Linden spoke of. And if we, like Linden, imagine that we are looking at that picture through *time-lapse photography*, taken over thousands of years, then we will *see* that motion.

Thirty centimetres of movement every year doesn't look like much in real time, but in time-lapse, glaciers become flowing rivers of ice, ice that moves with free-flowing grace and awesome, unstoppable power.

Awesome? I hear you scoff. *Thirty centimetres a year? What possible harm could that do?*

A lot of harm to your tax dollars, I would say. Did you know that the British government has had to replace Halley Station on *four* separate occasions? You see, like many other Antarctic research stations, Halley Station is built underground, buried in the ice but a mere thirty centimetres of shift every year cracks its walls and drastically skews its ceilings.

The point here is that the walls of Halley Station are under a lot of pressure, a *lot* of pressure. All of that ice, moving outwards from the pole, moving inexorably toward the sea, it *wants* to get to the sea – to see the world, you might say, *as an iceberg* – and it isn't going to let something as insignificant as a *research station* get in its way!

But then again, comparatively speaking, Britain has come off rather well when it comes to dramatic ice movement.

Consider when, in 1986, the Filchner Ice Shelf calved an iceberg the size of Luxembourg into the Weddell Sea. Thirteen *thousand* square kilometres of ice broke free of the mainland . . . taking with it the abandoned Argentine base station, Belgrano I, and the Soviet summer station, Druzhnaya. The Soviets, it seems, had planned to use Druzhnaya that summer. As it turned out, they spent the next three months searching for their missing base among the three massive icebergs that had formed out of the original ice movement! And they found it. Eventually.

The United States has been even less fortunate. *All five* of its 'Little America' research stations floated out to sea on icebergs in the sixties.

Ladies and gentlemen, the message to be taken from all of this is quite simple. What *appears* to be barren, may not really be so. What *appears* to be a wasteland, may not really be so. What *appears* to be lifeless, may not really be so.

No. For when you look at Antarctica, *do not be fooled.* You are not looking at an ice-covered rock. You are looking at a living, *breathing* continent.'

From: Goldridge, William
       Watergate
       (New York, Wylie, 1980)

'CHAPTER 6: THE PENTAGON

. . . What the literature is oddly silent about, however, is the strong bond Richard Nixon forged with his military advisers, most notably an Air Force Colonel named Otto Niemeyer . . .' [p. 80]

'. . . After Watergate, however, no one is quite sure what happened to Niemeyer. He was Nixon's liaison to the Joint Chiefs of Staff, his insider. Having risen to the rank of full colonel by the time Nixon resigned,

Niemeyer had enjoyed what few people could ever lay claim to: Richard Nixon's ear.

What *is* surprising, however, is that after Nixon's resignation in 1974, not much can be found in the statute books regarding Otto Niemeyer. He remained on the Joint Chiefs of Staff under Ford and Carter, a silent player, keeping much to himself, until 1979, when abruptly, his position became vacant.

No explanation was ever given by the Carter Administration for Niemeyer's removal. Niemeyer was unmarried; some suggested, homosexual. He lived at the military academy at Arlington, alone. He had few people who openly claimed to be his friends. He travelled frequently, often to "destinations unknown", and his work colleagues thought nothing of his absence from the Pentagon for a few days in December of 1979.

The problem was, Otto Niemeyer never returned . . .'
[p. 86]

ICE STATION

PROLOGUE

It had been three hours now since they'd lost radio contact with the two divers.

There had been nothing wrong with the descent, despite the fact that it was so deep. Price and Davis were the most experienced divers at the station, and they had talked casually over the intercom the whole way down.

After pausing halfway to re-pressurize, they had continued down to three thousand feet where they had left the diving bell and begun their diagonal ascent into the narrow, ice-walled cavern.

Water temperature had been stable at 1.9° Celsius. As recently as two years previously, Antarctic diving had been restricted by the cold to extremely shortlived, and scientifically speaking, extremely unsatisfactory, ten-minute excursions. However, with their new Navy-made thermal-electric suits, Antarctic divers could now expect to maintain comfortable body temperatures for at least three hours in the near-freezing waters of the continent.

The two divers had maintained steady conversation

9

over the intercom as they made their way up the steep underwater ice tunnel; describing the cracked, rough texture of the ice, commenting on its rich, almost angelic, sky-blue colour.

And then, abruptly, their talking had stopped.

They had spotted the surface.

The two divers stared at the water's surface from below.

It was dark, the water calm. Unnaturally calm. Not a ripple broke its glassy, even plane. They swam upward.

Suddenly they heard a noise.

The two divers stopped.

At first it was just a single, haunting whistle, echoing through the clear, icy water. Whale song, they thought.

Possibility: killers. Recently, a pod of killer whales had been seen lurking about the station. A couple of them – two juvenile males – had made a habit of coming up for air inside the pool at the base of Wilkes Ice Station.

More likely, however, it was a blue, singing for a mate, maybe five or six miles offshore. That was the problem with whale song. Water was such a great conductor, you could never tell if the whale was one mile away or ten.

Their minds reassured, the two divers continued upward.

It was then that the first whistle was answered.

All at once, about a dozen similar whistles began to

coo across the dense aquatic plane, engulfing the two divers. They were louder than the first whistle.

Closer.

The two divers spun about in every direction, hovering in the clear blue water, searching for the source of the noise. One of them unslung his harpoon gun and cocked the hammer and suddenly the high-pitched whistles turned into pained wails and barks.

And then suddenly, there came a loud *whump!* and both divers snapped upward just in time to see the glassy surface of the water break into a thousand ripples as something large plunged into the water from above.

The enormous diving bell broke the surface with a loud splash.

Benjamin K. Austin strode purposefully around the water's edge barking orders, a black, insulated wetsuit stretched tight across his broad, barrel chest. Austin was a marine biologist from Stanford. He was also the chief of station of Wilkes Ice Station.

'All right! Hold it there!' Austin called to the young technician manning the winch controls on C-deck. 'Okay, ladies and gentlemen, no time to waste. Get inside.'

One after the other, the six wetsuited figures gathered around the edge of the pool and dived into the icy water. They rose a few seconds later inside the big, dome-shaped diving bell that now sat half-submerged in the centre of the pool.

Austin was standing at the edge of the large, round pool that formed the base of Wilkes Ice Station. Five storeys deep, Wilkes was a remote, coastal research station, a giant underground cylinder that had literally been carved into the ice shelf. A series of narrow cat-walks and ladders hugged the circumference of the vertical cylinder, creating a wide circular shaft in the mid-dle of the station. Doorways led off each of the catwalks – *into* the ice – creating the five different levels of the station. Like many others before them, the resi-dents of Wilkes had long since discovered that the best way to endure the harsh polar weather was to live under it.

Austin shouldered into his scuba gear, running through the equation in his head for the hundredth time.

Three hours since the divers' radio link had cut out. Before that, one hour of hands-free diving up the ice tunnel. And one hour's descent in the diving bell . . .

In the diving bell, they would have been breathing 'free' air – the diving bell's own supply of heliox – so that didn't count. It was only when they left the diving bell and started using tank air that the clock began to run.

Four hours, then.

The two divers had been living off tank air for four hours.

The problem was their tanks contained only three hours' worth of breathing time.

And for Austin that had meant a delicate balancing act.

The last words he and the others had heard from the two divers – before their radio signal had abruptly cut to static – had been some anxious chatter about strange whistling noises.

On the one hand, the whistling could have been anything: blues, minkes, or any other kind of harmless baleen whale. And the radio cut-out could easily have been the result of interference caused by nearly half a kilometre of ice and water. For all Austin knew, the two divers had turned around immediately and begun the hour-long trip back to the diving bell. To pull it up prematurely would be to leave them stranded on the bottom, out of time and out of air.

On the other hand, if the divers actually had met with trouble – killers, leopard seals – then naturally Austin would have wanted to yank up the diving bell as quickly as possible and send others down to help.

In the end, he decided that any help he could send – after hauling up the diving bell and sending it back down again – would be too late anyway. If Price and Davis were going to survive, the best bet was to leave the diving bell down there.

That was three hours ago – and that was as much time as Austin had been willing to give them. And so he'd pulled up the diving bell, and now a second team was preparing to go down –

'Hey.'

Austin turned. Sarah Hensleigh, one of the palaeontologists, came up alongside him.

Austin liked Hensleigh. She was intelligent, while at the same time practical and tough; not afraid to get her hands dirty. It came as no surprise to him that she was also a mother. Her twelve-year-old daughter, Kirsty, had been visiting the station for the past week.

'What is it?' Austin said.

'The topside antenna's taking a beating. The signal isn't getting through,' Hensleigh said. 'It also looks like there's a solar flare coming in.'

'Oh shit . . .'

'For what it's worth, I've got Abby scanning all the military frequencies, but I wouldn't get your hopes up.'

'What about outside?'

'Pretty bad. We've got eighty footers breaking on the cliffs and a hundred-knot wind on the surface. If we have casualties, we won't be getting them out of here by ourselves.'

Austin turned to stare at the diving bell. 'And Renshaw?'

'He's still shut up in his room.' Hensleigh looked up nervously toward B-deck.

Austin said, 'We can't wait any longer. We have to go down.'

Hensleigh just watched him.

'Ben – ' she began.

'Don't even think about it, Sarah.' Austin began walking away from her, toward the water's edge. 'I need

14

you up here. So does your kid. You just get that signal out. We'll get the others.'

'Coming to three thousand feet,' Austin's voice crackled out from the wall-mounted speakers. Sarah Hensleigh was sitting inside the darkened radio room of Wilkes Ice Station. 'Roger that, *Mawson,*' she said into the microphone in front of her.

'There doesn't appear to be any activity outside, Control. The coast is clear. All right, ladies and gentlemen, we're stopping the winch. Preparing to leave the diving bell.'

One kilometre below sea level, the diving bell jolted to a halt.

Inside, Austin keyed the intercom. 'Control, confirm time at 2132 hours, please.'

The seven divers sitting inside the cramped confines of the *Douglas Mawson* looked tensely at each other.

Hensleigh's voice came over the speaker. *'I copy, Mawson. Time confirmed at 2132 hours.'*

'Control, mark that we are turning over to self-contained air supply at 2132 hours.'

'Marked.'

The seven divers reached up for their heavy face masks, brought them down off their hooks, clamped them to the circular buckles on the collarbones of their suits.

15

'Control, we are now leaving the diving bell.'

Austin stepped forward, pausing for a moment to look at the black pool of water lapping against the rim of the diving bell. Then he stepped off the deck and splashed into the darkness.

'Divers. Time is now 2220 hours, dive-time is forty-eight minutes. Report,' Hensleigh said into her mike.

Inside the radio room behind Sarah sat Abby Sinclair, the station's resident meteorologist. For the past two hours, Abby had been manning the satellite radio console, trying without success to raise an outside frequency.

The intercom crackled. Austin's voice answered. *'Control, we are still proceeding up the ice tunnel. Nothing so far.'*

'Roger, divers,' Hensleigh said. 'Keep us informed.'

Behind her, Abby keyed her talk button again. 'Calling all frequencies, this is station four-zero-niner, I repeat this is station four-zero-niner, requesting immediate assistance. We have two casualties, possibly fatalities, on hand and we are in need of immediate support. Please acknowledge.' Abby released the button and said to herself, 'Somebody, anybody.'

The ice tunnel was starting to widen.

As Austin and the other divers slowly made their way

upward, they began to notice several strange holes set into the walls on either side of the underwater tunnel.

Each hole was perfectly round, at least ten feet in diameter. And they were all set on an incline so that they *descended* into the ice tunnel. One of the divers aimed his flashlight up into one of the holes, revealing only impenetrable, inky darkness.

Suddenly Austin's voice cut across their intercoms. '*Okay people, stay tight. I think I see the surface.*'

Inside the radio room, Sarah Hensleigh leaned forward in her chair, listening to Austin's voice over the intercom.

'*The surface appears calm. No sign of Price or Davis.*'

Hensleigh and Abby exchanged a glance. Hensleigh keyed her intercom. 'Divers. This is Control. What about the noises they mentioned? Do you hear anything? Any whale song?'

'*Nothing yet, Control. Hold on now I'm coming to the surface.*'

Austin's helmet broke the glassy surface.

As the icy water drained off his face-plate, Austin slowly began to see where he was. He was hovering in the middle of a wide pool, which was itself situated at one end of a gigantic subterranean cavern.

Slowly, Austin turned in a complete circle, observing

one after the other, the sheer vertical walls that lined every side of the cavern.

And then he saw the final wall.

His mouth fell open.

'*Control, you're not going to believe this.*' Austin's stunned voice broke over the intercom.

'What is it, Ben?' Hensleigh said into her mike.

'*I'm looking at a cavern of some sort. Walls are sheer-sided ice, probably the result of some kind of seismic activity. Area of the cavern is unknown, but it looks like it extends several hundred feet into the ice.*'

'Uh-huh.'

'*There's, ah . . . there's something else down here, Sarah.*'

Hensleigh looked at Abby and frowned. She keyed the intercom. 'What is it, Ben?'

'*Sarah . . .*' There was a long pause. '*Sarah, I think I'm looking at a spaceship.*'

It was half buried in the ice wall behind it.

Austin stared at it, entranced.

Completely black, it had a wingspan of about ninety feet. Two sleek, dorsal tail fins rose high into the air above the rear of the ship. Both fins, however, were completely embedded in the ice wall behind the ship – two shadowy blurs trapped within the clear, frozen wall. It stood on three powerful-looking landing struts and it looked magnificent – the aerodynamics sleek to the extreme, exuding a sense of raw power that was almost tangible –

There came a loud splash from behind him and Austin spun.

He saw the other divers, treading water behind him, staring up at the spaceship. Beyond them, however, was a set of expanding ripples, the remnants, it seemed, of an object that had fallen into the water . . .

'What was that?' Austin said. 'Hanson?'

'Ben, I don't know what it was, but something just went past my – '

Austin watched as, without warning, Hanson was wrenched underwater.

'Hanson!'

And then there was another scream. Harry Cox.

Austin turned, just in time to see the slicked back of a large animal rise above the surface and plough at tremendous speed into Cox's chest, driving him underwater.

Austin began to swim frantically for the water's edge. As he swam, his head dipped below the surface and suddenly his ears were assaulted by a cacophony of sound – loud, shrill whistles and hoarse, desperate barks.

The next time his head surfaced, he caught a glimpse of the ice walls surrounding the pool of water. He saw large holes set into the ice, just above the surface. They were exactly the same as the ones he'd seen down in the ice tunnel before.

Then Austin saw something come out of one of the holes.

'Holy Christ,' he breathed.

Hideous screams burst across the intercom.

In the radio room of the ice station, Hensleigh stared in stunned silence at the blinking console in front of her. Beside her, Abby had her hand across her mouth. Terrified shouts rang out from the wall-mounted speakers:

'*Raymonds!*'

'*He's gone!*'

'*Oh shit, no –*'

'*Jesus, the walls! They're coming out of the fucking walls!*'

And then suddenly Austin's voice. '*Get out of the water! Get out of the water now!*'

Another scream. Then another.

Sarah Hensleigh grabbed her mike. 'Ben! Ben! Come in!'

Austin's voice crackled over the intercom. He was speaking quickly, in between short, shallow breaths. '*Sarah, shit, I . . . I can't see anybody else. I can't . . . they're all . . . they're all gone . . .*' A pause, and then, '*Oh sweet Jesus . . . Sarah! Call for help! Call for anything you ca –*'

And then a crash of breaking glass exploded across the intercom and the voice of Benjamin Austin was gone.

*

Abby was on the radio, yelling hysterically into the mike.

'For God's sake, somebody answer me! This is station 409, I repeat, this is station four-zero-niner. We have just suffered heavy losses in an underwater cavern and request immediate assistance! Can anybody hear me? Somebody, please answer me! Our divers – oh Jesus – our divers said they saw a spacecraft of some sort in this cavern, and now, now we've lost contact with them! The last we heard from them, they were under attack, under attack in the water . . .'

Wilkes Ice Station received no response to their distress signal.

Despite the fact that it was picked up by at least three different radio installations.

FIRST INCURSION

16 June 0630 hours

The hovercraft raced across the ice plain.

It was painted white, which was unusual. Most Antarctic vehicles are painted bright orange, for ease of visibility. And it sped across the vast expanse of snow with a surprising urgency. Nobody is ever in a hurry in Antarctica.

Inside the speeding white hovercraft, Lieutenant Shane Schofield peered out through reinforced fibreglass windows. About a hundred yards off his starboard bow he could see a second hovercraft – also white – whipping across the flat, icy landscape.

At thirty-two, Schofield was young to be in command of a Recon Unit. But he had experience that belied his age. At five-ten, Schofield was lean and muscular, with a handsome, creased face and closely cropped black hair. At the moment, his black hair was covered by a camouflaged kevlar helmet. A grey turtle-neck collar protruded from beneath his shoulderplates, covering his neck. Fitted inside the folds of the turtle-neck collar was a lightweight kevlar plate. Sniper protection.

It was rumoured that Shane Schofield had deep blue eyes, but this was a rumour that had never been confirmed. In fact, it was folklore at Parris Island – the legendary training camp for the United States Marine Corps – that no one below the rank of General had ever actually seen Schofield's eyes. He always kept them hidden behind a pair of reflective, silver, anti-flash glasses.

His call-sign added to the mystery, since it was common knowledge that it had been Brigadier-General Norman W. McLean himself who had given Schofield his operational nickname – a nickname which many assumed had something to do with the young lieutenant's hidden eyes.

'*Whistler One, do you copy?*'

Schofield picked up his radio. 'Whistler Two, this is Whistler One. What is it?'

'*Sir –*' the deep voice of Staff Sergeant Buck 'Book' Riley was suddenly cut off by a wash of static. Over the past twenty-four hours, ionospheric conditions over continental Antarctica had rapidly deteriorated. The full force of a solar flare had kicked in, disrupting the entire electromagnetic spectrum, and limiting radio contact to short-range UHF transmissions. Contact between hovercrafts one hundred yards apart was difficult. Contact with Wilkes Ice Station – their destination – was impossible.

The static faded and Riley's voice came over the speaker again. '*Sir, do you remember that moving contact we picked up about an hour ago?*'

'Uh-huh,' Schofield said.

For the past hour, Whistler Two had been picking up

emissions from the electronic equipment on board a moving vehicle heading in the opposite direction, back down the coast toward the French research station, Dumont d'Urville.

'What about it?'

'*Sir, I can't find it anymore.*'

Schofield looked down at the radio. 'Are you sure?'

'*We have no reading on our scopes. Either they shut down, or they just disappeared.*'

Schofield frowned in thought, then he looked back at the cramped personnel compartment behind him. Seated there, two to each side, were four Marines, all dressed in snow fatigues. White-grey kevlar helmets sat in their laps. White-grey body armour covered their chests. White-grey automatic rifles sat by their sides.

It had been two days since the distress signal from Wilkes Ice Station had been picked up by the US Navy landing ship, *Shreveport*, while it had been in port in Sydney. As luck would have it, only a week earlier it had been decided that the *Shreveport* – a rapid deployment vessel used to transport Marine Force Reconnaissance Units – would stay in Sydney for some urgent repairs while the rest of her group returned to Pearl Harbor. That being the case, within an hour of the receipt of Abby Sinclair's distress signal, the *Shreveport* – now up and ready to go – was at sea, carrying a squad of Marines due south, heading toward the Ross Sea.

Now, Schofield and his unit were approaching Wilkes Ice Station from McMurdo Station, another, larger, US research facility about nine hundred miles from Wilkes.

McMurdo was situated on the edge of the Ross Sea and was manned by a standing staff of 104 all year round. Despite the lasting stigma associated with the US Navy's disastrous nuclear power experiment there in 1972, it remained the US gateway to the South Pole.

Wilkes, on the other hand, was as remote a station as one would find in Antarctica. Six hundred miles from its nearest neighbour, it was a small American outpost, situated right on top of the coastal ice shelf not far from the Dalton Iceberg Tongue. It was bounded on the landward side by a hundred miles of barren, windswept ice plains, and to seaward, by towering three-hundred-foot cliffs which were pounded all year round by mountainous sixty-foot waves.

Access by air had been out of the question. It was early winter and a minus-thirty-degree blizzard had been assailing the camp for three weeks now. It was expected to last another four. In such weather, exposed helicopter rotors and jet engines were known to freeze in mid-air.

And access by sea meant taking on the cliffs. The US Navy had a word for such a mission: *suicide*.

Which left access by land. By hovercraft. The twelve-man Marine Recon Unit would make the eleven-hour trip from McMurdo to Wilkes in two enclosed-fan, military hovercrafts.

Schofield thought about the moving signal again. On a map, McMurdo, d'Urville and Wilkes stations formed something like an isosceles triangle. D'Urville and Wilkes on the coast, forming the base of the triangle.

McMurdo – further inland, on the edge of the enormous bay formed by the Ross Sea – the point.

The signal that Whistler Two had picked up heading back along the coast toward Dumont d'Urville had been maintaining a steady speed of about forty miles an hour. At that speed, it was probably a conventional hovercraft. Maybe the French had had people at d'Urville who'd picked up the distress signal from Wilkes, sent help, and were now on their way back . . .

Schofield keyed his radio again. 'Book, when was the last time you held that signal?'

The radio crackled. '*Signal last held eight minutes ago. Rangefinder contact. Identical to previously held electronic signature. Heading consistent with previous vector. It was the same signal, sir, and as of eight minutes ago it was right where it should have been.*'

In this weather – howling eighty-knot winds that hurled snow so fast that it fell horizontally – regular radar scanning was hopeless. Just as the solar flare in the ionosphere put paid to radio communications, the low pressure system on the ground caused havoc with their radars.

Prepared for such an eventuality, each hovercraft was equipped with roof-mounted units called rangefinders. Mounted on a revolving turret, each rangefinder swung back and forth in a slow one-hundred-and-eighty-degree arc, emitting a constant, high-powered focal beam known as a 'needle'. Unlike radar, whose straight-line reach has always been limited by the curvature of the earth, needles can hug the earth's surface and bend over the horizon for at least another fifty miles. As soon as any 'live' object – any object with chemical, animal or electronic properties – crosses the path of a needle, it is recorded. Or, as the unit's rangefinder operator, Private José 'Santa' Cruz, liked to put it, 'if it boils, breathes or beeps, the rangefinder'll nail the fucker'.

Schofield keyed his radio. 'Book, the point where the signal disappeared. How far away is it?'

'*About ninety miles from here, sir,*' Riley's voice answered.

Schofield stared out over the seamless expanse of white that stretched all the way to the horizon.

At last he said, 'All right. Check it out.'

'*Roger that.*' Riley responded immediately. Schofield had a lot of time for Book Riley. The two men had been friends for several years. Solid and fit, Riley had a boxer's face – a flat nose that had been broken too many times, sunken eyes and thick black eyebrows. He was popular in the unit – serious when he had to be, but relaxed and funny when the pressure was off. He had been the Staff Sergeant responsible for Schofield when Schofield had been a young and stupid second lieutenant. Then, when Schofield had been given command of a Recon unit, Book – then a forty-year-old, highly respected Staff Sergeant who could have had his choice of assignment within the Marine Corps establishment – had stayed with him.

'We'll continue on to Wilkes,' Schofield said. 'You find out what happened to that signal, and then you meet us at the station.'

'*Got it.*'

'Follow-up time is two hours. Don't be late. And set your rangefinder arc from your tail. If there's anybody out there behind us, I want to know.'

'*Yes, sir.*'

'Oh, and Book, one more thing,' Schofield said.

'*What?*'

'You play nice with the other kids, you hear.'

'*Yes, sir.*'

'One, out,' Schofield said.

'*Whistler Two, out.*'

And with that, the second hovercraft peeled away to the right and sped off into the snowstorm.

An hour later, the coastline came into view, and through a set of high-powered field glasses, Schofield saw Wilkes Ice Station for the first time.

From the surface, it hardly looked like a 'station' at all – more like a motley collection of squat, dome-like structures, half-buried in the snow.

In the middle of the complex stood the main building. It was little more than an enormous, round dome mounted on a wide square base. Above the surface, the whole structure was about a hundred feet across, but it couldn't have been more than ten feet high.

On top of one of the smaller buildings gathered around the main dome stood the remains of a radio antenna. The upper half of the antenna was folded downward, a couple of taut cables the only things holding it to the upright lower half. Ice crusts hung off everything. The only light, a soft white glow burning from within the main dome.

Schofield ordered the hovercraft to a halt half a mile from the station. No sooner had it stopped than the port-side door slid open, and the six Marines leapt down from the hovercraft's inflated skirt and landed with muffled whumps on the hard-packed snow.

As they ran across the snow-covered ground, they could hear, above the roar of the wind, the crashing of the waves against the cliffs on the far side of the station.

'Gentlemen, you know what to do,' was all Schofield said into his helmet mike as he ran.

Wrapped in the blanket of the blizzard, the white-clad squad fanned out, making its way toward the station complex.

Buck Riley saw the hole in the ice before he saw the battered hovercraft in it.

The crevasse looked like a scar on the icescape – a deep, crescent-shaped gash about forty metres wide.

Riley's hovercraft came to rest a hundred yards from the rim of the enormous chasm. The six Marines climbed out, lowered themselves gently to the ground, and cautiously made their way across the snow, toward the edge of the crevasse.

PFC Robert 'Rebound' Simmons was their climber, so they harnessed him up first. A small man, Rebound was as nimble as a cat, and weighed about the same. He was young, too, just twenty-three, and like most men his age, he responded to praise. He had beamed with pride when he'd overheard his Lieutenant once say to another platoon commander that his climber was so good, he could scale the inside of the Capitol building without a rope. His nickname was another story, a good-natured jibe bestowed upon him by his unit in reference to his less than impressive success rate with women.

Once the rope was secured to his harness, Simmons lay down on his stomach and began to shimmy his way forward, through the snow, towards the edge of the scar.

He reached the edge and peered out over the rim, down into the crevasse.

'*Oh shit . . .*'

Ten metres behind him, Buck Riley spoke into his helmet mike, 'What's the story, Rebound?'

'*They're here, sir,*' Simmons' voice was almost resigned. '*Conventional craft. Got somethin' in French written on the side. Thin ice scattered all about underneath it. Looks like they tried to cross a snow bridge that didn't hold.*'

He turned to face Riley, his face grim, his voice tinny over the short-range radio frequency. '*And sir, they's pretty fucked up.*'

The hovercraft lay forty feet below the surface, its rounded nose crumpled inward by the downward impact, every one of its windows either shattered or cracked into distorted spiderwebs. A thin layer of snow had already embarked upon the task of erasing the battered vehicle from history.

Two of the hovercraft's occupants had been catapulted by the impact right *through* the forward windshield. Both lay against the forward wall of the crevasse, their necks bent backwards at obscene angles, their bodies resting in pools of their own frozen blood.

Rebound Simmons stared at the grisly scene.

There were other bodies inside the hovercraft. He could see their shadows inside it, and could see star-shaped splatters of blood on the insides of the cracked windows of the hovercraft.

'*Rebound?*' Riley's voice came over his helmet inter-com. '*Anybody alive down there?*'

'Don't look like it, sir,' Rebound said.

'*Do an infra-red,*' Riley instructed. '*We got twenty minutes before we gotta hit the road and I wouldn't want to leave and find out later that there were some survivors down there.*'

Rebound snapped his infra-red visor down into place. It hung down from the brow of his helmet, covering both of his eyes like a fighter pilot's visor.

Now he saw the crashed hovercraft through a wash of electronic blue imagery. The cold had taken effect quickly. The whole crash site was depicted as a blue-on-black outline. Not even the engine glowed yellow, the colour of objects with minimal heat intensity.

More importantly, however, there were no blobs of orange or yellow *within* the image of the vehicle. Any bodies that were still inside the hovercraft were ice-cold. Everyone on board was most certainly dead.

Rebound said, 'Sir, infra-red reading is nega – '

The ground gave way beneath him.

There was no warning. No pre-emptive cracking of the ice. No sense of it weakening.

Rebound Simmons dropped like a stone into the crevasse.

It happened so fast that Buck Riley almost missed it. One second, he was watching Rebound as he peered out over the edge of the crevasse. The next second, Rebound simply dropped out of sight.

The black rope slithered out over the edge after Rebound, uncoiling at a rapid rate, shooting out over the rim.

'Hold fast!' Riley yelled to the two Marines anchoring the rope. They held the rope tightly, taking the strain, waiting for the jolt.

The rope continued to splay out over the edge until *whack!*, it went instantly taut.

Riley stepped cautiously over to the right, away from the edge of the crevasse, but close enough so that he could peer down into it.

He saw the wrecked hovercraft down at the bottom of the hole, and the two bloodied and broken bodies pressed up against the ice wall in front of it. And he saw Rebound, hanging from his rope, two feet above the hovercraft's banged-open starboard door.

'You okay?' Riley said into his helmet mike.

'*Never doubted you for a second, sir.*'

'Just hold on. We'll have you up in a minute.'

'*Sure.*'

*

Down in the crevasse, Rebound swung stupidly above the destroyed hovercraft. From where he hung he could see in through the open starboard door of the hovercraft.

'Oh, *Jesus* . . .' he breathed.

Schofield knocked loudly on the big wooden door.

The door was set into the square-shaped base structure that supported the main dome of Wilkes Ice Station. It lay at the bottom of a narrow ramp that descended about eight feet into the ice.

Schofield banged his fist on the door again.

He was lying flat on the parapet of the base structure, reaching down from *above* the door to knock on it.

Ten yards away, lying on his belly in the snow at the top of the ramp with his legs splayed wide, was Gunnery Sergeant Scott 'Snake' Kaplan. His M-16E assault rifle was trained on the unopened door.

There came a sudden *creak*, and Schofield held his breath as a sliver of light stretched out onto the snow beneath him and the door to the station slowly began to open.

A figure stepped out onto the snow ramp beneath Schofield. It was a man. Wrapped in about seven layers of clothing. Unarmed.

Suddenly, the man tensed, presumably as he saw Snake lying in the snow in front of him, with his M-16 pointed right at the bridge of the man's nose.

'Hold it *right there*,' Schofield said from above and behind the man. 'United States Marines.'

The man remained frozen.

'*Unit Two is in. Secure*,' a woman's voice whispered over Schofield's earpiece.

'*Unit Three. In and secure*.'

'All right. We're coming in through the front door.'

Schofield slid down from his perch and landed next to the man on the snow ramp, and began to pat him down.

Snake strode down the ramp toward them, his rifle up, pointed at the door.

Schofield said to the man, 'You American? What's your name?'

The man spoke.

'Non. Je suis Français.'

And then, in English. 'My name is Luc.'

There is a tendency among academic observers to view Antarctica as the last neutral territory on earth. In Antarctica, so it is said, there are no traditional or holy sites to fight over, no historical borders to dispute. What remains is something of a *terra communis*, a land belonging to the community.

Indeed, by virtue of the Antarctic Treaty, since 1961 the continent has been divided up into what looks like an enormous pie chart, with each party to the Treaty being allocated a sector of the pie. Some sectors overlap, as with those administered by Chile, Argentina and the United Kingdom. Others cover monumentally vast tracts of land – Australia administers a sector of the pie which covers nearly a whole quarter of the Antarctic land mass. There is even one sector – that which covers the Amundsen Sea and Byrd Land – which belongs to no one.

The general impression is one of a truly international land mass. Such an impression, however, is misguided and simplistic.

Advocates of the 'politically neutral Antarctica' fail to acknowledge the continuing animosity between

Argentina and Great Britain as to their respective Antarctic claims; or the staunch refusal of *all* of the parties to the Antarctic Treaty to vote on the 1985 UN Resolution that would have dedicated the Antarctic land mass to the benefit of the *entire* international community; or the mysterious conspiracy of silence among the Treaty nations that followed a little-known Greenpeace report in 1995 which accused the French government of conducting secret underground nuclear detonations off the coast of Victoria Land.

More importantly, however, such advocates also fail to recognize that a land without clearly defined borders has no means of dealing with hostile foreign incursions.

Research stations can often be a thousand miles apart. Sometimes, those research stations discover items of immense value – uranium, plutonium, gold. It is not impossible that a foreign state, desperate for resources, would, upon learning of such a discovery, send an incursionary force to appropriate that discovery before the rest of the world even knew it existed.

Such an incident – insofar as it could be known – had never happened in Antarctica before.

There's always a first time, Schofield thought as he was led into Wilkes Ice Station by the Frenchman named Luc.

Schofield had heard a recording of Abby Sinclair's distress signal, heard her mention the discovery of a spacecraft buried within the ice underneath Wilkes Ice Station. If the scientists at Wilkes had, in fact, discovered an extraterrestrial spacecraft, it would definitely be something other parties would be interested in. Whether or not they had the nerve to send a strike team in to get it was another question.

In any case, it made him more than a little uneasy to be greeted at the doors of an *American* research station by a *French* national, and as he walked down the dark, ice-walled entrance tunnel behind Luc, Schofield found himself gripping his automatic pistol a little more tightly.

The two men emerged from the darkened entry tunnel into brightly lit, wide open space. Schofield found himself standing on a thin metal catwalk overlooking a wide, cylindrical chasm of empty space.

Wilkes Ice Station opened in front of him, a giant subterranean structure. Narrow, black catwalks ran around the circumference of the underground cylinder, surrounding the wide, central shaft. At the base of the enormous cylinder, Schofield saw a circular pool of water, in the middle of which sat the station's diving bell.

'This way,' Luc said, guiding Schofield to the right. 'They're all in the dining room.'

As he entered the dining room preceded by Luc, Schofield felt like an adult entering a pre-school classroom: a stranger who by the simple fact of his size and bearing just doesn't fit in.

The group of five survivors sat in a tight circle around

41

the table. The men were unshaven, the women unkempt. They all looked exhausted. They looked up wearily as Schofield entered the room.

There were two other men in the room, standing behind the table. Unlike the people seated at the table, these two, like Luc, seemed alert, clean and fresh. One of them was holding a tray of steaming drinks. He froze in mid-step as soon as he saw Schofield walk into the room.

French scientists from d'Urville, Schofield thought. *Here in response to the distress signal.*

Probably.

At first, no one said anything.

Everyone in the room just looked at Schofield, taking in his helmet and his silver anti-flash glasses; his body armour and his snow fatigues; the MP-5 machine pistol slung over his shoulder; the .44 automatic in his hand.

Snake came in behind Schofield, and all eyes switched to him: similarly garbed, similarly armed. A clone.

'It's okay,' Luc said gently to the others. 'They are Marines. They are here to rescue you.'

One of the women let out a gasp of air. 'Oh, Jesus,' she said. Then she started to cry. 'Oh, thank *God*.'

American accent, Schofield noted. The woman pushed back her chair and came toward him, tears pouring down her cheeks. 'I knew you'd come,' she said. 'I knew you'd come.'

She clutched Schofield's shoulderplate and began sobbing into his chest. Schofield showed no emotion.

He held his pistol clear of her, as he'd been trained to do.

'It's okay, ma'am,' was all he said, as he guided her gently to a nearby seat. 'It's okay. You're all right now.'

Once she was seated, he turned to face the others. 'Ladies and gentleman. We are Reconnaissance Unit Sixteen of the United States Marine Corps. My name is Lieutenant Shane Schofield, and this is Sergeant Scott Kaplan. We are here in response to your distress signal. We have instructions to secure this station and ensure that each of you is unharmed.'

One of the men at the table let out a sigh of relief.

Schofield went on. 'So that you're under no illusions, I will tell you now that we are a *reconnaissance* unit. We will *not* be extracting you. We are a front-line unit. We travel fast, and we travel light. Our task is to get here quickly, and make sure that you are all okay. If there's an emergency situation, we will extract you, if not, our orders are to secure this station and wait for a fully equipped extraction team to arrive.'

Schofield turned to face Luc and the other two men standing behind the table. 'Now, I presume you gentlemen are from d'Urville. Is that correct?'

The man with the tray in his hands swallowed loudly, his eyes wide.

'Yes,' Luc said. 'That is correct. We heard the message on the radio, and we came as soon as we could. To help.'

As Luc spoke, a woman's voice crackled over Schofield's earpiece. '*Unit Two, sweep is clear.*'

'*Unit Three. We have found three – no, actually, make that four – contacts in the drilling room. We're on our way up now.*'

Schofield nodded at Luc. 'Your names?'

'I am Professor Luc Champion,' Luc said. 'This is Professor Jean-Pierre Cuvier, and holding the tray there is Dr Henri Rae.'

Schofield nodded slowly, taking the names in, comparing them to a list he'd seen on the *Shreveport* two days previously. It had been a list of the names of every French scientist stationed at d'Urville. *Champion*, *Cuvier* and *Rae* were on it.

There was a knock on the door and Schofield turned.

Senior Sergeant Morgan 'Montana' Lee stood in the doorway to the dining room. Montana Lee was a nugget of a man, stocky, and, at forty-six years of age, he was the oldest member of the unit. He had a pug nose and a heavy-set, weathered face. Ten yards behind him stood his partner, Corporal Oliver 'Hollywood' Todd. Tall, black and lean, Hollywood Todd was twenty-one years old.

And in between the two Marines stood the fruits of their sweep.

One woman.

One man.

One young girl.

And one seal.

'They got here about four hours ago,' Sarah Hensleigh said. Schofield and Hensleigh were standing on A-deck, out on the catwalk that looked out over the rest of the ice station.

As Hensleigh had already explained, Wilkes Ice Station was essentially a great, big, vertical cylinder that had been bored into the ice shelf. It dived five storeys straight down, all the way to sea level.

Indented at regular intervals on the walls of the cylinder were metal catwalks which ran around the circumference of the cylinder. Each catwalk was joined to the one above it by steep, narrow rung-ladders, so that the whole structure looked kind of like a fire-escape.

Branching out from each catwalk, burrowing *into* the icy walls of the cylinder, was a series of tunnels which formed the different levels of the station. Each level was made up of four straight tunnels that branched out from the central shaft to meet a curved outer tunnel that ran in a wide circle *around* the central well. The four straight tunnels roughly equated the four points on a compass, so they were simply labelled north, south, east and west.

Each catwalk/level of Wilkes Ice Station was labelled

45

A through E – A-deck being the highest, E-deck signi-
fying the wide metal platform that surrounded the large
pool of water at the base of the massive underground
structure. On C-deck, the middle level, Sarah said, a
narrow, retractable bridge was able to extend across the
wide, central shaft of the station.

'How many?' Schofield asked.

'There were five of them at first,' Sarah said. 'Four
stayed here with us, while the fifth guy took the others
back to d'Urville on their hovercraft.'

'You know them?'

Sarah said, 'I know Luc and I know Henri – who I
think wet himself when he saw you guys walk in – and
I know *of* the fourth one, Jacques Latissier.'

After Montana had led Hensleigh into the dining
room a few minutes earlier, it hadn't taken long for
Schofield to figure out that she was the person to speak
to about the previous week's events at Wilkes Ice
Station.

While all the others looked either dejected or tired,
Sarah had appeared collected and in control. Indeed,
Montana and Hollywood had said that they'd found her
while she had been showing one of the French scientists
the core-drilling room down on E-deck. His name had
been Jacques Latissier – a tall man with a thick black
beard – and he was also on Schofield's mental list.

Sarah Hensleigh stared out over the central shaft of
the station, deep in thought. Schofield looked at her.
She was an attractive woman, about thirty-five, with
dark brown eyes, black shoulder-length hair and high

arching cheekbones. Schofield noticed that around her neck she wore a glistening silver locket on a chain.

At that moment, the little girl came out onto the catwalk. Schofield guessed that she must have been about ten. She had short blonde hair, a small button nose, and she wore thick glasses that hung down awkwardly over her cheeks. She looked almost comical in the bulky pink parka that she wore – it had a terribly oversized wool-lined hood that flopped down over her face.

And behind the little girl, loping out onto the metal catwalk, came the seal.

'And who is this?' Schofield asked.

'This is my daughter, Kirsty,' Sarah said, putting her hand on the little girl's shoulder. 'Kirsty, this is Lieutenant Schofield.'

'Hi there,' Schofield said.

Kirsty Hensleigh just stood there for a moment and stared up at Schofield, taking in his armour, his helmet and his weapons.

'Cool glasses,' she said at last.

'Huh? Oh, yeah,' Schofield said, touching his silver anti-flash glasses. Combined with his snow fatigues and his white-grey body armour, he knew the reflective, single-lens glasses made him look particularly icy. A kid *would* like that. Schofield didn't take the glasses off.

'Yeah, I guess they are pretty cool,' he said. 'How old are you?'

'Twelve, almost thirteen.'

'Yeah?'

'I'm kind of short for my age,' Kirsty added matter-of-factly.

'Me, too,' Schofield said, nodding.

He looked down as the seal flopped forward and started sniffing at his knee. 'And your friend here. What's his name?'

'*She's* a girl, and her name is Wendy.'

Schofield reached down and let the seal sniff his hand. She wasn't very big, about the size of a medium-sized dog and she happily wore a cute red collar.

'Wendy. What kind of seal is she?' Schofield asked, as he began to pat Wendy on the head.

'*Arctocephalus gazella*,' Kirsty said. 'Antarctic fur seal.'

Wendy started winding her head around in Schofield's hand, forcing him to pat her behind her earflap. He did, and then suddenly Wendy dropped to the ground and rolled over onto her back.

'She wants you to rub her tummy,' Kirsty said, smiling. 'She likes that.'

Wendy lay on the catwalk, on her back, her flippers held out wide, waiting to be patted. Schofield bent down and gave her a quick rub on the stomach.

'You just won yourself a friend for life,' Sarah Hensleigh said, watching Schofield closely.

'Great,' Schofield said, rising.

'I didn't know Marines could be so friendly,' Sarah said suddenly, taking Schofield slightly off guard.

'We're not all heartless.'

'Not when there's something here that you want.'

The comment made Schofield stop and look at Sarah for a long second. Clearly, she was no fool.

Schofield nodded slowly, accepting the criticism. 'Ma'am, if you don't mind, if we could just get back to what we were discussing before: you know two of them, and you *know of* one of them, right?'

'That's right.'

'What about the fourth one, Cuvier?'

'Never met him.'

Schofield moved on. 'And how many did they take back to d'Urville?'

'They could only fit six people in their hovercraft, so one of their guys took five of our people back there.'

'Leaving the other four back here.'

'That's right.'

Schofield nodded to himself. Then he looked at Hensleigh. 'There are a couple of other things we need to talk about. Like what you found down in the ice. And the Renshaw . . . *incident*.'

Sarah understood what he was saying. Such matters were best discussed in the absence of a twelve-year-old.

She nodded. 'No problem.'

Schofield looked at the ice station around him: at the pool down at the bottom, at the catwalks set into the walls of the cylinder, at the tunnels that disappeared into the ice. There was something about it all that wasn't quite right, something that he couldn't quite put his finger on.

And then he realized, and he turned to face Sarah. 'Stop me if this is a stupid question, but if this whole station is carved into the ice shelf and all the walls are made of ice, why don't they melt? Surely, you must generate a lot of heat in here with your machinery and all. Shouldn't the walls be dripping constantly.'

Sarah said, 'It's not a stupid question. In fact, it's a very good question. When we first arrived here, we found that the heat from the exhaust of the core drilling machine was causing some of the ice walls to melt. So we had a cooling system installed on C-deck. It works off a thermostat which keeps the temperature steady at $-1°$ Celsius no matter what heat we produce. The funny thing is, since the surface temperature outside is almost thirty below, the *cooling* system actually *warms* the air in here. We love it.'

'Very clever,' Schofield said, as he looked around the ice station.

His gaze came to rest on the dining room. Luc Champion and the other three French scientists were in there, sitting at the table with the residents of Wilkes. Schofield watched them, deep in thought.

'Are you going to take us home?' Kirsty said suddenly from behind him.

For a long moment, Schofield continued to watch the four French scientists in the dining room. Then he turned to face the little girl.

'Not just yet,' he said. 'Some other people will be here soon to take you home. I'm just here to take care of you until they do.'

Schofield and Hensleigh walked quickly down the wide ice tunnel. Montana and Hollywood kept pace behind them.

They were on B-deck, the main living area. The ice tunnel curved around a wide bend. Doors were sunk into it on either side: bedrooms, a common room and various labs and studies. Schofield couldn't help noticing one particular door which had a distinctive three-ringed biohazard sign on it. A rectangular plate beneath the sign read: BIOTOXIN LABORATORY.

Schofield said, 'They said something about it when we got to McMurdo. That Renshaw claimed he did it because the other guy was stealing his research. Something like that.'

'That's right,' Hensleigh said, walking fast. She looked at Schofield. 'It's just crazy.'

They came to the end of the tunnel, to a door set into the ice. It was closed and it had a heavy wooden beam locked in place across it.

'James Renshaw,' Schofield mused. 'Isn't he the one who found the spaceship?'

'That's right. But there's a whole lot more to it than that.'

51

Upon arriving at McMurdo Station, Schofield had been given a short briefing on Wilkes Ice Station. On the face of it, the station seemed like nothing special. It contained the usual assortment of academics: marine biologists studying the ocean fauna; palaeontologists studying fossils frozen in the ice; geologists looking for mineral deposits; and geophysicists like James Renshaw who drilled deep down into the ice looking for thousand-year-old traces of carbon monoxide and other gases.

What made Wilkes Ice Station something special was that two days *before* Abby Sinclair's distress signal had gone out, *another* high-priority signal had been sent out from the station. This earlier signal, sent to McMurdo, had been a formal request seeking the dispatch to Wilkes of a squad of military police.

Although the details had been sketchy, it appeared that one of the scientists at Wilkes had killed one of his colleagues.

Schofield stared at the barred door at the end of the ice tunnel, and shook his head. He really didn't have time for this. His orders had been very specific:

Secure the station. Investigate the spacecraft. Verify its existence. And then guard it against all parties until reinforcements arrived.

Schofield remembered sitting in the closed briefing room on board the *Shreveport*, listening to the voice of the Undersecretary of Defence on the speakerphone. 'Other parties have almost certainly picked up that

52

distress signal, Lieutenant. If there really is an extrater-restrial vehicle down there, there's a good chance one of those parties might make a play for it. The United States Government would like to avoid that situation, Lieuten-ant. Your objective is the protection of the spacecraft, nothing else. I repeat. Your objective is the protection of the spacecraft. All other considerations are secondary. *We want that ship.*'

Not once had the safety of the American scientists at the station been mentioned, a fact that hadn't gone unnoticed by Schofield. It obviously hadn't slipped past Sarah Hensleigh either.

All other considerations are secondary.

In any case, Schofield thought, he couldn't afford to send any divers down to investigate the spacecraft while there existed the possibility that one of the residents of Wilkes might be a source of trouble.

'All right,' Schofield said, looking at the door, but addressing Hensleigh. 'Twenty-five words or less. What's his story?'

Sarah Hensleigh said, 'Renshaw is a geophysicist from Stanford, studying ice cores for his Ph.D. Bernie Olson is – *was* – his supervisor. Renshaw's work with ice cores was groundbreaking. He was digging core holes deeper than anybody had ever dug before, at times going nearly a kilometre below the surface.'

Schofield vaguely knew about ice core research. It involved drilling a circular hole about thirty centimetres wide down into the ice shelf and pulling out a cylinder of ice known as a core. Held captive within the core were pockets of gases that had existed in the air thousands of years before.

'Anyway,' Sarah said, 'a couple of weeks ago, Renshaw hit the big time. His drill must have hit a layer of upsurged ice – prehistoric ice that has been dislodged by an earthquake sometime in the past and pushed up toward the surface. Suddenly Renshaw was studying pockets of air that were as much as three hundred *million* years old. It was the discovery of a lifetime. Here was a chance to study an atmosphere that no one has ever known. To see what the earth's atmosphere was like *before* the dinosaurs.' Sarah Hensleigh shrugged. 'For an academic, something like that is like the pot of gold at the end of the rainbow. It's worth a fortune on the lecture circuit alone.

'Only then it got better.

'A few days ago, Renshaw adjusted his drilling vector slightly – that's the angle at which you drill down into the ice – and at 1500 feet, in the middle of a four-hundred-million-year-old section of ice, he hit *metal*.'

Sarah paused, allowing what she had just said to sink in. Schofield said nothing.

Sarah said, 'We sent the diving bell down, did some sonic-resonance tests of the ice shelf, and discovered that there was a *cavern* of some sort right where this piece of prehistoric metal was supposed to be. Further tests showed that there was a tunnel leading *up* to this cavern from a depth of 3000 feet. That was when we sent the divers down, and that was when Austin saw the space-craft. And that was when all the divers disappeared.'

Schofield said, 'So what does all this have to do with Bernard Olson's death?'

Sarah said, 'Olson was Renshaw's supervisor. He was always looking over Renshaw's shoulder while Renshaw was making these amazing discoveries. Renshaw started to get paranoid. He started saying that Bernie was stealing his research. That Bernie was using *his* findings to write a quickfire article himself and beat Renshaw to the punch.

'You see, Bernie had connections with the journals, knew some editors. He could get an article out within a month. Renshaw, as an unknown Ph.D student, would almost certainly take longer. He thought Bernie was trying to steal his pot of gold. And then when Renshaw discovered *metal* down in the cavern and he saw that Bernie was going to include *that* in his article too, Renshaw flipped.'

'And he *killed* him?'

'He killed him. Last Wednesday night. Renshaw just went to Bernie's room and started yelling at him. We all heard it. Renshaw was angry and upset, but we'd heard it all before so we didn't think much of it. But, this time, he killed him.'

'How?' Schofield continued to stare at the locked door.

'He – ' Sarah hesitated. 'He jabbed Bernie in the neck with a hypodermic needle and injected the contents.'

'What was in the syringe?'

'Industrial-strength drain-cleaning fluid.'

'Charming,' Schofield said. He nodded at the door. 'He's in here?'

Sarah said, 'He locked himself in after it happened. Took a week's worth of food in with him and said that if any of us tried to go in there after him he'd kill us, too. It was terrifying. He was crazy. So one night – the night before we sent the divers down to investigate the cave – the rest of us got together and bolted the door shut from the outside. Ben Austin fixed some runners to the wall on either side of the door while the rest of us slid the beam into place. Then Austin used a rivet gun to seal the door shut.'

Schofield said, 'Is he still alive?'

'Yes. You can't hear him now, which means he's probably asleep. But when he's awake, believe me, you'll know it.'

'Uh-huh.' Schofield examined the edges of the door, saw the rivets holding it to the frame. 'Your friend did a good job with the door.' Schofield turned around. 'If he's locked inside. That's good enough for me, *if* you're sure there's no other way out of that room.'

'This is the only entrance.'

'Yeah, but is there any other way out the room. Could he dig his way out, say, through the walls, or the ceiling?'

'The ceilings and the floors are steel-lined, so he can't dig through them. And his room's at the end of the corridor, so there aren't any rooms on either side of it –

56

the walls are solid ice,' Sarah Hensleigh gave Schofield a crooked smile. 'I don't think there's any way out of there.'

'Then we leave him in there,' Schofield said, as he started walking back down the ice tunnel. 'We've got other things to worry about. The first of which is finding out what happened to your divers down in that cave.'

The sun shone brightly over Washington, D.C. The Capitol practically glowed white against the magnificent blue sky.

In a lavish, red-carpeted corner of the Capitol Building, a meeting broke for recess. Folders were closed. Chairs were pushed back. Some of the delegates took off their reading glasses and rubbed their eyes. As soon as the recess was called, small clusters of aides immediately rushed forward to their bosses' sides with cellular phones, folders and faxes.

'What *are* they up to?' the US Permanent Representative, George Holmes, said to his aide, as he watched the entire French delegation – all twelve of them – leave the negotiating room. 'That's the fourth time they've called a recess today.'

Holmes watched France's Chef de Mission – a pompous, snobbish man named Pierre Dufresne – leave the room at the head of his group. Holmes shook his head in wonder.

George Holmes was a diplomat, had been all his life. He was fifty-five, short and, though he hated to admit it, a little overweight.

Holmes had a round, moon-like face and a horse-shoe of greying hair, and he wore thick, horn-rimmed glasses that made his brown eyes appear larger than they really were.

Holmes stood up and stretched his legs, looked around at the enormous meeting room. A huge, circular table stood in the centre of the room, with sixteen comfortable, leather chairs placed at equal distances around its circumference.

The occasion, the reaffirmation of an alliance.

International alliances are not exactly the friendly affairs the TV news makes them out to be. When Presidents and Prime Ministers emerge from the White House and shake hands for the cameras in front of their interlocking flags, they belie the deal-making, the promise-breaking, the nit-picking and the catfighting that goes on in rooms not unlike the one in which George Holmes now stood. The smiles and the handshakes are merely the icing on very complex, negotiated cakes that are made by professional diplomats like Holmes.

International alliances are not about friendship. They are about *advantage*. If friendship brings advantage, then friendship is desirable. If friendship does not bring advantage, then perhaps merely civil relations may be all that is necessary. International *friendship* – in terms of foreign aid, military allegiance and trade alignment – can be a very expensive business. It is not entered into lightly.

Which was the reason why George Holmes was in Washington on this bright summer's day. He was a negotiator. More than that, he was a negotiator skilled in the niceties and subtleties of diplomatic exchange.

And he would need all his skills in this diplomatic exchange, for this was no ordinary reaffirmation of an alliance.

This was a reaffirmation of what was arguably the most important alliance of the twentieth century.

The North Atlantic Treaty Organization.

NATO.

'Phil, did you know that for the last forty years, the one and only goal of French foreign policy has been to destroy the United States' hegemony over the western world?' Holmes mused as he waited for the French delegation to return to the meeting room.

His aide, a twenty-five-year-old Harvard Law grad named Phillip Munro, hesitated before he answered. He wasn't sure if it was a rhetorical question. Holmes swivelled on his chair and stared at Munro through his thick glasses.

'Ah, no, sir, I didn't,' Munro said.

Holmes nodded thoughtfully. 'They think of us as brutes, unsophisticated fools. Beer-swilling rednecks who through some accident of history somehow got our hands on the most powerful weapons in the world and, from that, became its leader. They French resent that. Hell, they're not even a full NATO member anymore, because they think it perpetuates US influence over Europe.'

Holmes snuffed a laugh. He remembered when, in 1966, France withdrew from NATO's integrated military command because it did not want French nuclear weapons to be placed under NATO – and therefore, US – control. At the time the French President, Charles de Gaulle, had said point blank that NATO was 'an American organization'. Now, France simply maintained a seat on NATO's North Atlantic Council, to keep an eye on things.

Munro said, 'I know a few people who would agree with them. Academics, economists. People who would say that that's *exactly* what NATO is designed to do. Perpetuate our influence over Europe.'

Holmes smiled. Munro was good value. College-educated and an ardent liberal, he was one of those let's-have-a-philosophical-debate-over-coffee types. The kind who argue for a better world when they have absolutely no experience in it. Holmes didn't mind that. In fact, he found Munro refreshing. 'But what do *you* say, Phil?' he asked.

Munro was silent for a few seconds. Then he said, 'NATO makes European countries economically and technologically dependent upon the United States for defence. Even highly developed countries like France and England know that if they want the best weapons systems, they have to come to us. And that leaves them with two options – come knocking on our door with their hats in their hands, or join NATO. And so far as I know, the United States hasn't sold any *Patriot* missile systems to non-NATO countries. So, yes, I think that NATO does perpetuate our influence over Europe.'

'Not a bad analysis, Phil. But let me tell you something, it goes a *lot* further than that, a lot further,' he said. 'So much so, in fact, that the White House maintains that the national security of the United States *depends* upon that influence. We want to keep our influence over Europe, Phil, economically and especially technologically. France, on the other hand, would like us to lose that influence. And for the last ten years successive French governments have been actively pursuing a policy of eroding US influence in Europe.'

'Example?' Munro said.

'Did you know that it was *France* who was the driving force behind the establishment of the European Union?'

'Well, no. I thought it was – '

'Did you know that it was *France* who was the driving force behind the establishment of a European Defence Charter?'

A pause.

'No,' Munro said.

'Did you know that it is *France* who subsidizes the European Space Agency so that the ESA can charge vastly cheaper prices for taking commercial satellites up into orbit than NASA can?'

'No, I didn't know that.'

Holmes turned in his chair, faced Munro.

'Son, for the last ten years, France has been trying to unite Europe like never before and sell it to the rest of the world. They call it regional pride. We call it an attempt to tell European nations that they don't need America anymore.'

'*Does* Europe need America anymore?' Munro asked quickly. A loaded question.

Homes gave his young aide a crooked smile. 'Until Europe can match us weapon-for-weapon, *yes*, they do need us. What frustrates France most about us is our defence technology. They can't match it. We're too far ahead of them. It *infuriates* them.

'And as long as we stay ahead of them, they know that they've got no option but to follow us. *But*,' Holmes held up a finger, 'once they get their hands on something *new*, once they develop something that tops our technology, *then* I think things may be different.

'This isn't 1966 anymore. Things have changed. The *world* has changed. If France walked out of NATO now, I think half of the other European nations in the Organization would walk out with her – '

At that moment, the doors to the meeting room opened and the French delegation, led by Pierre Dufresne, came back into the room.

As the French delegates returned to their seats, Holmes leaned close to Munro. 'What worries me most, though, is that the French may be closer to that new discovery than we think. Look at them today. They've recessed this meeting four times already. *Four* times. Do you know what that means?'

'What?'

'They're stalling the meeting. Drawing it out. You only stall like that when you're waiting for information.

That's why they keep recessing – so they can talk with their intelligence people and get an update on whatever it is they're up to. And by the looks of things, whatever that is, it could be the difference between the continued existence of NATO and its complete destruction.'

The sleek, black head broke the surface without a sound. It was a sinister head, with two dark, lifeless eyes on either side of a glistening, snub-nosed snout.

A few moments later, a second, identical head appeared next to the first, and the two animals curiously observed the activity taking place on E-deck.

The two killer whales in the pool of Wilkes Ice Station were rather small specimens, despite the fact that they each weighed close to five tons. From tip to tail, they were each at least fifteen feet long.

Having evaluated and dismissed the activity taking place on the deck around them – where Lieutenant Schofield was busy getting a couple of divers suited up – the two killer whales began to circle the pool, gliding around the diving bell which sat half-submerged in the very centre of the pool.

Their movements seemed odd, almost co-ordinated. As one killer would look one way, the other would look in the opposite direction. It was almost as if they were searching for something, searching for something in particular . . .

'They're looking for Wendy,' Kirsty said, looking

down at the two killers from the C-deck catwalk. Her voice was flat, cold – unusually harsh for a twelve-year-old girl.

It had been almost two hours since Schofield and his team had arrived at Wilkes, and now Schofield was down on E-deck, preparing to send two of his men down in the *Douglas Mawson* to find out what had happened to Austin and the others.

Fascinated, Kirsty had been watching Schofield and the two divers from up on C-deck when she had seen the two killer whales surface. Beside her, stationed on C-deck to work the winch controls, were two of the Marines.

Kirsty liked these two. Unlike a couple of the older ones who had merely grunted when she had said hello, these two were young and friendly. One of them, Kirsty was happy to note, was a woman.

Lance-Corporal Elizabeth Gant was compact, fit, and she held her MP-5 as though it were an extension of her right hand. Hidden beneath her helmet and her silver anti-flash glasses was an intelligent and attractive twenty-six-year-old woman. Her call-sign, 'Fox,' was a compliment bestowed upon her by her admiring male colleagues. Libby Gant looked down at the two killer whales as they glided slowly around the pool.

'They're looking for Wendy?' she asked, glancing down at the little black fur seal on the catwalk beside her. Wendy backed nervously away from the edge of the catwalk, trying, it seemed, to avoid being seen by the two whales circling in the pool forty feet below.

'They don't like her very much,' Kirsty said.

'Why not?'

'They're juveniles,' Kirsty said. '*Male* juveniles. They don't like anybody. It's like they have something to prove – prove that they're bigger and stronger than the other animals. Typical *boys*. The killer whales around these parts mostly eat baby crabeaters, but these two saw Wendy swimming in the pool a few days ago and they've been coming by ever since.'

'What's a crabeater?' Hollywood Todd asked from over by the winch controls.

'It's another kind of seal,' Kirsty said. 'A big, fat seal. Killers eat them in about three bites.'

'They *eat* seals?' Hollywood said, genuinely surprised.

'Uh-huh,' Kirsty said.

'Whoa.' Having barely graduated high school, Hollywood couldn't exactly claim to possess a love for books or academia. School had been a hard time. He'd joined the Marines two weeks after graduating and thought it was the best decision he'd ever made.

He looked down at Kirsty, assessing her size and age. 'How come you know all this stuff?'

Kirsty shrugged self-consciously. 'I read a lot.'

'Oh.'

Beside Hollywood, Gant began to laugh softly.

'What're you laughing at?' Hollywood asked.

'You,' Libby Gant said, smiling. 'I was just thinking about how much you read.'

Hollywood cocked his head. 'I read.'

'Sure you do.'

'I *do*.'

'Comic books don't count, Hollywood.'

'I don't just read comic books.'

'Oh, yeah, I forgot about your prized subscription to *Hustler* magazine.'

Kirsty began to chuckle.

Hollywood noticed, and frowned. 'Ha-ha. Yeah, well, 'least I *know* I ain't gonna be no college professor, so I don't try to be somethin' I'm not.' He raised his eyebrows at Gant. 'What about you, *Dorothy*, you ever try to be somethin' you're not?'

Libby Gant lowered her glasses slightly, revealing sky-blue eyes. She gave Hollywood a sad look. 'Sticks and stones, Hollywood. Sticks and stones.'

Gant replaced her glasses and turned back to look at the whales down in the pool.

Kirsty was confused. When she'd been introduced to Gant earlier, she'd been told that her real name was Libby and that her nickname was 'Fox'. After a few moments, Kirsty asked innocently, 'Why did he call you Dorothy?'

Gant didn't answer. She just kept looking down at the pool, and shook her head.

Kirsty spun to face Hollywood. He gave her a cryptic smile and a shrug. 'Everybody knows Dorothy liked the scarecrow better than the others.'

He smiled as if that explained everything, and went back about his work. Kirsty didn't get it.

Gant just leaned on the rail, watching the killer whales, determinedly ignoring Hollywood. The two killers were still scanning the station, looking for Wendy. For an instant one of them seemed to see Gant and it stopped. It cocked its head to one side, and just looked at her.

'It can see me from all the way down there?' Gant said, glancing at Kirsty. 'I thought whales were supposed to have poor eyesight out of the water.'

'For their size, killer whales have bigger eyes than most other whales,' Kirsty said, 'so their eyesight out of the water is better.' She looked at Gant. 'You know about them?'

'*I* read a lot,' Gant said, casting a sideways glance at Hollywood, before turning back to face the killers.

The two killer whales continued to prowl slowly around the pool. Gliding through the still water, they seemed patient, calm. Content to bide their time until their prey appeared. Down on the pool deck, Gant saw Schofield and the two Marine divers watching the killer whales as they ominously circled the pool.

'How do they get in here?' Gant said to Kirsty. 'What do they do – swim in under the ice shelf?'

Kirsty nodded. 'That's right. This station is only about a hundred yards away from the ocean, and the ice shelf out that way isn't very deep, maybe five hundred feet. The killers just swim in under the ice shelf and surface here inside the station.'

Gant looked down at the two killer whales on the far side of the pool. They seemed so calm, so cold, like a pair of hungry crocodiles searching for their next meal.

Their survey complete, the two killer whales slowly

began to submerge. In a moment they were gone, replaced by two sets of ripples. Their eyes had remained open the whole way down.

'Well, that was sudden,' Gant said.

Her eyes moved from the now empty pool to the diving platform beside it. She saw Montana emerge from the south tunnel with some scuba tanks slung over his shoulders. Sarah Hensleigh had told them that there was a small goods elevator in the south tunnel – a 'dumb waiter' – that they could use to bring their diving gear down to E-deck. Montana had been using it just now.

Gant's gaze moved to the other side of the platform, where she saw Schofield standing with his head bowed, holding a hand to his ear, as though he were listening to something on his helmet intercom. And then suddenly he was heading toward the nearest rung-ladder, speaking into his helmet mike as he walked.

Gant watched as Schofield stopped at the base of the rung-ladder on the far side of the station, and turned to look directly at her. His voice crackled over her helmet intercom. '*Fox. Hollywood. A-deck. Now.*'

As she hastened toward the rung-ladder nearest her, Gant spoke into her helmet mike, 'What is it, sir?'

Schofield's voice was serious. '*Something just set off the tripwire outside. Snake's up there. He says it's a French hovercraft.*'

Snake Kaplan drew a bead on the hovercraft.

The lettering on the side of the vehicle glowed bright

green in his night-vision gunsights. It read: 'DUMONT
D'URVILLE – 02'.

Kaplan was lying in the snow on the outskirts of the
station complex, bracing himself against the driving
wind and snow, following the newly arrived hovercraft
through the sights of his Barrett M82A1A sniper rifle.

Gunnery Sergeant Scott 'Snake' Kaplan was forty-five
years old, a tall man, with dark, serious eyes. Like
most of the other Marines in Schofield's unit, Kaplan
had customized his uniform. A weathered tattoo of a
fearsome-looking cobra with its jaws bared wide had
been painted onto his right shoulderplate. Underneath
the picture of the snake were the words: 'KISS THIS'.

A career soldier, Kaplan had been with the Marine
Corps for twenty-seven years, during which time he had
risen to the magic rank of Gunnery Sergeant, the highest
rank an enlisted Marine can reach while still getting his
hands dirty. Indeed, although further promotion was
possible, Snake had decided to stay at Gunnery Sergeant
rank, so that he could remain a senior member of a
Marine Force Reconnaissance Unit.

Members of Recon units don't care much for discus-
sions about rank. Membership of a Marine Force
Reconnaissance Unit alone gives one privileges to which
even some officers cannot lay claim. It is not unknown,
for instance, for a four-star general to consult a senior
Recon member on matters of combat technique and
weaponry. Indeed, Snake himself had been approached
on several such occasions. And besides, since most of
those who were selected for the Recons were sergeants

and corporals anyway, rank wasn't really an issue. They were with the Recons, the *elite* of the United States Marine Corps. That was rank in itself.

Upon the unit's arrival at Wilkes Ice Station, Snake had been put in charge of setting up the laser tripwire on the landward side of the station, about two hundred metres out. The tripwire was not really that much different from the rangefinder units on the hovercrafts. It was merely a series of box-like units through which a tiny, invisible laser beam was directed. When something crossed the beam, it triggered a flashing red light on Kaplan's forearm guard.

Moments ago, something had crossed the beam.

From his post on A-deck, Kaplan had immediately radioed Schofield who, sensibly, had ordered a visual check. After all, it might have just been Buck Riley and his team, returning from their check of that disappearing signal. Schofield had set follow-up time at two hours, and it had been nearly that long since Schofield's team had arrived at the station. Buck Riley and his crew were due here any minute now.

Only this wasn't Buck Riley.

'*Where is it, Snake?*' Schofield's voice said over Snake's helmet intercom.

'South-east corner. Coming through the outer circle of buildings now.' Snake watched as the hovercraft slowly made its way through the station complex, carefully negotiating its way between the small, snow-covered structures.

'Where are you?' Snake asked as he stood up, picked

up his rifle, and started jogging back through the snow toward the main dome.

'*I'm at the main entrance,*' Schofield's voice said. '*Just inside the front door. I need you to take up a covering position from the rear.*'

'Already on it.'

With the driving snow, visibility was limited, so the hovercraft proceeded slowly through the complex. Kaplan hurried along parallel to it, a hundred yards away. The vehicle came to halt outside the main dome of the ice station. It was slowly beginning to lower itself from its cushion of air when Snake dropped into the snow forty metres away and began to set up his sniper rifle.

He had just put his eye to his telescopic sight when the side door of the hovercraft slid open and four figures stepped out of it into the snowstorm.

'Good evening,' Schofield said with a crooked smile.

The four French scientists just stood there in the doorway to the ice station, dumbstruck. They stood in two pairs, with each pair carrying a large, white container between them.

In front of them stood Schofield, with his MP-5 held casually by his side. Behind Schofield stood Hollywood and Montana, with their MP-5s raised to shoulder height and their eyes looking straight down the barrels of their guns. Guns which were pointed right at their new visitors.

Schofield said, 'Why don't you come inside.'

'The others are safely back at d'Urville,' the leader of this new group said, as he sat down at the table in the dining room, alongside his French colleagues. Like the others, he had just passed a thorough pat-down search.

He had a lean face, hollow, with sunken eyes and high cheekbones. He had said his name was Jean Petard, and Schofield recognized the name from his list. He also remembered the short bio that had appeared under the name. It had said that Petard was a geologist, studying natural gas deposits in the continental shelf. The names of the other three Frenchmen were also on the list.

The four original French scientists were also there in the dining room – Champion, Latissier, Cuvier and Rae. The remaining residents of Wilkes were now back in their quarters. Schofield had ordered that they remain there until he and his squad had checked out the occupants of this newly arrived hovercraft. Montana and Lance-Corporal Augustine 'Samurai' Lau, the sixth and last member of Schofield's team, stood guard by the door.

'We hurried back as fast as we could,' Jean Petard added. 'We brought fresh food and some battery-powered blankets for the trip back.'

Schofield looked over at Libby Gant. She was over by the far wall of the dining room, examining the two white containers the Frenchmen had brought with them.

'Thank you,' Schofield said, turning back to face Petard. 'Thank you for all you have done. We arrived here only several hours after you did and the people here have told us how good you have been to them. We thank you for your efforts.'

'But of course,' Petard said, his English fluent. 'One must look after one's neighbours.' He offered a wry smile. 'You never know when you yourself might be in need of assistance.'

'No, you don't.'

At that moment Snake's voice crackled over Schofield's earpiece: '*Lieutenant, we have another contact crossing the tripwire.*'

Schofield frowned. Now things were starting to happen a little too fast. Four French scientists, he could handle. Another four, and the French were starting to show a little *too* much interest in Wilkes Ice Station. But now, if there were more of them –

'*Wait, Lieutenant, it's all right. It's one of ours. It's Riley's hovercraft.*'

Schofield let out a sigh of relief that he hoped nobody saw, and headed out of the room.

Over by the wall of the dining room, Libby Gant was sifting through the two large containers that the French scientists had brought with them. She pushed aside a couple of blankets, and some fresh bread. There was also some canned meat down at the bottom of the container. Corned beef, ham, that sort of thing. All were packed in sealed cans, the kind which have a key attached to the side which you use to peel back the lid.

Gant pushed a couple of the cans aside and was looking for more beneath them when suddenly one of the cans caught her eye.

There was something wrong about it.

It was a little larger than the other, medium-sized cans, and was roughly triangular in shape. At first Gant couldn't tell what it was that struck her about this particular can. It was just that something about it didn't look right . . .

And then Gant realized.

The seal on the can had been broken.

The peel-back lid, it seemed, had been opened and then set *back* into place. It was barely visible. Just a thin black line around the edge of the lid. If you were only giving the cans a cursory glance, you would almost certainly miss it.

Gant turned to look back at Schofield, but he had left the room. She looked up quickly at the French scientists, and as she did so, she saw Petard exchange a quick glance with the one named Latissier.

Schofield met Buck Riley at the main entrance. The two men stood out on the A-deck catwalk, about thirty feet away from the dining room.

'How was it?' Schofield asked.

'Not good,' Riley said.

'What do you mean?'

'That signal we lost, it was a hovercraft. French markings. From d'Urville. It had crashed into a crevasse.'

Schofield looked up sharply at Riley. 'Crashed into a crevasse?' Schofield looked back quickly at the French-men in the dining room. Only moments earlier, Jean Petard had said that the other hovercraft had arrived *safely* back at d'Urville.

'What happened,' Schofield said. 'Thin ice?'

'No. That's what we thought at first. But then Rebound got a closer look.'

Schofield turned back around. 'And?'

Riley gave him a serious look. 'There were five dead bodies in that hovercraft, sir. And all of them had been shot through the back of the head.'

Gant's voice exploded across Schofield's helmet intercom.

'Sir, this is Fox. There's something wrong here. Their food containers have been compromised.'

Schofield spun around and saw Libby Gant coming out of the dining room. She was walking quickly toward him, carrying a food can of some sort, peeling the lid back.

Behind her, Schofield saw Petard, in the dining room, rising to his feet, watching Gant, and then watching Schofield himself.

It was then that their eyes met.

It was only for an instant, but that was all either man needed. In that moment, there was a flash of understanding.

Gant cut across Schofield's line of sight with Petard. She had opened the can now and was pulling something out of it. The object she extracted from the can was small and black, and it looked a little like a small crucifix, the only difference being that the shorter, horizontal beam of the object was bent in a semi-circle.

Schofield's eyes widened when he saw it and he opened his mouth to shout, but it was too late.

In the dining room, Petard dived for the two white containers, just as Latissier – who hadn't been patted down since he had been at the station when the Marines had arrived – threw open his parka, revealing a short-barrelled, French-made FA-MAS assault rifle. At the same time, the one named Cuvier pulled both of his hands free of his pockets, revealing two models of the same weapon that Gant now had in her hand. Cuvier immediately fired one of them at Gant, and Schofield saw her head snap backward with the impact as she fell to the floor.

Deafening gunfire exploded through the silence as Latissier jammed his finger down on the trigger of his assault rifle and sprayed the dining room with a blanket of suppressing fire. His arc of gunfire cut through the air like a scythe, and it practically ripped Augustine Lau in two.

Latissier didn't let go for a full ten seconds and the sustained burst of machine-gun fire caused everybody else to hit the deck.

Wilkes Ice Station had become a battlefield.

And everything went to hell.

SECOND INCURSION

16 June 0930 hours

'This is Scarecrow! This is Scarecrow!' Schofield yelled into his helmet mike as he ducked into a doorway amid the cacophony of gunfire. 'I count eight hostiles! I repeat, eight hostile objects! I call it as six military, two civilians. Civilians are probably concealing weapons for use by the commandos. Marines, do not show prejudice!'

Chunks of ice rained down all around him as Latissier's stream of bullets impacted against the ice wall above him.

It was the sight of the crossbow that did it.

Each of the elite military units of the world has its own characteristic weapon. For the United States Navy SEALs, experts in close-quarter combat, it is the Ruger pump-action, 12-gauge shotgun. For the British Special Air Service – the famous SAS – nitrogen charges are the signature weapon. For US Marine Force Reconnaissance Units – the elite of the regular United States Marine Corps – it is the Armalite MH-12 Maghook, a grappling hook which also contains a high-powered magnet for adhesion to sheer, metallic surfaces.

Only one elite force, however, is known for carrying crossbows.

The Premier Régiment Parachutiste d'Infanterie de Marine, the crack French commando unit – known in English as the first marine parachute regiment. It is the French equivalent of the SAS or the SEALs.

Which is to say that it is not a regular force like, for example, the Marines. It is one step higher. It is an *offensive* unit, an attack team, an elite, covert force that exists for one reason and one reason only: to go in first, and to go in fast, and to kill everything in sight.

Which was why, when Schofield saw Gant lift the small, handheld crossbow from inside the food can, he knew that these men were not scientists from d'Urville. They were soldiers. Elite soldiers.

Cleverly, they had anticipated that he would know the names of all the scientists at d'Urville, so they had appropriated their names. To add to the illusion, they had also brought with them two *actual* scientists from the French research station – Luc Champion and Henri Rae – people whom the residents of Wilkes would know personally.

The final touch was probably the best touch of all: they had allowed Luc Champion, one of the civilians, to take the lead when the Marines had arrived at Wilkes Ice Station, bolstering the illusion that they were all merely scientists, following the lead of their superior.

That the French had taken five of the residents of Wilkes Ice Station – innocent civilians – out on a hovercraft under the pretence that they were being taken back to safety, and then *executed* them in the middle of the snow plains, made Schofield furious. In a detached corner of his mind, he conjured up a picture of what the scene must have looked like – the American scientists, men and women, crying, pleading, begging for their lives as the French soldiers moved among them, levelling their pistols at their heads and blasting their brains all over the inside of the hovercraft.

That at least two French scientists – Champion and Rae – had gone along with the French commandos made Schofield even more angry. What could they have been promised that would make them party to the murder of innocent academics?

The answer, unfortunately, was simple.

They would be given the first opportunity to study the spacecraft when the French got their hands on it.

Frantic voices shouted over Schofield's helmet intercom.

' – *return fire!*'

' – *Clear!*'

' – *Samurai is down! Fox is down!*'

' – *can't get a fucking shot –* '

Schofield looked out from behind the doorway and saw Gant lying flat on her back on the catwalk halfway between the dining room and the main entrance passageway. She wasn't moving.

His gaze shifted to Augustine Lau, lying sprawled out on the catwalk in the dining room doorway. Lau's eyes were wide open, his face covered in blood, blood that had sprayed up from his own stomach as Latissier's barrage of gunfire had assailed him from practically point-blank range.

Not far from Schofield, in the tunnel leading to the main entrance to the station, Buck Riley leaned out and returned fire with his MP-5, drowning out the tinny *rat-a-tat* sound of the French-made FA-MAS with the deep, puncture-like firing sound of the German-made MP-5. Next to him, Hollywood did the same.

Schofield snapped around to look over at Montana, huddled in the entrance to the western tunnel. 'Montana. You okay?'

When Latissier had opened fire a few moments earlier, Montana and Lau had been the closest men to him, standing in the doorway to the dining room. When Latissier's gun came up firing, Montana had been quick enough to duck back behind the doorway. Lau hadn't.

And while Lau had performed what infantry soldiers call 'the *danse macabre*' under the brutal weight of Latissier's fire, Montana had scrambled back along the catwalk to the nearest point of safety, the west tunnel.

Schofield saw Montana speak into his helmet mike fifty feet away. His gravelly voice came over Schofield's headset. '*Check that, Scarecrow. I'm a little shook up, but I'm okay.*'

'Good.'

More bullets slammed into the ice above Schofield's head. Schofield ducked back behind the doorway. Then, quickly, he peered out around the doorframe. But this time as he did so he heard a strange whistling sound.

With a sharp *thwump*, a four-inch-long arrow lodged into the ice barely five centimetres from Schofield's right eye.

Schofield looked up and saw Petard in the dining room, with his crossbow raised. No sooner had Petard fired his crossbow than Luc Champion hurled a short-barrelled sub-machine gun over to him and Petard rejoined the battle with a sharp volley of gunfire.

Peering around the doorframe, Schofield looked quickly over at Gant again. She was still lying motionless on the catwalk, halfway between the dining room and the main entrance tunnel.

And then suddenly her arm moved.

It must have been a reflex of some sort as she slowly regained consciousness.

Schofield saw it instantly and spoke into his helmet mike. 'This is Scarecrow, this is Scarecrow. Fox is still alive. I repeat, Fox is still alive. But she's out in the open. I need cover so I can go out there and get her. Confirm.'

Voices came in like a roll call. '*Hollywood, check that!*'

'*Rebound, check that!*'

'*Montana, check that.*'

'*Book, check that,*' Buck Riley said. '*You're all clear, Scarecrow. Go!*'

'All right, then, *now!*' Schofield yelled as he broke cover and scampered out onto the catwalk.

All around him, in perfect unison, the Marines whipped out from their cover positions and returned fire at the dining room. The noise was deafening. The ice walls of the dining room exploded into a thousand pock-marks. The combined strength of the assault forced Latissier and Petard to cease firing for a moment and dive for cover.

Out on the catwalk, Schofield fell to his knees next to Gant.

He looked down at her head. The arrow from Cuvier's crossbow had lodged in the forehead guard of her kevlar helmet and a narrow stream of blood ran out from her forehead and down the side of her nose.

Seeing the blood, Schofield leaned closer and saw that the force of the crossbow had been so strong that the arrow had penetrated Gant's helmet. Nearly a whole inch of the arrow had passed *through* the kevlar, so that now its glistening silver tip was poised right in front of Gant's forehead.

The helmet had held the arrow clear of her skull by millimetres.

Not even that. The razor-sharp point of the arrow had actually nicked her skin, drawing blood.

'Come on, let's go,' Schofield said, even though he was sure Gant couldn't hear him. The Marines' cover fire continued all around them as Schofield dragged Gant back along the catwalk, toward the main entrance passageway.

Suddenly, out of nowhere, one of the French commandos popped up from behind a hole in the wall of the dining room, with his rifle raised.

Still dragging Gant, Schofield quickly brought his pistol up, aimed through the sights and loosed two quick rounds. If the FA-MAS sounded tinny, and the MP-5 sounded like puncture noises, then Schofield's Colt 'Desert Eagle' automatic pistol sounded like a cannon. The French commando's head exploded in a splash of red as both rounds found their mark on the bridge of his nose. His head jolted back sharply – twice – and he dropped instantly out of sight.

'*Get out of there, Scarecrow! Move!*' Riley's voice yelled through Schofield's earpiece.

'I'm almost there!' Schofield yelled above the gunfire.

Suddenly another voice came over the intercom.

It was calm, clinical. There was no gunfire in the background behind it.

'*Marine Force, this is Snake. I am still at my post outside. I report that I now have visual on six more hostiles exiting the second French hovercraft. I repeat I am looking at six more armed men disembarking the French hovercraft and approaching the main entrance of the station.*'

A sudden, jarring shot rang out over the intercom. Snake Kaplan's sniper rifle.

'*Marine Force, this is Snake. Make that five more hostiles approaching the main entrance of the station.*'

Schofield looked back at the tunnel leading to the main entrance behind him. That was where he and Gant were heading. Riley and Hollywood were there right now, firing at the dining room. Beside them, Sergeant Mitch 'Ratman' Healy was doing the same.

And then suddenly, without warning, Healy's chest exploded. Shot from behind by a high-powered weapon.

Healy convulsed violently as a gout of blood spewed

out from his ribcage. The force of the impact and the subsequent nervous convulsion bent his back forward at an obscene angle and Schofield heard a sickening crack as the young soldier's spine broke.

Riley and Hollywood were out of the entrance passageway in a nanosecond. As they fired into the tunnel behind them, at some unseen enemy, they backed quickly toward the nearest rung-ladder that led down to B-deck.

Unfortunately, since they had only just arrived at the station, the six Marines who had gone with Riley to investigate the crashed hovercraft had been gathered around the main entrance passageway when the fighting had broken out. Which meant that now they were caught *in between* two hostile forces: one in the dining room in front of them, and another coming in through the main entrance behind them.

Schofield saw this. 'Book! Go down! Go down! Take your guys down to B-deck!'

'*Already on it, Scarecrow.*'

Schofield and Gant were in an even worse position.

Caught out on the catwalk between the dining room and the main entrance passageway, they had nowhere to go, no doorways to hide behind, no passageways to duck into. Just a metal catwalk three feet wide, bounded on one side by a sheer ice wall and on the other by a seventy-foot drop.

And any second now, the second French team would be bursting in through the main entrance passageway and Schofield and Gant would be the first thing they saw.

A chunk of ice exploded next to Schofield's head and he spun around. Petard was back on his feet in the dining room. Firing hard with his assault rifle, Schofield levelled his Desert Eagle at the dining room and fired six rapid shots back at Petard.

He looked back at the main entrance.

Ten seconds, at the most.

'Shit,' he said aloud, looking at Gant, limp in his arms. 'Shit.'

He looked down over the railing of the catwalk and saw the pool of water way down at the bottom of the station. It couldn't have been more than sixty or seventy feet. They could survive the fall . . .

No way.

Schofield looked at the catwalk on which he stood and then at the ice wall behind him.

Better.

'*Scarecrow, you better get out of there!*' It was Montana. He was now out on the catwalk, on the southern side of the station. From where he was standing he could see into the main entrance tunnel on the northern side. Whatever he saw there wasn't good.

'I'm trying, I'm trying,' Schofield said.

Schofield fired off two more shots at Petard in the dining room before holstering his pistol.

Then he quickly reached over his shoulder and pulled his Maghook from its holster on his back. The Armalite

MH-12 looks a little like an old-fashioned Tommy gun. It has two pistol grips: one normal grip with a trigger, and one forward, support grip below the muzzle. In effect the Maghook *is* a gun, a compact, two-handed launcher that fires a grappling hook from its muzzle at tremendous speed.

At Schofield's feet, Gant began to groan.

Schofield pointed his launcher at the ice wall and fired. A loud, metallic *whump* rang out as the grappling hook shot out from the muzzle and slammed into the ice wall. The hook exploded right *through* the wall, into the dining room. Once on the other side, its 'claws' snapped open.

'*Scarecrow! Get moving!*'

Schofield turned, just as Gant groggily got to her feet beside him.

'Grab my shoulders,' he said to her.

'Wha – huh?'

'Never mind. Just hold on,' Schofield said as he threw her arms over his shoulders. The two of them stood close, nose to nose. In any other circumstance, it would have looked like an intimate clinch, two lovers about to kiss – but not now. Holding Gant tightly, Schofield spun and leaned his butt up against the railing.

He looked back toward the main entrance tunnel and saw shadows moving quickly over the ice walls of the passageway. Gunfire began to spew out from within the passageway.

'Hold tight,' Schofield said to Gant.

And then, with both hands holding the launcher

behind Gant's back – and with her arms wrapped tightly around his neck – Schofield shifted his weight backwards and the two of them tumbled over the railing and fell out into space.

No sooner had Schofield and Gant fallen clear of the railing then it was assaulted by a torrent of bullets. A brilliant cascade of white-orange impact sparks exploded above their heads as they dropped clear of the catwalk.

Schofield and Gant fell.

The Maghook's cable splayed out above them. They whipped past B-deck, past Riley and Hollywood, who spun around at the unexpected sight of a pair of bodies dropping past them.

Then Schofield hit a black button on the forward grip of the launcher and a clamping mechanism inside the muzzle bit into the unspooling cable.

Schofield and Gant jolted to a sudden stop, just below B-deck, and the Maghook's cable began to swing them in toward the catwalk. They swung in fast, over the C-deck catwalk, and dropped down onto the metal gangway.

As soon as his feet hit the catwalk, Schofield pressed down twice on the trigger of the launcher. When he did so, up on A-deck, the grappling hook's claws responded by immediately collapsing inward with a sharp *snick*, and the hook was sucked back through the hole it had created in the dining room wall. The grappling hook fell down into the central shaft of the ice station, reeled in by the launcher. In a couple of seconds it was back in Schofield's hands, and he and Gant hurried inside the nearest doorway.

'*Grenade!*'

Riley and Hollywood ran flat out down the northern tunnel of B-deck, and dived around the corner.

Just as they cleared the corner a booming explosion rocked the ice tunnel behind them. Hard on the heels of the explosion came the concussion wave and then –

Riley and Hollywood ducked behind the corner as a swarm of dart-like objects shot past them at phenomenal speed and thudded into the opposite wall of the tunnel.

The two Marines looked at each other in astonishment.

A fragmentation charge.

A fragmentation charge is basically a conventional grenade which has been filled with hundreds of tiny pieces of metal – tiny *sharp-edged, skewed* pieces of metal designed to be as difficult as possible to extract from the human body. When the charge detonates, it sends a wave of these lethal fragments rocketing out in every direction.

'I've *always* said it,' Riley said wryly as he popped his clip and jammed a fresh magazine into the receiver of his MP-5. '*Always* said it: never trust the fucking French. There's just something about 'em. Maybe it's those beady little eyes they all got. Those assholes are supposed to be our goddam allies.'

'Fuckin' French,' Hollywood agreed thoughtfully, as he peered around the corner with one eye.

His jaw dropped. 'Oh *shit* – '

'What?' Riley spun around just in time to see a second grenade bounce around the corner and come to rest five feet away from them.

Five feet.

Out in the open.

There was nowhere to go. They couldn't get clear. Couldn't run down the corridor and get away in ti –

Riley launched himself forward. Toward the grenade. He slid along the frost-covered floor, feet first, soccer-style. When he was within range he let loose with a powerful kick, and sent the grenade skittling back down the north tunnel, back toward the central shaft.

As Riley kicked the grenade, Hollywood lunged forward and grabbed him by the shoulderplates and yanked him back behind the corner.

The grenade detonated.

Another deafening explosion boomed out.

A new wave of metal shards blasted out from the corridor, whipped past Riley and Hollywood, and slammed into the wall opposite them.

Hollywood turned and looked at Riley. 'Fuck my Roman sandals, man, this is some serious fucking catastrophe.'

Riley was already up on his feet. 'Come on, we're not staying here.'

He looked over toward the other side of the north tunnel and saw Rebound appear at the opposite corner.

With him were Corporal Georgio 'Legs' Lane and Sergeant Gena 'Mother' Newman. They must have come round from the western side of B-deck.

Riley said, 'All right everyone, listen up. As far as I'm concerned, this is now a split op. If we cluster and get cornered, we're all gonna be turned into strawberry fuckin' donuts. We have to split up. Rebound, Legs, Mother, you head back west, round the outer tunnel. Hollywood and I'll go east. Once we figure out where we are and what we can do with our position, then we can figure out how the hell we're going to regroup with the others and nail these fuckers. You all okay with that?'

There were no objections. Rebound and the others quickly got to their feet and hustled off down the opposite ice tunnel.

Riley and Hollywood began to run east, following the curve of the outer tunnel.

As he ran, Riley said, 'All right, what's this? B-deck, right. Okay. What's on B-deck?'

'I don't – ' Hollywood cut himself off as they cleared the bend in the tunnel and saw what lay ahead of them.

Both men stopped instantly and immediately felt their blood run cold.

Schofield fired up into the central shaft of Wilkes Ice Station with his Desert Eagle.

He and Gant were down on C-deck, inside a room which opened out onto the central catwalk. Schofield stood in the doorway, gun in hand, looking out across the central shaft and up at A-deck.

Behind him, inside whatever room this was, Gant was down on her haunches, shaking off her dizziness. She had taken off her helmet, revealing a short crop of snow-white, blonde hair.

Gant looked curiously at her helmet, at the arrow lodged in it. She shook her head, and put the helmet back on, arrow and all. She also donned her anti-flash glasses, concealing much of the thin line of dried blood that ran down from her forehead to her chin. Then she grabbed her MP-5 determinedly and joined Schofield at the doorway.

'You okay?' Schofield asked over his shoulder, as he aimed his pistol up at A-deck.

'Yeah, did I miss anything?'

'Did you see the part where that bunch of French *pricks* posing as scientists decided to pull guns on us?' Schofield fired off another round.

'Yeah, I caught that part.'

'What about the part where we found out that our new friends had six more guys stashed away in their hovercraft.'

'No, missed that.'

'Well that's the – ' he fired off another angry round ' – story so far.'

Gant looked at Schofield. Behind those opaque, silver glasses was a seriously pissed-off individual.

In fact, Schofield wasn't really angry at the French soldiers *per se*. Sure, at first, he'd been annoyed at himself for not picking that the French 'scientists' were actually soldiers. But then, they *had* got to Wilkes first, and they had brought with them two genuine scientists, a particularly clever ploy which had been enough to throw Schofield and his team off the scent.

What really made him angry, however, was that he'd lost the initiative in this battle.

The French had caught Schofield and his team off guard, taken them by surprise, and now *they* were dictating the terms of this fight. That was what really made Schofield pissed.

He tried desperately to fight his anger. He couldn't allow himself to be angry. He couldn't *afford* to feel that way.

Whenever he found himself beginning to feel angry or upset, Schofield always remembered a seminar he'd attended in London in late 1996 given by the legendary British commander, Brigadier-General Trevor J. Barnaby.

A burly man, with piercing dark eyes, a fully shaven head, and a severe, black goatee, Trevor Barnaby was the head of the SAS – had been since 1979 – and was widely regarded as the most brilliant front-line military tactician in the world. His strategic ability with regard to small incursionary forces was extraordinary. When it was executed by the finest elite military unit in the world, the SAS, it was invincible. He was the pride and joy of the British military establishment, and he had never failed on a mission yet.

In November 1996, as part of a USA–UK 'knowledge share agreement' it was decided that Barnaby would give a two-day seminar on covert incursionary warfare to the most promising American officers. In return, the United States would instruct British artillery units on the use of mobile *Patriot II* missile batteries. One of the officers chosen to attend Trevor Barnaby's seminar was Lieutenant Shane M. Schofield, USMC.

Barnaby had had a cocky, hard-edged lecture style that Schofield had liked – a rapid-fire series of questions and answers that had proceeded in a simple, logical progression.

'In any combat exchange,' Barnaby had said, 'be it a world war or an isolated two-unit stand-off, the first question you always ask yourself is this: *what is your opponent's objective?* What does he want? Unless you know the answer to that question, you'll never be able to ask yourself the second question: *how is he going to get it?*

'And I'll tell you right now, ladies and gentlemen,

the second question is of far greater importance to you than the first. Why? Because what he wants is unimportant insofar as strategy is concerned. What he wants is an object, that's all. The worldwide spread of communism. A strategic foothold on foreign territory. The ark of the covenant. *Who cares?* Knowing of it means nothing, in and of itself. *How he plans to get it*, on the other hand, means everything. Because that is action. And action can be stopped.

'So, once you have answered this second question, then you can proceed to question number 3: *what are you going to do to stop him?*'

When he had been speaking about command and leadership, Barnaby had repeatedly stressed the need for cool-headed reason. An angry commander, acting under the influence of rage or frustration, will almost certainly get his unit killed.

'As a leader,' Barnaby had said, 'you simply cannot *afford* to get angry or upset.'

Recognizing that no commanding officer was immune from feeling angry or frustrated, Barnaby had offered his three-step tactical analysis as a diversion from such feelings. 'Whenever you feel yourself succumbing to angry feelings, go through the three-step analysis. Get your mind off the anger and get it back on the job at hand. Soon, you'll forget about what pissed you off and you'll start doing what you're paid for.'

And as he stood there in the doorway on C-deck, in the freezing-cold, ice-covered world of Wilkes Ice

Station, Shane Schofield could almost hear Trevor Barnaby speaking inside his head.

Okay, then.

What is their objective?

They want the spaceship.

How are they going to get it?

They're going to kill everybody here, grab the spaceship and somehow get it off the continent before anybody even knows it existed.

All right. But there was a problem with that analysis. What was it – ?

Schofield thought for a moment. And then it hit him.

The French had arrived quickly.

So quickly, in fact, that they had arrived at Wilkes *before* the United States had been able to get a team of its own there. Which meant they'd been close to Wilkes when the original distress signal had gone out.

Schofield paused.

French soldiers had been at d'Urville when Abby Sinclair's signal had gone out.

But the distress signal could never have been anticipated. It was an emergency, a sudden occurrence.

And *that* was the problem with his analysis.

A picture began to form in Schofield's mind: *they had seen an opportunity, and they had decided to take it . . .*

The French had had their commandos at Dumont d'Urville, probably doing exercises of some sort. Arctic warfare, or something like that.

And then the distress signal from Wilkes had been

picked up. And suddenly the French would have realized that they had one of their elite military units within six hundred miles of the discovery of an extraterrestrial spacecraft.

The prospective gains were obvious: technological advances to be garnered from the propulsion system, the construction of the exterior shell. Maybe even weapons.

It was an opportunity too good to pass up.

And the beauty of the plan was that if the French did in fact manage to remove the spacecraft from Wilkes Ice Station, could the American government realistically go crying to the UN or the French Government and say that France had stolen *an alien spacecraft* from American custody? You can hardly complain when something you're not supposed to have in the first place is stolen from you.

But the French commandos faced two problems.

Firstly: the American scientists at Wilkes. They would have to be eliminated. There could be no witnesses.

The second problem was worse: it was almost certain that the United States would dispatch a protective reconnaissance unit to Wilkes. So a clock was ticking. In fact, the French had realized that, in all probability, US troops would arrive at Wilkes before they could get the spaceship off the continent.

Which meant there would be a firefight.

But the French were here by chance. They'd had neither the time nor the resources to prepare a full-strength assault on Wilkes. They were a small force facing the probability that the US would arrive on the scene, with a force of greater strength than theirs, before they could make good their escape with the spacecraft.

They needed a plan.

And so they'd posed as scientists, concerned neighbours. Presumably with the intention that they would earn the Marines' trust and then kill them while their backs were turned. It was as good a strategy as any for an impromptu force of inferior strength.

Which left one further question: *How were they going to get the spaceship out of Antarctica?*

Schofield decided that that question could wait. Better to tackle the battle at hand. So we ask again:

What is their objective?

To eliminate us and the scientists here at Wilkes.

How are they going to achieve that?

I don't know.

How would *you* achieve that?

Schofield thought about that. *I'd probably try to flush us all into the one place. That'd be much more efficient than attempting to search the whole station for us and pick us off one by* –

'Grenade!' Gant yelled.

Schofield was jolted back to the present as he saw a small, black grenade sail out over the A-deck railing and arc down toward him. Six similar grenades went flying down from A-deck and into the three ice tunnels that branched off into B-deck.

'Move!' Schofield said quickly to Gant as he ducked back inside the doorway and slammed the door shut.

He and Gant moved back to the far side of the room just in time to hear the grenade bounce up against the outside of the thick, wooden door.

Clunk, clunk.

And then the grenade exploded. White splinters shot out from the inside of the door as the pointed tips of a hundred, jagged metal shards instantly appeared in their place.

Schofield looked at the door, stunned.

The whole door, from floor to ceiling, was littered with tiny protrusions. What had once been a smooth wooden surface now looked like some kind of sinister medieval torture device. The whole thing was covered with sharp, spiked pieces of metal that had *almost* managed to rip right through the thick wooden door.

Other, similar, explosions rang out from the level above Schofield and Gant. They both looked up.

B-deck, Schofield thought.

I'd probably try to flush us all into the one place.

'Oh no,' Schofield said aloud.

'What?' Gant asked.

But Schofield didn't answer. Instead, he quickly yanked open the destroyed door and looked out into the central shaft of the ice station.

A bullet immediately rammed into the frost-covered doorframe next to his head. But it didn't stop him seeing them.

Up on A-deck, five of the French commandos were on their feet, laying down a suppressing fire over the whole of the station.

It was cover fire.

Cover fire for the other five commandos who were at that moment abseiling down from A-deck to B-deck. It was a short, controlled ride, and in a second the five commandos were on the B-deck catwalk, guns up and heading for the tunnels.

As he saw them, Schofield had a sickening realization. Most of his Marines were on B-deck, having retreated there after the second French team had charged in through the main entrance of the station.

And there was another thing.

B-deck was the main living area of Wilkes Ice Station. And Schofield himself had sent the American scientists back to their quarters while he and his team had gone to meet the newly arrived French hovercraft.

Schofield stared up at B-deck in horror.

The French had flushed them all into one place.

On B-deck, the world suddenly went crazy.

No sooner had Riley and Hollywood rounded the bend in the ice tunnel then they were confronted by the frightened faces of the residents of Wilkes Ice Station.

The instant he saw them, Riley suddenly remembered what B-deck was.

The living area.

Suddenly, a stream of submachine-gun fire raked the ice wall behind him.

At the same time, Schofield's voice came over Riley's

helmet intercom: '*All units, this is Scarecrow. I have a visual on five hostile objects landing right now on the B-deck catwalk. I repeat, five hostile objects. Marines, if you're on B-deck, look sharp.*'

Riley's mind went into overdrive. He quickly tried to remember the floor-plan of B-deck.

The first thing he recalled was that the layout of B-deck differed slightly from that of the other floors of Wilkes. All of the other floors were made up of four straight tunnels that branched out from the central well of the ice station to meet the circular outer tunnel. But because of an anomalous rock formation buried in the ice around it, B-deck didn't have a south tunnel.

It only had three straight tunnels, meaning that the outer, circular tunnel didn't form a complete circle as it did on every other floor. The result was a dead end at the southernmost point of the outer circle. Riley remembered seeing the dead end before: it housed the room in which James Renshaw was being held.

Right now, though, Riley and Hollywood found themselves in the outer tunnel, caught on the bend between the east tunnel and the north tunnel. With them were the scientists from Wilkes, who had obviously heard something going on outside, but who had dared not venture beyond the immediate vicinity of their rooms. Among the frightened faces in front of him, Riley saw a little girl.

Jesus.

'Take the rear,' Riley said to Hollywood, meaning that

part of the outer tunnel which lead back to the north tunnel.

Riley himself began to move past the group of scientists, so that he could take up a position in view of the east tunnel.

'Ladies and gentlemen! Could you please move back into your rooms!'

'What's going on?' one of the men asked angrily.

'Your friends upstairs weren't really your friends,' Riley said. 'There's now a team of French paratroopers inside your station and they will kill you if they see you. Now could you *please* get *back* in your *room*.'

'*Book! Grenade!*' Hollywood's voice echoed down the corridor.

Riley spun to see Hollywood come charging around the bend toward him. He also caught a glimpse of a fragmentation grenade bouncing into the tunnel twenty feet behind him.

'Oh, fuck.' Riley turned instantly, looking for cover in the opposite direction – in the east tunnel, ten yards away.

It was then that he saw two more grenades tumble out of the east tunnel, and come to rest against the wall of the outer tunnel.

'Oh, *really fuck*.' Riley's eyes went wide. There were now fragmentation grenades at *both* ends of the tunnel.

'Get inside! *Now!*' Riley screamed at the scientists as he began to throw open the nearest door. 'Get *back* in your rooms *now!*'

It took the scientists a second to grasp what Riley meant, but when they did get it, they immediately dived for their doorways.

Riley hurled himself inside the nearest doorway and peered back out to see what Hollywood was doing. The young corporal was running for all he was worth down the curved tunnel toward Riley.

And then suddenly he slipped. And fell.

Hollywood went sprawling – clumsily, head first – onto the frost-covered floor of the tunnel.

Riley watched helplessly as Hollywood frantically began to pick himself up off the floor, looking anxiously back at the fragmentation grenade in the tunnel behind him as he did so.

Maybe two seconds left.

And in an instant, Riley felt his stomach knot.

Hollywood wasn't going to make it.

Right in front of Hollywood – in the only doorway he could possibly get to in time – two of the scientists were desperately trying to get into the same room. One was pushing the other in the back, trying to get him to move inside.

Buck Riley watched in horror as Hollywood looked up at the two scientists and saw that he had no chance of getting into that room. Hollywood then swung back round to look at the fragmentation grenade thirty feet down the curved corridor behind him.

A final, desperate turn, and Hollywood's eyes met Riley's. Eyes white with fear. The eyes of a man who knows he is about to die.

He had nowhere to go. Nowhere at all.

And then, with thunderous intensity, the three grenades – one from the north tunnel, two from the east – unleashed their anger and Riley ducked back behind his doorway and saw a thousand glistening metal shards whip past him in both directions.

Another explosion rocked the outside of the thick wooden door and a new wave of metal shards slammed into it.

Schofield and Gant were at the back of the room on C-deck, taking cover behind an upturned aluminium table.

'Marines, call in,' Schofield said.

Voices came in over his intercom, gunfire rang out in the background.

'*This is Rebound! I'm with Legs and Mother! We are under heavy fire in the north-west quadrant of B-deck!*'

A burst of static suddenly cut across Schofield's ear-piece. '*– is Book – wood is down. I'm in – quadrant –*' Book's voice cut off abruptly, the signal gone.

'*This is Montana. Santa Cruz is with me. We're still on A-deck, but we're pinned down.*'

'*Lieutenant, this is Snake. I'm outside, approaching the main entrance right now.*'

There was no word from Hollywood. And Mitch Healy and Samurai Lau were already dead. Schofield did the math. If all three of them were dead, then the Marines were down to nine now.

Schofield thought about the French. They had started with twelve men, plus the two civilian scientists. Snake had said earlier that he'd killed one outside, and Schofield himself had capped another one upstairs. That meant the French were down to ten men – *plus* the two civilians, wherever the hell they were.

Schofield's thoughts returned to the present. He looked at the big wooden door in front of him, covered with dozens of protruding silver spikes.

He turned to Gant. 'We can't stay here.'

'I kind of already got that idea,' Gant replied deadpan.

Schofield spun to look at her, confused by her reply. Gant didn't say anything. She just pointed over his shoulder.

Schofield turned around and for the first time, really *looked* at the room around him.

It looked like a boiler room of some sort. Anodized black pipes covered the ceiling. Two enormous white cylinders – lying on their sides, one on top of the other – took up the entire right-hand wall of the room. Each cylinder was about twelve feet long and six feet high.

And in the middle of each cylinder was a large, diamond-shaped red sticker. On the sticker was a picture of a single flame and, in large bold letters, the words:

DANGER
FLAMMABLE PROPELLANT
L-5
HIGHLY FLAMMABLE

Schofield stared at the massive white cylinders. They appeared to be connected to a computer which sat on a table in the rear corner of the room. The computer was switched on, but at the moment the screen was filled with a *Sports Illustrated* Swimsuit screen saver: a buxom blonde in an impossibly small bikini lying provocatively on a tropical beach somewhere.

Schofield crossed the room quickly and stood in front of the computer. The sexy woman on the screen pouted at him.

'Maybe later,' Schofield said to the screen as he hit a key on the keyboard. The screen saver vanished instantly.

It was replaced by a coloured schematic diagram of the five floors of Wilkes Ice Station. Five circles filled the screen – three on the left, two on the right – each one comprised of the central well of the station surrounded by a larger, outer circle. The outer circle was connected to the central well by four straight tunnels.

Rooms were arrayed both *between* the outer tunnel and the central well, and *outside* the outer tunnel. Different rooms were painted different colours. A colour chart on the side of the screen explained that each colour indicated a different temperature. The temperatures ranged from $-5.4°$ to $-1.2°$ Celsius.

'It's the air-conditioning system,' Gant said, taking up a position by the door. 'L-5 means it uses chlorofluorocarbons as propellant. Must be pretty old.'

'Why doesn't that surprise me,' Schofield said as he walked over toward the door and grabbed the handle.

He opened the door a crack –

– just in time to see a black, baseball-sized object come rocketing toward him.

A long finger of white smoke traced a line through the air behind it, revealing its source: Petard up on A-deck, with a FA-MAS assault rifle equipped with an underslung 40mm grenade launcher.

Schofield ducked just as the gas-propelled grenade shot through the narrow gap in the doorway above his head, banked upward slightly, and slammed into the back wall of the air-conditioning room.

'*Out! Now!*' Schofield yelled.

Gant didn't need to be told. She was already on her way out the door, MP-5 up and firing.

Schofield dived out through the doorway after her, just as the air-conditioning room exploded behind him. The heavy, spike-ridden door almost blew off its hinges as the concussion wave flung it outward like a twig. The door whipped around in a full 180-degree arc before banging into the ice wall out on the catwalk, right next to Schofield. An enormous fireball then blasted out from the doorway and shot past Schofield out into the open space in the centre of Wilkes Ice Station.

'Scarecrow! Come on!' Gant called as she fired up at A-deck from further down the catwalk.

Schofield leapt to his feet and cut loose an extended burst from his MP-5, aiming up at where he had seen Petard only moments before.

Gant and Schofield raced around the C-deck catwalk – out in the open – Schofield with his gun trained up to the left, Gant taking the right. Long tongues of bright, yellow flames burst out from the muzzles of their MP-5s. Return fire from the French raked the ice walls all around them.

Schofield saw a small alcove set into the wall about ten yards ahead of them.

'Fox! *There!*'

'Got it!'

Schofield and Gant threw themselves into the small alcove just as a second, more powerful, explosion boomed out from the air-conditioning room.

From the second it erupted, Schofield knew that this detonation was different to the first one. It wasn't like the short, contained blast of a grenade. It had more resonance to it, more substance. It was the sound of something large exploding . . .

It was the sound of one of the air-conditioning cylinders exploding.

The walls to the air-conditioning room cracked instantly under the weight of the massive explosion. Like a cork being popped from a champagne bottle, a length of black piping shot clear of the air-conditioning room and careered at phenomenal speed across the one-hundred-foot space in the middle of the station, and lodged itself into the ice wall on the far side.

Schofield pressed himself flat against the wall of the alcove as a hail of bullets slammed into the ice next to him. He looked at the alcove around him.

It was just a small nook sunken into the wall, designed, it seemed, for the sole purpose of housing the control console which drove the enormous winch which raised and lowered the station's diving bell. The console itself, Schofield saw, was little more than a series of levers, dials and buttons arranged on a panel.

In front of the console, sat an abnormally large, steel-plated chair. Schofield immediately recognized the chair as a pilot's ejection seat from an F-14 fighter. The black exhaust marks beneath the seat's booster and the sizeable dent in its large steel headrest told Schofield that this ejection seat had, in a former life, been used for its given purpose. Someone at Wilkes had cleverly mounted the enormous seat on a rotating stand and then bolted the whole thing down to the floor, turning four hundred pounds of military junk into heavy duty furniture.

Suddenly, a new barrage of automatic gunfire thundered down from the north-west corner of A-deck and Gant jumped onto the ejection seat and ducked behind the headrest, curling her small frame into a ball so that she was completely covered by the big seat's steel-lined backplate.

The burst of gunfire lasted a full ten seconds and pummelled the rear of the ejection seat. Gant pressed her head up against the headrest, keeping her eyes shielded from the onslaught of ricocheting bullets.

As she did so, however, some movement caught her eye.

It was off to her left. *Down* to her left.

Down in the pool at the base of the station. *Under* the surface. A glistening black and white shape, unbelievably huge, cruising slowly, ominously, beneath the surface. It must have been deeper than it appeared because the high dorsal fin wasn't breaking the surface.

The first dark shape was joined by a second shape, then a third, and then a fourth. The lead one must have been at least forty feet long. The others were smaller.

Females, Gant thought. She had read once that for every one male there were usually eight or nine females.

The water was choppy and it served only to make their blurred black and white outlines look all the more sinister. The leader rolled on its side and Gant caught a side-on glimpse of the white underbelly and the wide open mouth and the two terrifying rows of teeth and suddenly the picture was complete.

It was then that Gant saw the two juveniles, swimming behind the enormous lead male. They were the two killers she had seen earlier, before the battle with the French had erupted, the two killers who had been searching for Wendy.

Now they were back . . . *and they had brought the rest of the pack with them.*

The full pod of killer whales began to circle the pool at the base of Wilkes Ice Station and as she huddled behind the headrest of the ejection seat, Gant felt a new sense of dread begin to crawl up the back of her spine.

Hollywood had never stood a chance.

The shards from the three fragmentation grenades had rained down on him with terrifying intensity – from in front and behind.

Book could only watch helplessly as his young partner – on the floor, on his knees – put a feeble hand over his face and then fell under the weight of the hailstorm of metal fragments.

The scientist who had been trying to push his colleague into the nearby doorway hadn't been fast enough either. Like Hollywood, he was now unrecognizable. The wave of metal shards had cut him down where he stood. And while Hollywood's body armour had been effective in protecting *his* chest and shoulders from the blast, the scientist hadn't been so lucky. His whole body – unprotected by any kind of armour – was a hideous, bloodstained mess.

No exposed tissue could have survived such a bombardment. None had. The storm of shards had ripped every inch of exposed skin from the two men's bodies.

And for a moment, a brief moment, Buck Riley could

do nothing but stare at the broken body of his fallen friend.

On the other side of B-deck, Rebound was charging around the curved outer tunnel, gun up.

Legs Lane and Mother Newman ran behind him, firing desperately back at the three shadows coming down the tunnel after them.

Legs Lane was a thirty-one-year-old Corporal, olive-skinned, square-jawed, Italian in both looks and manner. For her part, Mother Newman was the second of the two women in Schofield's unit – and she couldn't have been more different from Libby Gant.

Whereas Gant was twenty-six, compact and had a short crop of straight blonde hair, Mother was thirty-four, six-foot-two and had a fully shaven head. She weighed in at nearly two hundred pounds. Her call sign 'Mother' wasn't supposed to mean 'maternal figure'. It was short for motherfucker.

Mother spoke into her helmet mike. 'Scarecrow. This is your Mother speaking. We are experiencing heavy fire on B-deck. I repeat. We are experiencing heavy fire on B-deck. We have enemy troops behind us. and frag grenades bouncing all over the fucking place. We are approaching the west tunnel and are going to head for the central shaft. If you or anyone out there has a visual on the shaft, we'd really love to hear about it.'

Schofield's voice came over their helmet intercoms. *Mother. This is Scarecrow. I have a visual on the central shaft. There are no hostile objects out on the catwalk right now. We spotted five on your level before, but they're all in the tunnels now.*

'*I can also confirm five more hostiles up on A-deck, and at least one of those has a 40 mil grenade launcher. If you have to break out onto the catwalks, we'll cover you from below. Montana, Santa Cruz? You out there?*'

'*We're here,*' came Montana's voice.

'*You still on A-deck?*'

'*Affirmative that.*'

'*You still pinned down?*'

'*We're working on it.*'

'*Just keep doing what you're doing. Draw their fire. We're gonna have three of our people stepping out into the open on B-deck in about ten seconds.*'

'*No problem, Scarecrow.*'

Mother said, 'Thanks, Scarecrow. We're moving into the western tunnel now. Coming to the central shaft.'

In the alcove on C-deck, Schofield keyed his helmet mike again. 'Book! Book! Come in!'

There was no reply.

'Jesus, Book. Where are you?'

Inside the women's shower room on B-deck, Sarah Hensleigh snapped around at the sound of a door being kicked in.

For one terrifying instant, she thought the French

soldiers were storming the women's shower room. But they weren't. The sound had come from the next room, the men's shower room.

The French were in the next room!

With Sarah inside the women's shower block were Kirsty, Abby Sinclair and a geologist named Warren Conlon. When Buck Riley had ordered them back to their rooms, the four of them had immediately scrambled in here. They had only just made it, with Conlon just managing to squeeze in through the doorframe and jam the door shut a split second before the fragmentation grenades had gone off in the tunnel outside.

The women's shower block was situated in between the outer tunnel and the central shaft, in the north-eastern corner of B-deck. It had three doors: one leading to the north tunnel, one leading to the outer tunnel and one leading to the men's shower room next door.

More sounds echoed out from the men's shower room.

The sounds of French soldiers kicking open cubicle doors, looking for anyone who had attempted to hide in the cubicles.

Sarah pulled Kirsty toward the door that led to the north tunnel. 'Come on, honey, keep moving.'

Sarah looked back over her shoulder.

Beyond the row of six shower recesses, she could see the top quarter of the door that led to the men's shower room.

It was still closed.

The French soldiers would be coming through that door any second now.

Sarah reached the door leading out to the north tunnel and grabbed the handle.

She hesitated. There was no way of knowing what lay on the other side.

'*Sarah!* What are you *doing*? Come *on*,' Warren Conlon said in a desperate, hissing whisper. Tall and thin, he was a timid man, nervous at the best of times. Now he was positively terrified.

'Okay, okay,' Sarah said. She began to turn the handle.

There was a loud bang as the door to the men's shower room suddenly burst open behind them.

'*Go!*' Conlon yelled.

Sarah threw open the door and, pulling Kirsty with her, charged out into the north tunnel.

She hadn't gone more than a couple of steps when she stopped dead in her tracks –

– and found herself looking into the eyes of a man with a gun pointed right at her head.

The man cocked his head to one side and shook his head. 'Jesus.' He lowered his gun.

'It's okay, it's okay,' Buck Riley said as he ran up to Sarah and Kirsty. 'You scared the shit out of me, but it's okay.'

Abby Sinclair and Warren Conlon joined them out in the tunnel, slamming the door shut behind them.

'They in there?' Riley asked, nodding at the women's shower block.

'Yeah,' Sarah said.

'Are the others okay?' Warren Conlon asked stupidly.

'I don't think they'll be leaving their rooms again in a hurry,' Riley said as he scanned the tunnel behind him. Automatic gunfire echoed out from the outer tunnel. As Riley looked behind him, Sarah noticed a thin line of blood trickling out from a large cut on his right ear. Riley himself didn't seem to notice it. The earpiece that he had in that ear had a jagged sliver of metal lodged in it.

'We may have a slight problem,' Riley said, as his eyes searched the tunnel around them. 'I've lost contact with the rest of my team. My radio gear got hit by some ricocheting fragments before, so I'm off the air. I can't hear the others and they can't hear me.'

Riley snapped round and looked the other way, out over Sarah's head, toward that end of the tunnel that led to the catwalks and the massive shaft in the centre of the station.

'Come with me,' was all he said as he brushed past Sarah and led the way toward the central well of Wilkes Ice Station.

'Book!' Schofield whispered into his helmet mike, as he kept his eyes locked on the western tunnel of B-deck. '*Book!* Where are you? God damn it.'

'No Book?' Gant asked.

'Not yet,' Schofield said. He and Gant were still crouched in their alcove on C-deck, on the eastern side of the station. They were waiting tensely for Rebound, Mother and Legs to come out from the western tunnel of B-deck.

Rebound emerged first. Quickly but cautiously, gun up, eyes looking down his gunsights, sweeping his MP-5 in a brisk 180-degree arc, searching for any sign of trouble.

As soon as he saw Rebound emerge, Schofield immediately opened fire on A-deck, forcing whoever was up there to take cover. Gant came up five seconds later and did the same.

Schofield pulled back behind the alcove's wall to reload. As he did so, he watched as Gant fired off three short bursts.

It was then that he saw something strange happen.

The yellow tongue of fire that flashed out from the

muzzle of Gant's gun suddenly leapt forward a full two metres. It was only for a second, but it looked incredible. For a short moment, Gant's compact MP-5 machine pistol had looked like a flame-thrower.

Schofield was momentarily confused. *What the hell had caused that?* Then, suddenly, it hit him, and he spun and looked back at the –

All of a sudden, Gant yelled, 'I'm dry!' and Schofield snapped back to the present. He immediately opened fire on the A-deck catwalk while she reloaded.

As he lay down a suppressing fire on A-deck, Schofield saw Legs and Mother hurry out onto the B-deck catwalk behind Rebound. They were firing for all they were worth back into the tunnel from which they had come.

Legs went dry. Schofield watched as Legs popped his clip and let it drop to the catwalk, and then grabbed a fresh magazine. No sooner had he jammed it into the lower receiver of his gun than he was hit in the neck by some unseen opponent inside the western tunnel.

Legs flailed backwards, losing his balance for a second, before turning his gun back toward the enemy and letting loose with an extended burst of gunfire that would have woken the dead. In 2.2 seconds thirty rounds were spent and that clip was dry, too. Mother grabbed him and yanked him out onto the catwalk, away from the tunnel.

Now wounded and dripping with blood, Legs began to fumble with a new clip. The clip slipped through his bloody fingers and fell out over the railing, dropping fifty feet through the air until it splashed into the pool at the bottom of the station. At that point, Legs cut his losses, tossed his MP-5 and pulled out his Colt .45. Single fire from here.

Schofield and Gant continued to sweep the uppermost deck with their fire. Gant had watched as Legs' clip dropped all the way down into the pool; had watched as one of the killer whales banked upward to see what it was that had fallen into its domain.

Mother went dry. She cut the empty clip and reloaded fast.

Schofield watched anxiously as the three of them – Mother, Rebound and Legs – moved along the catwalk between the west and the north tunnels of B-deck, heading toward the north tunnel.

They were almost there when suddenly Buck Riley burst out from the north tunnel with four civilians in tow behind him.

Right in front of Mother, Rebound and Legs!

Schofield saw it as it happened and his jaw dropped.

'Oh, *Jesus*,' he breathed.

This was a disaster. Now *four* of his people were out in the open, with four innocent civilians! And any second now, the French would appear and cut them to ribbons.

'Book! Book!' Schofield yelled into his helmet mike. 'Get out of there! *Get off the catwa* –'

And then it happened and Schofield's horror was complete.

In perfect synchronization, five French commandos burst out onto the B-deck catwalk.

Three from the west tunnel. Two from the east.

They opened fire without the slightest hesitation.

What happened next almost happened too fast for Schofield to comprehend.

The five French commandos on B-deck had just pulled off a perfect pincer manoeuvre. They'd flushed Mother, Rebound and Legs out onto the catwalk and now they were about to finish it off by firing upon them from both flanks.

The appearance of Buck Riley and the four civilians was an added bonus. It obviously hadn't been expected – when they had appeared out on the catwalk, all five of the French soldiers had had their guns firmly trained on Mother, Rebound and Legs.

As it turned out, however, they never got a chance to turn their fire on Riley and the civilians anyway.

The three French commandos who had emerged from the *western* tunnel fired first. White-hot tongues of fire shot out from the muzzles of their guns.

At point-blank range, Legs, Mother and Rebound were all hit. Mother in the leg, Rebound in the shoulder. Legs took the brunt of it – two to the head, four to the chest – his whole body becoming a shuddering explosion of blood. He was dead before he hit the ground.

But that was all Schofield saw.

Because that was when it happened.

Schofield watched in amazement as, at the *exact* moment that the French commandos on the western side of the station fired their rifles, two enormous fingers of fire shot out in both directions from where they stood.

They looked like twin comets. Two seven-foot-tall balls of fire that rocketed around the circumference of the B-deck catwalk, leaving in their wake a wall of blazing flames.

The whole of the B-deck catwalk disappeared in an instant as the spectacular curtain of flames shot up from every point on the circular metal catwalk, concealing from view everybody who had been standing on the deck.

For a full second, Schofield could do nothing but stare. It had happened so fast. It was as if somebody had laid down a trail of gasoline on the B-deck catwalk and then lit a match.

Then the penny dropped and Schofield immediately spun around to face –

– the air-conditioning room.

And in that instant, it all suddenly made sense.

The air-conditioning cylinders had no doubt been substantially damaged by the detonation of the rocket-grenade minutes earlier. Thus punctured, they had immediately started spewing out their store of chloro-fluorocarbons.

Highly flammable chlorofluorocarbons.

That was what had happened when Schofield had seen the two-metre length of fire spew forward from the muzzle of Gant's machine pistol only moments earlier. It had been a warning of things to come. But at that time, the CFCs hadn't yet filled the station. Hence, the small, two-metre flame.

But now . . . now the amount of flammable gas in the station's atmosphere had multiplied considerably. So much so that when the French had opened fire on the Marines on B-deck, the whole deck had gone up in flames.

Schofield's eyes widened.

The air-conditioning cylinders were still spewing out CFCs. Soon the whole station would be contaminated with flammable . . .

The horror of the realization hit Schofield hard.

Wilkes Ice Station had become a gas oven.

All it needed was one spark, one flame – or one gunshot – and the whole station would spontaneously combust.

Rivets began to pop out of their sockets on B-deck.

Spot fires burned all over the B-deck catwalk. Agonized screams echoed out across the open space of the ice station as soldiers and civilians alike lay writhing on the catwalk, their bodies alight.

It looked like a scene from Hell itself.

The three French soldiers on the western side of the station – the ones who had opened fire on Mother,

Rebound and Legs – had been the first to go up in flames, the gaseous air around them having been ignited by the white-hot tongues of fire that had burst forth from the muzzles of their guns.

The twin fireballs had immediately shot out from the barrels of their guns. One had surged forward while the other had turned on them and rushed with all its fury *back* at their faces.

Now two of those French soldiers lay on the floor, screaming. The third was frantically banging himself against the ice wall nearby in a desperate attempt to put out the flames on his fatigues.

Mother and Rebound were also alight. Beside them, Legs was already dead. His motionless body lay flat on the catwalk as it was slowly devoured by crackling, orange flames.

Over by the north tunnel, Buck Riley was trying to smother out the flames on Abby Sinclair's pants by rolling her over on the metal catwalk. Beside them, Sarah Hensleigh slapped frantically at a cluster of flames that had ignited on the back of Kirsty's bulky pink parka. Warren Conlon just screamed. His hair was on fire.

And then, suddenly, there came a sickening sound. The lurching, wrenching sound of bending steel.

Riley looked up from what he was doing.

'Oh, no,' he moaned.

Schofield also looked up at the sound.

He scanned the catwalk above him, and saw a series

of triangular steel supports that fastened the underside of the B-deck catwalk to the ice wall.

Slowly, almost imperceptibly, those supports began to slide out from the wall.

Under the intense heat from the fire on B-deck, the long rivets that fastened the supports to the wall were starting to heat up. *They were melting the ice around them*, and were now starting to slide out from the wall!

The rivets began to expand – *thwack! thwack! thwack!* – and in rapid succession began to crack open the ice-cold notches of their steel supports and fall to the catwalk below.

The rivets clanked loudly as they dropped down onto the C-deck catwalk.

One.

Then two. Then three.

Then five. Then ten.

There were rivets everywhere, raining down on the C-deck catwalk. And then suddenly a new sound filled Wilkes Ice Station.

The unmistakable, high-pitched squeal of rending metal.

'Oh, *shit*,' Schofield said. 'It's gonna go.'

B-deck went. Suddenly. Without warning.

The entire catwalk – the whole, flaming circle – just fell away, dropping with a sudden jolt, taking everybody who was still on it down with it.

Some sections of the catwalk managed to stay

attached to the ice walls. Their fall ended abruptly, almost as soon as it had begun. They ended up pointing downward at a 45-degree angle.

The remaining sections just slid out from the ice walls and dropped down into the central shaft of the station.

Nearly everyone who had been standing on B-deck dropped with the collapsed sections of catwalk – eleven people in all.

A tangled mix of civilians, soldiers and three broken sections of metal catwalk sailed down the central shaft of Wilkes Ice Station.

They fell a full fifty feet.

And then they landed.

Hard.

In water.

In the pool at the bottom of the station.

Sarah Hensleigh plunged underwater.

A stream of bubbles shot up past her face and the world suddenly went silent.

Cold. Absolute, unforgiving cold assailed all of her senses at once. It was so cold it hurt.

And then suddenly, she heard noises.

Noises that broke the ghostly, underwater silence – a series of muffled *whumps* in the water all around her. It was the sound of the others falling into the pool with her.

Slowly, the curtain of bubbles in front of her face began to disperse, and Sarah began to make out a number of unusually large shapes moving smoothly through the water around her.

Large, *black* shapes.

They appeared to glide effortlessly through the silent, freezing water – each one frightening in its size; as large and as wide as a car. At that moment, a wash of white cut across Sarah's field of vision and suddenly an enormous mouth, full of razor-sharp teeth, opened wide in front of her eyes.

Pure fear shot through her body.

Killer whales.

Suddenly, Sarah broke the surface. Gulped in air. The

cold of the water meant nothing now. One after the other, huge, black dorsal fins began to rise above the choppy surface of the pool.

Before Sarah could even get a bearing on exactly where in the pool she was, something burst up out of the water next to her and she spun.

It wasn't a killer whale.

It was Abby.

Sarah felt her heart start again. A second later, Warren Conlon also came up beside her.

Sarah spun around in the water. All five of the French soldiers who had been on B-deck when it blew were scattered around the pool. Three Marines were also in the pool. One of them, Sarah noticed, was floating face-down in the water.

A scream echoed down through the central shaft of the station.

A shrill, high-pitched squeal.

The scream of a little girl.

Sarah's head snapped to look upward. There, high above her, hanging by one hand from the downturned railing of the B-deck catwalk, was Kirsty. The Marine who had been with them when the catwalk had collapsed was lying face-down on the broken metal platform, reaching down desperately, trying to grab Kirsty's hand.

Just then, as she was looking up at Kirsty, Sarah felt the immense weight of one of the killers rush through the water between her and Conlon. The massive animal brushed against the side of her leg.

And then suddenly, Sarah heard a shout.

It had come from the other side of the pool, and Sarah spun around just in time to see one of the French commandos – his face blistered and scorched from the fireball – swimming frantically for the edge of the pool, his terrified, panicked whimpers interrupted only by short, desperate breaths.

It was the only movement in the whole pool. Nobody else had even dared to move.

Almost immediately, a towering, black dorsal fin appeared alongside the desperate swimmer. After a second, it slowed, and then it ominously sank below the surface behind him.

The result was as violent as it was sudden.

With a hideous *crack*, the French commando's body suddenly snapped backwards in the water. He turned in the water and opened his mouth to scream but nothing came out. His eyes just went wide. He must have seen that the whale had crushed the whole of his lower body with its bite and was now holding him firmly within its mighty jaws.

The whale's second yank was even more powerful than the first. It pulled the Frenchman under with such force that the man's head jolted backwards and slapped down hard against the water as he went under and disappeared forever.

Sarah Hensleigh gasped. 'Oh, Jesus . . .'

*

Buck Riley's section of catwalk was still attached to the ice wall. Just. It hung downward at a steep angle, out over the central shaft.

The three scientists – Riley didn't know their names – had all been too slow. The sudden collapse of the catwalk had caught all three of them by surprise. Too slow to get a handhold, they had all fallen down into the shaft.

Riley's reflexes had been quicker. When the catwalk had fallen away beneath him, he had hit the deck and immediately garnered a fingerhold in the grating of the catwalk itself.

The little girl had also been fast.

As soon as the floor had dropped away beneath her, she had fallen to the catwalk and immediately started to slide toward the edge.

Her feet had gone over the edge first, followed quickly by her waist, and then her chest. Just as her head fell clear of the railing, she threw out a desperate hand and miraculously caught hold of the hand railing.

The railing held for a second but, weakened by the force of the gas explosion, it suddenly buckled and snapped and swung out over the edge of the catwalk, so that it now hung *upside-down* out over the shaft.

And so the little girl hung there, one-handed and screaming, from the upside-down railing of the catwalk, fifty feet above the killer-whale-infested pool.

'Don't look down!' Riley yelled, as he reached down for her hand. He had already seen the killer whales down in the pool, had just seen one of them take the French commando. He didn't want the little girl seeing them.

The little girl was crying, sobbing, 'Don't let me fall!'

'I won't let you fall,' Riley said as he lay on his stomach and stretched out as far as he could, trying to grab her wrist. Small, isolated spot fires burned on the remnants of the catwalk all around him.

His hand was about a foot away from the girl's when he saw her frightened eyes begin to dart around.

'What's your name?' Riley said suddenly, trying to distract her.

'My *hand* is hot,' she whimpered.

Riley looked back along the railing. About five yards to his left, a small spot fire licked at the point where the downturned railing met the catwalk.

'I know it's hot, honey. I know it is. Just keep holding on. What did you say your name was?'

'Kirsty.'

'Hi, Kirsty. My name's Buck, but you can just call me Book like everybody else does.'

'Why do they call you that?'

Riley cast a sideways glance at the spot fire licking against the railing.

Not good.

Under the intense heat of the explosion, the black paint on the railing had broken out into dry, paper-like flakes. If the fire came into contact with those flakes, the whole railing would go up in flames.

Riley kept reaching out for Kirsty's hand, stretched harder. Half a foot away. He almost had her.

'Do you always,' Riley breathed a weak half-laugh, 'ask this many questions?' He grimaced as he stretched. 'If you,' – breath – 'really wanna know,' – breath – 'it's because, once,' – breath – 'one of my friends found out I was writing a book.'

'Uh-huh . . .' Kirsty's eyes began to wander again.

'Kirsty. Now listen to me, honey. I want you to keep your eyes looking right at me now, okay. Right at me.'

'O-*kay*,' she said.

Then she looked down.

Riley swore.

Rebound had been less than three yards away from the French commando when he had been taken under. The sheer violence of the Frenchman's death had scared the living shit out of him.

Now, the whole pool was silent.

Rebound hovered in the pool, looking desperately about himself. The water was cold and the bullet wound in his shoulder stung, but he barely even noticed them now.

Mother was treading water next to him, her face watchful. Waiting, with tense anticipation. Legs' body floated face-down in the water next to her, a halo of blood slowly fanning out from its head, seeping into the clear, blue water around it.

The four remaining French commandos were also still

in the pool. They completely ignored Rebound and Mother, their battle forgotten, at least for the moment.

Last of all, Rebound saw the scientists – two women and one man.

Ten people in all were in the pool, and not one of them moved.

Not one of them *dared* to move.

They had all seen the French commando go under moments before.

The lesson: *if you don't move, they might not take you.*

Rebound held his breath as three massive shadows glided slowly through the water beneath him.

He heard a sudden click, and turned to see Mother holding her MP-5 poised above the surface.

Jesus, Rebound thought. If there was anyone in the world who had the balls to take down a killer whale with a gun, it *had* to be Mother.

More silence.

Don't move . . .

And then suddenly there came an incredible roar as one of the whales exploded out from beneath the surface, right next to Mother.

It lifted half of its enormous body out of the water, turned onto its side in mid-air, and then ploughed into Legs' motionless body. There was a series of sickening crunches as it caught the dead body in its mouth and clamped down hard with its teeth, breaking nearly every bone in it. And then the whale's head went under and its tail appeared, and then the tail disappeared and only frothing water remained.

And Legs' body was gone.

Rebound just stayed where he was, hovering in the water, his mouth agape. And then, slowly, it dawned on him.

Legs hadn't been moving.

An unspoken understanding instantly spread throughout the nine remaining people in the pool.

The killers didn't care whether they were moving or not . . .

The nine people in the pool moved as one, breaking out into frantic swimming strokes as the killer whales rose to the surface beneath them and commenced their feeding frenzy.

Up on what was left of B-deck, Book Riley swore again.

When Kirsty had seen the pool, seen the enormous black and white shapes in it, her lower jaw had started to quiver. Then, when she saw the first killer leap up out of the water and crunch through Leg's dead body, she started to hyperventilate.

'*OhmyGod, ohmyGod,*' she sobbed.

Riley began to hurry. He quickly lowered his upper body out over the edge of the downturned catwalk, so that he was now practically hanging upside down, reaching down for Kirsty with his free right hand.

Their hands were now only two inches apart.

He almost had her.

And then all of a sudden, he heard a soft *whooshing* sound from somewhere to his left.

Riley's head snapped round.

'*No . . .*'

The spot fire had ignited the flakes on the railing. The response was instantaneous. A small, orange flame began to race along the length of the railing, devouring the dried paint flakes in its path, leaving a tiny trail of fire in its wake.

Riley's eyes went wide.

The trail of fire was rocketing along the length of the railing.

And heading right for Kirsty's hand!

Kirsty was still looking down at the killer whales in the pool. She swung her head up to look at Riley and in an instant their eyes met and Riley saw the absolute terror in her eyes.

Riley stretched down as far as he could, his whole upper body dangling upside-down, off the downturned catwalk, in a desperate effort to grab her hand.

The orange flame raced along the black hand railing, its firetrail lighting up the railing behind it.

Riley's hand was an inch away from Kirsty's.

He stretched again and felt the tips of his fingers brush against the top of her hand.

Another inch. Just another inch . . .

'*Mister Book! Don't let me fall!*'

And then suddenly the bright orange line of fire cut across Riley's field of vision and he yelled in frustration.

'*No!*'

The firetrail sped across the railing in front of him, right underneath Kirsty's hand.

Riley watched in helpless horror as the little girl squealed with pain, and then did the only thing her body knew to do when it came into contact with fire.

She let go.

Kirsty dropped fast.

But as she did so, Buck Riley released his grip on the catwalk above him and lunged forward after her. He dropped three feet straight down – one arm pointed down, the other pointed up. His lower hand snatched the wool-lined hood of Kirsty's pink parka, while his upper hand caught the flaming railing behind him.

Both of their bodies jerked to a sudden halt, and Riley did a jarring 180-degree spin that nearly pulled his arm out of its socket. He was now right-side-up, hanging from the same burning railing that had, only seconds earlier, caused Kirsty to fall.

And oddly, despite the searing heat seeping through his leather-gloved hand, he managed a relieved smile.

'I gotcha, baby,' he breathed, almost laughing. 'I gotcha.'

Kirsty just hung there below him with her arms held out awkwardly on either side of her body, held up only by Riley's grip on the wool-lined hood of her parka.

'All right,' Riley said to himself, 'how the hell are we gonna get out of this – '

There came a sudden popping sound and abruptly

Kirsty lurched downwards. She only dropped an inch, and for an instant Riley couldn't understand what had happened.

Then he saw it.

His eyes zeroed in on the join between Kirsty's pink parka and its pink, wool-lined hood.

Riley's eyes went wide.

The hood wasn't actually part of the parka.

It was one of those removable hoods that could be connected to the collar of the parka whenever the wearer so desired. It was only attached to Kirsty's parka by six clasp-like buttons.

The popping sound that he had heard had been the sound of one of those buttons *unclasping*.

Riley began to feel sick.

'Oh, that's not fair. That's not fucking fair,' he said.

Pop!

Another button unclasped.

Kirsty dropped another inch.

Riley was at a loss. He didn't know what to do. There was nothing he *could* do. He was already hanging from the lowest point on the railing, so he couldn't lower himself any further. And Kirsty was hanging from his other hand, so he couldn't *reach* any further either.

Pop! Pop!

Two more buttons unclasped and Kirsty screamed in horror as she dropped sharply and then jolted to a sudden stop.

The pink hood began to stretch. Only two buttons held it to the parka's collar now.

Riley thought about swinging Kirsty in toward the C-deck catwalk below them, about four yards away. But he quickly dispelled the thought. The wool-lined hood was now only tenuously connected to the parka. Any movement would almost certainly unclasp the remaining two buttons.

'*God damn it!*' Riley yelled. 'Can't anybody *help* me!'

'Hold on!' another voice yelled from somewhere nearby. 'I'm coming!'

Riley turned his head, and saw Schofield on the far side of the C-deck catwalk, inside a small alcove of some sort. Next to him was Fox. Schofield seemed to be directing her to go down the nearest rung-ladder and head for the pool deck while he took care of Riley and Kirsty.

Pop!

One of the last two buttons snapped open and Riley turned his attention back to Kirsty. Grimacing, he held tight and he looked down at her. The little girl was scared out of her mind. Her eyes were red, filled with tears. She stared into his eyes, and spoke through teary sniffles: '*I don't want to die. Oh my God, I don't want to die.*'

One button left.

The hood was stretched taut, straining under Kirsty's weight.

It wasn't going to hold . . .

A second before it happened, Buck Riley felt the weight of the little girl pull on the hood and he said softly, 'I'm sorry.'

With a sudden *pop*, the final button snapped open and Riley watched helplessly as Kirsty fell away from him in a kind of nightmarish slow motion. Her wide eyes looked right into his as she fell, her face the picture of pure, unspeakable terror. Those wide eyes became smaller and smaller, and Buck Riley felt sick to his stomach as he saw the little girl splash into the icy pool fifty feet below.

The pool at the base of Wilkes Ice Station had become a slaughterhouse. From his alcove on C-deck, Shane Schofield looked down at it in horror.

Blood had so clouded the icy water that nearly half of the enormous pool was now no more than a maroon haze. Even the massive killer whales disappeared when they swam through the murky patches.

Schofield surveyed the scene.

On one side of the pool were the French. They had suffered the worst. They had already lost two men to the killers.

On the other side of the pool were the two remaining Marines – Rebound and Mother – and the three scientists from Wilkes who had been with Book when B-deck had given way. All five of them were swimming desperately for the metal deck that surrounded the pool.

It was into this that Schofield saw the tiny, pink-clad figure of Kirsty drop with an ugly splash. She landed back-first, and immediately went under. Her high-pitched scream had followed her all the way down.

Schofield snapped around to look over at Buck Riley, hanging from the downturned B-deck railing.

Their eyes met for an instant. Book looked beaten, dejected, exhausted. His eyes said it all. He couldn't do any more. He had done all he could.

Schofield hadn't.

He pursed his lips, took in the situation.

Kirsty was on the far side of the pool, on the other side of the diving bell, out in the open. Everybody else was near the edges of the pool, trying to get out. In their own efforts to escape, none of them had seen her land in the pool.

As he looked down at the pool, Schofield could hear Montana's voice on the intercom yelling at Snake and Santa Cruz in their gunless battle with the French soldiers still up on A-deck.

' – *Keep 'em moving round south –* '

' – *Can't use their guns either –* '

Schofield spun around where he stood, looking for something he could use.

He was still in the alcove, alone. Moments earlier, he'd sent Gant down to the pool deck, while he'd intended to go over and help Book Riley. But before he'd even had a chance to get over there, the little girl had fallen. And now she was down in the pool.

Schofield saw the array of buttons on the console behind him, saw some words underneath a lever: DIVING BELL – WINCH.

No, that was no help.

But then he saw another, large, rectangular button, on which was written a single word: BRIDGE.

Schofield stared at the button for a moment, per-plexed. And then he remembered. The retractable bridge. This must have been the control switch for the retractable bridge that Hensleigh had told him about earlier, the bridge that extended out from C-deck, out across the open space in the centre of the station.

Without even thinking, Schofield hit the long rectan-gular button and immediately he heard a loud, clanking noise from somewhere beneath his feet.

An engine somewhere within the wall next to him suddenly hummed to life and Schofield watched as a narrow, elongated platform began to extend out over the enormous empty space in the middle of the station.

On the far side of the shaft, Schofield saw another, identical, platform begin to extend out from underneath the catwalk. Presumably, the two platforms would meet in the middle and form one bridge spanning the width of the station.

Schofield didn't miss a beat. He charged out onto the bridge as it extended out over the centre of the station. It extended quite quickly, in a telescope-like motion, smaller extensions being born out of larger ones, and fast enough so that it stayed ahead of him as he ran. It wasn't very wide, only about two feet, and it had no hand railing.

Schofield ran across the extending bridge as it grew forward in front of him. And then just as his platform was about to join with its twin from the other side, he took a deep breath, increased his speed, and leapt diagonally off the bridge.

Riley watched in amazement as Schofield sailed through the air, over the massive diving bell, and arced down toward the icy pool.

He fell fast. But as he did so, Schofield did a strange thing. He raised his right hand and upholstered something from behind his shoulder.

When he hit the water, his feet entered first – with both legs splayed wide so that he wouldn't go far underwater – while both of his hands held the object he had pulled from behind his back.

Kirsty instinctively turned away as the water next to her exploded.

At first she thought it was one of the killer whales bursting out from beneath the surface to take her under, but as the water fell back down on top of her and she was able to see again, all she saw was a man hovering in the water next to her.

It was one of the Marines. In fact, it was the one she had met before, the nice one, the leader. The one who wore the cool, reflective silver sunglasses. She tried to remember his name. Seinfeld, she thought, or something like that.

'You okay?' he said

She nodded dumbly.

His silver glasses hung askew from his nose, dislodged by his landing in the water. He swiped them off quickly and for a brief second Kirsty saw his eyes and she gasped.

Suddenly one of the killers whooshed past them and Kirsty didn't care about Schofield's eyes anymore.

The towering, black dorsal fin sailed right past both of their faces and then slowly, very slowly, lowered itself into the water until finally the tip of the massive fin dipped below the surface and disappeared.

Kirsty began to breathe very fast.

Beside her, Schofield immediately started to look down into the water beneath them. They were treading water in one of the sections of the pool that hadn't yet been contaminated with blood. The water beneath them was crystal clear.

Kirsty followed his gaze and looked down into the water beneath her –

– just in time to see the wide open mouth of the killer whale rushing up at her feet!

Kirsty screamed like the banshee but beside her, Schofield stayed calm. He quickly lowered his Maghook beneath the surface and for a terrifying half-second, *waited* until the killer was right up close . . .

And then he fired.

The grappling hook, with its bulbous magnetic head, thundered out of its launcher into the water and slammed into the killer whale's snout, stopping the massive creature dead in its tracks.

Four thousand pounds per square inch of thrust had launched the grappling hook. Whether or not it had truly been enough to stun a full-grown, seven-ton killer whale wasn't entirely clear to Schofield. Hell, the whale was probably just shocked that something had dared to fight back.

Schofield quickly pressed down twice on the trigger of the launcher and the grappling hook immediately began to reel itself in.

He turned to face Kirsty again. 'You still in one piece? Got all your fingers and toes?'

Kirsty just stared at him, saw those eyes again, nodded dumbly.

'Come on then,' Schofield said as he pulled her through the water.

Sarah Hensleigh reached the edge of the pool and clambered up onto the deck as fast as she could. She turned back and saw Conlon and Abby splashing through the water toward her.

'Hurry up!' Sarah yelled. '*Hurry up!*'

Abby got there first. Sarah grabbed her hand and yanked her up onto the deck.

Conlon was still two yards away, swimming hard.

'Come *on*, Warren!'

Conlon swam for all he was worth.

One yard away.

He looked up desperately at Sarah, and she dropped to her knees at the edge of the deck.

He got there. Slammed into the metal rim of the deck like a Olympic swimmer hitting the wall at the end of a race. He reached up, grabbed Sarah's outstretched hand. Sarah was just beginning to haul Conlon up onto the deck when suddenly the water behind him parted and one of the killer whales burst up out of it. The big whale opened its mouth wide and enveloped Conlon's body from foot to chest.

Conlon went bug-eyed as the killer clamped down hard on his chest and Sarah tried desperately to hold onto his hand, but the killer was too strong. When it dropped back down into the water it yanked so hard on Conlon's body that Sarah felt the terrified scientist's fingernails scratch her skin and draw blood, and then suddenly his hand was out of her grasp and she fell to the deck and watched in horror as Warren Conlon disappeared under the water right in front of her eyes. A few yards away, Mother and Rebound were also approaching the deck.

Rebound swam hard as Mother turned in the water and fired her MP-5 under the surface. One of the first things they teach you at Parris Island, the legendary training camp of the United States Marine Corps, is the resistance that water offers against gunfire. Indeed, the average bullet will lose nearly all of its velocity in less than two metres of water. After that it will just slow to a halt and sink to the bottom.

Such physical laws, however, didn't seem to be bothering Mother right now. She just waited until the killers got close and then she fired hard. The bullets appeared to penetrate the outer skin, but they didn't seem to do much damage. Mother fired and hit, and the killers momentarily darted away, but they always seemed to come back, unhurt, undeterred.

Rebound hit the deck and was about to climb up onto it when he turned and saw Mother behind him.

She was looking down to her left, her gun arm jolting repeatedly as she fired at something under the water. And then suddenly her gun arm stopped its jolting movement and Mother looked confused. Her gun wasn't firing anymore.

Frozen ammo.

Rebound watched as Mother shook her MP-5 in disgust, as if shaking it would somehow make it work again.

It was then that Rebound saw a ominous dark shadow slithering upwards underneath the surface, silently approaching Mother from her right.

'Mother! Check right!'

Mother heard him and spun instantly and saw the killer whale rising beneath her. Her gun now useless, Mother just pivoted in the water and lifted her legs up sharply and the killer barrelled past her, missing her feet by inches.

But then, just when Rebound thought it had passed Mother by, the killer whale abruptly changed course and broke the surface of the water and wrapped its jaws around Mother's gun hand.

Mother yelled in pain and released her MP-5, yanking her hand free just as the whale bit down on the gun.

A gash of red appeared instantly above her wrist. Blood slicked her entire forearm.

But her hand was still there.

Mother didn't care. Now gunless, she just swam like hell for the water's edge.

Rebound hoisted himself onto the deck and turned and urged Mother on.

'*Move it, Mother! Pick it up, baby!*'

Mother swam.

Rebound knelt at the edge of the deck.

Black shadows cut back and forth behind Mother's frantically swimming frame.

Black shapes everywhere. Too many of them.

And then, suddenly, it dawned on Rebound.

Mother wasn't going to get to the deck in time.

And then, as if right on cue, a massive black silhouette appeared in the water right behind Mother's frantically kicking legs.

It closed in slowly, through the rippling translucent water, and Rebound saw a pink slit appear across its enormous black and white jawline.

Its mouth was opening.

Teeth appeared and Rebound felt his blood run cold.

Through the crystalline water he saw the black shadow slowly rise and rise behind Mother until it overtook her legs and allowed them to kick inside its wide open mouth.

And then with an ominous sense of finality, the big whale's jaws closed slowly around Mother's knees.

The jolt that Mother experienced was incredible in its ferocity.

Rebound watched in horror as the killer whale yanked her under. The water around Mother started to froth and bubble and blood began to fan out, but Mother was struggling fiercely, putting up a hell of a fight.

Suddenly, she broke the surface and so did the killer. Somehow, during their underwater scuffle, Mother must have managed to get one of her legs free from the killer's jaws, because now she was using it to kick down hard on the big whale's snout.

'You *motherfucker*!' she screamed. 'I'm gonna fucking kill you!' But it had her by the other leg and it wasn't letting go.

Abruptly, Mother shot forward in the water, raising a wash of white waves in front of her. The whale was pushing her forward, toward Rebound and the deck.

And then – *clang!* – Mother slammed down hard against the edge of the deck and, amazingly, managed to get a handhold on the metal grating.

'Fucking *kill you*! You son of a *bitch*!' Mother yelled through clenched teeth.

Rebound dived forward and grabbed Mother's hand as she grimly held the deck and struggled with the killer whale in a tug-of-war over her own body.

Then Rebound saw Mother draw her powerful Colt automatic pistol from its holster and level it at the killer whale's head.

'Oh, fuck me . . .' Rebound said.

'You want to eat something, baby?' Mother said to the whale. 'Eat *this*.'

She fired.

A small blast of yellow light flared out from the muzzle of Mother's gun as the flash of her pistol ignited the gaseous air around her. Both she and Rebound were hurled a full five yards backwards onto the deck by the concussion wave.

The whale wasn't so lucky. As soon as the bullet entered its brain, the killer convulsed violently backwards, snapping upward. Then it just fell limply back into the water amid a cloud of its own blood, its final prize – garnered in the split second before it died – a portion of Mother's left leg. Everything from the left knee down.

Schofield and Kirsty were still out in the middle of the pool, caught halfway between the diving bell in the centre and the deck twenty-five feet away.

With their backs pressed against each other, they both looked fearfully about themselves. The water around them was ominously still. Quiet. Calm.

'Mister,' Kirsty said, her voice barely a whisper. Her jaw was quivering, a combination of fear and cold.

'What?' Schofield kept his eyes trained on the water around him.

'I'm scared.'

'Scared?' Schofield said, not exactly hiding his own fear very well. 'I didn't think kids these days were afraid of anything. Don't they have this kind of stuff at Sea World – '

At that moment, one of the killer whales shot up out of the water right in front of Schofield. It rose out of the water and arced down fast, heading *right* for him and Kirsty!

'Go under!' Schofield yelled as he saw the two rows of jagged, white teeth open wide in front of him.

Schofield held his breath and ducked underwater, pulling Kirsty down with him.

The world suddenly went silent as the killer whale's immense white underbelly thundered over the top of them at incredible speed. It brushed roughly against the top of Schofield's helmet as it pounded back into the water right above their heads.

Schofield and Kirsty burst back up above the surface, gasped for air.

Schofield quickly looked left: saw Rebound and Mother on the deck. Looked right: saw Sarah and Abby, also safely up on the deck, quickly moving away from the edge.

He spun around: saw another Frenchman get yanked under. The two remaining French commandos were just reaching the edge of the pool. They'd had to swim further than everyone else, having landed closest to the middle of the pool.

Serves them right, Schofield thought.

He looked up: and immediately saw the retractable bridge that spanned the width of the station from either side of C-deck.

Just then, a deafening explosion boomed out from the alcove on the C-deck catwalk, and an unbelievably huge tongue of fire shot out over the whole of the central shaft of the station.

Schofield knew what had happened immediately – the French soldiers up on A-deck, deprived of the use of their guns, were now tossing grenades down into the shaft. Sharp thinking. A grenade detonating in this flammable atmosphere would do twice as much damage as it would normally. Their first target, Schofield noticed, had been the alcove he and Gant had been hiding in before.

Suddenly something emerged from the fireball that had consumed the alcove.

It was large and grey, square-shaped, and it tumbled end-over-end out into the central shaft of the station. It fell fast, cutting through the air, its immense weight driving it downwards. With a thunderous crash, the four-hundred-pound ejection seat that had been sitting in front of the console in the C-deck alcove came smashing down onto the deck that surrounded the pool at the bottom of the station. It weighed so much and it landed so hard that it dented the thick metal deck when it hit.

Despite the chaos all around him, Shane Schofield kept his eyes locked on the retractable bridge three storeys above him. He took in the distance.

Thirty feet. Maybe thirty-five.

He wasted no time, raised his Maghook, flicked a switch marked 'M' with his thumb – and saw a red light on the head of the grappling hook activate – aimed and fired.

The grappling hook shot up into the air. However, this time, the claws of the hook didn't spring outward. This time it was set on magnet.

The bulbous magnetic head of the Maghook thunked into the underside of the retractable steel bridge, and stuck there.

Schofield did some quick calculations in his head. 'Shit,' was all he said when he finished.

Then he handed the launcher to Kirsty and said, 'Three words, honey: *don't let go.*'

She took the launcher in both hands and looked at Schofield, puzzled.

Schofield smiled at her reassuringly. 'Just hold on.'

Then he pressed down firmly on a small black button on the grip of the Maghook.

Suddenly, Kirsty flew up out of the water as the Maghook reeled her upwards like some bizarre kind of fishing rod.

She was light, so the Maghook had little difficulty whisking her up to the bridge. Schofield knew it would have been considerably slower if his weight were also being –

A killer whale shot up out of the water after Kirsty.

Schofield's jaw dropped as he saw the massive whale lift its entire body out of the water in a magnificent vertical leap.

Kirsty was still moving rapidly upward, pulled up by the Maghook. She looked down and saw the whale emerge from the water beneath her like the Devil coming out of Hell itself. Saw it come roaring up toward her, its body rotating as it rose into the air.

And then all of a sudden Kirsty came to a jarring halt.

The whale kept coming upward.

Kirsty squealed in surprise, looked up, and saw that she had hit the underside of the bridge.

She couldn't go any further up!

The whale opened its jaws wide as it reached the zenith of its leap . . .

Kirsty gripped the Maghook as hard as she could and quickly brought her legs up tightly against her chest just as the killer's teeth jammed shut with a loud *crunch*, coming together barely a foot below her butt, the lowest part of her body.

Kirsty watched as the huge black and white whale fell away beneath her, diminishing in size until it disappeared back into the pool below. The animal must have been at least thirty feet long, and it had lifted its entire body vertically out of the wat –

Suddenly a hand appeared in front of Kirsty's face and she almost had a heart attack, almost let go of the Maghook.

'It's okay,' a voice said. 'It's me.'

161

Kirsty looked up and found herself looking into the friendly eyes of the Marine she knew as Mr Book. She took his hand and he hauled her up onto the retractable bridge.

She was breathing heavily, almost crying. Buck Riley held her, looked at her in amazement. After a second, Kirsty reached into her pocket and pulled out a plastic puffer for her asthma.

She drew in two long puffs, and caught her breath. When, finally, she was able to speak she looked at Riley, shook her head, and said, 'They definitely don't have *that* at Sea World.'

Schofield was still down in the pool. Two of the killer whales circled him ominously. Schofield noticed that these two appeared to be smaller than the other killers. Juveniles, maybe.

Schofield tilted his head upward, and yelled 'Book! I need my Maghook!'

Up on the bridge, Riley immediately dropped to his belly and leaned out over the edge of the narrow, metal platform. He reached out underneath the platform and tried to deactivate the magnet on Schofield's grappling hook.

'I need it *now*, Book!' Schofield's voice sailed up through the shaft of the ice station.

'I'm trying! I'm trying!' Riley said.

'Try *faster*!'

Riley stretched his arm out under the platform, tried

to reach the switch marked 'M' on the grip that activated and deactivated the Maghook's powerful magnet.

As he did so, however, a strange thing happened.

For a brief second, Riley could have sworn that he heard Kirsty speaking to someone on the bridge above him.

'Help the diver, Wendy. *Help the diver.*'

Riley blinked to himself. Must be hearing things.

Down in the pool, Schofield thought it was all over. The two killers on either side of him were closing in as they circled, shutting off any possible escape route.

Suddenly one of them seemed to break out of its circle and swing around. Schofield swallowed. *It was coming round for the kill.*

The killer turned in a slow, wide arc until it was pointing right at Schofield. Its body was only a foot or so beneath the surface, and its high, dorsal fin sliced easily through the waves in the pool. It was moving at such powerful speed that it created a rolling bow wave in front of its submerged, black and white head.

The bow wave raced across the water, on a collision course with Shane Schofield.

Schofield looked around himself. There was nowhere to go this time, no weapon to use.

Out of sheer desperation he pulled out his Desert Eagle pistol, raised it above the water.

If it had to come to this, he thought, *then it had to come to this.*

The killer charged toward him.

And then suddenly, a black missile-like object plunged into the water right in front of Schofield's face, right *in between* him and the killer whale.

Whatever it was, it was so sleek that it entered the water with barely even a splash, and once in, it zoomed away from him at phenomenal speed.

Both killers saw it instantly and immediately lost interest in Schofield. Even the one that had been charging at him only seconds before abruptly altered its path and raced off in pursuit of this new quarry.

Schofield was stunned. What had it been? It had looked almost like a . . . a seal of some sort.

And then, miraculously a Maghook dropped into the water right in front of Schofield.

Schofield grabbed it before it sank and immediately looked upward. Up on the bridge, he saw Book Riley lying on his belly, with one arm stretched out underneath the bridge.

Schofield looked at the Maghook and suddenly felt a new lease of life come over him.

Just then, a small, pointed, black head popped up out of the water right in front of him and he fell backwards in surprise.

It was Wendy. Kirsty's little Antarctic fur seal.

Her cute red collar glistened with wetness and her soft black eyes looked right into his. If it were possible, Schofield could have sworn that the little seal was *smiling* – having a ball of a time swimming around in the pool, evading the less agile killer whales.

Then he realized. Wendy must have been the object that had dived into the pool in between him and the charging killer whale.

Suddenly Wendy's head snapped left.

She'd heard something, sensed something.

Then she gave what looked like a final, happy nod to Schofield before she ducked back under the water and sped off down the length of the pool.

She swam fast. Speeding just underneath the surface of the water like a tiny, black torpedo. Cutting left, ducking right, and then disappearing suddenly as she dropped into a steep vertical dive. No sooner had she moved then three black dorsal fins appeared behind her and immediately gave chase, before they themselves vanished beneath the surface in hot pursuit.

Schofield took the opportunity and swam for the nearest edge. He was three feet from the deck when a sudden surge of water rocked him and Schofield rolled in the water as the giant body of one of the killers swept past him at a frightening speed. Schofield immediately tensed for another fight but the whale just barrelled past him, in search of the elusive Wendy.

Schofield breathed again, swam forward, and grabbed hold of the deck. He climbed up out of the water, and saw the battered ejection seat lying crumpled on its side on the deck in front of him. Schofield turned around, surveyed the chaos around him.

Sarah and Abby were long out of the water and were now hurrying into the tunnels of E-deck. Not far from them were Rebound and Mother. Rebound was kneeling over Mother. He appeared to be applying pressure to a wound of some kind on Mother's leg.

On the other side of the pool, Schofield saw the two surviving French commandos, also safely out of the water. Soaking wet, they were just getting to their feet on the deck. One of them saw Schofield and began to reach for his crossbow.

Just then, a sudden movement caught Schofield's eye and he turned and saw a familiar, black shadow whipping down the length of the pool.

Wendy.

Three larger black and white shapes raced through the water behind her. The killers in pursuit.

Wendy was travelling at tremendous speed, just below the surface. Her flippers would occasionally sweep backwards with a powerful stroke and then fall in by her sides so that her body remained as streamlined as possible. She looked like a bullet shooting through the pool, alternately appearing and disappearing in the murky, red clouds that stained the icy water.

She was heading for the deck, for that part of the deck on which the two French commandos stood. And she wasn't slowing down.

In fact, it looked to Schofield like she was *picking up* speed as she raced toward the deck with the three black and white spectres racing through the water behind her.

Schofield then watched in amazement as, within a metre of the deck, Wendy suddenly launched herself out of the water. It was a flat, graceful leap, and she landed smoothly on her belly on the deck and slid forward a full three metres. She slid right past the two bewildered Frenchmen standing next to her.

But she didn't stop there. No sooner had she stopped sliding then she was up on her fore-flippers and galloping as fast as she could, away from the water's edge.

For a fleeting instant, Schofield wondered why she would do that. Surely once you were out of the water, you were safe from the killers.

And then Schofield discovered why Wendy did what she did.

Like a demon rising from the depths, one of the pursuing killer whales roared out of the water and hurled its massive body up onto the deck, landing on the thick metal grating with an enormous crash. The huge whale slid fast across the deck, carried forward by the weight of its own inertia. It rolled smoothly onto its side as it moved, so that its jaws opened vertically, and then, with almost effortless grace, it caught one of the Frenchmen in its mouth and bit down hard.

The big animal's sliding movement stopped and it ground to a halt, with the French soldier – screaming madly, blood pouring from his mouth – held tightly within its jaws. The whale then began to shuffle its enormous frame awkwardly backwards along the deck. After a few moments, it reached the edge and fell back into the water, taking the screaming Frenchman down with it.

Wendy had known. You weren't truly safe from the killers until you were *well clear* of the water's edge.

The six people remaining on the deck understood at once.

Get away from the edge.

Schofield saw Gant join Rebound on the other side of the pool. Saw them both hurriedly pick up Mother by the shoulders and start to drag her away from the edge. As they did so, Schofield caught a fleeting glimpse of Mother's lower body. The bottom half of one of her legs was missing.

At that moment there came a sudden, resounding *whump!* from behind Schofield and he felt the deck beneath him shudder violently. He spun instantly, faced the pool, and saw the smiling face of one of the killer whales sliding across the deck toward him!

The whale slid across the deck fast.

Schofield was still on his knees.

The whale rolled onto its side, opened its mouth wide.

Schofield dived away from the massive creature, saw the battered ejection seat lying on the deck four feet behind him. If he could just get to it, and leap over it, he'd be safe. Schofield scrambled across the deck on his hands and knees, toward the big ejection seat.

The whale kept coming. Fast.

Schofield clawed at the deck, crawled as fast as he could. Not fast enough. He wasn't going to make it. He wasn't going to be able to get over the ejection seat in time.

Schofield saw water spread out on the deck all around him. The wash from the advancing killer whale.

It was *right behind him*!

Schofield's adrenalin surged and he dived forward. He knew he wasn't going to make it *over* the chair so he slammed himself, back first, *into* the ejection seat.

He was now facing the pool, 'sitting' in the battered ejection seat as it lay crumpled on its side. He looked up and the killer whale filled his entire field of vision.

It was right on top of him! Less than a metre away. It came roaring toward him.

There was no chance of it slowing down.

No chance of it missing him.

And Shane Schofield shut his eyes as the killer whale's jaws came slamming down around his head.

There came a sudden, otherworldly *clang!*, a noise louder than anything Schofield had ever heard in his life.

Schofield had expected to feel pain – sharp, sudden, burning pain – as the killer whale's teeth chomped down hard on his head. But strangely, he didn't feel any pain.

Bewildered, he opened his eyes . . .

. . . and saw two, long rows of razor-sharp teeth stretching away from him into darkness. In between the two, long rows of teeth sat an obscenely fat, pink tongue.

It took a second for Schofield's brain to put it all together.

His head was inside the killer whale's mouth!

But for some reason – some unfathomable, incredible reason – he was still alive.

It was then that Schofield looked up and saw that his head was surrounded on three sides by the battered, steel headrest of the ejection seat.

The killer whale's ferocious bite had come down hard on the headrest, on either side of Schofield's head. But the steel headrest had been strong enough to withstand the incredible force of the bite – it had halted the big whale's teeth only millimetres short of Schofield's ears. Now, two severe dents in the headrest jutted inwards on either side of his head. One of them – sharp and jagged – had drawn a tiny bead of blood from Schofield's left ear.

Schofield couldn't see anything else. His entire upper body, from chest to head, was completely covered by the killer whale's mouth.

Suddenly, the ejection seat jolted beneath him.

It scraped loudly against the metal deck, and Schofield fell back into the seat as the whole thing lurched forward.

The movement stopped suddenly, almost as soon as it had begun, and Schofield rocked forward and shuddered to a halt. He suddenly realized what was happening.

The whale was dragging him back toward the pool.

The ejection seat jolted once again and Schofield felt the seat slide another three feet across the deck.

In his mind's eye, Schofield could picture the whale's movements. It was probably shuffling backwards – as the other one had done before with the Frenchman – undulating its massive body back across the deck as it dragged the four-hundred-pound ejection seat toward the edge of the deck.

The ejection seat moved again and Schofield felt a sudden rush of warm air wash over his face.

It had come from within the whale.

Schofield couldn't believe it. The killer whale was huffing and puffing, breathing hard as it held this unusually heavy prize within its jaws and dragged it back toward the water! Schofield wriggled in his seat as another rush of warm air hit his face and the seat jolted once again.

His feet were still sticking out from the base of the ejection seat, out from the side of the whale's propped-open mouth. If he could just wriggle down that way, Schofield thought, he might be able to slip out of the chair – and out of the whale's mouth – before it reached the water.

Schofield moved slowly, gingerly, easing himself down in the ejection seat, not wanting to alert the whale to his plan.

Suddenly, the seat lurched sideways. It screeched hideously as it slid across the metal deck. Schofield quickly grabbed hold of the armrests to stop himself falling forward onto the big animal's teeth.

He lowered himself further. Now his waist was out of the chair and his eyes were level with the whale's sharp, pointed teeth. The whale grunted as it heaved on the heavy, steel chair.

Slowly, Schofield lowered himself an inch further out of the chair.

And then he encountered a problem.

He was now sitting so low in the ejection seat that he couldn't keep a hold on the armrests anymore. He needed something to hold onto, something from which he could push himself out of the seat. Schofield desperately looked around himself, searching for something to grab onto.

Nothing.

There was absolutely nothing to hold onto.

And then Schofield's gaze fell upon the killer whale's teeth in front of him.

I don't believe this, Schofield thought as he reached up with both hands and took hold of two of the killer whale's enormous, white teeth.

Suddenly the ejection seat jolted and slid again and Schofield felt it lift slightly off the deck. He had a sudden, horrifying thought.

It's reached the edge of the deck.

And now it's tipping over it . . .

Holy shit.

Schofield gripped the whale's teeth tightly and pushed hard off them, and hurled himself clear of the ejection seat. He slid out from the chair, out from the side of the big whale's mouth, and fell clumsily onto the deck just in time to see the killer whale's rear end drop back into the pool. As its tail entered the water, the big whale's body tipped upward, and its head lifted up, lifting the entire ejection seat off the deck. Then the killer whale's enormous black and white frame began to slide downward, into the water, and the great predator took its prize to a watery grave.

Schofield was on his feet in seconds, moving quickly across the deck toward Rebound, Gant and Mother.

He spoke into his helmet mike as he ran. 'Montana, this is Scarecrow, report.'

'*Still up on A-deck, Scarecrow. Snake and Santa Cruz're up here with me.*'

'How many up there?' Schofield asked.

'*I count it as five military and two civilian,*' Montana's voice said. '*But two of the military guys just made a break for one of the ladders and went down a level. What? Oh, fuck –*'

The connection cut off. Schofield heard a scuffle.

'Montana –'

Suddenly, a French commando stepped out onto the deck in front of Schofield himself.

He was the last of the five French soldiers who had fallen into the pool, the only one of them to come out of it alive. He looked like death warmed up – dripping wet, scowling, and mad as hell. He glared at Schofield, then raised his crossbow.

Without missing a beat, Schofield drew a throwing knife from a sheath strapped to his knee and threw it underhanded. The knife whistled through the air and thudded into the Frenchman's chest. He dropped instantly. The whole thing took two seconds. Schofield never stopped walking. He stepped over the slumped body, retrieved his knife and the dead French commando's crossbow, and kept moving.

He spoke into his helmet mike again, 'Montana, I say again, are you all right?'

'*I copy, Scarecrow. I'm okay. Revision on my previous count: make that four military and two civilians. Put me down for one more frog.*'

'Put me down for one, too,' Schofield said.

Schofield arrived at the entrance to the south tunnel, where he found Gant and Rebound. They were dragging Mother into the tunnel.

Schofield saw Mother's leg immediately. A bloody, jagged piece of bone protruded from where her left knee should have been.

'Put her somewhere safe, stop the flow and give her a hit of methadone,' Schofield said quickly.

'Got it – ' Gant said, looking up at him. She cut herself off abruptly.

Schofield's anti-flash glasses had been lost in the water in the battle with the killer whales and Gant saw his eyes for the first time.

Two prominent, vertical scars cut down across both of his eyes. They were unmissable, hideous. Each scar stretched downward in a perfectly straight line from eyebrow to cheekbone, scarring the eyelid in between.

Gant winced when she saw them and regretted it

175

as soon as she did so. She hoped Schofield didn't notice.

'How are you feeling, Mother?' Schofield asked as they dragged Mother into the tunnel.

'Nothing one good kiss from a fine lookin' man like you wouldn't fix,' Mother growled through clenched teeth. Despite her pain, she too saw Schofield's scarred eyes.

'Maybe later,' Schofield said, as he saw a door set into the tunnel wall ahead of them. 'In there,' he said to Gant and Rebound.

They opened the door and dragged Mother inside, all four of them dripping wet. They were in a storeroom of some sort. Rebound immediately set to work on Mother's leg.

Schofield spoke into his helmet mike, 'Marines, call in.'

Names came in over the intercom as each Marine identified him or herself.

Montana, Snake and Santa Cruz. All up on A-deck.

Rebound and Gant, E-deck. They called in formally over their helmet intercoms even though they were standing right next to Schofield, so that the others would hear their voices and know for a fact that they were still alive. Even Mother said her name, just for the record.

There was no word from Book, Hollywood, Legs, Samurai or Ratman.

'Okay, everyone, listen up,' Schofield said. 'By my count these bastards are down to four now, plus the two civilians they brought along with them to jerk my chain.

'This has gone far enough. It's time to end it. We have a numerical advantage, seven against four. Let's use it. I want a flush of this entire facility from the top down. I want these assholes pushed into a corner so we can finish them off without losing any more of our people. All right, this is how it's gonna happen. I want – '

There came a sudden thunking noise from above him and Schofield immediately looked upwards.

There was a long silence.

Schofield saw a line of fluorescent lights bolted to the ceiling above him. They stretched away at regular intervals down the southern tunnel to his right.

And then, at that moment, as Schofield watched them, every single fluorescent light in the tunnel went out.

The world glowed incandescent green.

Night vision.

With his scarred eyes masked by his night-vision goggles, Shane Schofield climbed up one of the rung ladders between E-deck and D-deck. He moved slowly and carefully, deliberately. He remembered Book saying once that wearing night-vision goggles is like wearing a pair of low-powered binoculars strapped to your head – you see something and you reach out to grab it, only to find that it's actually a lot closer than you think and you knock it over.

The whole station was cloaked in darkness.

And silence.

Cold, eerie silence.

With the entire station filled with the flammable propellant from the air-conditioners, all gunfire had ceased. The occasional shuffle of movement and the odd, low whisper of someone speaking into a helmet microphone were all that could be heard in the pitch darkness.

Schofield surveyed the green-lit station through his night-vision goggles.

The battle had entered a new phase.

Somehow, one of the French commandos must have managed to find the station's fuse box and turn off all the lights. It was a desperate ploy, but a good one nonetheless.

Darkness has long been the ally of numerically inferior forces. Even the advent of ambient-light technology – night-vision goggles and gunsights – hasn't diminished the average military tactician's opinion of the advantages of a small operation carried out under cover of darkness. It's a simple maxim of warfare – landed, naval or airborne – nobody likes to fight in the dark.

'Marines, stay alert. Watch for flashers,' Schofield whispered into his helmet mike. One of the great dangers of night-vision fighting is the use of stun grenades, or 'flashers' – grenades that emit a sudden blinding flare of light which is designed to temporarily disorient an enemy. Since night-vision goggles *magnify* any given light source, if one sees a flasher go off through a pair of night-vision goggles, blindness won't be temporary. It will be permanent.

Schofield peered up into the station's central shaft. No light entered the station from outside the enormous frosted-glass dome that topped the wide, central shaft. It was June – early winter in the Antarctic. Outside, it would be twilight for the next three months.

Blackness. Total blackness.

Schofield felt Gant's weight on the ladder behind him. They were heading up the shaft.

As soon as the lights had gone out, Schofield had

immediately ordered his team to 'go to green'. Then he had outlined his plan.

It was no use playing defence in a darkened environment. They had to stay on the attack. *Had* to. The team that would win this battle would be the one that used the darkness to its advantage, and the best way to do that was to stay on the offensive. As such, Schofield's plan was simple.

Keep the French on the run.

They were down on numbers. Only *four* of the original twelve French commandos were still alive. And Montana had just said that two of those four had just evacuated A-deck. So they were also split into two groups of two.

But most importantly of all, they were running.

Schofield's team, on the other hand, was also split, but in a much more advantageous way.

Schofield had three Marines up on A-deck – Montana, Snake and Santa Cruz – and another three down on E-deck – Gant, Rebound and himself.

If the Marines up on A-deck could flush the remaining French commandos down through the station, soon those French soldiers would run right into the Marines from the lower decks. And then the Marines – a force of superior numbers, attacking from two flanks – would finish them.

But Schofield didn't want to get carried away, didn't want to get ahead of himself, because this would be no ordinary battle.

The fighting would be different.

For in the highly flammable, gaseous atmosphere of the station, neither side could use guns.

This would be old-fashioned, close-quarter fighting.

Hand to hand combat.

In near total darkness.

In other words, it would be knives in the dark.

But as he'd thought about it more closely, Schofield had suddenly seen a problem with his plan.

The French had crossbows.

Schofield had looked at the crossbow he had taken from the dead French commando on E-deck. Since it didn't create a spark of any kind, a crossbow could be fired safely inside the gaseous atmosphere of the station. Schofield tried to think back to his early weapons training at the Basic School at Quantico, tried to remember the vital stats for a handheld crossbow. He remembered that the standard range of accuracy for a small-size crossbow was not great, about the same as that for a conventional six-shooter, roughly twenty feet.

Twenty feet.

Damn it, Schofield thought. Knives would be useless if the French had a twenty-foot safety zone around themselves. With no corresponding projectile-firing weapon, the Marines wouldn't stand a chance. The thing was, they didn't *have* such a weapon. At least, nothing that they could use safely in the station's flammable, gaseous environment.

181

And then it occurred to Schofield.

Maybe they did . . .

Schofield stepped up onto D-deck with his Maghook held out in front of him at shoulder height, ready to fire. In his other hand, he held the dead Frenchman's crossbow.

Although not exactly designed for accuracy, the Armalite MH-12 Maghook launcher has the ability to shoot its magnetic grappling hook quite substantial distances – over a hundred feet.

Initially, the MH-12 Maghook was intended for use in urban warfare and anti-terrorist operations – its chief purpose was to provide a self-contained rope and grappling hook that could be used for scaling the sides of buildings, or providing zip lines along which anti-terrorist units could slide and make rapid forced entries.

That being the case, the Maghook's small, handheld launcher had to have the power to shoot its hook to great heights. The answer was a state-of-the-art hydraulic launching system that provided four-thousand-pounds per square inch of enhanced vertical thrust. The way Schofield figured it, if he fired his Maghook at an enemy soldier from a distance of twenty feet, four-thousand-pounds per square inch of thrust had to have *some* chance of scoring a hit.

And indeed, as Schofield himself had discovered in the pool before, at close range, *underwater*, a Maghook had the capacity to stun a seven-ton killer whale. When fired at a one-hundred-and-eighty-pound man at similar range, *above* water, the Maghook would probably crack his skull.

Thus armed, the Marines were confident that they could handle the French commandos' crossbows.

So the plan would go ahead.

Montana, Snake and Santa Cruz would work their way down through the station from A-deck, forcing the Frenchmen down, while Schofield, Gant and Rebound worked their way up from E-deck. They would hopefully meet halfway and the rest would write itself.

Schofield and Gant had departed right away.

Rebound was to join them as soon as he had stemmed the flow of blood from Mother's leg and started her up on a intravenous line of methadone.

The three Marines on A-deck began their attack.

They moved quickly, using a textbook three-man flushing formation known as 'leap-frogging'. One Marine would move forward, ahead of his partners and fire his Maghook. Then, while he reeled his hook in to reload, a second Marine would move in front of him – 'leap-frogging' him – and fire his Maghook at the enemy. By the time the third man stepped forward and fired, the first man was ready to fire again and the cycle continued.

The two French soldiers on A-deck responded as they were supposed to – they retreated, hastened away from the rolling wave of powerful Maghook fire. They hurried for the ladders, climbed down the shaft.

However, as he fielded reports from Montana about the French soldiers' movement, Schofield noticed something odd about their evasive manoeuvres.

They were moving too fast.

In their retreat down the shaft, the four French soldiers had completely avoided the destroyed B-deck catwalk and continued straight down to C.

They moved fluidly, in a swift, two-by-two, cover formation – the lead two men covering the forward flank, the rear two covering their pursuers behind, with a space of about ten yards between the two pairs.

Earlier, Montana had reported that all four of the French commandos were wearing night-vision goggles. They had come prepared.

They continued to move down the shaft fast.

Schofield had expected them to waste time in the tunnels as they tried to adopt a defensive position. But the French soldiers seemed to have other ideas. They darted into the C-deck tunnels only for so long as it took the Marines pursuing them from the levels above to join them. Then suddenly, they appeared on the catwalk again and made for the rung-ladder leading down to D-deck.

At that moment, Schofield recalled something Trevor Barnaby had once said about strategy.

Good strategy is like magic, Barnaby had said. *Make your enemy look at one hand, while you're doing something with the other.*

'*They're moving for the south-west ladder*,' Montana's

voice said in Schofield's earpiece. '*Scarecrow, you down there?*'

Schofield moved forward along the D-deck catwalk, the world green before his eyes. 'We're on it.'

He and Gant approached the south-west corner of D-deck, saw the rung-ladder that led up to C-deck.

Schofield spoke into his mike, 'Rebound, where *are* you?'

'*Finishing up now, sir,*' Rebound's voice replied from the storeroom down on E-deck.

'*Flanking west, Sarge,*' the voice of José 'Santa' Cruz said over the intercom.

Montana's voice: '*Keep 'em coming, 'Cruz. Then send 'em down to the Scarecrow.*'

On D-deck, Schofield and Gant arrived at the rung-ladder. They crouched, levelled their weapons at the empty ladder. They heard boots stomping fast on the metal catwalk above them, heard the distinctive *snap-phew!* of a crossbow being fired.

'*They're coming to the ladder,*' Santa Cruz's voice said.

More footsteps clanged on the metal grating.

Any second now . . .

Any second . . .

And then suddenly, *clunk, clunk.*

What the hell –

'*Marines! Eyes shut! Flasher on the ground!*' Santa Cruz's voice yelled suddenly.

Schofield immediately squeezed his eyes shut just as

he heard the stun grenade bounce on the metal deck above him.

The stun grenade went off – like a flashbulb on a camera – and for a brief instant the whole of Wilkes Ice Station flared white.

Schofield was about to open his eyes when suddenly, there came a new noise from his right. It sounded like someone doing up a zipper really, really fast.

Schofield spun right and opened his eyes and his green world streaked laterally. His eyes searched the empty shaft, but he saw nothing.

'*Ah, shit!*' Cruz said. '*Sir! One of them just went over the railing!*'

The zipping sound that Schofield had just heard suddenly made sense. It had been the sound of someone rappelling down the central shaft on a rope.

Schofield froze for a split second.

Such a move wasn't a defensive move at all.

It was a co-ordinated move, a planned move, an *attacking* move.

The French weren't actually on the run.

They were carrying out a plan of their own.

Make your enemy look at one hand while you're doing something with the other . . .

Like a chess player caught in check a second before he intends to play his own killing move, Schofield felt his mind start to spin.

What were they up to?

What was their plan?

In the end he didn't have time to think about it,

because no sooner had he heard Santa Cruz's message than a volley of arrows thudded into the ice wall all around him. Schofield ducked and spun and saw Gant dive to the floor behind him and then he spun back round and before he knew what was happening, a figure slid down the rung-ladder in front of him and Schofield found himself standing face-to-face with the Frenchman he knew as Jacques Latissier.

Rebound was crouched over Mother in the storeroom on E-deck.

Mother had tough veins, and, to make it even more difficult, Rebound was wearing his night-vision goggles as he tried to get the needle into her arm. He'd missed the vein on his first four attempts, and he had only now just managed to get the IV line flowing into Mother's arm.

The IV done, Rebound stood up and was about to leave Mother when, strangely, he heard the sound of soft footsteps hurrying down the tunnel outside the darkened storeroom.

Rebound froze.

Listened.

The sound of the footsteps faded as they hurried off down the southern tunnel outside.

Rebound stepped forward and grabbed the door-knob, and slowly, quietly, turned it. The door opened and, Rebound peered out into the tunnel through his night-vision goggles.

He looked left and saw the pool. Small waves lapped against the sides of the deck.

He looked right, and saw a long, straight tunnel stretching away from him into darkness. He recognized it immediately as the elongated southern tunnel of E-deck that led to the station's drilling room.

Since it was the lowest level in the ice station, E-deck housed the station's drilling room – the room from which the scientists drilled down into the ice to obtain their ice cores. So as to maximize the depths to which the scientists could drill, the drilling room had been constructed as far *into* the ice shelf as possible – to the south of the station, where the ice was deepest. The room was connected to the main station complex by a long, narrow tunnel that stretched for at least forty metres.

Rebound heard the soft footsteps disappear down the long tunnel to his right.

After a short moment of pause, he raised his Mag-hook and ventured out into the tunnel after them.

Schofield fired his Maghook at Latissier.

The Frenchman ducked fast and the grappling hook thundered over the top of him and flew through the rung-ladder behind him. The hook looped itself over one of the rungs and knotted itself tight against the ladder.

Schofield threw his Maghook down and raised his crossbow at the same time as Latissier levelled his own at Schofield.

The two men fired at the same time.

The arrows whistled through the air, crossing each other in mid-flight.

Latissier's arrow slammed into Schofield's armoured shoulderplate. Schofield's arrow lodged in Latissier's hand as the big Frenchman covered his face with his forearm. He roared with pain as he frantically began to reload his crossbow with his good hand.

Schofield quickly looked down at his own crossbow.

The French crossbows had five, circular, rubber slots on their sides in which spare arrows were kept for quick reloading. Schofield's crossbow had five empty slots.

The commando he had taken it from must have used all but the last of his arrows earlier. Now there were none left.

Schofield didn't hesitate.

He took five quick steps forward and hurled himself at Latissier. He slammed into the Frenchman and the two soldiers went sprawling onto the catwalk behind the rung-ladder.

Gant was still lying face down on the catwalk about five yards away when she saw Schofield tackle Latissier. She leapt to her feet and was about to go over and help Schofield when suddenly, another French commando slid down the rung-ladder in front of her and, through a pair of black night-vision goggles, stared right into her eyes.

Rebound slowly made his way down the long, narrow tunnel.

There was a door at the very end of the tunnel. The door to the drilling room. It was ajar.

Rebound listened carefully as he approached the half-open door. He heard soft, shuffling sounds from inside the drilling room. Whoever had run past the storeroom earlier was now inside the drilling room, doing something.

He heard the man speak softly into a microphone of some sort. He said, '*Le piège est tendu.*'

Rebound froze.

It was one of the French commandos.

Rebound pressed himself flat against the wall next to the door and – still wearing his night-vision goggles – slowly peered around the doorframe.

It was like looking through a video camera. First, Rebound saw the doorframe, saw it slide out to the right of his green viewscreen. Then he saw the room open up beyond it.

And then he saw the man – also wearing night-vision goggles – standing right there in front of him, with a crossbow pointed directly at Rebound's face.

Even though the French commando standing in front of her was wearing night-vision goggles, Gant could tell that it was the one named Cuvier.

Jean-Pierre Cuvier. The one who had shot her in the head with his crossbow right at the start of all this. Even now, she could see the tip of that same arrow sticking out from the front of her helmet. The bastard seemed to smile when he realized that he was facing off against the American woman he had shot earlier.

In a blur of green, he brought his crossbow up and fired.

Gant was about twenty feet away and she actually saw the arrow dip in the air as it covered the distance between them. She sidestepped quickly, her gun hand flailing behind her, and then suddenly – *smack!* – she felt that hand jolt sharply as the arrow thudded into her Maghook and sent it flying from her hand.

And then before she knew it, Cuvier was right in front of her with his Bowie knife drawn. He came in fast, his long-bladed hunting knife arcing down towards Gant's throat –

There came a sudden, metallic *zing* as Cuvier's blade came to a jarring halt.

Gant had caught his blow with her own knife.

The two soldiers separated and began to circle each other warily. Cuvier held his knife underhanded. Gant held hers backhanded, SEAL-style. Both still wore their night-vision goggles.

Suddenly, Cuvier lunged and Gant swatted his blade away. But the Frenchman had a longer reach and as they separated again he swiped at Gant's goggles and dislodged them from her head.

For a single, terrifying moment, Gant saw nothing.

Just blackness.

Total blackness.

In this darkness, without her goggles she was *blind*.

Gant felt the catwalk beneath her vibrate. Cuvier was lunging at her again.

Still blind, she ducked instinctively, not knowing whether it was the right move or not.

It was the right move.

She heard the swish of Cuvier's knife as it sliced through the darkness above her helmet.

Gant somersaulted in the darkness, across the catwalk, away from Cuvier. She quickly leapt to her feet and hit a button on the side of her helmet and, immediately, her helmet's infra-red visor snapped down into place in front of her eyes.

It wasn't night vision but it was almost as good.

Now Gant saw the catwalk around her as an electronic, blue-on-black image.

Both the catwalk and the rung-ladder were depicted as blue outlines – cold, lifeless bodies. Beyond the blue rung-ladder, Gant saw two multicoloured figures rolling around on the catwalk – Schofield and Latissier, still struggling desperately.

Gant turned, and on the catwalk in front of her, saw a vibrant, man-shaped, red-green-and-yellow blob moving quickly toward her.

It was Cuvier.

Or at least a graphic representation of the heat patterns inside Cuvier's body.

He swung his knife. Gant parried the blow with her own knife and then let loose with a powerful side-kick to the Frenchman's solar plexus. The kick connected and Cuvier fell, but as he did so, he lashed out with his hand and managed to grab Gant's knife arm and pull her to the catwalk with him.

They hit the floor together.

Gant fell on top of Cuvier, rolled clear, slammed her back against the icy wall surrounding the catwalk. She reached out to steady herself and her hand hit something on the ground next to her.

The Mag –

And then suddenly, the coloured blob that was Cuvier leapt up into her field of vision.

Cuvier had thrown himself at her, had his knife at her throat. Gant threw up her hands to defend herself, dropping her knife so that she could grab Cuvier's knife hand with both of her hands.

With all her strength Gant held Cuvier's knife hand at bay, inches away from her throat.

But he was too strong.

The knife came closer to her throat.

Cuvier's face was right in front of Gant's and through her infra-red visor, Gant saw past his facial features – saw the macabre image of his skull and his teeth, surrounded by pulsating colours. It was as if she were being attacked by a demented skeleton.

And he was close, so close that Gant felt his night-vision goggles brush against her helmet.

The goggles.

Without even thinking, Gant suddenly let go of Cuvier's knife hand with one of her hands, reached up and ripped his night-vision goggles roughly off his head.

Cuvier yelled. Gant threw the goggles over the edge of the catwalk.

Now it was Cuvier who was blind.

But he continued to fight.

The French commando desperately tried to push his knife down into Gant's throat, but Gant suddenly shifted her weight and allowed herself to slide under him, so that her helmet was now level with his eyes.

'You remember giving this to me,' Gant said, seeing the blue outline of the arrow sticking out from the front of her helmet. 'Well, now you can have it back.'

And with that Gant rammed her head forward.

The arrow jutting out from the front of her helmet penetrated Cuvier's right eye and he let out a hideous, inhuman scream and Gant felt a sudden splash of warm blood explode all over her face.

She kicked Cuvier away from her and saw – through her infra-red visor – a computer-generated fountain of yellow-red liquid spraying out from his right eye socket.

Cuvier screamed as he fell backwards, clutching his bloody eye socket.

Gant had poked his eye out, but he wasn't dead yet. He began to thrash about wildly, trying to hit her despite his total blindness.

Gant grabbed the Maghook from the catwalk beside her and levelled it at the Frenchman's bleeding head. He was moving erratically, but Gant had all the time she needed now.

She aimed carefully, at the head of this wailing, multicoloured blob that represented a man.

And then she fired.

The Maghook struck the screaming Frenchman square in the face and a split second before he dropped to the catwalk, Gant heard Cuvier's skull crack in two.

While Gant fought with Cuvier, Schofield and Latissier rolled around on the catwalk.

As they fought, Schofield heard noises everywhere. Voices spoke frantically over his helmet intercom:

' – *They're going round the other side!*'

' – *going for the other ladder!*'

Footsteps clanged on the catwalk above him.

A crossbow fired somewhere nearby.

Schofield heard a sudden snap as Latissier managed to lock another arrow into the bolt of his crossbow. Schofield quickly elbowed the big Frenchman hard in the face, up under his night-vision goggles, breaking his nose. Blood splattered everywhere, all over Schofield's arm, all over the lenses of Latissier's goggles.

The Frenchman grunted with pain as he flung Schofield away from him, toward the edge of the catwalk. The two men separated and Latissier – still lying on the catwalk, half-blinded by the splotches of blood on his night-vision goggles – angrily brought his crossbow around toward Schofield's head.

Schofield was right at the edge of the catwalk, up against the railing. He thought fast.

He caught Latissier's weapon hand as it came round

toward him and then, in a very sudden movement, rolled himself *off the edge of the catwalk*!

Latissier had never expected it.

Schofield kept his grip on Latissier's weapon hand as he fell and, hanging from it, he swung down onto the empty deck below. Like a cat, Schofield landed on his feet and immediately raised Latissier's crossbow up at the underside of the D-deck catwalk and pulled the trigger.

Latissier was lying face down on the catwalk – with his arm stretched awkwardly out over the edge – when the crossbow discharged. At point-blank range, the arrow shot up through a gap in the steel grating, penetrated Latissier's night-vision goggles, and lodged itself right in the middle of the Frenchman's forehead.

Down in the drilling room, Rebound faced the crossbow-wielding French commando.

The Frenchman thought he had the upper hand, thought he had Rebound dead to rights. He only forgot one thing.

Night vision is hell on peripheral vision.

He was standing *too close.*

Which was why he never saw the Maghook that Rebound was holding at his hip.

Rebound fired. The Maghook shot out from its launcher and slammed into the Frenchman's chest from a range of three feet. There came a series of instantaneous *cracks* as the French commando's ribcage collapsed in on his heart. He was dead before he hit the ground.

Rebound took a deep breath, sighed with relief, looked at the drilling room in front of him.

He saw what the Frenchman had been doing and his mouth fell open. And then he remembered what the Frenchman had said earlier.

Le piège est tendu.

Then Rebound looked at the room again.

And he smiled.

'*South tunnel*,' Montana's voice said over Schofield's helmet intercom.

Schofield was down on E-deck now, having swung down there on Latissier's arm. He looked across the pool and saw a black figure running into the south tunnel. It was the last French commando – save for the one who had rappelled down the shaft earlier.

'I see him,' Schofield said, taking off in pursuit.

'*Sir, this is Rebound*,' Rebound's voice suddenly cut across the airwaves. '*Did you just say the south tunnel?*'

'That's right.'

'*Let him come*,' Rebound said firmly. '*And follow him down.*'

Schofield frowned. 'What are you talking about, Rebound?'

'*Just follow him, sir*,' Rebound was whispering now. '*He wants you to.*'

Schofield paused for a moment.

Then he said, 'Do you know something that I don't, Corporal?'

'*That I do, sir*,' came the reply.

Montana, Snake and Gant joined Schofield on E-deck, at the entrance to the south tunnel. They'd all heard Rebound over their helmet intercoms.

Schofield looked at them as he spoke into his helmet mike. 'All right, Rebound, it's your call.'

Schofield, Montana, Snake and Gant edged cautiously down the long, southern tunnel of E-deck. At the end of the tunnel, they saw a door, saw the silhouette of the last French soldier disappear behind it, a shadow in the green darkness.

Rebound was right. The soldier was moving slowly. It was almost as if he *wanted* them to see him go into the drilling room.

Schofield and the others pressed forward down the tunnel. They were about ten yards away from the door to the drilling room when suddenly a hand reached out from the shadows and grabbed Schofield by the shoulder. Schofield spun instantly and saw Rebound emerge from a cupboard set into the wall. There seemed to be another body in the cupboard behind Rebound. Rebound pressed his finger against his lips and led Schofield and the others down the tunnel toward the drilling room door.

'It's a trap,' Rebound mouthed as they reached the door.

Rebound pushed open the door. It creaked loudly as it swung open in front of them.

The door swung wide and the Marines saw the last Frenchman standing over on the far side of the drilling room.

It was Jean Petard. He looked forlornly at them. He was caught in a dead end and he knew it. He was trapped.

'I . . . I surrender,' he said meekly.

Schofield just stared at Petard. Then he turned to Rebound and the others, as if calling for advice.

Then he stepped forward into the drilling room.

Petard seemed to smile, relieved.

At that moment, Rebound suddenly stuck his arm out in front of Schofield's chest, stopping him. Rebound had never taken his eyes off Petard.

Petard frowned.

Rebound stared at him and said, '*Le piège est tendu.*'

Petard cocked his head, surprised.

'The trap is set,' Rebound said in English.

And then Petard suddenly averted his gaze and looked at something else, something on the floor in front of him and his smile went flat. He looked up at Rebound, horrified.

Rebound knew what Petard had seen.

He had seen five French words, and as soon as he had seen them, Petard knew that his fight was over.

Those five words were: BRAQUEZ CE CÔTÉ SUR L'ENNEMI.

Rebound stepped forward and Petard yelled '*No!*'

but it was too late. Rebound stepped through the trip-wire in front of the door and the two concave mines in the drilling room exploded with all their terrifying force.

THIRD INCURSION

16 June 1130 hours

The highway stretched away into the desert.

A thin, unbroken strip of black overlaying the golden-brown floor of the New Mexico landscape. Not a single cloud appeared in the sky.

A lone car raced along the desert highway.

Pete Cameron drove, sweating in the heat. The air-conditioner in his 1977 Toyota had long since given up the fight for life, and now the car was little more than an oven on wheels. It was probably ten degrees hotter inside his car than it was outside.

Cameron was a reporter for *The Washington Post*, had been for three years now. Before that, he had made a name for himself doing features for the respected investigative-reporting journal, *Mother Jones*.

Cameron had fitted in well at *Mother Jones*. The journal has one all-encompassing goal: to expose mis-leading government reports. Cover-ups. And to a large extent, it had been successful in achieving this goal. Pete Cameron loved it, thrived on it. In his last year at *Mother Jones*, he had won an award for an article he had written on the loss of five nuclear warheads from a crashed B-2 stealth bomber. The bomber had crashed into the

Atlantic Ocean just off the coast of Brazil and the US Government had issued a press release saying that all five warheads had been recovered, safely and intact. Cameron had investigated the story, had queried the methods used to find the missing nukes.

The truth soon emerged. The rescue mission had not been about the recovery of the warheads at all. It had been about recovering all evidence of the *bomber*. The nuclear warheads had been a secondary priority and they had never been found.

It was that article and the award that followed it that had brought Cameron to the attention of *The Washington Post*. They offered him a job and he took it with both hands.

Cameron was thirty years old, and tall, really tall – six-feet-five. He had messy, sandy-brown hair and wire-frame glasses. His car looked like a bomb had hit it – empty Coke cans were strewn about the floor, intermingled with crumpled cheeseburger wrappers; pads and pens and scraps of paper stuck out from every compartment in the car. A pad of Post-Its rested in the ashtray. Those that had been used were stuck to the dashboard.

Cameron drove through the desert.

His cellular rang. It was his wife, Alison.

Pete and Alison Cameron were something of celebrities among the Washington press community, the famous – or infamous – husband-and-wife team of *The Washington Post*. When Pete Cameron had arrived at the *Post* from *Mother Jones* three years ago, he had been assigned to work with a young reporter named Alison

Greenberg. The chemistry between them had ignited immediately. It was electric. In one week, they were in bed together. In twelve months they were married. They didn't have any kids yet, but they were working on it.

'Are you there yet?' Alison's voice said over the speaker phone. Alison was twenty-nine and had shoulder-length, auburn hair, enormous sky-blue eyes and a beaming smile that made her face glow. Pete loved it. Alison wasn't conventionally beautiful, but she could stop traffic with that smile. At the moment, she was working out of the paper's D.C. office.

'I'm almost there,' Pete Cameron replied.

He was on his way to an observatory out in the middle of the New Mexico desert. Some technician at the SETI Institute there had called the paper earlier that day claiming to have detected some chatter over an old spy satellite network. Cameron had been sent to investigate.

It was nothing new. The Search for Extraterrestrial Intelligence Institute, or SETI, picked up stuff all the time. Their radio satellite array was very powerful and extraordinarily sensitive. It wasn't uncommon for a SETI technician, in his search for extraterrestrial transmissions, to 'cross beams' with a stray spy satellite and pick up a few, garbled words from a restricted military transmission.

Those pick-ups were disparagingly labelled 'SETI sightings' by the reporters at *The Washington Post*. Usually they amounted to nothing – just incomprehensible, one-word transmissions – but the theory was that, maybe, one day, one of those garbled messages would provide the starting point for a story. The kind of story that ended in the word Pulitzer.

Alison said, 'Well, call me as soon as you're done at the Institute.' She put on a mock-sexy voice, 'I have a *thing* for SETI sightings.'

Cameron smiled. 'Very provocative. Do you do house calls?'

'You never know your luck in the big city.'

'You know,' Cameron said, 'in some states, that could qualify as sexual harassment.'

'Honey, being married to you *is* sexual harassment,' Alison said.

Cameron laughed. 'I'll call you when I'm done,' he said before hanging up.

An hour later, Cameron's Toyota pulled into the dusty parking lot of the SETI Institute. There were three other cars parked in the lot.

A squat, two-storey office building stood adjacent to the parking lot, nestled in the shadow of a three-hundred-foot-tall radio telescope. Cameron counted twenty-seven other, identical, satellite dishes stretching away from him into the desert.

Inside, Cameron was met by a geeky little man wearing a white lab coat and a plastic pocket protector. He said his name was Emmett Somerville and that it was he who had picked up the signal.

Somerville led Cameron down some stairs to a wide, underground room. Cameron followed him silently as they negotiated their way through a maze of electronic radio equipment. Two massive Cray XMP supercomputers took up an entire wall of the enormous, subterranean room.

Somerville spoke as he walked, 'I picked it up at around two-thirty this morning. It was in English, so I knew it couldn't be alien.'

'Good thinking,' Cameron said, dead-pan.

'But the accent was definitely American, and considering the content, I called the Pentagon right away.' He turned to look at Cameron as he walked. 'We have a direct number.'

He said it with nerdy pride: the government thinks we're so important that they gave us a direct line. Cameron figured that the number Somerville had was probably the number for the Pentagon's PR desk, a number that SETI could have found by looking up the Department of Defence in the phone book. Cameron had it on his speed-dial.

'Anyway,' Somerville said, 'when they said that it wasn't one of their transmissions, I figured it was okay to give you guys at the paper a call.'

'We appreciate it,' Cameron said.

The two men arrived at a corner console. It consisted of two screens mounted above a keyboard. Next to the screens was a broadcast quality, reel-to-reel recording machine.

'Wanna hear it?' Somerville asked, his finger poised above the 'PLAY' button on the reel-to-reel machine.

'Shoot.'

Emmett Somerville hit the switch. The reels began to rotate.

At first Cameron heard nothing, then static. He looked expectantly at Emmett the Geek.

'It's coming,' Somerville said.

There was a wash of some more static and then, suddenly, voices.

' – *copy, one-three-four-six-two-five* – '

' – *contact lost due to ionospheric disturbance* – '

' – *forward team* – '

' – *Scarecrow* – '

' – *minus sixty-six point five* – '

' – *solar flare disrupting radio* – '

' – *one-fifteen, twenty minutes, twelve seconds east* – '

' – *how* – ' static, ' – *get there so* – '

' – *secondary team en route* – '

Pete Cameron slowly shut his eyes. It was another bum steer. Just more indecipherable military gobbledygook.

The transmission ended and Cameron turned and saw that Somerville was watching him eagerly. Clearly, the SETI technician wanted something to come of his discovery. He was a nobody. Worse, a nobody out in the middle of nowhere. A guy who probably just wanted to see his name in *The Washington Post* in anything other than an obituary. Cameron felt sorry for him. He sighed.

'Could you play it again for me,' he said, reluctantly pulling out his notepad.

Somerville practically leaped for the rewind button.

The tape played again and Cameron dutifully took notes.

It was ironic, Schofield thought, that Petard, the last French commando, should be killed by one of his own weapons. Especially when it was a weapon that France had obtained from the United States by virtue of their alliance under NATO.

The M18A1 mine is better known throughout the world as the 'Claymore'. It is made up of a concave porcelain plate which contains hundreds of ball bearings embedded in a six-hundred-gram wad of C-4 plastic explosive. In effect, a Claymore is a *directable* fragmentation grenade. If one sits behind it, one will not be harmed by its blast. If one is caught in front of it, one will be shredded to pieces

The most well-known characteristic of the Claymore, however, is the simple instruction label which one finds embossed on the forward face of the mine. It reads: THIS SIDE TOWARD ENEMY.

Or, in French: BRAQUEZ CE CÔTÉ SUR L'ENNEMI.

If you ever found yourself looking at those words, you knew you were looking at the wrong end of a Claymore.

The two Claymores in the drilling room had been

central to the French commandos' last ditch plan to beat the Marines. After it was all over, Schofield pieced together that plan:

They had sent someone down to the drilling room, ahead of the others. Once there, that person had set up the two Claymores so that they faced the door. The Claymores would then be connected to a tripwire.

Then, the other French commandos would pretend to retreat to the drilling room, *deliberately* allowing the Marines to follow them.

Of course, the Marines would know that the drilling room was a dead end, so they would *think* that the French, in their desperate attempt to flee, had run themselves into a corner, into a trap.

Surrender would be inevitable.

But as the Marines entered the drilling room to secure the French troops, they would break the tripwire and set off the two Claymores. The Marines would be cut to ribbons.

It was an audacious plan. A plan that would have changed the course of the battle.

And it was cunning, too. It turned a full-scale retreat – hell, *a total surrender* – into a decisive counterattack.

But what Petard and the French had *not* accounted for was that one of the American soldiers might come upon their trap while they were setting it.

Schofield was proud of Rebound. Proud of how the young soldier had handled the situation.

Rather than blow the lid on the French plan and continue with unpredictable hand-to-hand fighting,

Rebound had coolly *allowed* the French to believe that their plan was still on foot.

But he had changed one thing.

He had turned the Claymores around.

That was what Petard had seen when Rebound had spoken to him in the drilling room. He had seen those chilling words.

THIS SIDE TOWARD ENEMY.

Pointing at him.

Rebound had got the better of him.

And when Rebound stepped forward across the trip-wire, it was to be the last thing that Petard ever saw.

The battle, at last, was over.

An hour later, all of the bodies, French and American, had been found and accounted for. At least those bodies that *could* be found.

The French had lost four men to the killer whales, the Americans, one. Eight other French commandos and two more US Marines – Hollywood and Ratman – had been found in various locations around the ice station. They had all been confirmed dead.

The Americans also had two wounded, both quite seriously. Mother, who had lost one of her legs to the killer whale, and, rather surprisingly, Augustine 'Samurai' Lau, the very first Marine to have been gunned down by the French.

Mother was faring better than Samurai. Since her wound was a localized one – confined to the lower extremity of her left leg – she was still conscious. In fact, she still had full movement in all of her other limbs. The flow of blood from the wound had been stopped and the methadone took care of what pain there was. The only enemy that remained was shock. As such, it was decided that Mother would remain in her storeroom on E-deck, under constant supervision. To move her might trigger a fit.

Samurai, on the other hand, was in a much worse state. He was in a self-induced coma, his stomach having been ripped to shreds by Latissier's barrage of gunfire at the very beginning of the battle.

The young Marine's body had responded to the sudden trauma in the only way it knew how – it had switched itself off. At the time they found him alive, Schofield had marvelled at the ability of the human body to take care of itself in the face of such extreme crisis. No amount of methadone or morphine could have quelled the pain of that many gunshot wounds. So Samurai's body had done the next best thing: it had simply turned off its sensory apparatus and was now awaiting external help.

The problem was whether or not Schofield could provide that external help.

Anything greater than basic medical knowledge is rare in a front-line unit. The closest thing such units have to a doctor is the team medic, who is usually a low-level corporal. Legs Lane had been Schofield's medic, and he was now deader than dead.

Schofield walked quickly around the A-deck catwalk.

He'd just come up from E-deck where he had checked on Mother, and he was now wearing a new pair of silver anti-flash glasses. Mother had given them to him. She'd said that in her state, she wouldn't be needing them anymore.

Schofield poked his head around the dining room door. 'What do you think, Rebound?' he said.

Inside the dining room, Rebound was working feverishly over Samurai's inanimate body. The body lay flat on its back on a table in the centre of the room. Blood dripped off the edges of the table, forming a red puddle on the cold porcelain floor.

Rebound looked up from what he was doing. He shook his head in exasperation.

'I can't keep up with the blood loss,' he said to Schofield. 'There's just too much internal damage. His whole gut's been blown apart.'

Rebound wiped his forehead. A slick of blood appeared above his eyes. He looked hard at Schofield. 'This is way out of my league, sir. He needs someone who knows what he's doing. He needs a doctor.'

Schofield stared at Samurai's prone body for a few seconds.

'Just do what you can,' he said, and then he left the room.

'Okay, people, listen up,' Schofield said. 'We don't have much time, so I'm going to keep this short.'

The six remaining able-bodied Marines were gathered

around the pool on E-deck. They all stood in a wide circle. Schofield stood in the middle.

Schofield's voice echoed up through the shaft of the empty station. 'This station is obviously a lot hotter than we originally thought. I'm thinking that if the French were willing to take a chance to grab it, others will, too. And whoever those others might be, by now they've had some time to get their shit together and prepare for a full-scale attack. Have no doubt, people, if anyone else decides to hit this station they will almost certainly be better prepared and more heavily armed than those French pricks we just exterminated. Opinions?'

'Concur,' Buck Riley said.

'Same,' Snake said. Book Riley and Snake Kaplan were the two most senior enlisted men in the unit. It meant something that they both agreed with Schofield's assessment of the situation.

Schofield said. 'All right, then. What I want to happen now is this. Montana . . .'

'Yes, sir.'

'I want you to go topside and position our two hovercrafts so that their rangefinders are pointed outward, so that they cover the entire landward approach to this station. I want maximum coverage, no gaps. Tripwires aren't going to cut it anymore with this place, we use the rangefinders from here. As soon as anyone comes within fifty miles of this station, I want to know about it.'

'Got it,' Montana said.

'And while you're up there,' Schofield said, 'see if

you can get on the radio and raise McMurdo. Find out when our reinforcements are coming. They should've been here by now.'

'You got it,' Montana said. He hurried away.

'Santa Cruz . . .' Schofield said, turning.

'Yes, sir.'

'Eraser check. I want this whole facility swept from top to bottom for any kind of eraser or delay switch, okay. There's no knowing what kinds of little surprises our French friends left behind for us. Got it.'

'Yes, sir,' Santa Cruz said. He broke out of the circle and headed for the nearest rung-ladder.

'Snake . . .'

'Sir.'

'The winch that lowers the diving bell. Its control panel is up on C-deck, in the alcove. That control panel was damaged by a grenade blast during the fight. I need those winch controls working again. Can you handle it?'

'Yes, sir,' Snake said. He, too, left the circle.

When Snake had gone, Riley and Gant were the only ones left on the deck.

Schofield turned to face them. 'Book. Fox. I want you two to do a full prep of our dive gear. Three divers, four-hour dive compression, low-audibility gear, plus some auxiliaries for later.'

'Air mix?' Riley asked.

'Saturated helium-oxygen. Ninety-eight to two,' Schofield said.

Riley and Gant were momentarily silent. A compressed air mix of 98% helium and 2% oxygen was very rare. The almost negligible amount of oxygen indicated a dive to a very high-pressure environment.

Schofield handed Gant a handful of blue capsules. They were N-67D anti-nitrogen blood-pressure capsules, developed by the Navy for use during deep-dive missions. They were affectionately known to military divers as 'the pills'.

By retarding the dissolution of nitrogen in the bloodstream during a deep dive, the pills prevented decompression sickness – better known as the bends – among divers. Since the pills neutralized nitrogen activity in the bloodstream, Navy and Marine Corps divers could *descend* as quickly as they liked without fear of nitrogen narcosis, and *ascend* without the need for making time-consuming decompression stops. The pills had revolutionized military deep-diving.

'Planning a deep dive, sir?' Gant said, looking up from the blue pills in her hand.

Schofield looked at her seriously, 'I want to find out what's down in that cave.'

Schofield walked quickly around the curved outer tunnel of B-deck, deep in thought.

Things were moving fast now.

The French attack on Wilkes had taught him a lot. Wilkes Ice Station – or more precisely, whatever lay buried in the ice *beneath* Wilkes Ice Station – was now officially worth killing for.

But it was the implications of that lesson that gave Schofield a chill. If France had been willing to launch an impromptu snatch-and-grab for whatever was down in that cave, it was highly probable that other countries would be willing to do the same.

There was one additional factor, though, about possible further attacks on Wilkes that caused Schofield particular concern: if someone was going to launch an attack on Wilkes, they would have to do it *soon* – before a full-strength US force arrived at the station.

The next few hours would be very tense.

It would be a race to see who would arrive first.

American reinforcements, or a fully-equipped enemy force.

Schofield tried not to think about it. There were a lot

of things to do, and one matter in particular required his attention first.

After the battle with the French had concluded, the remaining scientists from Wilkes – there were five of them, three men and two women – had retired to their living quarters on B-deck. Schofield was heading for those living quarters now. He was hoping to find among those scientists a doctor who might be able to help Samurai.

Schofield continued to walk around the curved outer tunnel. His clothes were still wet, but he didn't care. Like all of the other Marines in his unit, he was wearing a thermal wetsuit under his fatigues. It was practically standard attire for Recon units working in arctic conditions. Wetsuits were warmer than long-johns and they didn't get heavy if they got wet. And by *wearing* one's wetsuit instead of *carrying* it, a Recon Marine lightened his load, something very important for a rapid-response unit.

Just then, a door to Schofield's right opened and a cloud of steam wafted out into the corridor. A sleek black object slid out of the haze and into the corridor in front of Schofield.

Wendy.

She was dripping with water. She looked up at Schofield with a goofy seal grin.

Kirsty emerged from the steamy haze. The shower room. She saw Schofield instantly and she smiled.

'Hi,' she said. She was wearing a new set of dry

clothes, and her hair was tousled, wet. Schofield guessed that Kirsty had just had the hottest shower of her life.

'Hey, there,' Schofield said.

'Wendy loves the shower room,' Kirsty said, nodding at Wendy. 'She likes to slide through the steam.'

Schofield suppressed a laugh and looked down at the little black fur seal at his feet. She was cute, very cute. She had also saved his life. Her soft brown eyes glistened with intelligence.

Schofield looked at Kirsty. 'How are *you* feeling?'

'Warm now,' she said.

Schofield nodded. From the look of her, Kirsty seemed to have bounced back well from her ordeal in the pool. Kids were good like that, resilient. Schofield wondered what sort of therapy an adult would need after falling into a pool filled with ferocious killer whales.

Schofield gave a lot of the credit to Buck Riley. Riley had been up on C-deck when Kirsty had been whizzed up there on Schofield's Maghook, and for the remainder of the battle, Riley had kept Kirsty by his side, safe and sound.

'Good,' Schofield said. 'You're one tough kid, you know that? You ought to be a Marine.'

Kirsty beamed. Schofield nodded down the tunnel. 'You going my way?'

'Yeah,' she said, falling into step beside him as he began walking down the tunnel. Wendy loped down the corridor behind them.

'Where are you going?' Kirsty asked.

'I'm looking for your mom.'

'Oh,' Kirsty said, a little softly.

It was a strange response, and, through his reflective silver glasses, Schofield cast a sideways glance at Kirsty. She just stared at the floor as she walked. Schofield wondered what it meant.

There was an awkward silence and Schofield searched for something to say. 'So, uh, how old did you say you were? Twelve, right.'

'Uh-huh.'

'What is that, seventh grade?'

'Mmm.'

'Seventh grade,' Schofield mused. He was at a total loss for something to say now, so he just said, 'I guess you must be starting to think about a career, then.'

Kirsty seemed to perk up at the question. She looked across at Schofield as they walked.

'Yeah,' she said seriously, as though career thoughts had been weighing heavily on her twelve-year-old mind lately.

'So what do you want to do when you leave school?'

'I want to be a teacher,' Kirsty said. 'Like my dad.'

'What does your dad teach?'

'He taught geology at a big college in Boston,' Kirsty said. 'Harvard,' she added importantly.

'And what do you want to teach?' Schofield asked.

'Math.'

'*Math?*'

'I'm good at math,' Kirsty said, shrugging self-consciously, embarrassed and proud at the same time.

'My dad used to help me with my homework,' she went on. 'He said I was much better at math than most other kids my age, so sometimes he would teach me stuff that the other kids didn't know. Interesting stuff, stuff that I wasn't supposed to learn until I was a *senior*. And sometimes he'd teach me stuff that they don't teach you at all in school.'

'Yeah?' Schofield said, genuinely interested. 'What sort of stuff?'

'Oh, you know. Polynomials. Number sequences. Some calculus.'

'Calculus. Number sequences,' Schofield repeated, amazed.

'You know, like triangular numbers and Fibonacci numbers. That sort of stuff.'

Schofield shook his head in astonishment. This was impressive. Very impressive. Kirsty Hensleigh, twelve years old and a little short for her age, was apparently a very smart young lady. Schofield looked at her again. She seemed to walk on her toes, with a kind of spring in each step. She just looked like a regular kid.

Kirsty said, 'We used to do a lot of stuff together. Softball, hiking, once he even took me scuba diving, even though I hadn't done the course.'

Schofield said, 'You make it sound like your dad doesn't do that sort of thing anymore?'

There was a short silence. Then Kirsty said softly, 'He doesn't.'

223

'What happened?' Schofield asked gently. He was waiting to hear a tale about fighting parents and a divorce. It seemed to happen a lot these days.

'My dad was killed in a car wreck last year,' Kirsty said flatly.

Schofield stopped in mid-stride. He turned to look at Kirsty. The little girl was staring down at her shoelaces.

'I'm sorry,' Schofield said.

Kirsty cocked her head to one side. 'It's okay,' she said, and then resumed walking.

They came to a door sunken into the outer tunnel and Schofield stopped in front of it. 'Well, this is my stop.'

'Mine, too,' Kirsty said.

Schofield opened the door and let Kirsty and Wendy enter in front of him. He followed them inside.

It was a common room of some sort. Some ugly orange couches, a stereo, a television, a VCR. Schofield guessed that they didn't get regular TV transmissions down here so they just watched videos on the television.

Sarah Hensleigh and Abby Sinclair sat on one of the orange couches. They were also now wearing dry clothes. The three other scientists from Wilkes – three men named Llewellyn, Harris and Robinson – were there, too. After seeing what the fragmentation grenades had done to Hollywood and one of their colleagues they had spent the remainder of the battle holed up in their rooms. Now they looked tired and weary, afraid.

Kirsty went over and sat down on the couch next to Sarah Hensleigh. She sat down silently and didn't say anything to her mother. Schofield remembered the first time he had seen Sarah and Kirsty together – back before the French had arrived at Wilkes. Kirsty hadn't said much then either. Schofield hadn't noticed any tension between them then, but he noticed it now. He put it out of his mind as he walked over to Sarah.

'Is anyone here a medical doctor?' Schofield asked her.

Sarah shook her head. 'No. No, Ken Wishart was the only doctor at the station. But he – ' She cut herself off.

'But he what?'

Sarah sighed. 'But he was on board the hovercraft that was *supposed* to be heading back to d'Urville.'

Schofield shut his eyes, once again imagined the fate of the five scientists who had been on board the doomed hovercraft.

A voice crackled over his helmet intercom. '*Scarecrow, this is Montana.*'

'What is it?' Schofield said.

'*I've set up the rangefinders around the outer perimeter just like you wanted. You wanna come up and check it out?*'

'Yes, I do,' Schofield said, 'I'll be up in a minute. Where are you?'

'*South-west corner.*'

'Wait for me,' Schofield said. 'Have you had any luck getting through to McMurdo?'

'*Not yet. There's a shitstorm of interference on every frequency. I can't get through.*'

'Keep trying,' Schofield said. 'Scarecrow, out.'

Schofield turned and was about to leave the common room when someone tapped him lightly on the shoulder. He turned. It was Sarah Hensleigh. She was smiling.

'I just remembered,' she said. 'There *is* a medical doctor at this station after all.'

After the battle was over, the Marines had found the two French scientists, Luc Champion and Henri Rae, cowering in a cupboard in the dining room on A-deck.

They had not offered any resistance. Indeed, as they had been dragged unceremoniously out of the cupboard to face their conquerors, the horror on their faces had said it all. They had backed the wrong side in this fight. The men they had deceived were now their captors. The price for their treachery would be high.

Both men had been taken down to E-deck where they were handcuffed to a pole in plain view. Schofield's team had work to do and Schofield didn't want to waste any of his manpower guarding the two French scientists. By cuffing the two Frenchmen to a pole out in the open, the Marines down on E-deck could work as well as keep an eye on them.

Schofield stepped out onto the B-deck catwalk. He was about to speak into his helmet mike when Sarah Hensleigh came out onto the catwalk behind him.

'I have something I have to ask you,' she said. 'Something I couldn't ask you back in the common room.'

Schofield held up a hand, spoke into his helmet mike: 'Rebound. This is Scarecrow. How's Samurai?'

Rebound's voice came in over his earpiece. '*I've managed to stop the bleeding for the moment, sir, but he's still pretty bad.*'

'Stable?'

'*As stable as I'm gonna get him.*'

'All right, listen. I want you to go down to E-deck and grab that French scientist named Champion, Luc Champion,' Schofield said. He looked at Sarah as he spoke. 'I've just been informed that our good friend Monsieur Champion is a surgeon.'

'*Yes, sir,*' Rebound said eagerly. He seemed relieved that someone more qualified might be able to take over Samurai's care. But then he seemed to check himself. '*Uh, sir . . .*'

'What is it?'

'*Can we trust him?*'

'No,' Schofield said firmly, as he began to climb up the rung-ladder toward A-deck. He motioned for Sarah to follow him up. 'Not a wit. Rebound, you just tell him that if Samurai dies, so does he.'

'*Gotcha.*'

Schofield reached the top of the rung-ladder and stepped up onto the A-deck catwalk. He helped Sarah up behind him. Almost immediately, he saw Rebound emerge from the dining room doorway not far away and jog for the opposite rung-ladder. He was going down to E-deck to get Champion.

Schofield and Sarah headed for the main entrance to

the station. As they walked along the catwalk, Schofield looked down at the station beneath him and thought about his people.

They were scattered everywhere.

Montana was outside. Riley and Gant were down on E-deck, getting the scuba gear ready for the dive down to the cave. Snake was smack in the middle, in the alcove on C-deck, fixing the winch controls. And Santa Cruz was nowhere to be seen, since he was off conducting a search of the station for erasers.

Christ, Schofield thought, they were spread all over the place.

Schofield's helmet intercom crackled. It was Santa Cruz.

'What is it, Private?' Schofield said.

'*Sir, I've conducted a search of the station and I've found no sign of any erasing device.*'

'No erasers?' Schofield frowned. 'Nothing at all?'

'*Not a thing, sir. My guess is they didn't expect things to happen so fast, so they didn't get a chance to lay any.*'

Schofield thought about that.

Cruz was probably right. The French team's plan had undoubtedly been cut short by Buck Riley's arrival at the station and his accidental discovery of what had really happened to the crashed French hovercraft. The French commandos' plan had been to win the Americans' trust and then shoot them in the back. Since that plan hadn't come to fruition, it was no surprise that they hadn't been able to set any erasers.

'*But I did find something, sir,*' Santa Cruz said.

'What?'

'I found a radio, sir.'

'A radio?' Schofield said dryly. It was hardly a mind-blowing discovery.

'Sir, this ain't no ordinary radio. It looks like a portable VLF transmitter.'

That got Schofield's attention. A VLF, or very low frequency transmitter is a rare device. It has a frequency range of between 3 kHz and 30 kHz, which, in real terms, amounts to an unbelievably long wavelength. It is so long – or, in radio terms, so 'heavy' – that the radio signal travels as a ground signal that follows the curvature of the earth's surface.

Until only very recently, signals travelling at such low frequencies required very high-powered transmitters, which were, of course, very large and cumbersome. As such, they weren't often used by ground forces. Recent developments in technology, however, had resulted in heavy, but nonetheless man-portable, VLF transmitters. They looked and weighed about the same as the average backpack.

The fact that the French had brought such a transmitter to Wilkes bothered Schofield. There was really only one use for VLF radio signals and that was –

No, that's ridiculous, Schofield thought. *They couldn't have done that.*

'Cruz, where did you find it?'

'Down in the drilling room,' Santa Cruz's voice said.

'Are you there now?'

'Yes, sir.'

'Bring it out to the pool deck,' Schofield said. 'I'll come down after I check on Montana outside.'

'*Yes, sir.*'

Schofield clicked off his intercom. He and Sarah came to the entrance passageway.

'What are erasers?' Sarah asked.

'What? Oh,' Schofield said. He only just remembered that Sarah wasn't a soldier. Schofield took a deep breath. ' "Eraser" is the term used to describe an explosive device that is planted in a battlefield by a covert incursionary force for use in the event that their mission fails. Most of the time, an eraser is set off by a delay switch, which is just an ordinary timer.'

'Okay, wait a minute. Slow down,' Sarah said.

Schofield sighed, slowed down. 'Small crack units like these French guys we met tonight usually find themselves fighting in places where they're not supposed to be, right. Like, there would probably be an international incident if it could be proved that French troops were in a US research station trying to kill everybody, right?'

'Yeah . . .'

'Well, there's no guarantee that these crack units are gonna *succeed* in getting what they came for, is there?' Schofield said. 'I mean, hey, they might come up against a team of tough hombres like us and wind up dead.'

Schofield grabbed a parka off a hook on the wall, and began to put it on.

He said, 'Anyway, these days, nearly all elite teams – the French parachute regiment, the SAS, the Navy SEALs – nearly all of them carry contingency plans just in case they fail in their missions. We call those contingency plans "erasers" because that's exactly what they're designed to do: *erase* that whole team's existence. Make it look like that team was never there. Sometimes they're called cyanide pills, because if any of the enemy are caught, the eraser will ultimately act as their suicide pill.'

'So, you're talking about explosives,' Sarah said.

'I'm talking about special explosives,' Schofield said. 'Most of the time erasers are either chlorine-based explosives, or high-temperature liquid detonators. They're designed to wipe off faces, vaporize bodies, destroy uniforms and dogtags. They're designed to make it look like you were never there.

'Erasers are actually a relatively recent phenomenon. No one had ever really heard about them until a couple of years ago when a German sabotage team was caught in an underground missile silo in Montana. They were cornered so they pulled the pin on three liquid-chlorine grenades. After those things went off, there was *nothing* left. No soldiers. No silo. We think the Germans were there to disable some ballistic nuclear missiles that we said didn't exist.'

'A German sabotage unit. In Montana,' Sarah said in diselief. 'Correct me if I'm wrong, but isn't Germany supposed to be our ally?'

'Isn't France supposed to be our ally?' Schofield replied, raising his eyebrows. 'It happens. More often than you think. Attacks from so-called "friendly" countries. They even have a term for it at the Pentagon, they call them "Cassius Ops", after Cassius, the traitor in "Julius Caesar".'

'They have a *term* for it?'

Schofield shrugged into his coat. 'Look at it this way. America used to be one of two superpowers. When there were two superpowers, there was a balance, a check. What one did, the other countered. But now the Soviets are history and America is the only real superpower left in the world. We have more weapons than any other nation in the world. We have more money to *spend* on weapons than any other nation in the world. Other countries would go broke trying to keep up with our defence spending. The Soviets did. There are a lot of countries out there – some of whom we call friends – who think that America is too big, too powerful, countries who would really like to see America take a fall. And some of those countries – France, Germany and to a lesser extent, Great Britain – aren't afraid to give us a little push either.'

'I never knew,' Sarah said.

'Not many people do,' Schofield said. 'But it's one of the main reasons my unit was sent to this station. To defend it against any of our "allies" who might decide to make a play for it.'

Schofield pulled his parka tight around himself, and grabbed the handle to the main door leading outside.

'You said you wanted to ask me about something,' he said. 'Can you talk as you walk?'

'Uh, yeah, I guess so,' Sarah said as she quickly grabbed a parka off one of the hooks.

'Then let's go,' Schofield said.

Down on E-deck, Libby Gant was checking the calibration on a depth gauge.

She and Riley were on the outer perimeter of the deck that surrounded the pool. It had been a good forty-five minutes since they had seen a killer whale, but they weren't taking any chances. They stayed well away from the water's edge.

Gant and Riley were checking the unit's scuba gear, in preparation for the dive that would be made in the station's diving bell.

They were alone on E-deck, and they worked in silence. Every now and then, Riley would wander over to the storeroom in the south tunnel and check on Mother.

Gant put down the depth gauge she was holding and grabbed another. 'What happened to his eyes?' she asked quietly, not looking up from what she was doing.

Riley stopped working for a moment, and looked up at Gant. When he didn't speak immediately, Gant raised her own eyes.

For a while, Riley seemed to evaluate her. Then, abruptly, he looked away.

'Not many people know what happened to his eyes,' Riley said. 'Hell, until today, not that many people had even *seen* his eyes.'

There was a short silence.

'Is that why his call-sign is Scarecrow?' Gant said softly. 'Because of his eyes?'

Riley nodded. 'Norman McLean gave it to him.'

'The *general?*'

'The general. When McLean saw Schofield's eyes, he said he looked like a scarecrow McLean had once had guarding his cornfield back in Kansas. Apparently, it was one of those scarecrows that had two slits for each eye, you know, like a plus sign.'

'Do you know how it happened?' Gant asked gently.

At first Riley didn't answer. Then, finally, he nodded. But he didn't say anything.

'What happened?'

Riley took a deep breath. He put down the helium compressor he was holding in his hand and looked at Gant. 'Shane Schofield wasn't always in command of a ground Recon unit,' he began. 'He used to be a pilot, based on the *Wasp*.'

The USS *Wasp* is the flagship of the United States Marine Corps. It is one of seven Landing Helicopter Dockships in the Corps, and it is the battle centre for any major Marine expedition. Most casual observers mistake it for an aircraft carrier.

What a lot of people don't know about the Marine Corps is that it maintains a sizeable aviation wing. Although this air wing is used primarily to transport troops it is also used to support ground attacks. For this purpose, it is equipped with lethal AH-1W Cobra Attack Helicopters – instantly recognizable because of their skinny shape – and British-made (but American-modified) AV-8B Harrier 11 fighter jets, or, as they are more widely known throughout the world, Harrier jumpjets. Harriers are the only attack planes in the world with the ability to take off and land vertically.

'Schofield was a Harrier pilot on the *Wasp*. One of the best, so they tell me,' Riley said. 'He was in Bosnia in 1995, during the worst of the fighting there, flying patrol missions over the no-fly-zone.'

Gant watched Riley closely as he spoke. He was staring off into space as he recounted the story.

'One day, late in 1995, he got shot down by a mobile Serbian missile battery that Intelligence said didn't exist. I think they found out later that it was a two-man strike team in a jeep with six American-made Stingers in the back seat.

'Anyway,' Book said, 'Schofield managed to eject a second before the Stingers took out his fuel tanks. He came down bang in the middle of Serb-held territory.'

Riley turned to face Gant.

'Our lieutenant survived for nineteen days in the Serbian woodlands – alone – while over a hundred Serbian troops swept the forest looking for him. When they found him, he hadn't eaten in ten days.

'They took him to a deserted farmhouse and tied him to a chair. Then they beat him with a wooden plank with nails stuck into it and asked him questions. Why was he flying over this area? Was he a spy plane? They wanted to know how much he knew about their positions because they thought he was up there providing air support for US ground forces inside Serb territory.'

'US ground forces were *inside* Serbian territory?' Gant asked.

Riley nodded silently. 'There were two SEAL teams in there. Carrying out covert surgical hits on Serbian leadership positions. Night hits. Good hits. They'd been causing chaos among the Serbs, absolute chaos. They'd be in and out before anyone knew they even existed. They'd go in, slash their victims' throats and then they'd vanish into the night. They were so good that some of the locals started saying they were ghosts come to haunt them for what they were doing to their own people.'

Gant said, 'Did Scarecrow know about them? The SEAL teams inside Serb territory?'

Book was silent for a moment. Then he said, 'Yes. Officially, Schofield was patrolling the no-fly-zone. Unofficially, he was sending grid co-ordinates of Serb leadership farmhouses to the SEALs on the ground. It didn't make any difference anyway. He never said a word.'

Gant watched intently as Riley took a deep breath. He was building up to something.

'In any case,' Book said, 'the Serbs decided that Schofield *had* been carrying out reconnaissance for the SEAL teams; that he *had* been spotting strategic targets from the air and transmitting their co-ordinates to men on the ground. They decided that since he'd been seeing things that he wasn't supposed to be seeing, they would cut his eyes out.'

'*What?*' Gant said.

Riley said, 'They pulled a razor blade out of a drawer and they held him down. Then one of them stepped forward and slowly cut two vertical lines down across Schofield's eyes. Apparently, as he did it, the man with the razor blade quoted something from the Bible. Something about if your hand sins, cut it off, and if your eyes sin, cut them out.'

Gant felt sick. They had *blinded* Schofield. 'What did they do then?' she asked.

'They locked him in a cupboard and they let him bleed.'

Gant was still shocked. 'So how did he get out?'

'Jack Walsh sent a Recon team to go in and get him,' Riley said.

Gant's ears pricked up at the name. Every Marine knew of Captain John T. Walsh. He was the captain of the *Wasp*, the most revered Marine in the Corps.

Some thought he should have been Commandant, the highest ranking officer in the United States Marine Corps, but Walsh's history of disdain for any kind of politician had prevented that. The Commandant is required to liaise regularly with members of Congress and everyone knew – Walsh more than anyone – that Jack Walsh wouldn't be able to stomach that. Besides, Walsh had said, he would rather command the *Wasp* and liaise with soldiers. The Marines loved him for it.

Riley went on. 'When Scott O'Grady got lifted out of Bosnia on June 8 1995, they put him on the cover of *Time* magazine. He met the President. He did the whole PR thing.

'When Shane Schofield got lifted out of Bosnia five months later, nobody heard a thing. There were no TV cameras waiting on the deck of the *Wasp* to photograph him as he stepped off that helicopter. There were no newspaper reporters there to take down his story. Do you know why?'

'Why?'

'Because when Shane Schofield landed on the *Wasp* after being extracted from that farmhouse in Bosnia by a team of United States Marines, he was the worst looking thing you have *ever* seen.

'The extraction had been bloody. Fierce as hell. The Serbs hadn't wanted to give up their prized American pilot and they'd fought hard. When that chopper resumed and hit the tarmac on the *Wasp*, it had four seriously wounded Marines on board. It also had Shane Schofield.

'The medics and the doctors and the support crews charged out and got everybody off the chopper as fast as they could. There was blood everywhere, wounded men screaming. Schofield was taken away on a gurney. He had blood *pouring* out of both of his eyes. The extraction had been so fast – so *intense* – that no one had even had a chance to put gauze patches over his eyes.'

Riley paused. Gant just stared.

'What happened after that?' she asked.

'Jack Walsh copped shit from the White House *and* the Pentagon. They hadn't wanted him to send anyone in for Schofield because Schofield wasn't supposed to be there in the first place. The White House didn't want the "political damage" that would follow from an American search-and-rescue mission for a downed spy plane. Walsh told them where to shove it, said they could fire him if they wanted to.'

'What about Scarecrow? What happened to him?'

'He was blinded. His eyes had been ripped to shreds. They took him to Johns Hopkins University Hospital in Maryland. It's got the best eye surgery unit in the country, or so they tell me.'

'And?'

'And they fixed his eyes. Don't ask me how, 'cause I don't know how. Apparently, the razor blade cuts were fairly shallow, so there was no damage to his retinas. The real damage, they said, was to the outer extremities of his eyes – the irises and the pupils. Purely physical defects, they said. Defects which could be fixed.' Riley shook his head. 'I don't know what they did – some fancy new laser-fusing procedure, someone told me – but they did it, they fixed his eyes. Hell, all I know is that if you can afford it – and in Scarecrow's case, the Corps could – you don't need glasses these days.

'Of course, there *was* still the scarring on his skin, but otherwise, they did it. Schofield could see again. Twenty-twenty.' Riley paused. 'There was only one hitch.'

'What was that?'

'The Corps wouldn't let him fly again,' Riley said. 'It's standard procedure across all the armed forces: once you've had eye trauma of *any* kind, you can't fly a military airplane. Hell, if you wear reading glasses, you're not allowed to fly a military kite.'

'So what did Scarecrow do?'

Riley smiled. 'He decided to become a line animal, a ground Marine. He was already an officer from his flying days, so he kept his commission. But that was all he kept. He had to start all over again. He went from flight status, lieutenant-commander, to ground force, lieutenant second class in an instant.

'And he went back to school. Back to the Basic School at Quantico. And he did every course they had. He did tactical weapons training. He did strategic planning. Small arms, Scout/Sniper. You name it, he did it. He did it *all*. Apparently, he said he wanted to be like those men who'd come in and got him out of Bosnia. What they'd done for him, he wanted to be able to do.'

Riley shrugged. 'As you can probably imagine, it didn't take long for him to get noticed. He was too clever to stay a second lieutenant for long. After a few months, they upped him to full lieutenant, and before long, they offered him a Recon unit. He took it. That was almost two years ago, now.'

Gant had never known. She had been selected for Schofield's Recon unit only a year ago and it had never occurred to her to wonder how Schofield himself had become the team's commander. That sort of thing was officer stuff, and Gant wasn't an officer. She was enlisted, and enlisted troops know only what they are told to know. Things like the choice of team commander are left to the higher-ups.

'I've been in his team ever since,' Riley said proudly.

Gant knew what he meant. Riley respected Schofield, trusted his judgement, trusted his appraisal of any given situation. Schofield was Riley's commander and Riley would follow him into hell.

Gant would, too. Ever since she had been in Schofield's Recon team, she had liked him. She respected him as a leader. He was firm but fair, and he didn't mince words. And he had never treated her any differently from any of the men in the unit.

'You like him, don't you?' Riley said softly.

'I trust him,' Gant said.

There was a short silence.

Gant sighed. 'I'm twenty-six years old, Book. Did you know that?'

'No.'

'Twenty-six years old. God,' Gant said, lost in thought. She turned to Book. 'Did you know I was married once?'

'No, I didn't.'

'Got married at the ripe old age of nineteen, I did. Married the sweetest man you'd ever meet, the catch of the town. He was a new teacher at the local high school, just arrived from New York, taught English. Gentle guy, quiet. I was pregnant by the time I was twenty.'

Book just watched Gant silently as she spoke.

'And then one day,' Gant said, 'when I was two-and-a-half months pregnant I arrived home early to find him doing it doggy-style on the living room floor with a seventeen-year-old cheerleader who'd come round for tutoring.'

Book winced inwardly.

'I miscarried three weeks later,' Gant said. 'I don't know what caused it. Stress, anxiety, who knows. I hated men after my husband did that to me. *Hated* them. That was when I enlisted in the Corps. Hate makes you a good soldier, you know. Makes you plant every single shot right in the middle of the other guy's head. I couldn't bring myself to trust a man after what my husband did. And then I met *him*.'

Gant was staring off into space. Her eyes were beginning to fill with water.

'You know, when I was accepted into this unit, the selection committee put on this big celebration lunch at Pearl. It was beautiful, one of those great Hawaiian BBQ lunches – out on the beach, in the sun. He was there. He was wearing this horrible, blue Hawaiian shirt and, of course, those silver sunglasses.

'I remember that at one point during the lunch, everybody else was talking, but he wasn't. I watched him. He just seemed to bow his head and go into this inner world. He seemed so lonely, so *alone*. He caught me looking and we talked about something inane, something about what a great place Pearl Harbor was and what our favourite holiday spots were.

'But my heart had already gone out to him. I don't know what he was thinking about that day, but whatever it was, he was thinking *hard* about it. My guess is it was a woman, a woman he couldn't have.

'Book, if a man *ever* thought about me the way he was thinking about her . . .' Gant shook her head. 'I would just . . . Oh, I don't know. It was just so *intense*. It was like . . . like nothing I have ever seen.'

Book didn't say anything. He just stared at Gant.

Gant seemed to sense his eyes on her and she blinked twice and the water in her eyes disappeared.

'Sorry,' she said. 'Can't go showing my emotions now, can I? If I start doing that, people'll start calling me "Dorothy" again.'

'You should tell him how you feel about him,' Book said gently.

'Yeah, *right*,' Gant said. 'Like I'd do that. They'd kick me out of the unit before I could say "That's why you can't have women in front-line units." Book, I'd rather be close to him and *not* be able to touch him, than be far away and *still* not be able to touch him.'

Book looked hard at Gant for a moment, as if he were appraising her. Then he smiled warmly. 'You're all right . . . Dorothy, you know that. You're all right.'

Gant snuffed a laugh. 'Thanks.'

She bowed her head, and shook it sadly. Then suddenly she looked up at Book.

'I have one more question,' she said.

'What?'

Gant cocked her head. 'How is it that *you* know all that stuff about him? All the stuff about Bosnia and the farmhouse and his eyes and all that?'

Riley smiled sadly.

Then he said, 'I was on the team that got him out.'

'Any sort of palaeontology is a waiting game,' Sarah Hensleigh said as she trudged through the snow next to Schofield toward the outer perimeter of the station. 'But now with the new technology, you just set the computer, walk away and do something else. Then you come back later and see if the computer has found anything.'

The new technology, Sarah had been saying, was a long-wave sonic pulse that the palaeontologists at Wilkes shot down into the ice to detect fossilized bones. Unlike digging, it located fossils without damaging them.

Schofield said, 'So what do you do while you wait for the sonic pulse to find your next fossil?'

'I'm not just a palaeontologist, you know,' Sarah said, smiling, feigning offence. 'I was a marine biologist before I took up palaeontology. And before all *this* happened, I was working with Ben Austin in the Bio Lab on B-deck. He was doing work on a new antivenom for *Enhydrina schistosa*.'

Schofield nodded. 'Sea snake.'

Sarah looked at Schofield, surprised, 'Very good, Lieutenant.'

'Yeah, well, *I'm* not just a grunt with a gun, you know,' Schofield said, smiling.

The two of them came to the outer perimeter of the station where they found Montana standing on the skirt of one of the Marine hovercrafts. The hovercraft was facing out from the station complex.

It was dark – that eerie eternal twilight of winter at the poles – and through the driving snow, Schofield could just make out the vast, flat expanse of land stretching out in front of the stationary hovercraft. The horizon glowed dark orange.

Behind Montana, on the roof of the hovercraft, Schofield saw the hovercraft's rangefinder. It looked like a long-barrelled gun mounted on a revolving turret, and it swept from side to side in a slow one-hundred-and-eighty-degree arc. It moved slowly, taking about thirty seconds to make a complete sweep from left to right before beginning the return journey.

'I set them just like you said,' Montana said, stepping down from the skirt so that he stood in front of Schofield. 'The other LCAC is at the south-east corner.' LCAC was the official name for a Marine hovercraft. It stood for 'Landing Craft – Air Cushioned'. Montana was a stickler for formalities.

Schofield nodded. 'Good.'

Positioned as they were, the rangefinders on the hovercrafts now covered the entire landward approach to Wilkes Ice Station. With a range of over fifty miles, Schofield and his team would know well in advance if anybody was heading toward the station.

'Have you got a portable screen?' Schofield asked Montana.

'Right here,' Montana offered Schofield a portable viewscreen that displayed the results of the rangefinders' sweeps.

It looked like a miniature TV with a handle on the left-hand side. On the screen, two thin green lines clocked slowly back and forth like a pair of windscreen wipers. As soon as an object crossed the rangefinders' beams, a blinking red dot would appear on the screen and the object's vital statistics would appear in a small box at the bottom of the screen.

'All right,' Schofield said. 'I think we're all set. I think it's time we found out what's down in that cave.'

The trudge back to the main building took about five minutes. Schofield, Sarah and Montana walked quickly through the falling snow. As they walked, Schofield told Sarah and Montana about his plans for the cave.

First of all, he wanted to verify the existence of the spacecraft itself. At this stage, there was no proof that anything was down there at all. All they had was the report of a single scientist from Wilkes who was himself now probably dead. Who knew what he had seen? That he had also been *attacked* soon after his sighting of the spacecraft – by enemies unknown – was another question that Schofield wanted answered.

There was a third reason, however, for sending a

small team down to the cave. A reason that Schofield didn't mention to Sarah or Montana.

If anyone else *did* happen to make a play for the station – especially in the next few hours when the Marines were at their most vulnerable – and if they also managed to overcome what was left of Schofield's unit up in the station proper, then a second team stationed down in the cave might be able to provide an effective last line of defence.

For if the only entrance to the cave was by way of an underwater ice tunnel, then anybody wanting to penetrate it would have to get there by an underwater approach. Covert incursionary forces hate underwater approaches and for good reason: *you never know what's waiting for you above the surface*. The way Schofield saw it, a small team already stationed inside the cave would be able to pick off an enemy force, one by one, as they broke the surface.

Schofield, Sarah and Montana came to the main entrance of the station. They trudged down the rampway and headed inside.

Schofield stepped onto the A-deck catwalk and immediately headed for the dining room. Rebound should have been back there by now – with Champion – and Schofield wanted to see if the French doctor had anything to say about Samurai's condition.

Schofield came to the dining room door and stepped inside.

He immediately saw Rebound and Champion standing at the table on which Samurai lay.

Both men looked up quickly as Schofield entered, their eyes wide as saucers. They looked like thieves caught with their hands in the till, caught in the middle of some illegal act.

There was a short silence.

And then Rebound said, 'Sir. Samurai's dead.'

Schofield frowned. He knew Samurai's condition was critical and that death was a possibility, but the way Rebound said it was –

Rebound stepped forward and spoke seriously. 'Sir, he was dead when we got here. And the doc here says he didn't die from his injuries. He says . . . he says it looks like Samurai was suffocated.'

Pete Cameron was sitting in his car in the middle of the SETI parking lot. The searing desert sun beat down on him. Cameron pulled out his cellular and called Alison in D.C.

'How was it?' she asked.

'Riveting,' Cameron said, flicking through his notes of the SETI recording.

'Anything to go on?'

'Not really. Looks like they got a few words off a spy satellite, but it's all Greek to me.'

'Did you write any of it down this time?'

Cameron looked at his notes.

'Yes, dear,' Cameron said. 'But I'm not so sure it's worth anything.'

'Tell me anyway,' Alison said.

'All right.' Cameron said, looking down at his notes.

COPY 134625
CONTACT LOST –> IONOSPHERIC DISTURB.
FORWARD TEAM
SCARECROW
– 66.5

SOLAR FLARE DISRUPT. RADIO
115, 20 MINS, 12 SECS EAST
HOW GET THERE SO – SECONDARY TEAM EN
ROUTE

Cameron read his notes aloud for her, word for word, substituting English for his own shorthand symbols.

'That's it?' Alison said when he was finished. 'That's all?'

'That's it.'

'Not much to go on.'

'That's what I thought,' Cameron said.

'Leave it with me,' Alison said. 'Where are you off to now?'

Cameron plucked a small, white card off his dashboard. It was almost covered over by Post-Its. It was a business card.

ANDREW WILCOX
Gunsmith
14 Newhury, Lake Arthur, NM.

Cameron said, 'I thought that since I was down here in the Tumbleweed State, I'd check out the mysterious Mr Wilcox.'

'The mail box guy?'

'Yeah, the mail box guy.'

Two weeks ago, someone had left this business card in Cameron's mail box. Just the card. Nothing else. No

251

message came with it and nothing was written on it. At first, Cameron almost threw it in the trash as errant junk mail – *really* errant junk mail since it had come from New Mexico.

But then Cameron had received a phone call.

It was a male voice. Husky. He asked if Cameron had got the card.

Cameron said he had.

Then the man said that he had something that Cameron might like to look into. Sure, Cameron had said, would the man like to come to Washington to talk about it?

No. That was out of the question. Cameron would have to come to him. The guy was a real cloak and dagger type, super-paranoid. He said he was ex-Navy, or something like that.

'You sure he's not just another of your fans?' Alison said.

Pete Cameron's reputation from his investigative days at *Mother Jones* still haunted him. Conspiracy theorists liked to ring him up and say that they had the next Watergate on their hands, or that they had the juice on some corrupt politician. Usually they asked for money in return for their stories.

But this Wilcox character had not asked for money. Hadn't even mentioned it. And since Cameron *was* in the neighbourhood . . .

'He may well be,' Cameron said. 'But since I'm down here anyway, I might as well check him out.'

'All right,' Alison said. 'But don't say I didn't warn you.'

Cameron hung up and slammed the door of his car.

In the *Post*'s offices in D.C., Alison Cameron hung up her phone and stared into space for a few seconds.

It was mid-morning and the office was a buzz of activity. The wide, low-ceilinged room was divided by hundreds of chest-high partitions, and in every one, people were busily working away. Phones rang, keyboards clattered, people scurried back and forth.

Alison was dressed in a pair of cream pants, a white shirt and a loosely tied black tie. Her shoulder-length, auburn hair was pulled back in a neat ponytail.

After a few moments, she looked down at the slip of paper on which she'd jotted down everything her husband had told her over the phone.

She read over each line carefully. Most of it was indecipherable jargon. Talk about Scarecrows, ionospheric disturbances, forward teams and secondary teams.

Three lines, however, struck her.

– 66.5
SOLAR FLARE DISRUPTING RADIO
115, 20 MINS, 12 SECS EAST

Alison frowned as she read the three lines again. Then she got an idea.

She quickly reached over to a nearby desk and grabbed a brown, folio-sized book from the shelf above it. She looked at the cover: *Bartholemew's Advanced Atlas of World Geography*. She flipped some pages and quickly found the one she was looking for.

She ran her finger across a line on the page.

'Huh?' she said aloud. Another reporter at a desk nearby looked up from his work.

Alison didn't notice him. She just continued to look at the page in front of her.

Her finger marked the point on the map designated latitude 66.5 degrees south, and longitude 115 degrees, 20 minutes and 12 seconds east.

Alison frowned.

Her finger was pointing at the coastline of Antarctica.

The Marines gathered around the pool on E-deck in silence.

Montana, Gant and Santa Cruz wordlessly shouldered into scuba tanks. All three wore black, thermal-electric wetsuits.

Schofield and Snake watched them as they suited up. Rebound stood behind them. Book Riley walked off in silence toward the E-deck storeroom, to check on Mother.

A large, black backpack – the French team's VLF transmitter that Santa Cruz had found during his search of the station – sat on the deck next to Schofield's feet.

The news of Samurai's death had rocked the whole team.

Luc Champion, the French doctor, had told Schofield that he had found traces of lactic acid in Samurai's trachea, or windpipe. That, Champion had said, was almost certain proof that Samurai had not died of his wounds.

Lactic acid in the trachea, Champion explained, evidenced a sudden lack of oxygen to the lungs, which the lungs then tried to compensate for by burning sugar, a process known as lactic acidosis. In other words, lactic acid in the trachea pointed to death due to a sudden lack of oxygen to the lungs, otherwise known as asphyxiation, or suffocation.

Samurai had not died from his wounds. He had died because his lungs had been deprived of oxygen. He had died because someone had cut off his air.

Someone had murdered Samurai.

In the time it had taken Schofield and Sarah to go out and meet with Montana at the perimeter of the station – the same time it took for Rebound to climb down to E-deck and collect Luc Champion – someone had gone into the dining room on A-deck and strangled Samurai.

The implications of Samurai's death hit Schofield hardest of all.

Someone among them was a killer.

But it was a fact that Schofield had *not* told the rest of the unit. He had only told them that Samurai had died. He hadn't told them how. He figured that if someone among them was a killer, it was better that that person not be aware that Schofield knew about him. Rebound and Champion had been sworn to silence.

As he watched the others suit up, Schofield thought about what had happened.

Whoever the killer was, he had expected that Samurai's death would probably be attributed to his wounds. It was a good assumption. Schofield figured that had he been told that Samurai hadn't made it, he would have immediately assumed that Samurai's body had simply given up the fight for life and died from its wounds.

That was why the killer had *suffocated* Samurai. Suffocation left no blood, no tell-tale marks or wounds. If there were no other wounds on the body, the story that Samurai had simply lost the battle with his bullet wounds gained credence.

What the killer had not known, however, was that asphyxiation did, in fact, leave a telltale sign – lactic acid in the trachea.

Schofield had no doubt that had he not had a doctor present at the station, the lactic acid would have gone unnoticed and Samurai's death *would* have been attributed to his bullet wounds. But there *had* been a doctor at the station. Luc Champion. And he had spotted the acid.

The implications were as chilling as they were endless.

Were there French soldiers still at large somewhere inside the station? Someone the Marines had missed. A lone soldier, maybe, who had decided to pick off the Marines one by one, starting with the weakest of their number, Samurai.

Schofield quickly dismissed the thought. The station, its surrounds, and even the remaining French hovercraft outside had been swept thoroughly. There were no more enemy soldiers either inside or outside Wilkes Ice Station.

That created a problem.

Because it meant that whoever had killed Samurai was someone Schofield thought he could trust.

It couldn't have been the French scientists, Champion and Rae. Since the end of the battle with the

French, they had been handcuffed to the pole on E-deck.

It could have been one of the scientists from Wilkes – while Schofield was outside with Montana and Hensleigh, they were all in their common room on B-deck, unguarded by any of the Marines. *But why?* Why on earth would one of the scientists want to kill a wounded Marine? They had nothing to gain from killing Samurai. The Marines were here to help them.

There still remained one other alternative.

One of the Marines had killed Samurai.

The mere possibility that that might have happened sent a chill down Schofield's spine. The fact that he had even *considered* it chilled him even more. But he considered it nonetheless, because aside from the residents of Wilkes, a Marine was the only other person in the station who'd had the opportunity to kill Samurai.

Schofield, Sarah and Montana had been outside when it had happened, so Schofield was at least sure about them.

As for the other Marines, however, there were difficulties.

They had all been, more or less, working alone at different places in the station when the murder had occurred. Any one of them could have done it without being detected.

Schofield checked them off one by one.

Snake. He had been on C-deck, in the alcove, working on the destroyed winch controls that raised and lowered the station's diving bell. He had been alone.

Santa Cruz. He had been searching the station for French erasing devices. That search had turned up nothing but the VLF transmitter that now sat silently at Schofield's feet. He had also been alone.

Rebound. Schofield thought about the young private. Rebound was the prime suspect. Schofield knew it, Rebound himself knew it. He was the one who had said to Schofield that Samurai was stable enough for him to go down to E-deck and fetch Champion. He was also the only one who had been with Samurai since the battle had ended. For all Schofield knew Samurai had been dead for over an hour, killed by Rebound long ago.

But *why?* It was this question that Schofield just couldn't figure out. Rebound was young, twenty-one. He was fresh and green and eager. He followed orders immediately, and he wasn't old enough to be jaded or cynical. The kid loved being a Marine, and he was as genuine a kid as Schofield had ever met. Schofield had thought that he had a good measure of Rebound's character. Maybe he hadn't.

The thought of Rebound as the killer did, however, trigger one *other* unusual thought in Schofield's mind. It was a memory, a painful memory that Schofield had tried to bury.

Andrew Trent.

Lieutenant First Class Andrew X. Trent, USMC.

Peru. March, 1997.

Schofield had gone through Officer Candidate School with Andy Trent. They were good friends and after OCS they had risen to the rank of first lieutenant together. A brilliant strategic thinker, Trent was given command of a prized Atlantic-based Marine Reconnaissance unit. Schofield – not quite the tactical genius that Trent was – was awarded a Pacific-based one.

In March of 1997, barely a month after he had taken command of his Recon unit, Schofield and his team were ordered to attend a battle scene in the mountains of Peru. Apparently, something of tremendous importance had been discovered in an ancient Incan temple high in the Andes mountains and the Peruvian President had called upon the United States for aid. Bands of murderous treasure hunters are rife in the mountains of Peru; they have been known to kill whole teams of university researchers in order to steal the priceless artefacts that the researchers find.

When Schofield's unit arrived at the mountain-top site, they were met by a squad of American troops, a single platoon of US Army Rangers. The Rangers had formed a two-mile perimeter around a particular, rain-forest-covered mountain. On top of the mountain stood the crumbling ruins of a pyramid-shaped Incan temple, half-buried in the mountainside.

A Marine Recon unit was already inside the temple, the captain of the Rangers informed Schofield.

Andy Trent's unit.

Apparently, it had been the first unit to arrive on the scene. Trent and his team had been doing some exercises in the jungles of Brazil when the alarm had been raised, so they had been the first to arrive.

The Army Ranger captain didn't know anything else

about what was going on inside the ruined temple. All he knew was that all *other* units arriving at the scene had been ordered to secure a two-mile perimeter around the temple and *not* to enter it for any reason.

Schofield's unit went about doing what they had been ordered to do and before long they had reinforced the two-mile perimeter around the temple.

It was then that a new unit arrived on the scene.

This unit, however, was allowed to pass through the perimeter. It was a SEAL team, someone said, a bomb squad of some kind that was going in to defuse some mines that had been laid by whoever was in there with Trent's Marines. Apparently, there had been heavy fighting in there. Trent and his team had prevailed, Schofield was pleased to hear.

The SEAL team went inside. Time passed slowly.

And then suddenly, Schofield's earpiece had exploded to life. A garbled voice cut through waves of static.

It said, 'This is Lieutenant Andrew Trent, Commander of United States Marine Force Reconnaissance Unit Four. I repeat, this is Andrew Trent of US Marine Force Reconnaissance Unit Four. If there are any Marines out there, please respond.'

Schofield responded.

Trent didn't seem to hear him. He could transmit, but he obviously couldn't receive.

Trent said, 'If there are any Marines outside this temple, *raid it now*! I repeat, raid it now! They planted men in my unit! They planted men inside my God damn unit! Marines, those SEALs who came in here before,

261

they said that they were here to help me. They said they were a special unit, sent by Washington to assist me in securing this site. Then they pulled their guns and shot one of my Corporals right in the fucking head! And now they're trying to kill me! Fuck! Some of my own men are helping them, for God's sake! *They planted fucking men in my unit*! They planted men in my own God damned unit! I'm being attacked by my own – '

The signal cut off abruptly.

Schofield had quickly looked about himself. No one else, it seemed, had heard the short, sharp message. Trent must have transmitted it over the 'Officer-Only' frequency, which meant that only Schofield had heard it.

Schofield didn't care. He immediately ordered his unit to mobilize, but as soon as they were ready and starting to head for the temple, they were cut off by the Army Rangers. The Rangers were a force of fifty men. Schofield's was only twelve.

The Ranger captain spoke firmly. 'Lieutenant Schofield, my orders are clear. No one goes in there. *No one*. If anyone tries to enter that building, my orders are to shoot them on sight. If you try to enter that building, Lieutenant, I will be forced to open fire on you.' His voice went cold. 'Have no doubt that I will, Lieutenant. I won't think twice about offing a dozen, faggot Marines.'

Schofield had glared at the Ranger captain.

He was a tall man, about forty, a career front-line soldier, fit but barrel-chested, with a full head of crew-cut, grey hair. He had cold, lifeless eyes and a weathered, sneering face. Schofield remembered his name – would always remember it – remembered the bastard stating it in a robotic, staccato manner after Schofield had demanded it from him: Captain Arlin F. Brookes, United States Army.

And so Schofield and his team were held back at the perimeter, while Andrew Trent's voice continued to shout desperately over Schofield's helmet intercom.

The more Trent shouted, the more furious and frustrated Schofield became.

The SEAL team that had gone inside had killed more of his men, Trent said. *Some of his own men* had then joined them and turned on him and killed others in his unit from point-blank range. Trent didn't know what was going on.

The last thing Schofield heard over his helmet intercom that day was Trent saying that he was the last one left.

Andrew Trent never came out of the temple.

About a year later, after making some enquiries, Schofield was told that Trent's unit had arrived at that temple only to find no one there. There was no battle, Schofield was told, no fighting with *anyone*. No 'mysterious discovery' in the first place. Upon arriving at the temple and finding it empty, Trent and his team had investigated the dark, dank ruins. It was during that search that a few men – Trent included – fell down a concealed plug hole. It was estimated that the plug hole was at least a hundred feet deep, with sheer rock walls.

No one had survived the fall. A search had apparently been made and all the bodies had been recovered.

Except Trent's, Schofield had been told. Andrew Trent's body was never found.

It made Schofield furious. Officially, nothing had ever happened at that temple. Nothing but a tragic accident that had claimed the lives of twelve United States Marines.

Schofield knew he was the only one who had heard Trent's voice over the radio system; knew no one would believe him if he ever questioned what had happened. If he said anything, it would probably only win him a quiet court martial and an even quieter dishonourable discharge.

And so Schofield had never mentioned the incident to anyone.

But now, in the cold confines of an underground ice station in the Antarctic, it was coming back to haunt him.

They planted men in my unit! They planted fucking men in my unit!

Trent's words echoed inside Schofield's head as he thought about whether Rebound had killed Samurai.

Had they also planted men inside *his* unit?

And who were 'they' anyway? The US Government? The US military?

It sounded like something that might have happened in the old Soviet Union. A government planting 'special' men inside elite units. But then, as Schofield knew, the United States and the USSR had not really been all that different. The US had always accused the Soviets of indoctrination, while at the same time they played 'Star Spangled Banner' every single morning in schools across America.

The thought of disloyal men inside his unit made Schofield's skin crawl.

He continued with his mental checklist.

Hell, even Riley and Gant – engaged in the preparation of the scuba gear down on E-deck – had occasionally separated. Every so often, Riley would go and check on Mother.

Schofield couldn't believe that Book Riley was a traitor. He had known him for too long.

But Gant? Schofield thought he knew Libby Gant, thought he had her measure, too. He had chosen Gant himself for the unit. Could that have been anticipated by someone else? By someone who had *wanted* her in Schofield's unit. No . . .

The only other Marine alive at the station was Mother. And the mere prospect that she could have killed Samurai was absurd.

Schofield's head was spinning. All he knew for sure was that Samurai Lau was dead and that someone among them had killed him. The problem was, they *all* could have done it.

Montana, Gant and Santa Cruz were ready to dive.

Strapped to their backs were Navy-made, low-audibility air tanks, or as they are more colloquially known in the Marine Corps, 'stealth tanks'.

Water is a great conductor of sound, and regular scuba tanks make a lot of noise as they pump compressed air through their hoses to a diver's mouthpiece. Any commecial underwater microphone will detect a diver by the loud *hisssssing* noise that his breathing gear makes.

With this in mind, the US Navy has spent millions of dollars developing a *silent* self-contained underwater breathing apparatus. The result is a scuba system known as LABA – low-audibility breathing apparatus. Scuba tanks that are all but noiseless underwater. LABA tanks are undetectable to conventional audio detection systems, hence the comparison with stealth aircraft.

Schofield watched the three Marines as they reached for their face masks and prepared to jump into the murky pool. Then he turned and scanned the pool, empty save for the diving bell that hovered out in the centre. The pod of killer whales had left the area about forty minutes ago and hadn't been seen since. As he gazed at the pool, however, he felt someone tap him on the shoulder. Schofield turned.

And saw Sarah Hensleigh standing in front of him. Dressed in a figure-hugging, blue and black thermal-electric wetsuit. Schofield was momentarily taken aback. For the first time that day, he noticed just how shapely Sarah Hensleigh was – the woman had a *great* body.

Schofield raised his eyebrows.

'This is what I wanted to ask you about before,' Sarah said. 'When we were outside. But I never got a chance. I want to go down with them.'

'I can see that,' Schofield said.

'This station lost nine people down in that cave. I'd like to know why.'

Schofield looked from Hensleigh to the three Marine divers on his left. He frowned, doubtful.

'I can help,' Sarah said quickly. 'With the cave, for example.'

'How?'

'Ben Austin – one of the divers who went down there at the very start – said it was an underground cavern of some sort, right,' Sarah said. 'He said it had sheer ice walls and that it stretched off for several hundred feet.' Sarah stared at Schofield. 'My guess is that if the walls in that cave are sheer, then it's a good bet that the cave was formed by some kind of seismic event in the past, some kind of earthquake or undersea volcanic eruption. Sheer walls are created by sudden upthrusts of rock, not slow, gradual movement.'

'I'm sure my men will be safe from sudden upthrusts of rock, Dr Hensleigh.'

'All right then. I can tell you what's down there,' Sarah said.

That got Schofield's attention. He turned to the three divers standing by the edge of the pool. 'Montana, Gant, Cruz. Just hold on a minute will you.' Schofield turned back to face Sarah Hensleigh, his eyes serious. 'All right, Dr Hensleigh, tell me what's down there.'

'All right,' Sarah said, as she collected her thoughts. She'd obviously thought about this a lot, but now Schofield had put her on the spot.

'Theory One,' she said. 'It's alien. It's a spacecraft from another planet, from another civilization. Now, that's not really my field – it's not really anyone's field. But if that thing is alien then I'd give my right arm to see it.'

'Mother already gave her left leg. What else?'

'Theory Two,' Sarah said, 'it's not alien.'

'It's *not* alien?' Schofield raised an eyebrow.

'That's right,' Sarah said. 'It's not alien. Now this theory, this theory really *is* my field. This is pure palaeontology. It's not a new theory by any means, but until now, no one's been able to find any evidence to prove it.'

'Prove what?'

Sarah took a deep breath. 'The theory goes that once, a long time ago, there was civilized life on earth.'

She paused, not for effect, but rather to wait for Schofield's reaction.

At first, Schofield didn't say anything, he just thought about it for a moment. Then he looked at Sarah. 'Go on.'

'I'm talking about a *long* time ago,' Sarah said, gaining momentum. 'I'm talking *before* the dinosaurs. I'm talking *four hundred million* years ago. Now, when you think about it . . . when you think about it in terms of human evolution, it's really very possible.

'Human life as we know it has been on earth for less than a million years, right. Historically speaking, that's not a long time. If the history of the earth were the twenty-four hours in a day, then the period of modern human presence would amount to about three seconds. What we would call *civilized* human life – human life in its *homo sapien* form – has been here for an even shorter period of time, not even twenty thousand years. That's less than a second on the world's time clock.'

Schofield watched Sarah Hensleigh closely as she spoke. She was excited, speaking quickly. She was in her element.

'What palaeontologists usually say,' she said, 'is that a whole matrix of factors contributed to the rise of the mammals, and hence the rise of human life on earth. The right distance from the sun, the right temperature, the right atmosphere, the right oxygen levels *in* the atmosphere, and, of course, the extinction of the dinosaurs. We all know about the Alvarez theory, how an asteroid slammed into the earth and killed all the dinosaurs and how the mammals rose out of the darkness and took their place as the rulers of the world. What if I was to tell you that there is evidence that there were at least *four* other such asteroid impacts on this planet in the last 700 million years.'

'Asteroid impacts,' Schofield said.

'Yes. Sir Edmund Halley once suggested that the entire Caspian Sea was created by an asteroid collision hundreds of millions of years ago. Alexander Bickerton, the famous New Zealand physicist who taught Rutherford, hypothesised that the sea bed of the entire south Atlantic Ocean – between South Africa and South America – was one great big bowl-shaped crater, caused by a *massive* asteroid impact over three hundred million years ago.

'Now, if we assume – as we so readily do in the case of the dinosaurs – that every time one of these cataclysmic asteroids hit the earth, a civilization died, we can only ask, what *other* kinds of civilizations, like that of the dinosaurs, have also been destroyed? What several academics have suggested in recent years – Joseph Sorenson from Stanford is the most well-known – is that one of these civilizations may have been human.'

Schofield looked at the other Marines on the deck around him. They were all listening to Sarah intensely, rapt in her story.

Sarah went on. 'You see, on average, the earth tilts on its vertical axis half a degree every 22,000 years. What Sorenson postulated was that about four hundred million years ago, the earth was tilted at an angle not unlike the angle it's tilted on today. It was also no further from the sun than it is now, so it had similar mean temperatures. Ice core samples, like the ones we get from this station, have shown that the air was a mix of oxygen, nitrogen and hydrogen, in quantities very similar to that of our own atmosphere today. Don't you see it? The matrix was the *same* then as it is now.'

Schofield was slowly beginning to believe what Sarah was saying.

Sarah said, 'That cavern down there is *fifteen hundred feet* below sea level, that's two and a half *thousand* feet below the average land level of Antarctica. The ice down there is easily four hundred million years old. If it's *upthrusted* ice from deeper down – ice that was raised by an earthquake or something – then it could be a lot, *lot* older.

'I think that whatever is down there is something that was frozen a long time ago. A *long* time ago. It could be alien, it could be human, from human life that existed on this planet millions of years ago. Either way, Lieutenant, it'll be the greatest palaeontological discovery this world has ever known and I want to see it.'

Sarah stopped, took a deep breath.

Schofield just stood there, silent.

Sarah spoke softly. 'Lieutenant, this is my life. This is my *whole* life. Whatever's down there is perhaps the greatest discovery in the history of mankind. I've been studying my whole life for this – '

Schofield looked curiously at her and she cut herself off, sensing that he was about to speak.

'What about your daughter?' he said.

Sarah cocked her head. She hadn't expected him to ask that.

Schofield said, 'You're willing to leave her up here alone?'

'She'll be safe,' Sarah said evenly. Then she smiled. 'She'll be up here with you.'

Schofield hadn't seen Sarah Hensleigh smile before. It illuminated her face, lit up the whole room.

Sarah said, 'I'll also be able to identify our divers who went down to that cave before, which might be – '

Schofield held up his hand. 'It's all right, you convinced me. You can go. But you use *our* scuba gear. I don't know what happened to your people down there before, but I have a sneaking suspicion that whatever's down there heard the noise of their breathing gear and I don't want the same thing to happen to us.'

'Thank you, Lieutenant,' Sarah said seriously. 'Thank you.' Then she took off the glistening silver locket that she wore around her neck and offered it to Schofield. 'I'd better not dive with this on. Can you keep it for me until I get back?'

Schofield took the locket, put it in his pocket. 'Sure.'

Just then, there came a sudden groaning sound from the pool to Schofield's left.

Schofield spun, just in time to see an enormous, black shadow rise to the surface of the pool amid a cloud of frothing, white bubbles.

At first Schofield thought the black shadow was one of the killer whales, returning to the pool in search of more food. But whatever it was, it wasn't swimming. It was just floating, rising up and up toward the surface.

And then the enormous black object breached the surface with a loud *shooshing* sound. Waves and bubbles shot out from every side of it. White froth expanded all around it. Narrow rivulets of blood snaked their way through the froth. The massive, black object bobbed on the surface. Everyone on the deck took a step forward.

Schofield stared at the black object in awe.

It *was* a killer whale.

But it was dead. Well and truly dead. The huge black and white carcass just floated limply in the water, alongside the deck. It was one of the larger ones, too, possibly even the male of the pack. It must have been at least thirty feet long. Seven tons in weight.

At first Schofield thought it must have been the killer whale that Mother had shot in the head during the battle – since that was the only whale that he knew for sure was dead. He quickly changed his mind.

This dead whale had no visible wound in its head. The one Mother had shot would have had a hole the size of a basketball in its skull. This one's forehead was unmarked.

And there was another thing.

This one had floated to the surface.

An animal killed in water will initially float, until its body fills with water. Only then will it sink. The killer whale that Mother had killed would have long since sunk to the bottom. This whale, on the other hand, had been killed recently.

The dead carcass rolled slowly in the water. Schofield and the other Marines on the deck just stared at it, entranced.

And then, slowly, it rolled belly-up and Schofield saw the great whale's white underbelly and his jaw dropped.

Two long, bloody gashes ran down the length of the big whale's underbelly.

They ran in parallel. Two jagged, uneven slashes that ran all the way up the centre of the whale's body, from its midsection right up to its throat. Sections of the big whale's intestines had fallen out through the gashes – long, ugly, cream-coloured coils that were as thick as a man's arm.

They weren't clean cuts either, Schofield saw. Each gash was a tear, a rip. Something had punctured the whale's belly and then ripped up the entire length of its body, tearing the skin apart.

Everyone on the deck stared at the bloody carcass, the understanding visible on their faces.

There was something down in that water.

Something that had killed a killer whale.

Schofield took a deep breath and turned to face Sarah. 'Want to reconsider?' he said.

Sarah stared at the dead killer whale for a few seconds. Then she looked back at Schofield.

'No,' she said. 'No way.'

Schofield paced nervously around the pool deck, alone.

He watched as in the middle of the pool the winch's cable plunged into the water. At the end of that cable was the diving bell, and inside the diving bell were three of his Marines plus Sarah Hensleigh. The cable entered the water at a steady speed, as fast as it could go.

The winch had been lowering the diving bell into the water for almost an hour now. Three thousand feet was a long way, almost a kilometre and Schofield knew it would take some time before it reached that depth.

Schofield stood on the deserted deck. Twenty minutes earlier, he had sent Book, Snake and Rebound topside to try to raise McMurdo Station on the portable radio again – he *had* to know when a full-strength American force was going to arrive at Wilkes.

Now he stood alone on E-deck, the station around him silent save for the rhythmic mechanical thumping of the winch mechanism up on C-deck. The repetitive *thump-thump-thump* of the winch had an almost soothing effect on him.

Schofield pulled Sarah Hensleigh's silver locket out of his pocket. It glistened in the white fluorescent light of the station. He turned it over in his hand. There was some writing engraved on the back of it –

And then suddenly there came a noise and Schofield's head snapped round. It had only lasted for an instant, but Schofield had definitely heard it.

It had been a voice. A male voice. But a voice that had been speaking in . . .

. . . *French.*

Schofield's eyes fell instantly upon the VLF transmitter that sat on the deck a few feet away from him.

Suddenly, the transmitter emitted a shrill whistling sound. And then the voice came again.

'*La hyène, c'est moi, le requin,*' the voice said. '*La hyène, c'est moi, le requin. Présentez votre rapport. Je renouvele. Présentez votre rapport.*'

Rebound, Schofield thought. *Shit. I need Rebound.* But he was outside with the others and Schofield needed a French speaker now.

'Rebound,' Schofield said into his helmet mike.

The reply came back immediately. '*Yes, sir?*' Schofield could hear the swirling wind in the background.

'Don't say a word, Rebound. Just listen, okay,' Schofield said, pressing a button on his belt that kept his helmet microphone switched on. He leaned in close to the VLF transmitter so that his helmet mike was near the transmitter's speaker.

The French voice came again.

'*La hyène. Vous avez trois heures pour présenter votre rapport. Je renouvele. Vous avez trois heures pour présenter votre rapport. Si vous ne le présentez pas lorsque l'heure*

nous serons contraint de lancer l'engine d'efface. Je ren-
ouvele. Si vous ne le présentez pas lorsque l'heure nous
serons contraint de lancer l'engine d'efface. C'est moi, le
requin. Finis.'

The signal cut off and there was silence. When he was
sure that it was finished, Schofield said, 'Did you get all
that, Rebound?'

'*Most of it, sir.*'

'What did they say?'

'*They said: Hyena. You have three hours to report. If*
you do not report by that time we will be compelled to
launch the "*l'engine d'efface*", *the erasing device.*'

'The erasing device,' Schofield said flatly. 'Three
hours. You sure about that, Rebound?'

Schofield grabbed his wristwatch as he spoke. It was
an old Casio digital. He started the stopwatch on it. The
seconds began to tick upward.

'*Very sure, sir. They said it all twice,*' Rebound said.

Schofield said, 'Good work, Private. All right. Now
all we have to do is figure out where these guys are – '

'*Uh, excuse me, sir?*' It was Rebound again.

'What is it?'

'*Sir, I think I have an idea where they might be.*'

'Where?'

'*Sir, at the end of that transmission we just heard, they*
said "C'est moi le requin." *Now, I missed the start of the*
transmission. Did they say that at the very beginning?
"*C'est moi le requin?*"'

Schofield didn't know, he didn't speak French. It had
all sounded the same to him. He tried to replay the

radio message in his head. 'They may have,' he said. 'No, wait, yes. Yes, I think they did say that. Why?'

Rebound said, '*Sir*, "le requin" *is French for "shark".* "C'est moi le requin" *means "This is Shark." You know, like a military codename. The French unit here at the station was called "Hyena" and that one we just heard was called "Shark". You know what I'm thinking, sir –* '

'Oh, damn,' Schofield said.

'*That's right. I'm thinking they're out on the water somewhere. Somewhere off the coast. I'll bet you a million bucks that "Shark" is a warship or something sailing off the coast of Antarctica.*'

'Oh, *damn*,' Schofield said again, this time with feeling.

It made sense that whoever sent that message was a ship of some kind. And not just because of its codename. As Schofield knew, because of their extraordinarily long wavelengths, VLF transmissions were commonly used by surface vessels or submarines out in the middle of the ocean. That was why the French commandos had brought the VLF transmitter with them. To keep in contact with their warship off the coast.

Schofield started to feel ill.

The prospect of a frigate or a destroyer patrolling the ocean a hundred miles off the coast was bad. *Very* bad. Especially if it was aiming some kind of weapon – in all likelihood, a battery of nuclear-tipped cruise missiles – at Wilkes Ice Station.

It had never occurred to Schofield that the French might not bring an erasing device *with* them, but would rather leave it with an outside agent – like a destroyer off the coast – with instructions to fire upon the station if that destroyer did not receive a report by a given time.

Shit, Schofield thought. *Shit. Shit. Shit.*

There were only two things in the world that could stop the launch of that erasing device. One, a report coming in from twelve dead Frenchmen sometime within the next three hours. *That* wasn't going to happen.

Which meant the second option was the *only* option.

Schofield *had* to get in contact with the US forces at McMurdo Station. And not just to find out when American reinforcements would be arriving at Wilkes. No, now he had to tell the Marines at McMurdo about a French warship sailing somewhere off the coast with a battery of cruise missiles trained on Wilkes Ice Station. It would then be up to the people at McMurdo to take out that warship – *within* three hours.

Schofield keyed his mike again. 'Book, you hear all that?'

'*Yeah,*' Book Riley's voice said.

'Any luck with McMurdo?'

'*Not yet.*'

'Keep trying,' Schofield said. 'Over and over. Until you get them on the line. Gentlemen, the stakes in this game have just been raised. If we don't get through to McMurdo in less than three hours, we're all gonna be vaporized.'

'*Scarecrow, this is Fox,*' Gant's voice said. '*I repeat. Scarecrow, this is Fox. Hey, Scarecrow? Are you out there?*'

Schofield was out on the pool deck on E-deck, watching the cable descend into the pool, thinking about cruise missiles. It had been about ten minutes since he had heard the transmission from the French vessel, 'Shark'. Book, Rebound and Snake were all still outside trying to raise McMurdo.

Schofield keyed his mike. 'I hear you, Fox. How are you doing down there?'

'*We are coming to three thousand feet. Preparing to stop the cable.*'

There was a short pause.

'*Okay. We are stopping the cable . . . now.*'

As Gant said the word 'now', the cable plunging into the water suddenly jolted to a stop. Gant had stopped its descent from inside the diving bell.

'*Scarecrow, I have the time as 1410 hours,*' Gant said. '*Please confirm.*'

'I confirm the time as 1410 hours, Fox,' Schofield said. It was standard deep-diving practice to confirm the time at which a dive was to start. Schofield didn't know that he was following exactly the same procedure that the scientists from Wilkes had followed only two and a half days earlier.

'*Copy time at 1410 hours. Turning over to self-contained air. Preparing to leave the diving bell.*'

Gant kept Schofield updated on the dive.

The four divers – Gant, Montana, Santa Cruz and Sarah Hensleigh – turned over to self-contained air without incident and left the diving bell. A few minutes later, Gant reported that they had found the entrance to the underwater ice tunnel, and that they were beginning their ascent.

Schofield continued to pace around the deck, deep in thought.

He thought about the divers from Wilkes who had disappeared down in the cavern, about the cavern itself and what was in it, about the French and their snatch-and-grab effort to seize whatever was down there, about erasing devices being fired from warships off the coast, about the possibility that one of his own men had killed Samurai, and about Sarah Hensleigh's smile. It was all too much.

His helmet intercom crackled to life. '*Sir, Book here.*'

'Any luck?'

'*Not a goddamn thing, sir.*'

For the last quarter of an hour, Book, Snake and Rebound had been trying to raise McMurdo Station on the unit's portable radio. They were doing it from just outside the main entrance to the station, as if being outside the structure might somehow help the signal get through.

'Interference?' Schofield asked.

'*Mountains of it*,' Book said sadly.

Schofield thought for a moment. Then he said, 'Book. Cancel that option and come back inside. I want you to go and find the scientists who are still here. I think they're in that common room on B-deck. See if you can find out if any of them are familiar with the radio system here.'

'*I copy that, sir.*'

Book's voice switched off and Schofield's intercom was silent again. Schofield stared at the pool of water at the base of the station and resumed his thoughts.

He thought about Samurai's death and who could have done it. At the moment, he trusted only two people: Montana and Sarah Hensleigh, since they had been with him when Samurai had been murdered. They were the only two people whom Schofield knew for certain were not involved in Samurai's murder. As far as everybody else was concerned, they were all under suspicion.

Which was why Schofield had decided to keep Book, Snake and Rebound all together. If one of them was the killer, he wouldn't be able to kill again with the other two around . . .

Suddenly, a new thought hit Schofield and he keyed his mike again. 'Book, you still out there?'

'*Yes, sir.*'

'Book, while you're down on B-deck, I want you to ask those scientists something else,' Schofield said. 'I want you to ask if any of them knows anything about weather.'

The radio room at Wilkes Ice Station is situated in the south-east corner of A-deck, directly across the shaft from the dining room. It houses the station's satellite telecommunications gear and short-range radio transmitters. Four radio consoles – each consisting of a microphone, a computer screen and keyboard, and some frequency dials – were in the room, two to each side.

Abby Sinclair was sitting at one of the radio consoles when Schofield entered the radio room.

The first thing Schofield noticed was that Abby Sinclair had not borne the recent events at Wilkes Ice Station at all well. Abby was a pretty woman in her late thirties, with long, frizzy brown hair, and large, brown eyes. Long, vertical streaks of black mascara ran down from beneath both of her eyes. They reminded Schofield of the two scars that cut down across his own eyes – now hidden once again behind his opaque, silver glasses.

Next to Abby stood the three other Marines – Riley, Rebound and Snake. Abby Sinclair was the only scientist in the room.

Schofield turned to Book. 'Nobody knows anything about weather?'

'On the contrary,' Book said. 'You're in luck. Lieutenant Shane Schofield, I'd like you to meet Miss Abby

Sinclair. Miss Sinclair is both the radio expert at this station *and* its resident meteorologist.'

Abby Sinclair said, 'Actually, I'm not the real radio expert. Carl Price was, but he . . . *disappeared* down in the cave before. I just help him out with the radio gear, so I guess I'm it now.'

Schofield smiled reassuringly at her. 'That's good enough for me, Miss Sinclair. Is it okay if I call you Abby?'

She nodded.

Schofield said, 'All right. Abby, I have two problems, and I'm hoping that you can help me with both of them. I need to get in contact with my superiors at McMurdo as soon as possible. I need to tell them what's happened here so that they can send in the cavalry, if they haven't done so already. Now, we've been trying to raise McMurdo on our portable radio, but we can't get through. Question One: does the radio system here work?'

Abby smiled weakly. 'It *was* working. I mean, before all this started. But then the solar flare kicked in and disrupted all our transmissions. In the end, though, that didn't matter because our antenna went down in the storm and we never got a chance to fix it.'

'That's okay,' Schofield said. 'We can fix that.'

Something else that she had said, however, troubled him. Schofield had been told about the 'solar flare' phenomenon on his way to Wilkes, but he didn't know exactly what it was. All he knew was that it disrupted

284

the electromagnetic spectrum, and in doing so, prevented any sort of radio communication.

'Tell me about solar flares,' he said to Abby.

'There isn't really much to tell,' Abby replied. 'We don't really know that much about them. "Solar flare" is actually the term used to describe a brief, high temperature explosion on the surface of the sun, what most people would call a sunspot. When a sunspot occurs, it emits a huge amount of ultraviolet radiation. A *huge* amount. Like ordinary heat from the sun, this radiation travels through space towards the earth. When it gets here, it contaminates our ionosphere, turning it into a thick blanket of electromagnetic mayhem. Satellites become useless because radio signals from the earth can't penetrate the contaminated ionosphere. Similarly, signals coming *from* satellites down to the earth can't get through the ionosphere either. Radio communication becomes impossible.'

Abby suddenly looked about herself. Her eyes fell on one of the computer screens next to her. 'Actually. We have some weather-monitoring gear in here. If you'll just give me a minute, I might be able to show you what I mean.'

'Sure,' Schofield said as Abby switched on the computer next to her.

The computer hummed to life. Once it was up and running, Abby clicked through various screens until she came to the one she wanted. It was a satellite map of southeastern Antarctica, overlaid with multicoloured

285

patches. A barometric weather map. Like the ones on the evening news.

'This is a snapshot of the eastern Antarctic weather system for – ' Abby looked at the date in the corner of the screen, ' – two days ago.' She looked around at Schofield. 'It was probably one of the last ones we got before the solar flare moved in and cut us off from the weather satellite.'

She clicked her mouse. Another screen came up. 'Oh, wait, here's another one. There it is,' Abby said.

It filled half the screen.

An enormous yellow-white blob of atmospheric disturbance. It filled the entire left-hand side of the map, smothering nearly half of the pictured Antarctic coastline. In real terms, Schofield thought, the solar flare must have been absolutely enormous.

'And *that* is your solar flare, Lieutenant,' Abby said. She turned to look at Schofield. 'It must have moved eastward after this shot was taken and covered us, too.'

Schofield stared at the yellow-white blob superimposed on the Antarctic coastline. There were slight discolourations in it, red and orange patches, even some black ones.

Abby said, 'Since they usually explode in one section of the sun's surface, solar flares usually only affect defined areas. One station might have a total radio blackout while another, two hundred miles away, will have all of its systems working just fine.'

Schofield stared at the screen. 'How long do they last?'

Abby shrugged. 'A day. Sometimes two. However long it takes for all the radiation to make the trip from the sun to the earth. Depends on how large the original sunspot was.'

'How long will *this* one last?'

Abby turned back to face her computer. She looked at the depiction of the solar flare on the screen, pursed her lips in thought.

'I don't know. It's a big one. I'd say about five days,' she said.

A short silence followed as what she said sank in to everyone in the room.

'Five days,' Rebound breathed from behind Schofield.

Schofield was frowning in thought. He turned to Abby. 'You say it disrupts the ionosphere, right?'

'Right.'

'And the ionosphere is . . .'

'The layer of the earth's atmosphere about 50 to 250 miles up,' Abby said. 'It's called the ionosphere because the air in it is filled with ionized molecules.'

Schofield said, 'Okay. So, a solar flare explodes on the surface of the sun and the energy it emits travels down to earth where it disrupts the ionosphere, which turns into a shield through which radio signals can't pass, right?'

'Right.'

Schofield looked at the screen again, and stared at the black splotches on the yellow-white graphic representation of the solar flare. There was one, larger, black hole in the middle of the yellow-white blob that held his attention.

'Is it uniform?' Schofield asked.

'Uniform?' Abby blinked, not comprehending.

'Is the shield uniform in its strength? Or does it have weak points, inconsistencies, *breaks* in the shield that could be penetrated by radio signals? Like these black spots here.'

Abby said, 'It would be *possible* to penetrate them, but it would be difficult. The break in the flare would have to be directly over this station.'

'Uh-huh,' Schofield said. 'Is there any way that you could figure out when or if one of those breaks would be directly over us? Like, maybe, this one here.'

Schofield pointed at the large black hole in the centre of the yellow-white blob.

Abby studied the screen, evaluated the possibilities.

Finally, she said, 'There *might* be a way. If I can bring up some previous images of the flare, I should be able to plot how fast it's travelling across the continent and in what direction. If I can do that, then I should be able to make a rough plot of its course.'

'Just do what you can,' Schofield said, 'and call me if you find anything. I want to know when one of those breaks is going to pass over this station, so we can be ready to send a radio signal to McMurdo when it does.'

'You'll have to fix the antenna outside – '

'I'm already on it,' Schofield said. 'You just find me a break in that flare. We'll get your antenna up again.'

In Washington, Alison Cameron was also sitting in front of a computer.

She was in a small computer lab in the *Post*'s offices. A microfilm viewing machine sat in the corner. Filing cabinets lined two of the four walls. Half a dozen computers filled the rest of the space in the small lab.

Alison found the screen she was looking for. The All-States Library Database.

There is a popular urban myth that the FBI has a tap on every library borrowing computer in the country, and that they use this facility to track down serial killers. The killer quotes Lowell at a homicide scene, so the FBI check up on every library in the country to see who's been borrowing Lowell. Like all good urban myths, this is only a half-truth. There *is* a system (it is an updatable CD-Rom service) which crosslinks every library computer in the country, telling the user where a certain book can be found. It doesn't list the names of every person who has borrowed that book. It just tells you where a particular book is located. You can search for a book in several ways: by the author, by the book's title, or even by any unusual keywords that appear in the text of a book. The All-States Library Database was one such service.

Alison stared at the screen in front of her. She tabbed down to the 'SEARCH BY KEYWORD' button. She typed:
ANTARCTICA.

The computer whirred for about ten seconds, and the results of the search came up on the screen:
1,856,157 ENTRIES FOUND. WOULD YOU LIKE TO SEE A LIST?

Great. One million, eight hundred and fifty thousand books contained the word 'Antarctica' in some way or another. That was no help.

Alison thought for a second. She'd need a narrower keyword, something a lot more specific. She got an idea. It was a long shot, perhaps a little too specific. But Alison thought it was worth a try anyway. She typed:
LATITUDE − 66.5° LONGITUDE 115° 20′ 12″

The computer whirred as it searched. This time the search didn't take long at all. The results came up on the screen:
6 ENTRIES FOUND. WOULD YOU LIKE TO SEE A LIST?

'You bet your ass I'd like to see a list,' Alison said. She hit the 'Y' key for 'Yes' and a new screen appeared. On it was a list of book titles and their locations.

ALL-STATES LIBRARY DATABASE
SEARCH BY KEYWORD
SEARCH STRING USED: LATITUDE − 66.5°
                                    LONGITUDE 115° 20′ 12″

NO. OF ENTRIES FOUND: 6

TITLE	AUTHOR	LOCATION	YEAR
DOCTORAL THESIS	LLEWELLYN, D.K.	STANFORD, CT	1998
DOCTORAL THESIS	AUSTIN, B.E.	STANFORD, CT	1997
POST-DOCTORAL THESIS	HENSLEIGH, S.T.	USC, CA	1997
FELLOWSHIP GRANT RESEARCH PAPER	HENSLEIGH, B.M.	HARVARD, MA	1996
'THE ICE CRUSADE – REFLECTIONS ON A YEAR SPENT IN ANTARCTICA'	HENSLEIGH, B.M.	HARVARD, MA AVAIL: AML	1995
PRELIMINARY SURVEY	WAITZKIN, C.M.	LIBCONG	1978

Alison stared at the list.

Every one of these entries, in some way or another, mentioned Latitude −66.5 degrees and Longitude 115 degrees, 20 minutes and 12 seconds.

They were mainly university papers. None of the names meant anything to Alison: Llewellyn, Austin, and the two Hensleighs, S and B.

It looked like the latter Hensleigh – B.M. Hensleigh – had written a book on Antarctica. Alison looked at its location reference. It had been printed at Harvard University, but it was available at 'AM' – all major libraries.

Unlike all of the other entries – a collection of single issue, privately published theses – this Hensleigh guy's book was widely available. Alison decided she'd check it out.

There was, however, one other entry that caught her attention.

The last one.

PRELIMINARY
SURVEY   WAITZKIN, C.M.   LIBCONG   1978

Alison frowned at the final entry. She checked a quick reference list that was affixed to the side of the computer monitor. It was a list of all of the abbreviations used in the database. Alison found 'LibCong.'

'Ah-*ha*,' she said aloud.

'LibCong' stood for the Library of Congress. The Library of Congress was situated across the road from the Capitol Building, not far from Alison's office.

Alison looked at the final entry again. She wondered what a preliminary survey was. She looked at the date of the entry.

1978.

Well, whatever it was, it was over twenty years old, so it was worth checking out.

Alison smiled as she hit the button marked 'PRINT SCREEN'.

'All right! Hoist her up!' Book called.

Rebound and Snake pulled on the stabilizing cables and Wilkes Ice Station's battered radio antenna – a long, black pole thirty feet high, with a blinking, green beacon light at its tip – rose slowly into the air. The intermittent flash-flash of the green beacon light illuminated all of their faces.

'How long do you think it will take?' Schofield asked Book, yelling above the wind.

'It won't take us long to hoist it up, that's the easy part,' Book replied. 'The hard part will be reconnecting all the radio wiring. We've got the power going again, but there's still another fifteen or so radio wires to solder back together.'

'Ballpark?'

'Thirty minutes.'

'Get to it.'

Shane Schofield trudged back down the entrance ramp of the station and headed inside. He had come back inside to check on two things: Abby Sinclair and Mother.

Abby met him on the A-deck catwalk. While Schofield

and the others had been outside, she had been in the radio room looking at weather maps on the computer, trying to find a break in the solar flare.

'Any luck?' Schofield asked.

'Depends on what you mean by luck,' Abby said. 'How soon did you want it?'

'*Soon.*'

'Then I'm afraid it's not that good,' Abby said. 'By my calculations, a break in the solar flare will pass over this station in about sixty-five minutes.'

'*Sixty-five* minutes,' Schofield said. 'How long will it last?'

Abby shrugged. 'Ten minutes. Maybe fifteen. Long enough to get a signal through.'

Schofield bit his lip as he took all of this in. He had been hoping to get a window in the solar flare a lot sooner than that. He desperately needed to get in contact with McMurdo Station to tell them about the French warship that was sailing off the coast of Antarctica aiming a battery of missiles at Wilkes Ice Station.

Schofield asked, 'Will there be any more breaks coming over the station?'

Abby smiled. 'I thought you'd ask that, so I checked it out. There will be two more breaks in the flare after the first one, but there's a long wait for them. Okay. The time is now 2:46 p.m. so the first window period won't be until 3:51 p.m., sixty-five minutes from now. The other two will be a lot later, at approximately 7:30 p.m. and 10:00 p.m. tonight.'

Schofield sighed. This wasn't good at all.

'Good work, Abby,' he said. 'Good work. Thank you. If you want something else to do, I was hoping you might like to man the radio room while my men fix your antenna outside. Just in case anything comes through.'

Abby nodded. 'I'd like that.'

'Good,' Schofield said. Abby wanted something to do, *needed* something to do. The events of the previous few hours had hit her hard, but once she had something to occupy her, she seemed to be okay.

Schofield smiled at her and headed for the rung-ladder.

Mother was sitting on the floor with her back up against the, cold, ice wall when Schofield entered the storeroom on E-deck. Her eyes were closed. She appeared to be sleeping.

'Hey there,' she said, without opening her eyes.

Schofield smiled as he came over and crouched beside her. 'How you feeling?' he asked.

Mother still didn't open her eyes. 'Methadone's good.'

Schofield looked down at what was left of Mother's left leg. Book had bandaged up the jagged protrusion at her knee quite well. The bandages, however, were soaked through with blood.

'Guess I won't be playing football anymore,' Mother said.

Schofield looked at her face and he saw her open her eyes.

'That fucking fish took my leg,' she said indignantly.

'I noticed. Could have been worse, though.'

'Don't I know it,' Mother snorted.

Schofield laughed.

Mother looked him over as he laughed. 'Scarecrow. Have I ever told you that you are one *damn* fine lookin' man?'

Schofield said, 'I think that's the methadone talking.'

'I know a good man when I see one,' Mother said as she leaned back against the wall and closed her eyes slowly.

Schofield spoke softly, 'I'm not certain of many things, Mother, but one thing I am certain of is that I am *not* much to look at.'

Schofield began to think about the two scars that cut down across his eyes and how hideous they were. People instinctively winced when they saw them. When he was back home, Schofield almost always wore sunglasses.

As he thought about his eyes, Schofield must have looked away from Mother for an instant, because when he looked back at her he found that she was staring at him. Her eyes were hard and sharp, not glazed or drugged out. They bored right through his reflective, silver glasses.

'Any woman who won't have you 'cause of your eyes doesn't deserve you, Scarecrow.'

Schofield said nothing. Mother let it go.

'All right, then,' she said. 'Now that we got all these pleasantries out of the way,' she raised her eyebrows suggestively, 'what brings you down to my neck of these woods? I'm hoping it wasn't just to check up on my health.'

'It wasn't.'

'Well . . .?'

'Samurai's dead.'

'What?' Mother said seriously. 'They told me he was stable.'

'He was murdered.'

'By the French?'

'No, later. Much later. The French were all dead when he was killed.'

'It wasn't one of their scientists?'

'Accounted for.'

Mother spoke evenly, 'One of *our* scientists?'

'If it was, I can't figure out why,' Schofield said.

There was a short silence.

Then Mother said, 'What about the one that was shut up in his room when we got here. You know, what's-his-name. Renshaw.'

Schofield's head snapped up.

He had completely forgotten about James Renshaw. Renshaw was the scientist Sarah Hensleigh had said had killed one of his fellow scientists only days before the Marines had arrived at Wilkes. He was the man the residents of Wilkes had locked inside his room on B-deck. After Samurai's death, Schofield hadn't even checked to see if Renshaw was still in his room. If Renshaw had escaped, then maybe *he* had . . .

'Shit, I forgot all about him,' Schofield said. He quickly keyed his helmet mike. 'Book, Rebound, Snake, you out there?'

'*Copy, Scarecrow*,' Snake's voice replied.

'Snake, I need someone up there to go down to B-deck right away and make sure that that guy who was shut up in his room is still there, okay.'

'*I'm on it*,' Snake said.

Schofield clicked off his intercom.

Mother smiled, spread her arms wide. 'Honestly, where would you be without your Mother, Scarecrow?'

'Lost,' Schofield said.

'Don't you know it,' Mother said. 'Don't you know it.' She eyed Schofield carefully; he was staring at the floor. 'What's wrong?' she said softly.

Schofield kept his head down. He shook his head slowly.

'I should have known they were soldiers, Mother. I should have *anticipated* it.'

'What are you talking about?'

'I should have locked them up as soon as I saw them – '

'You couldn't do that.'

'We lost *three men*.'

'Honey, we won.'

'We got lucky,' Schofield said seriously. 'We got very, very lucky. They'd flushed five of my men out onto that catwalk and were about to slaughter them when they dropped into that pool. Christ, look at what happened down in the drilling room. They had a plan *right up to the end*. If Rebound hadn't caught wind of it before-hand, they would have got us, Mother, even at the very end. We were on the back foot the whole damn time. *We didn't even have a plan at all.*'

'Scarecrow. Listen to me,' Mother said firmly. 'You wanna know something?'

'What?'

Mother said, 'Did you know that about six months ago, I was offered a place in an Atlantic Recon Unit?'

Schofield looked up at that. No. He hadn't known.

'I still have the letter back home if you want to see it,' Mother said. 'It's signed by the Commandant him-self. You know what I did after I got that letter, Scarecrow?'

'What?'

'I wrote back to the Commandant of the United States Marine Corps and said thank you very much but I would like to stay with my current unit, under my commanding officer, Lieutenant First Class Shane M. Schofield, USMC. I said that I could find no better unit, under no better commander, than the one I was cur-rently in.'

Schofield was momentarily stunned. That Mother would do such a thing was quite incredible. To reject an offer to join an Atlantic Recon unit was one thing, but to politely decline the personal invitation of the Com-mandant of the United States Marine Corps to join such a unit was something else.

Mother looked Schofield squarely in the eye. 'You are a great officer, Scarecrow, a *great* officer. You are smart and you are brave and you are something that is very, very rare in this world: you are a good man.

'That's why I stayed with you. You've got a heart, Scarecrow. You *care* about your men. And I'll tell you right now, that puts you above every other commander I have ever known. I am prepared to risk my life at your judgement because I know that whatever the plan is, you're still worried about me.

'A lot of commanders, they're just looking for glory, looking for a promotion. They ain't gonna care if that dumb ol' bitch Mother gets herself killed. But you *do* care and I like that. Shit, look at you now. You're beating up on yourself because we almost got our asses capped. You are *smart*, Scarecrow, and you are *good* and don't you ever doubt that. Ever. You just have to believe in yourself.'

Schofield was taken aback by the force of Mother's words. He nodded. 'I'll try.'

'Good,' Mother said, her tone now a little more upbeat. 'Now. Was there anything else you wanted to hear from "Dear Abby" while you were down here?'

Schofield snuffed a laugh. 'No. That's it. I better get going, check on this Renshaw guy.' He stood up and headed for the doorway. When he reached the doorway, however, he stopped suddenly and turned.

'Mother,' he said, 'do you know anything about men being planted in units?'

'What do you mean?'

Schofield hesitated. 'When I found out Samurai had been murdered, I remembered something that happened a couple of years ago to a friend of mine. At the time, this friend had said something about people planting men inside his unit.'

Mother looked hard at Schofield. She licked her lips, didn't speak for a very long time.

'It's not something I like to talk about,' she said quietly. 'But, yes, I have heard about it.'

'What have you heard?' Schofield stepped back into the storeroom.

'Only rumours. Rumours that get bigger and bigger each time you hear 'em. As an officer, you probably don't hear this shit, but I'll tell you, if there's one thing about enlisted men, it's that they gossip like a bunch of old women.'

'What do they say?'

'Enlisted grunts like to talk about infiltrators. It's their favourite myth. A campfire story designed by senior line animals to scare the booties off the junior troops and make them trust one another. You know, if we can't trust each other, who can we trust, or something like that.

'You hear all kinds of theories about where these infiltrators come from. Some folks reckon they're inserted by the CIA. Deep-cover agents enlist with the armed forces with the sole purpose of infiltrating elite units – so that they can keep tabs on us, make sure we're doin' what we're supposed to be doin'.

'Others say it's the Pentagon that does it. Others still say it's the CIA *and* the Pentagon. I heard one guy – a real fruitloop named Hugo Boddington – say once that he'd heard that the National Reconnaissance Office and the Joint Chiefs of Staff had a joint subcommittee that they called the Intelligence Convergence Group, and that *it* was the office that was in charge of infiltrating American military units.

'Boddington said the ICG was some kind of ultra-secret committee charged with hoarding intelligence. Charged with *ensuring* that only the right people in the right places knew about certain stuff. That's why they have to infiltrate units like ours. If we're on a mission and we find something we're not supposed to – I don't know, like an alien or something – those ICG guys are there to wipe us out and make sure that we don't tell anybody about what we saw.'

Schofield shook his head. It sounded like a ghost story. Double agents among the troops.

But in the back of his mind there was a single doubt. A doubt that took shape in the form of Andrew Trent's voice screaming over Schofield's helmet radio from inside that Incan temple in Peru: 'They planted men inside my unit! *They planted fucking men inside my unit!*' Andrew Trent was no ghost story.

'Thanks, Mother,' Schofield said as he headed back for the door. 'I better get going.'

'Ah, yes,' Mother said. 'A unit to run. People to organize. Responsibility to take. I wouldn't be an officer for all the money in the world.'

'I wish you'd told me that ten years ago.'

'Ah, yes, but then tonight wouldn't have been anywhere near as much fun. You take care, you hear me, Scarecrow. Oh, and hey,' she said. 'Nice glasses.'

Schofield paused for a moment in the doorway. He realized that he was wearing Mother's anti-flash glasses. He smiled. 'Thanks, Mother.'

'Hey, don't thank me,' she said. 'Hell, the Scarecrow without his silver glasses, it's like Zorro without his mask, Superman without his cape. It just ain't right.'

'Call me if you need anything,' Schofield said.

Mother gave him a wicked grin. 'Oh, I *know* what I need, *baby*,' she said.

Schofield shook his head. 'You never quit, do you?'

Mother smiled. 'You know what,' she said coyly. 'I don't think you realize it when someone has their eye on you, honey.'

Schofield raised an eyebrow. '*Does* someone have their eye on me?'

'Oh, yes, Scarecrow. Oh, yes.'

Schofield shook his head, smiled. 'Good*bye*, Mother.'

'Goodbye, Scarecrow.'

Schofield left the storeroom and Mother sank back against the wall.

When Schofield was gone, she closed her eyes and said softly to herself, 'Does someone have their eye on you? Oh, Scarecrow. Scarecrow. If only you could see the way she looks at you.'

Schofield stepped out onto the pool deck.

The whole station was deserted. The cavernous shaft was silent. Schofield stared at the pool, at the stationary cable that stretched down into it.

'*Scarecrow, this is Fox,*' Gant's voice said over his earpiece. '*Are you still up there?*'

'I'm still here, where are you?'

'*Dive time is fifty-five minutes. We are proceeding up the ice tunnel.*'

'Any sign of trouble?'

'*Nothing yet – whoa, wait a minute, who's this?*'

'What is it, Fox?' Schofield said, alarmed.

'*No. It's nothing,*' Gant's voice said. '*It's all right. Scarecrow, if that little girl's up there with you, you might want to tell her that her friend is down here.*'

'What do you mean?'

'*That fur seal, Wendy. She just joined us in the tunnel. Must have followed us down here.*'

Schofield pictured Gant and the others swimming up the underwater ice tunnel, covered in their mechanical breathing apparatus, while beside them Wendy swam happily, not needing any such equipment.

'How far have you got to go?' Schofield asked.

'*Hard to say. We've been going extra slow, just to be careful. I'd say it'll be another five minutes or so.*'

'Keep me posted,' Schofield said. 'Oh, and Fox. Use caution.'

'*You got it, Scarecrow. Fox, out.*'

The radio clicked off. Schofield stared at the water in the pool. It was still stained red. At the moment, it was calm, glassy. Schofield took a step forward, toward it.

Something crunched beneath his feet.

He froze, looked down at his boots, bent down.

On the metal deck beneath his feet lay some broken shards of glass. White, frosted glass.

Schofield frowned at the glass.

And then, with frightening suddenness, a voice cut across his helmet intercom: '*Scarecrow, this is Snake. I'm on B-deck. I just checked Renshaw's room. There was no answer when I banged on his door, so I busted it open. Sir, there was no one in there. Renshaw is gone. I repeat, Renshaw is gone.*'

Schofield felt a chill run down his spine.

Renshaw wasn't in his room.

He was somewhere inside the station.

Schofield was about to move, about to go and find the others when he heard a soft puncture-like sound, followed by a faint whistling through the air. There came a sudden thwacking noise and Schofield immediately felt a stinging, burning sensation on the back of his neck and then, to his horror, Schofield suddenly realized that the thwacking noise had been the sound of something impacting against his neck at extremely high speed.

Schofield's knees buckled. He suddenly felt very weak.

He immediately put his hand to his neck and then held it out in front of his face.

His hand was slicked with blood.

Blackness slowly overcame him and Schofield dropped to his knees. The world went black around him and as his cheek thudded down against the ice-cold steel of the deck, Shane Schofield had a single, terrifying thought.

He had just been shot in the throat.

And then suddenly the thought vanished and the world went completely and utterly black.

Shane Schofield's heart . . .

. . . had stopped.

FOURTH INCURSION

16 June 1510 hours

Libby Gant swam up the steep underwater ice tunnel.

It was quiet here, she thought, peaceful. The whole world was tinted pale blue.

As she swam, Gant could hear nothing but the soft, rhythmic hiss of her low-audibility breathing gear. There were no other sounds – no whistling noises, no whale song, no nothing.

Gant stared out through her full-face diving mask. The icy walls of the tunnel glowed white. The other divers – Montana, Santa Cruz and the scientist woman, Sarah Hensleigh – swam alongside her in silence.

All of a sudden the ice tunnel began to widen dramatically and Gant saw several large, round holes set into the walls on either side of her.

They were larger than Gant had expected them to be – easily ten feet in diameter. And they were round, perfectly round. Gant counted eight such holes and wondered what kind of animal could possibly have made them.

And then, abruptly, Gant forgot about the holes set

into the ice walls. Something else had seized her attention.

The surface.

Gant keyed her intercom. 'Scarecrow. This is Fox,' she said. 'Scarecrow. This is Fox. Scarecrow, are you out there?'

There was no reply.

'Scarecrow, I repeat, this is Fox. Come in.'

Still no reply.

That was strange, Gant thought. Why would Scarecrow not answer her? She had only spoken to him a few minutes ago.

Suddenly a voice crackled over Gant's earpiece.

It wasn't Schofield.

'*Fox, this is Rebound.*' He seemed to be shouting above some wind. He must have been outside the station. '*I read you. What's up?*'

'We're approaching the surface now,' Gant said. 'Where's Scarecrow?' she added a little too quickly.

'*He's inside the station somewhere. Down with Mother, I think. Must have taken his helmet off or something.*'

Gant said, 'Well, it might be a good idea to go find him and tell him what's going on down here. We're about to surface inside the cavern.'

'*Got it, Fox.*'

Gant clicked off her radio and resumed her swim upward.

The water's surface looked strange from below.

It was glassy. Still. It looked like a warped glass lens of some sort, completely distorting the image of whatever it was that lay beyond it.

Gant swam toward it. The others rose slowly in the water beside her.

They all broke the surface together.

In an instant, the world around Gant changed and she found herself treading water in the centre of an enormous pool situated at one end of a massive underground cavern. She saw Montana and Santa Cruz hovering in the water beside her, with Sarah Hensleigh behind them.

The cavern was absolutely huge. Its ceiling was easily a hundred feet high, its walls perfectly vertical.

And then Gant saw it.

'I'll be damned . . .' she heard Santa Cruz say.

For a full minute, Gant could do nothing but stare. Slowly, she began to make her way toward the edge of the pool. When she finally stepped up on to solid ground, she was totally entranced. She couldn't take her eyes off it.

It looked like nothing she had ever seen before. Like something out of a movie. The mere sight of it took her breath away.

It was a ship of some sort.

A black ship – completely black from nose to tail – about the same size as a fighter jet. Gant saw that its two enormous tail fins were embedded in the ice wall behind it. It looked as if they had been *consumed* by the ice as it had crept slowly forward through the ages.

The huge black spacecraft just stood there – in stark contrast to the cold, white cavern around it – standing high on three powerful-looking, hydraulic landing struts.

It looked fantastic, otherworldly.

And it looked *mean*.

Black and pointed, sleek and sharp, to Gant it looked like a huge preying mantis. Its two black wings swooped down on either side of its fuselage so that it looked like a bird in flight with its wings at the lowest extremity.

The most striking feature of all, however, was the nose.

The ship had a hooked nose, a nose that pointed sharply downward, like the nose on the Concorde. The cockpit – a rectangular, reinforced tinted-glass canopy – was situated right above the hooked nose.

A huge preying mantis, Gant thought. *The sleekest, fastest – biggest – preying mantis that anyone has ever seen.*

Gant realized that the others were also out of the water now, standing beside her on the frost-covered floor of the cavern, also staring up at the magnificent spacecraft.

Gant looked at her companions' faces.

Santa Cruz's mouth hung open.

Montana's eyes were wide.

Sarah Hensleigh's reaction, however, struck Gant as strange. Hensleigh's eyes had narrowed and she stared at the spacecraft in an unusual way. Despite herself, Gant felt a sudden chill. Sarah Hensleigh's eyes glowed with what looked dangerously like ambition.

Gant shook the thought off and, with the initial spell of the spacecraft broken, her eyes began to take in the rest of the gigantic cavern.

It took all of ten seconds for her to see them.

Gant froze instantly.

'Oh, God . . .' she said, her voice low. 'Oh, *God* . . .'

There were nine of them.

Bodies.

Human bodies, although at first, it was hard to tell.

They were laid out on the floor on the far side of the pool – some lay flat on their backs, other lay draped over large rocks by the edge of the pool. Blood was *everywhere*. Puddled on the floor, splashed against the walls, lathered all over the bodies themselves.

It was carnage.

Limbs had been torn from their sockets. Heads had been wrenched from shoulders. Circular chunks of flesh had been ripped from the chests of some of the bodies. Exposed bones lay all over the floor, some of them splintered, others with ragged pieces of flesh still clinging to them.

Gant swallowed hard, tried desperately to keep herself from throwing up.

The divers from the station, she thought.

Santa Cruz stepped up alongside Gant and stared at the mutilated bodies on the far side of the pool.

'What the hell happened down here?' he said.

Schofield dreamed.

At first there was nothing. Nothing but black. It was like floating in outer space.

And then all of a sudden – *whack* – a glaring white light shattered Schofield's very existence, jarred him like an electric shock, and Schofield felt searing pain like he had never felt before.

And then, just as suddenly as it had come, the shock vanished and Schofield found himself lying on a floor somewhere – cold and alone, asleep but awake.

It was dark. There were no walls.

Schofield felt a wetness against his cheek.

It was a dog. A large dog. Schofield couldn't tell what type. He could only tell that it was big. Very, *very* big.

The dog nuzzled against his cheek, sniffed inquisitively. Its cold, wet nose brushed against the side of his face. Its whiskers tickled his nose.

It seemed curious, not at all threatening –

And then suddenly, the dog barked. Loud as hell.

Schofield jumped. The dog was barking madly now at some unseen foe. It seemed impossibly angry – frenzied, furious – baring its teeth at this new enemy.

Schofield continued to lie on the cold floor of the wall-less room unable – or just unwilling – to move. And then, gradually, the walls around him began to take shape, and soon Schofield realized that he was lying on the metal decking of E-deck.

The big dog was still standing over him, barking ferociously, snarling. The dog, it seemed, was defending him.

But from what? What could it see that he could not?

And then suddenly the dog turned and ran away and Schofield lay alone on the cold steel deck.

Asleep but awake, unable to move, Schofield suddenly felt vulnerable. Exposed.

Something was approaching him.

It came from the direction of his feet. He couldn't see it, but he could hear its footsteps as they clanged – slowly, one after the other – on the cold steel deck.

And then suddenly it was over him and Schofield saw an evil, smiling face appear above his head.

It was Jacques Latissier.

His face was covered in blood, contorted in an obscene sneer. Ragged pieces of flesh hung loosely from an open wound in his forehead. His eyes were alive, burning with hate. The French commando raised his glistening knife so that it was right in front of Schofield's eyes.

And then he brought the knife down in a violent slashing –

'Hey,' someone said gently.

Schofield's eyes darted open and he awoke from his dream.

He was lying on his back. In a bed of some sort. In a room with dazzling white fluorescent lights. The walls were white, too, made of ice.

A man stood over him.

He was a small man, about five-foot-three. Schofield had never seen him before.

The man was short and wiry, and he had two enormous blue eyes that seemed way too big for his small head. Large, black bags hung beneath both of his eyes. He had messy brown hair that looked like it hadn't been brushed in months, and two, huge front teeth that were horribly askew. He wore a K-Mart wash-and-wear shirt and a pair of blue, polyester trousers; in fact, he looked decidedly underdressed for the near-freezing conditions inside Wilkes Ice Station.

And he was holding something.

A long-bladed scalpel.

Schofield stared at it.

The scalpel had blood on it.

The man spoke in a flat, nasal voice, 'Hey. You're awake.'

Schofield squinted in the light, tried to lift himself up off the bed. He couldn't do it. Something stopped him. He saw what it was.

Two leather straps bound his arms to the sides of the bed. Two more straps bound his legs. When Schofield tried to raise his head to further examine his situation, he found that he couldn't even do that. It, too, was strapped tightly down against the bed.

Schofield's blood went instantly cold.

He was completely tied down.

'Just hold on a minute,' the short man said in his irritating, nasal voice. 'This will only take one . . . more . . . second.'

He raised his bloody scalpel and ducked out of Schofield's field of vision.

'Wait!' Schofield said quickly.

The short man returned instantly to Schofield's field of vision. He raised his eyebrows questioningly. 'Yes?'

'Where – where am I?' Schofield said. It hurt to speak. His throat was parched, dry.

The man smiled, revealing his crooked front teeth. 'It's okay, Lieutenant,' he said. 'You're still at Wilkes Ice Station.'

Schofield swallowed. 'Who are you?'

'Why, Lieutenant Schofield,' the man said, 'I'm James Renshaw.'

'Welcome back from the grave, Lieutenant,' Renshaw said as he unbound the leather strap around Schofield's head. Renshaw had just finished removing the last three bullet fragments from Schofield's neck with his scalpel.

Renshaw said, 'You know, you were very lucky you were wearing this kevlar plate inside your collar. It didn't stop the bullet entirely, but it took most of the speed off it.'

Renshaw held up the circular kevlar insert that had previously been fitted inside Schofield's grey turtle-neck collar. Schofield had forgotten all about his neck protector. To him, it was just another part of his uniform. Kevlar neck protectors were issued exclusively to Marine officers, as an extra defence against snipers. Enlisted men received no such protection, since enemy snipers rarely cared for corporals and sergeants.

With the leather strap around his forehead now removed, Schofield raised his head and looked at the kevlar insert that Renshaw held in his hand.

It looked like a priest's white collar – curved and flat, designed to encircle its wearer's neck while remaining hidden inside his turtle-neck collar. On one side of the circular, kevlar insert, Schofield could see a jagged, gaping hole.

The bullet hole.

'That bullet would have killed you for sure if it weren't for your insert,' Renshaw said. 'Would've cut right through your carotid. After *that* there would have been nothing anyone could have done for you. As it happened, the bullet shattered as it passed through your kevlar insert, so only a few small fragments of it lodged in your neck. Still, that would have been enough to kill you, and as a matter of fact, I actually think it did, at least for a short time.'

Schofield had stopped listening. He was taking in the room around him. It looked like someone's living quarters. Schofield saw a bed, a desk, a computer, and, strangely, a pair of black and white TV monitors mounted on top of two video recorders.

He turned to face Renshaw. 'Huh?'

'Several fragments of the bullet lodged in your neck, Lieutenant. I'm pretty sure – in fact, I'm absolutely certain – that for at least thirty seconds, you lost your pulse. You were clinically dead.'

'What do you mean?' Schofield said. He instinctively tried to raise his hand to feel his neck. But he couldn't move his arm. His arms and legs were still firmly tied down to the bed.

'Oh, don't worry, I fixed it up,' Renshaw said. 'I took the bullet fragments out and I cleaned the wound. You actually got a couple of kevlar fragments in there, too, but they weren't a problem. In fact, I was just trying to get them out when you woke up.' Renshaw indicated the bloody scalpel on a silver tray next to Schofield's bed. Beside the scalpel lay seven tiny metal fragments, all of them covered in blood.

'Oh, and don't worry about my qualifications,' Renshaw said with a smile, 'I did two years of medicine before I dropped out and took up geophysics.'

'Are you going to untie me?' Schofield said evenly.

'Oh, yeah. Right. Listen. I'm terribly sorry about that,' Renshaw said. He seemed nervous now. 'At first I just had to keep your head still while I extracted the bullet fragments from your neck. Did you know that you move around a lot in your sleep? Probably not. Well, you do. But anyway, to cut to the chase, I figured, what with all I have to tell you and all, it would be better if you were, well, a *captive* audience. So to speak.' Renshaw smiled weakly at the pun he'd just made.

Schofield just stared at him, unsure of what to make of this man named James Renshaw. After all, this was the man who only a week before had killed one of his fellow scientists. If nothing else, Schofield was certain of one thing. He did *not* want to remain tied up at this man's mercy.

'What do you have to tell me?' Schofield said. His eyes swept the room as he spoke. The door on the far side of the room was firmly shut. All of the other walls in the room were ice.

'Lieutenant, what I have to tell you is this: I am not a murderer. I did not kill Bernie Olson.'

Schofield didn't say anything.

He tried to remember what Sarah Hensleigh had told him earlier – way back when he had arrived at Wilkes – about the death of the scientist, Bernard Olson.

Sarah had said that on the night Olson was killed, Renshaw had been heard arguing loudly with Olson. It was after that argument that Renshaw had stabbed Olson in the throat with a hypodermic syringe filled with liquid drain cleaner. Then he had injected the contents of the syringe into Olson's bloodstream. The other residents of Wilkes had found Olson dead soon after, with the syringe hanging loosely from his neck.

'Do you believe me?' Renshaw said in a low voice, eyeing Schofield suspiciously.

Schofield still said nothing.

'Lieutenant, *you have to believe me*. I can only imagine what you've been told, and I know it must look bad, but you have to listen to me. *I didn't do it*. I swear, I didn't do it. I could never do something like that.'

Renshaw took a deep breath, spoke slowly.

'Lieutenant, this station is not what it appears to be. Things have been happening here – *strange* things – long before you and your men got here. You can't trust anyone at this station, Lieutenant.'

'But you expect me to trust you?' Schofield said.

'Yes. Yes, I do,' Renshaw said pensively. 'And that obviously creates a problem, doesn't it? After all, as far as you're concerned, four days ago I killed a man with a hypodermic needle filled with industrial strength Draino. Right? Hmmm.' Renshaw took a step forward, toward Schofield. 'But I intend to rectify this situation,

Lieutenant Schofield. Conclusively. Which is why . . .
I'm going to do this.'

Renshaw stood right next to the bed, towering over
Schofield, his eyes hard.

Schofield tensed. He was totally defenceless. He had
no idea what Renshaw was about to –

Snap! The leather strap around Schofield's left arm
suddenly went limp and fell to the floor. A second later,
the strap around his right arm did the same.

Schofield's arms were free again. Renshaw had released
the leather straps that had bound them to the bed.

Schofield sat up as Renshaw moved further down the
bed and unclipped the clasps that fastened the straps
around his legs.

For a long moment, Schofield just looked at Renshaw. Finally, he said, 'Thank you.'

'Don't thank me, Lieutenant,' Renshaw said. 'Believe
me. And promise me this: promise me that when this is
all over, you'll check out Bernie Olson's body. Look at
his tongue and his eyes. They will explain everything.
You're my only hope, Lieutenant. You're the only person who can prove my innocence.'

Now that he was free to move again, Schofield sat up on
the bed. He touched his neck. It throbbed with pain.
He looked at his throat in a nearby mirror. Renshaw had
sutured the wound well. Nice, close stitches.

Renshaw offered Schofield a rectangular length of

adhesive gauze. 'Here. Put this on over the stitches. It'll act like a Band-Aid, keep the wound tightly closed.'

Schofield took the adhesive gauze and fastened it firmly over the wound on his neck. He looked down at the rest of his body. Renshaw had removed most of his body armour – he was dressed only in his full-body camouflage fatigues, with his grey turtle-neck shirt underneath. He was still wearing his boots and his battered ankle/knee guards. His weapons – his pistol, his knife, his MP-5 and his Maghook – and his silver anti-flash glasses all sat on a table on the far side of the room.

Schofield saw the room's closed door again and something twigged in his memory. He remembered being told that the door to Renshaw's room had been sealed shut, riveted to its frame by Renshaw's fellow scientists. But he also remembered something else, something that someone had said only moments before he had been shot. Something about Renshaw's door being *broken down* . . .

Suddenly Schofield asked, 'How did I get here?'

'Oh, easy. I just stuffed your body inside the dumb waiter and sent it up to this level,' Renshaw said.

'No, I mean, I thought you were locked in this room? How did you get out?'

Renshaw offered Schofield a sly smile. 'Just call me Harry Houdini.'

Renshaw crossed to the other side of the room, and stood in front of the two television monitors. 'Don't worry, Lieutenant. I'll show you how I got out of here in a minute. But first, I've got something here that I think you'll want to see.'

'What?'

Renshaw smiled again. The same sly smile as before.

'How would you like to see the man who shot you?' he said.

Schofield stared at Renshaw for a long moment.

Then, slowly, he swung his legs off the bed. His neck stung and he had a monster of a headache from the concussion. Schofield walked gingerly across the room and stood next to Renshaw in front of the two television monitors.

'Aren't you cold?' Schofield asked, looking at Renshaw's rather casual attire.

Renshaw pulled open his shirt, Superman-style, revealing a blue, wetsuit-like undergarment. 'Neoprene bodysuit,' he said proudly. 'They use 'em on the shuttle, for spacewalks and the like. It could be a hundred below in here and I wouldn't notice it.'

Renshaw flicked on one of the monitors and a black and white image appeared on the screen.

The image was grainy, but after a few seconds, Schofield realized what he was looking at.

It was a view of the pool at the base of the ice station.

It was a strange view, however – taken from an overhead camera somewhere – one that looked directly *down* on a section of the pool and its surrounding deck.

'This is a live feed,' Renshaw said. 'It comes from a

camera mounted on the underside of the bridge that spans C-deck. It looks straight down on the pool.'

Schofield squinted as he looked at the black and white image on the screen.

Renshaw said, 'The scientists who work at this station come down on six-monthly rotations, so we just inherit each other's rooms. The guy who had this room before me was a crazy old marine biologist from New Zealand. Strange guy. He just loved killer whales, couldn't get enough of them. God, he'd watch them for hours, liked to watch them when they came up for air inside the station. Gave them names and everything. God, what was his name . . . Carmine something.

'Well anyway, old Carmine attached a camera to the underside of the bridge – so he could keep an eye on the pool from his room. When he'd see them on his monitor, he'd hustle on down to E-deck and watch them up close. Hell, sometimes the old bastard would watch 'em from inside the diving bell, so he could get right up close.'

Renshaw looked at Schofield and laughed. 'I guess you're the last person in the world I should be talking to about having a *close* look at killer whales.'

Schofield turned, remembering the terrifying battle with the killer whales earlier. 'You saw all that?'

'Did I?' Renshaw asked. 'Are you kidding? You bet I saw it. Hell, I got it all on *tape*. I mean, *yikes*, did you *see* those big bastards? Did you see the way they hunted. Did you see the *complexity* of their hunting behaviour?

Like the way they would always make a pass by their intended victim *before* they came in for the kill?'

'I must have missed that,' Schofield said flatly.

'I tell you, they did it. Every time. Every single time. I've read about it before. You know what I think it is? It's the whale staking his claim. It's the whale telling all the other whales that this person is his kill. Hey, I could show it to you if you – '

'You said there was something else I should see,' Schofield said. 'Something about the man who shot me.'

'Oh, yeah, right. *Right*. Sorry.' Schofield just stared at Renshaw as the little man grabbed a video cassette and thrust it into the second video recorder. He was a strange man. Manic, nervous, and yet obviously very intelligent. And he talked a lot. It seemed that when he spoke, it all just came gushing out. Schofield found it difficult to determine exactly how old he was. He could have been anything from twenty-nine to forty.

'*That's* it!' Renshaw exclaimed suddenly.

'What? What's it?' Schofield said.

'Yaeger. Carmine Yaeger. That was his name.'

'Play the video, would you,' Schofield said, exasperated.

'Oh, yeah, right,' Renshaw hurriedly hit the 'PLAY' button on the VCR.

An image came up on the second monitor. It was almost identical to the one that was on the first monitor, from the same high-mounted camera looking down on the pool and its surrounding deck.

There was only one difference.

On the second monitor's screen, someone was standing on the deck.

Schofield stared at the screen intently.

The person on the screen was a man, one of the Marines. He was alone.

Schofield couldn't tell who it was because the camera was positioned directly above him. All he could see was the top of the man's helmet and his armoured shoulderplates.

And then suddenly the man looked up, slowly scanning the shaft of the station, and Schofield saw his face.

Schofield frowned.

He was looking at his own face.

Schofield turned immediately to Renshaw. 'When did you record this – '

'Just keep watching.'

Schofield turned back to the screen.

He saw himself stop next to the pool and speak into his helmet mike. There was no sound, he could just see his own mouth moving. He stopped talking, and took a step across the deck.

And then he stopped.

He had stepped on something.

Schofield saw himself bend down and examine some broken glass on the deck. He seemed to look about himself. And then suddenly, his head cocked to the side. He was listening to something. Listening to someone speaking over his helmet intercom.

The Shane Schofield on the screen then stood up and

was starting to turn when suddenly his whole body jolted violently and a small spray of blood exploded out from his neck. He stopped instantly, and swayed slightly, and then he raised his hand to his neck and held it out in front of his face. It had blood all over it.

And then his knees buckled and he fell in a heap to the deck. He just lay there on the deck, motionless.

Schofield stared at his own image on the screen.

He had just seen himself get shot . . .

Schofield turned to Renshaw.

Renshaw just nodded back at the screen. 'There's more,' he said quietly. 'A lot more.'

Schofield swung back to face the screen.

He saw his own body lying on the pool deck, unmoving. It lay there for a while.

Nothing happened.

And then suddenly someone stepped into the frame.

Schofield felt his adrenalin rush as he watched the screen. He was about to see the person who had shot him.

The first thing he saw was the helmet.

It was another Marine.

A man. Schofield could tell by the way he walked. But he couldn't see his face.

The Marine walked slowly over to Schofield's unmoving body. He was in no hurry. He pulled his automatic pistol from his holster as he approached Schofield's body, pulled back the slide, cocking the gun.

Schofield stared at the screen intently.

The Marine, his face still obscured by his helmet,

bent down over Schofield's body and placed two fingers on Schofield's blood-covered throat.

'He's checking your pulse,' Renshaw whispered.

That was exactly what he was doing, Schofield saw. The Marine on the screen waited several seconds with his finger on Schofield's neck.

Schofield didn't take his eyes off the screen.

The Marine on the screen stood up, satisfied that Schofield had no pulse. He uncocked his pistol, put it back in its holster.

'And ... look at that,' Renshaw said. 'There's nothing there.' Renshaw turned to face Schofield. 'Lieutenant, I do believe your heart just stopped beating.'

Schofield didn't even look at Renshaw as he spoke. His eyes were glued to the screen.

'Now look at what he does here,' Renshaw said. 'This is his fatal mistake ...'

Schofield watched as on the screen the Marine – his face still masked by his helmet – shoved Schofield's dead body across the deck with his foot.

He was shoving the body towards the pool.

After two strong kicks, Schofield's body was lying on the edge of the deck, right next to the water. The Marine then kicked Schofield's body one last time and the body fell limply into the water.

'He doesn't know it,' Renshaw said 'but that guy just kickstarted your heart.'

'How?'

'The way I figure it, that water's so cold, it acted like a defibrillator – you know, those electric-shock paddles they use on TV to restart peoples' hearts. The shock your body received when it hit that water – and let me tell you, that would have been one *hell* of a shock to a body that wasn't prepared for it – was enough to jolt your heart back into action.'

Schofield watched the screen.

The Marine stood at the edge of the deck for a while, watching the circle of ripples that indicated the spot where Schofield's body had entered the inky water. After about thirty seconds, the Marine turned and looked around himself.

And at that moment, as the Marine turned, Schofield saw something that made his blood run cold.

Oh, no . . . he thought.

The Marine then turned on his heel and quickly walked out of the frame.

Schofield turned to Renshaw, his mouth agape.

'It's not over yet,' Renshaw said, interrupting him before he spoke. 'Keep watching.'

Schofield turned back to face the screen.

He saw the image of the deck and the pool. Otherwise there was nothing.

Nothing was happening.

Nothing at all.

There was no one on the deck. No movement in the water.

A full minute passed.

And then Schofield saw it.

'*What the hell* . . .' he said.

At that moment, the water in the pool seemed to part

of its own accord and suddenly, in a wash of bubbles and froth, Schofield's body – limp and lifeless – emerged from the water.

Schofield watched, stunned.

But it was what came *after* his body that truly laid him cold.

Whatever it was, it was absolutely huge, at least as big as a killer whale.

But this was no killer whale.

It lifted Schofield's lifeless body out of the water and deposited it gently onto the deck. Water washed out onto the deck all around Schofield's limp body as the animal leapt up onto the deck after him. The whole deck shuddered under its immense weight.

It was *huge*. It dwarfed Schofield's body. Schofield watched it, entranced.

It was a seal of some sort.

An enormous, *gigantic* seal.

It had a huge blubbery body, layer upon layer of undulating fat, and it propped itself up on two massive fore-flippers. The impression that Schofield got of the animal's strength was overwhelming – to hold up that enormous body required phenomenal musculature. It must have weighed at least eight tons.

The strangest feature of all, however, was the animal's teeth. This enormous seal had two, long, inverted fangs – fangs that protruded from its lower jaw and rose up in front of its nose.

'What the hell is that?' Schofield said softly.

'I have no idea,' Renshaw said. 'The nose, the eyes,

the shape of the head. It *looks* like an elephant seal. But I've never seen one so big. Or with teeth like that. Elephant seals have large lower canines, but I've never seen one with lower canines *that* big before.'

The seal on the screen was on the deck now. It ducked its head over Schofield's body. It seemed to be sniffing him. It slowly made its way up his inanimate body, until finally its long whiskers brushed against his nose. Schofield didn't move at all.

And then, slowly, very slowly, the big seal began to open its mouth.

Right in front of Schofield's face!

Its jaws parted – a hideous, obscene yawn – revealing the animal's enormous lower fangs. The massive seal leaned forward, and lowered its head. Its mouth began to close *around* Schofield's head . . .

Schofield stared at the screen, his eyes went wide.

The seal was about to bite his head off.

It was going to *eat* him!

And then suddenly the giant seal spun. At first, Schofield was surprised at how quickly the big animal moved. The deck beneath it shook as it turned its hulking frame around.

It had seen something offscreen.

The seal began to bark.

There was no sound on the monitor, but Schofield could see it barking. It bared its teeth. Barked and barked. It shuffled around, agitated, adopted an aggressive stance. The muscles on its huge fore-flippers bulged as it moved.

And then suddenly, the big seal turned and dived back into the pool. The huge splash it created sent waves sloshing up over the deck, all over Schofield's unmoving body.

'Wait for it,' Renshaw said. 'Here's my big entrance.'

At that moment, Schofield saw another man step into the frame. This man was not wearing a Marine helmet and his face was clearly visible. It was Renshaw.

On the screen, Renshaw hurried forward and grabbed Schofield's body by the armpits and dragged him quickly out of the camera's field of vision –

Renshaw hit the stop button on the video recorder.

'And that's all there is,' he said.

At first, Schofield didn't say anything. It was all just too overwhelming.

First, the Marine shooting him and checking his pulse – *to make sure that he was dead* – and then kicking him into the pool so that there would be no trace.

And then the elephant seal.

The massive creature that had lifted Schofield's body out of the water and placed it gently on the poolside deck, and which had then disappeared back into the murky water.

Renshaw said, 'Now, do you understand what I was saying about you being clinically dead? That guy we just saw, I think he was pretty sure that you were dead.'

Schofield said, 'He was ready to put a bullet in my head if he wasn't sure.'

Schofield shook his head at the thought of what he

had just seen. Death, it seemed, had just saved him from death. 'Holy shit . . .' he breathed.

Schofield stared blankly into space for a few moments, taking it all in. Then he blinked quickly, returning to the present.

'Can you rewind that tape, please,' he said to Renshaw. He had just remembered something about the image of the Marine who had shot him, something that the sight of the elephant seal had temporarily pushed from his mind.

Renshaw rewound the tape, pressed 'PLAY'.

Schofield saw himself walk out onto the deck.

'Fast-forward through this,' he said.

Renshaw fast-forwarded through the tape. Schofield watched as he walked around the deck in fast motion and then suddenly fell to the ground, shot.

The Marine arrived. Checked Schofield's pulse. He then stood up and started rolling the body toward the pool with his foot.

'Okay, slow down here,' Schofield said.

The image returned to normal speed just as the Marine kicked Schofield's body a final time and the body dropped into the water.

'Okay, get ready to stop it,' Schofield said, watching the screen intently.

On the screen, the Marine was standing at the water's edge, looking down into the pool at the spot where Schofield's body had entered the water.

Then the Marine turned and looked about himself.

'*There!*' Schofield said. 'Stop it there!'

Renshaw quickly hit the 'PAUSE' button on the VCR and the image on the screen froze.

The screen showed the top portion of the Marine's helmet. The man's shoulders had also rotated upward slightly as he had turned to look about himself.

'I don't get it,' Renshaw said. 'You still can't see his face.'

'I'm not looking at his face,' Schofield said.

And he wasn't.

He was looking at the man's shoulders. At the man's right shoulderplate.

The image on the screen was grainy but Schofield could see the shoulderplate clearly.

A picture had been painted onto it.

Schofield felt a sliver of ice run down his spine as he stared at the picture that had been tattooed onto the man's shoulderplate.

It was a picture of a cobra, with its jaws bared wide.

In the dark storeroom down on E-deck, Mother rested her head gently against the cold, icy wall.

She shut her eyes. It had been about a half hour since anyone had come to check on her and she expected Buck Riley to come by soon. Her leg was starting to ache and she was itching for another hit of methadone.

She took a deep breath, tried to shut out the pain.

After a moment, however, she had a strange sensation that someone else was in the room with her . . .

Slowly, Mother opened her eyes.

Someone was standing in the doorway.

A man. A Marine.

He just stood there, like a statue, silhouetted in the doorway. His face was cloaked in shadow. He didn't say a word.

'Book?' Mother said, sitting upright. She squinted, took a closer look, tried to see who it was.

She stopped, startled.

It wasn't Book.

Book was shorter than whoever this was, more rounded.

This Marine was tall and lean.

The Marine still didn't speak. He just stood there, staring at Mother, his features covered in darkness. Mother realized who it was.

'Snake,' she said. 'What's the matter? Don't you talk anymore? Cat got your tongue?'

Snake didn't move from the doorway. He just kept staring at Mother.

When he spoke, Mother didn't see his mouth move. His voice was low, rough. 'I'm here instead of Book,' he said. 'I'm here to take care of you, Mother.'

'Good,' Mother said, sitting up straighter, preparing herself for another shot of methadone. 'I could use another shot of that kickapoo joy juice.'

Snake still didn't move from the doorway.

Mother frowned. 'Well?' she said. 'What are you waiting for – a gilt-edged invitation?'

'No,' Snake said, his voice cold.

He stepped forward into the storeroom and Mother's eyes widened in horror as she saw the light from the corridor outside glint off the knife in his hand.

Mother pushed herself back against the icy wall of the storeroom as Snake stepped through the doorway, brandishing his long Bowie knife.

'Snake, what the fuck are you doing?'

'I'm sorry, Mother,' he said coldly. 'You're a good soldier. But you're too close to this.'

'What the hell is that supposed to mean?'

Snake stepped slowly closer.

Mother's eyes were glued to the glistening knife in his hand.

'National security,' Snake said.

'*National security?*' Mother scoffed. 'What the fuck are you, Snake?'

Snake smiled a thin, evil smile. 'Come on, Mother, you've been around. You've heard the stories. What do you think I am?'

'A fucking whacko, that's what I think,' Mother said, as her eyes fell upon her helmet, lying on the floor of the storeroom halfway between her and Snake. It was lying upside down, with the microphone pointed up in the air.

Slowly, Mother began to slide her left hand down toward her belt.

'I do what's necessary to be done,' Snake said.

'Necessary for what?' Mother said, as she flicked a button on her belt. The button that switched on her helmet mike.

In Renshaw's room on B-deck, Schofield now had his body armour back on.

He reached for his various weapons. His pistol went into its holster, his knife went back into its sheath on his ankle guard. He slung his MP-5 over his shoulder and holstered his Maghook behind his back. Lastly, Schofield reached for his helmet and slid it over his head.

He heard voices immediately.

' – *the national interest.*'

'*Snake, put that fucking* – '

And then suddenly static cut across the signal and there was nothing.

But Schofield had heard enough.

Mother.

Snake was down with Mother.

'*Jesus,*' Schofield said.

He spun to face Renshaw. 'Okay, Harry Houdini, you've got exactly five seconds to show me how you got out of this room.'

Renshaw immediately ran towards the door. 'Why? What's going on?' he said.

Schofield hurried alongside him. 'Somebody's about to get killed.'

Down in the storeroom, Snake lifted his foot off what was left of Mother's helmet.

The small microphone at the jawline of her helmet lay crumpled and bent, broken beyond repair.

'Come on, Mother,' Snake said in an admonishing tone. 'I expected more from you. Or did you just forget that I receive your transmissions, too.'

Mother scowled at him. 'Did *you* kill Samurai?'

'Yes.'

'You fuck.'

Snake was almost on top of her now. Mother shifted against the wall.

'Time to die, Mother,' Snake said.

Mother snorted at him. 'Snake. I've just got to know.

What sort of sick, twisted, two-faced, son of a bitch are you?'

Snake smiled. 'The only kind, Mother. I'm ICG.'

Schofield watched tensely as Renshaw stepped up to the thick, wooden door of his room.

Up until that time, Schofield hadn't noticed that the door was made up of about ten vertical wooden planks. Renshaw immediately placed his fingers up against one of these vertical planks.

'The horizontal beams are on the outside,' Renshaw said. 'Which meant that no one outside this room saw the cuts I made on the inside of these vertical planks.'

Schofield's eyes widened when he saw them.

Two thin horizontal lines stretched across the width of the heavy, wooden door – like two scars in the wood – cutting *across* the wide vertical planks. The two horizontal lines ran in parallel, approximately three feet away from each other – at precisely those points where the horizontal beams on the *other side* of the door would have been.

Schofield marvelled at Renshaw's ingenuity.

Anyone standing on the other side of the door would never have known that Renshaw had managed to saw right through the vertical wooden planks.

'I used a steak knife to saw through the planks,' Renshaw said. 'Three actually. The wood wears them down pretty fast.' He reached off to his right and grabbed a worn-down steak knife. Renshaw inserted the blade of the knife into the narrow gap between two of the vertical planks. Then he worked the knife like a crowbar until suddenly one of the planks popped clear of the rest of the door.

Renshaw pulled the plank clear of the door and a long, rectangular *hole* appeared in the door where the plank had been. Through that rectangular hole, Schofield could see the curved outer tunnel of B-deck stretching away from him.

Renshaw worked quickly. He grabbed the next plank with his bare hands and hurriedly pulled it away.

The hole in the door got wider.

Renshaw had manufactured a square-shaped 'hole' in the middle of the door. Schofield started removing the vertical planks with him and soon the hole was wide enough for a man to fit through.

'Stand back,' Schofield said.

Renshaw took a step back as Schofield dived, head-first, through the hole in the door. He rolled to his feet on the other side and immediately ran off down the tunnel.

'Wait!' Renshaw yelled. 'Where are you going!'

'*E-deck!*' Schofield's voice echoed back.

And then suddenly Schofield was gone and Renshaw was alone in his room, staring at the empty, square-shaped hole he had made in the door.

He peered out through it after Schofield.

'I never dived through it like *that*,' he said.

*

Schofield ran.

The walls of the curved outer tunnel streaked past him. He was breathing hard. His heart pounded loudly inside his head. He turned left, headed towards the central shaft.

A thousand thoughts ran through his mind as he raced through the tunnels of B-deck.

He thought of the tattoo on the shoulderplate of the man who had shot him. A cobra. A snake.

Snake.

The mere concept was too bizarre for Schofield to comprehend. Snake was a highly decorated Marine. One of the longest serving members in the Corps, let alone Schofield's unit. Why would he throw it all away by doing something like this? Why would he kill his own men?

And then Schofield thought about Mother.

Snake was down on E-deck with Mother.

It made sense. Snake had already killed Samurai, the weakest member of Schofield's team. Mother – with one leg, and heavily dosed up on methadone – would be another easy target.

Schofield hit the B-deck catwalk on the fly. He ran for the rung-ladder, and slid down it fast. C-deck. He slid down the next rung-ladder – D-deck – and then the next.

He was on E-deck now. Schofield ran across the pool deck, past the lapping waves of the pool, and headed for the south tunnel.

He entered the south tunnel and saw the door to Mother's storeroom.

Schofield approached the open doorway to the store-room cautiously. He upholstered his Maghook – he still couldn't use his pistol in the gaseous environment of the station – and held it out in front of him like a gun.

He approached the open doorway, came to it. Then he took one, last, deep breath and then . . .

. . . Schofield turned fast into the doorway, his Mag-hook up and ready.

He saw the scene inside.

And his jaw dropped.

'Holy shit,' he breathed.

They were on the floor of the storeroom.

Mother and Snake.

At first, Schofield just stared at them, stared at the scene.

Mother was stretched out on the floor, with her back up against one of the walls. She had her good leg extended across the room, pressed up against Snake's throat, pinning him to a thick wooden shelf filled with scuba tanks. Her boot was pressed *hard* against his throat, pushing his chin upwards, squeezing his face back against the sturdy wooden shelf. She also held her Colt automatic pistol cupped in her hands, extended in the perfect shooting position. Pointed right at Snake's face.

The gaseous environment of the station obviously didn't bother *her*.

Mother glared at Snake down the barrel of her gun.

Blood dripped freely from two deep gashes above her left eye. It dripped down off her eyebrow, smacking down onto her left cheek like droplets of water from a leaking tap. Mother didn't notice the blood – she just stared right *through* it – into the eyes of the man who had tried to kill her.

For his part, Snake was pinned to the wooden shelf. Every now and then he would attempt to struggle, but Mother had all the leverage. Whenever he tried to wriggle out of her hold, she would press down hard on his Adam's apple with her big size 12. Mother was choking him with her foot.

The room around them looked like a bomb had hit it.

Wooden shelves lay twisted on the floor, splintered and shattered. Scuba tanks rolled aimlessly across the floor. A knife – Snake's – lay on the floor. Blood dripped off its blade.

Slowly, Mother turned her head and looked over at Schofield who was still just standing in the doorway, stunned.

Her chest heaved up and down. She was still breathing hard from the fight.

'Well, Scarecrow,' she said, taking another breath, 'are you just gonna fucking stand there, or what?'

Pete Cameron pulled his Toyota to a stop outside 14 Newbury St, Lake Arthur, New Mexico.

14 Newbury was a pleasant-looking, white, weatherboard cottage. Its front garden was immaculate – perfectly cut grass, a rock garden, even a small pond. It looked like the home of a retiree – the home of someone who had the time, and the inclination, to take loving care of it.

Cameron looked at the business card again. 'All right, Andrew Wilcox, let's see what you've got to say.'

Cameron stepped up onto the porch and knocked on the screen door.

Thirty seconds later, the inner door opened and a man of about thirty-five appeared behind the screen. He looked young and fit, clean-shaven. He smiled pleasantly.

'Mornin',' the young man said. 'How can I help you?' He had a broad southern drawl. When he said 'I' it sounded like 'Ah' – *How can ah help you.*

Cameron said, 'Yes, hi, I'm looking for a Mr Andrew Wilcox,' Cameron held up the business card. 'My name

346

is Peter Cameron. I'm a writer for *The Washington Post*. Mr Wilcox sent me his card.'

The smile on the young man's face vanished instantly.

His eyes swept Cameron's body, as if evaluating him. Then they swept the street outside, as if to see whether anyone was watching the house.

And then suddenly the man's attention returned to Cameron.

'Mr Cameron,' he said, opening the screen door. 'Please, come inside. I was hoping you'd come, but I didn't expect to see you so soon. Please, please, come inside.'

Cameron stepped through the doorway.

It didn't occur to him until he was fully inside the house that the man's southern accent had completely disappeared.

'Mr Cameron, my real name is not Andrew Wilcox,' the young man now sitting opposite him said. The drawl was gone, replaced by a voice that was clear and precise, educated. East Coast.

Pete Cameron had his pad and pen out. 'Can you tell me your real name?' he asked gently.

The young man seemed to think about that for a moment, and as he did so, Cameron got a better look at him. He was a tall man, handsome, too, with blond hair and a square jaw. He had broad shoulders and he looked physically fit. But there was something wrong about him.

It was the eyes, Cameron realized.

They were tinged with red. Heavy, black sacks hung beneath both of them. He looked like a man on the edge, a man who hadn't slept in days.

And then at last, the man spoke. 'My real name,' he said, 'is Andrew Trent.'

'I used to be a First Lieutenant in the Marines,' Andrew Trent explained, 'in command of an Atlantic-based Reconnaissance Unit. But if you examine the official USMC records, you'll find that I died in a accident in Peru in March, 1997.'

Trent spoke in a low, even voice, a voice tinged with bitterness.

'So, you're a dead man,' Pete Cameron said. 'Nice, very nice. Okay, first question: why me? Why did you contact me?'

'I've seen your work,' Trent said. 'I like it. *Mother Jones*. The *Post*. You tell it straight. You also don't just write down the first thing you hear. You check things out and because of that, people believe you. I need people to believe what I'm going to tell you.'

'If it's worth telling in the first place,' Cameron said. 'All right, then, how is it that according to the United States Government you are officially dead?'

Trent offered Cameron a half-smile, a smile totally devoid of humour. 'If it's worth telling in the first place,' he repeated. 'Mr Cameron, what if I were to tell you

349

that the Government of the United States of America ordered that my whole unit be killed.'

Cameron was silent.

'What if I were to tell you that *our* government – yours and mine – planted men inside my unit for the sole purpose of killing me and my men in the event that we found something of immense technological value during a mission.

'What if I were to tell you that that was *exactly* what happened in Peru in March, 1997. What would you think then, Mr Cameron? If I told you all that, then do you think my story would be worth telling?'

Trent told Cameron his story, told him about what had happened inside the ruins of the Incan temple high in the mountains of Peru.

A team of university researchers who had been working inside the temple had apparently discovered a series of frescoes chiselled into its stone walls. Magnificent, coloured, frescoes that depicted scenes from Incan history.

One of the frescoes in particular had captured their attention.

It depicted a scene not unlike the famous painting of the Incan emperor, Atahualpa, meeting the Spanish conquistadors.

On the left-hand side of the fresco stood the Incan emperor, in full ceremonial dress, surrounded by his people. He was holding a golden chalice in his out-stretched hands. A gift.

On the right-hand side of the fresco stood four strange-looking men. Unlike the olive-skinned Incans, their skin was bone white. And they were thin, unnaturally thin – tall, emaciated. They had large, black eyes and round-domed foreheads. They also had pointed, narrow chins and – bizarrely – no mouths.

In the carved stone picture, the leader of this delegation of tall, white 'men' was holding a silver box in his outstretched hands, reciprocating the gesture of the Incan emperor in front of him.

It was an exchange of gifts.

'How long did it take them to find it?' Cameron asked dryly.

'Not long,' Trent said.

As Trent explained, they found the object of their search mounted on a pedestal not far from the fresco itself, a small, stone pedestal sunken into the wall of the temple.

It just sat there. All on its own. It was about the size of a shoebox, and the colour of chrome.

It was the silver box from the fresco.

'Those scientists couldn't believe their luck,' Trent said. 'They called their university back in the States right away, and told them what they'd found. Told them that they may have discovered a gift from an alien civilization.'

Trent shook his head. 'Stupid bastards. They did it

over a telephone line. An open goddam telephone line. Hell, *anyone* could have heard them. My unit was sent in to protect them from anyone who did.'

Trent leaned forward in his chair.

'The problem was, it wasn't really *my* unit.'

Trent went on to tell Cameron about what had happened after his unit's arrival at the temple – in particular, how several of his own men had turned on him when the SEAL team had arrived at the temple.

'Mr Cameron. The order to plant men in my unit came from a government committee called the Intelligence Convergence Group,' Trent said. 'It's a joint committee made up of members of the Joint Chiefs of Staff and the National Reconnaissance Office. Put simply, its primary objective is to secure for America technological superiority over the rest of the world.

'They killed my unit, Mr Cameron. My *whole* unit. And then they hunted me. For twelve days, they scoured that temple looking for me. *American* soldiers, hunting *me*. I stood squeezed into a small fissure in a wall, being dripped on by stinking seepage, for twelve days before they gave up and left.'

Cameron said, 'What happened to the university researchers?'

Trent shook his head. 'The SEALs took them away. They were never heard from again.'

Cameron fell silent.

Trent went on. 'Eventually, I got out of that temple and made it back to the States. It took a while but I got

352

there in the end. The first place I went was my parents' house. But when I got there I saw two guys sitting in a van across the street, watching the house. They had people there, *waiting for me to come back*.'

Trent's face went cold. 'That was when I decided to find out who'd been behind it all. It didn't take me long to find a trail, and at the end of that trail, I found the ICG.'

Cameron found that he was staring at Trent. He blinked out of it.

'Okay. Right,' Cameron said, regaining his composure. 'This ICG, you say it's a joint committee, right. Made up of members of the Joint Chiefs of Staff and the National Reconnaissance Office, right.'

'That's correct,' Trent said.

'Okay.' Cameron knew about the Joint Chiefs of Staff, but he knew little about the National Reconnaissance Office. It was the intelligence agency charged with procuring, launching and operating all of America's spy satellites. Its secrecy was legendary; it was one of the few agencies that was allowed to operate under a 'black' budget – a budget that, because of the sensitivity of its subject matter, did not have to be disclosed to Senate Finance Committees. Throughout the Cold War, the US Government had consistently refused to acknowledge the NRO's existence. It was only in 1991, in the face of mounting evidence, that the Government finally called in and acknowledged that it did exist.

Trent said, 'The ICG is a marriage of two of the most

powerful agencies in this country – the supreme commanding body of all of our armed forces and the most secret arm of our intelligence community.'

'And its job is – what did you say – "to secure technological superiority" for America?'

'Its job,' Trent said, 'is to ensure that *every* major breakthrough in technology – be it the compact disc or a computer chip or stealth technology – *belongs* to the United States of America.'

Trent took a deep breath. 'Mr Cameron, I don't think I'm explaining this very well. Let me put it another way. The ICG's job is intelligence gathering, or as they call it in Government-speak, "intelligence convergence".

'Its job is to hoard valuable information. To make sure that *no one* knows about it except us. And the ICG will not hesitate to kill in order to achieve that goal. Its job – its reason for being – is to ensure that certain information is for American eyes only. Because in the end, the ICG has only one ambition: to keep America in the lead – way out in the lead – ahead of the rest of the world.'

'Uh-huh,' Cameron said, 'And you claim it does this by inserting men into elite military units?'

'Compromising front-line military units is only one part of the ICG's overall strategy, Mr Cameron. It's also one of the easiest parts. Think about it,' Trent said. 'The Joint Chiefs of Staff are part of the ICG. They can ensure that men of their choosing – *ultra-loyal* men; usually older, enlisted men, senior sergeants, gunnery sergeants; the *career* soldiers – get placed in the right units. And by "the right units" I mean the rapid-response units, the front-line units that get to battle scenes first. The Marine Recons, the Navy SEALs, the Army Rangers.

'But having men inside front-line military units is only good for getting *sudden* things like enemy spy satellites that fall out of the sky or meteorites that crash down to earth.

'Look at it this way: a meteorite lands in the middle of the Brazilian jungle. We send in the Marines. The Marines secure the area and grab the meteorite. Then, if something of value is found inside that meteorite, you eliminate the Marines who found it.'

'You *eliminate* them?'

'Think about it,' Trent said bitterly. 'You can't have a team of high-school-educated grunts running around with the most highly prized national secrets – secrets that could put the United States *twenty years ahead* of the rest of the world – bouncing around inside their heads, now can you?

'Hell, you don't need sodium nitrate to get that sort of information out of a low-level soldier. You give him a few beers, a pretty girl and the slightest hint that he has a *chance* of getting a blow job and your average Marine corporal will be telling Miss Big Tits everything he knows about the glowing green meteorite he found on a mission in the jungles of Brazil.

'Don't forget the value of these secrets, Mr Cameron,'

Trent said. 'The loss of a couple of foot soldiers does not even *begin* to compare with the value of a twenty-year head start on the rest of the world.'

Pete Cameron interrupted him. 'All right, then, how often does something like this happen? The elimination of an entire unit. I mean, it's got to be pretty rare.'

Trent nodded. 'It is rare. I only know of it happening on four occasions in the last fifteen years.'

'Uh-huh,' Cameron cocked his head doubtfully. 'Mr Trent, I see what you're saying, but something like this would require a whole *network* of well-placed people. High-ranking soldiers who aren't just part of the Joint Chiefs but who are well-placed in the bureaucracy – '

'Mr Cameron, do you know who Chuck Kozlowski is?'

'I've heard the name – '

'Sergeant Major Charles R. Kozlowski is Sergeant Major of the Marine Corps. Do you know what the Sergeant Major of the Marine Corps is, Mr Cameron?'

'What?'

'The Sergeant Major of the Marine Corps is the highest-ranking non-commissioned officer in the Corps. An *enlisted* man, Mr Cameron, the *highest-ranking* enlisted man. Chuck Kozlowski has been a Marine for thirty-three years. He's one of the most decorated soldiers in the country.'

Trent paused. 'He's also ICG.'

Cameron stared at Trent for a long moment, then he wrote down the name.

Chuck Kozlowski.

Trent said, 'He's the guardian angel of every crooked soldier in the Corps. Someone told me he even came down to Peru after my incident and *personally* escorted the surviving Marines – the traitors; all of them *senior enlisted* men – back home. He reassigned them without even a blink. I'm told he even recommended one for a fucking medal.'

'Jesus . . .'

'That's your network, Mr Cameron. A network that has infiltrated the enlisted ranks of the United States Marine Corps all the way to the very top – to the extent that it even determines which *units* its men are assigned to. But it doesn't stop there. Like I said before, compromising elite military units is only one part of the ICG's overall programme. The ICG compromises a whole lot more than just the military.'

'Like what?'

'Like other sources of breakthrough technology,' Trent said.

'Such as?'

'Well, for one thing, business.'

'Business? You mean *private* companies?'

Trent nodded.

'You're telling me that the Government of the United States has *planted* people inside private corporations to spy on them?'

'Microsoft. IBM. Boeing. Lockheed,' Trent said, deadpan. 'Plus, of course, all of the other major Navy, Army and Air Force contractors, especially if they have contracts with other countries.'

'Holy shit,' Cameron said.

'There are other places, too.'

'Like . . .'

'Like universities,' Trent said. 'Universities are high on the list of ICG-compromised organizations. Cloning sheep – ICG knew about in 1993. Cloning humans – ICG knew about it last year.' Trent shrugged. 'It makes sense. Universities are the cutting edge. If you want to find out what's in the pipeline, it's best to put your people in the pipe.'

Cameron didn't say anything for a full minute.

The sheer concept of an America-wide intelligence-gathering conspiracy made his spine tingle. An octopus-like network, with its tentacles stretching out from a small boardroom in the Pentagon to all the corners of the country, penetrating every major business and university. It was worth checking out some more.

Andrew Trent interrupted his thoughts.

'Mr Cameron,' Trent said seriously. 'The ICG is a dangerous organization. A *very* dangerous organization. It owes its allegiance to one thing and one thing only. The United States of America. So long as America wins, the ICG doesn't care what it has to do. It will kill to achieve that goal. It will kill *you* and it will kill *me*. Mr Cameron, patriotism is the virtue of the vicious. An organization that is prepared to infiltrate its own armed forces and kill its own men to keep this country's secrets safe is not one you want to mess with lightly.'

Cameron nodded solemnly. Then he said, 'Mr Trent,

do you have anything, anything at all, with names or something that I could – '

Trent grabbed a sheet of A4 paper from the table beside him.

'The results of my search so far,' he said. 'Names, positions held, and rank, if any.' Trent handed the sheet to Cameron.

Cameron took it, scanned it quickly. It read:

TRANSMIT NO. 767-9808-09001
REF NO. KOS-4622
SUBJECT: THE FOLLOWING IS AN ALPHABETICAL LIST OF PERSONNEL
AUTHORIZED TO RECEIVE SECURE TRANSMISSIONS.

NAME	LOCATION	FIELD/RANK
ADAMS, WALTER K.	LVRMRE LAB	NCLR PHYSCS
ATKINS, SAMANTHA, E	GSTETNR	CMPTR SFTWRE
BAILEY, KEITH H.	BRKLY	AERONTL ENGNR
BARNES, SEAN M.	N. SEALS	LTCMMDR
BROOKES, ARLIN F.	A.RNGRS	CPTN
CARVER, ELIZABETH R.	CLMBIA	CMPTR SCI
CHRISTIE, MARGARET V.	HRVRD	IDSTRL CHMST
DAWSON, RICHARD K.	MCROSFT	CMPTR SFTWRE
DELANEY, MARK M.	IBM	CMPTR HRDWRE
DOUGLAS, KENNETH A.	CRAY	CMPTR HRDWRE
DOWD, ROGER F.	USMC	CPRL
EDWARDS, STEPHEN R.	BOEING	AERONTL ENGNR
FAULKNER, DAVID G.	JPL	AERONTL ENGNR
FROST, KAREN S.	USC	GNTC ENGNR
GIANNI, ENRICO R.	LCKHEED	AERONTL ENGNR
GRANGER, RAYMOND K	A. RANGERS	SNR SGT
HARRIS, TERENCE X.	YALE	NCLR PHYSICS
JOHNSON, NORMA E.U.	ARIZ	BIOTOXNS
KAPLAN, SCOTT M.	USMC	GNNY SGT

KASCYNSKI, THERESA E.	3M CORP	PHSPHTES
KEMPER, PAULENE J.	JHNS HPKNS	DRMTLGY
KOZLOWSKI, CHARLES R.	USMC	SGT MJR
LAMB, MARK I.	ARMALTE	BLLSTCS
LAWSON, JANE R.	U.TEX	INSCTCIDES
LEE, MORGAN T.	USMC	SNR SGT
MAKIN, DENISE E.	U.CLRDO	CHMCL AGNTS
McDONALD, SIMON K.	LVRMRE LAB	NCLR PHYSICS
NORTON, PAUL G.	PRNCTN	AMNO ACD CHNS
OLIVER, JENNIFER F.	SLCN STRS	CMPTR SFTWRE
PARKES, SARAH T.	USC	PLNTLGST
REICHART, JOHN R.	USMC	SNR SGT
RIGGS, WAYLON J.	N.SEALS	CMMDR
SHORT, GREGORY J.	CCA CLA	LQD SCE
TURNER, JENNIFER C.	UCLA	GNTC ENGNR
WILLIAMS, VICTORIA D.	U.WSHGTN	GEOPHYS
YATES, JOHN F.	USAF	CMMDR

Cameron glanced up at Trent. 'How did you get this?'

Trent smiled. It was the first real smile Cameron had seen from Trent for the hour that he had known him.

'You remember those guys I told you about who were parked in the van outside my parents' house?'

'Yes . . .'

'Well, I followed one of them home. Stopped him in the doorway to his apartment and asked him a few questions. He was very co-operative, once he was . . . properly motivated.'

'What happened to him?' Cameron asked warily.

When he answered, Trent's voice was hard, cold, entirely devoid of emotion.

'He died.'

Snake stood handcuffed to the same pole as Henri Rae and Luc Champion on E-deck. His weapons and body armour had been removed. He just stood there, cuffed to the pole, dressed in his camouflaged, full-body combat fatigues.

Schofield, Riley and Rebound stood on the deck in front of him, looking at him. Mother was also out on the pool deck, sitting in a chair, looking like Cleopatra on a chaise. Schofield had had Book and Rebound carry her out onto the deck for this.

Last of all, behind Schofield, stood James Renshaw. He was the only civilian on the pool deck.

The atmosphere was tense. No one spoke.

Schofield looked at his watch.

It was 3:42 p.m.

He remembered what Abby Sinclair had said about the solar flare in the atmosphere above Wilkes Ice Station. A break in the solar flare would be passing over the station at 3:51.

Nine minutes.

He would have to make this quick. Gant and the others were still down in the cavern and he wanted to contact them and find out exactly what was down there before he called McMurdo.

Schofield pressed a button on the side of his watch and the display changed. The stopwatch screen appeared. It displayed numbers ticking upward:

1:52:58

1:52:59

1:53:00

Damn, Schofield thought.

It was going to be close. After he spoke with the people at McMurdo at 3:51, they would have *less* than an hour to figure out a way to seek out and destroy the French warship hovering off the coast waiting to fire its missiles at Wilkes Ice Station.

'All right,' Schofield said, turning to the group assembled around him. 'Book. Rebound. You first.'

Book and Rebound told their story.

They had both been outside, working on the station's antenna, out by one of the outer buildings.

'And then you called and asked for one of us to go and check on Mr Renshaw,' Book said. 'Snake took the call, so he went to do it. He came back after about fifteen minutes and said that everything was fine; said that Mr Renshaw was still in his room and that it had just been a false alarm.'

Schofield nodded – that was when he had been shot.

Book said, 'A little later, I got up to go and check on Mother, but Snake stopped me and said that he'd do it. I didn't think anything of it at the time, so I said sure, if he wanted to.'

Schofield nodded again – that was when the attack on Mother had happened.

He stepped forward so that he stood right in front of Snake. 'Sergeant,' he said. 'Would you care to explain yourself.'

Snake said nothing.

Schofield said, 'Sergeant, I said, would you like to tell me what in *fucking hell* is going on here.'

Snake didn't flinch. He just sneered coldly at Schofield.

Schofield hated him, hated the very sight of him.

This was the man who had shot him – killed him – and then *checked* to make sure that he was dead.

Schofield had thought about his own shooting.

In the end, it was the frosted glass on the deck that explained it. The white, frosted glass that Schofield had stepped on only moments before he had been shot.

It explained two things: *why* Snake was able to fire a gun safely in the gaseous atmosphere of Wilkes Ice Station, and *where* he had fired it from.

The answer, in the end, was simple.

Snake hadn't fired his sniper rifle from inside the station at all. He had fired it from *outside* the station. He had broken a tiny, round hole in the white, frosted glass dome that towered above the central shaft of the station and he had then shot down *through* that hole at Schofield. The glass which he had dislodged from the dome to make the hole in it had fallen all the way down through the shaft to E-deck. The same glass that

Schofield had stepped on only moments before he had been shot.

Schofield just stared at Snake.

Mother said softly, 'He said he was ICG.'

Book and Rebound turned instantly at Mother's words.

'Well, Sergeant?' Schofield said.

Snake said nothing.

Schofield said, 'Not very talkative, huh?'

'He was pretty fucking talkative when he was getting ready to fillet me,' Mother said. 'I say we cut his balls off and make him watch as we feed 'em to the fucking whales.'

'Good idea,' Schofield said as he glared at Snake. Snake just sneered smugly back at him.

Schofield felt the anger well up inside him. He was furious. Right now he just wanted to slam Snake up against the wall and wipe that smug look off his fucking face –

As a leader, you simply cannot afford to get angry or upset.

Once again, Trevor Barnaby's words rang through Schofield's head.

Schofield wondered whether Barnaby had ever had an infiltrator in his unit. He wondered what the famous SAS commander would have done in *these* circumstances.

'Book,' Schofield said. 'Opinions?'

Buck Riley just stared sadly at Snake and shook his

head. He seemed to be the most deeply affected by the revelation that Snake was an ICG plant.

'I didn't think you were a traitor, Snake,' Book said. Then he turned to Schofield. 'It's not for you to kill him. Not here. Not now. Take him home. Send him to jail.'

As Book spoke, Schofield just glared at Snake. Snake stared defiantly back at him.

There was a long silence.

Schofield broke it. 'Tell me about the Intelligence Convergence Group, Snake.'

'That's a nice wound,' Snake said softly, slowly, looking at the stitched wound on Schofield's neck. The wound Snake himself had inflicted. 'You ought to be dead.'

'It didn't suit me,' Schofield said. 'Tell me about the ICG.'

Snake smiled a cold, thin smile. Then he began to laugh softly.

'You're a dead man,' Snake said quietly. Then he turned to face the others. 'You're all going to die.'

'What do you mean?' Schofield said.

'You wanted to know about the ICG,' Snake said. 'I just told you about the ICG.'

'The ICG is going to kill us?'

'The ICG will never let you live,' Snake said. 'It's not possible. Not after what you've seen here. When the United States Government gets their hands on that spaceship, it can't possibly allow a handful of *grunts* like you to know about it. You're all going to die. Count on it.'

Snake's words hung in the air. Everyone on the deck was silent.

Their reward for arriving at Wilkes Ice Station so quickly and defending it against the French was to be a death sentence.

'Wonderful,' Schofield said. 'That's just wonderful. I bet you're pretty fucking proud of yourself,' he said to Snake.

'My loyalty to my country is greater than my loyalty to you, Scarecrow,' Snake said defiantly.

Schofield's teeth began to grind. He stepped forward. Book held him back.

'Not now,' Book said quietly. 'Not here.'

Schofield took a step back.

'*Lieutenant!*' a woman's voice yelled from somewhere high up in the station.

Schofield looked up.

Abby Sinclair was leaning out over the railing of A-deck.

'Lieutenant!' she yelled. 'It's time!'

Schofield strode into the radio room on A-deck. Book and James Renshaw came in behind him. Rebound had stayed down on E-deck to keep an eye on Snake.

Abby was already seated at the radio console. She did a double take when she saw Renshaw enter the room.

'Hello, Abby,' Renshaw said.

'Hello, James,' Abby said, cautiously.

Abby turned to Schofield. 'The break should be over us any second now.' She flicked a switch on the console. The sound of static began to wash out from two wall-mounted speakers.

Shhhhhhhhh.

'That's the sound of the solar flare,' Abby said. 'But if you wait just . . . a . . . few . . . seconds . . .'

Abruptly, the shooshing sound cut off and there was silence.

'And there it is,' Abby said. 'There's your break, Lieutenant. Go for it.'

Schofield sat down at the console and grabbed the microphone.

He hit the talk button, but just as he was about to speak, a strange, high-pitched whistling sound suddenly blared out from the wall-mounted speakers. It sounded like feedback, interference.

Schofield released the microphone instantly, looked at Abby. 'What did I do? Did I press something?'

Abby frowned, flicked a couple of switches. 'No. You didn't do anything.'

'Is it the solar flare? Could you have got the timing wrong?'

'No,' Abby said firmly.

She flicked some more switches.

Nothing happened.

The system didn't seem to be responding to what she was doing. The high-pitched whistling sound filled the radio room.

Abby said, 'There's something wrong, this isn't inter- ference from the flare. This is something else. This is different. It's almost as if it's *electronic*. As though someone was jamming us . . .'

Schofield felt a chill run up the length of his spine.

'Jamming us?'

'It's as if there's someone *between* us and McMurdo, stopping our signal getting through,' Abby said.

'Scarecrow . . .' a voice said from somewhere behind Schofield.

Schofield spun.

It was Rebound.

He was standing in the doorway to the radio room.

'I thought I told you to stay down with – '

'Sir, you better see this,' Rebound said. 'You better see this *now*.' Rebound held up his left hand.

In it was the portable viewscreen that Schofield had brought inside from the hovercrafts earlier. The small TV screen that displayed the findings of the two range- finders mounted on top of the hovercrafts outside.

Rebound crossed the radio room quickly, and handed the viewscreen to Schofield.

Schofield looked at the screen and his eyes instantly widened in horror.

'Oh, *Christ*,' he said.

The screen was filled with red blips.

They looked like a swarm of bees, converging on a point; they were all approaching the centre of the screen.

Schofield counted twenty red blips.

Twenty . . .

All of them converging on Wilkes Ice Station.

'Good God . . .'

And then suddenly Schofield heard a voice.

A voice that made his blood run cold.

It came from the speakers that lined the walls of the radio room. Loud and hard, as if it were a message from God himself.

'*Attention Wilkes Ice Station. Attention,*' the voice said.

It was a crisp voice, clipped and cultured.

'*Attention American forces at Wilkes Ice Station. As you will now no doubt be aware, your communication lines have been intercepted. It is no use attempting to contact your base at McMurdo – you will not get through. You are advised to lay down your arms immediately. If you do not lay down your defences before our arrival, we will be forced to make an offensive entry. Such an entry, ladies and gentlemen, will be painful.*'

Schofield's eyes went wide at the sound of the voice. The English accent was all too apparent.

It was a voice that Schofield knew well. A voice from his past.

It was the voice of Trevor Barnaby. Brigadier-General Trevor J. Barnaby of Her Majesty's SAS.

FIFTH INCURSION

16 June 1551 hours

FIFTH INCURSION

'Oh, Jesus,' Rebound said.

'How long till they get here?' Book asked.

Schofield's eyes were glued to the portable view-screen. He looked at the box at the bottom of the screen. In it was a wire-frame picture of a hovercraft. The wire-frame hovercraft rotated within the box. Beneath it were the words: 'BELL TEXTRON SR.N7-S – LANDING CRAFT AIR CUSHIONED (UK).'

'It's the SAS,' Rebound said in disbelief. 'It's the fucking SAS.'

'Take it easy, Rebound,' Schofield said. 'We're not dead yet.'

Schofield turned to Book. 'Thirty-four miles out. Coming in at eighty miles an hour.'

'Definitely not friendly,' Book said.

Schofield said, 'Thirty-four miles at eighty miles an hour. That gives us, what – '

'Twenty-six minutes,' Abby said quickly.

'Twenty-six minutes,' Schofield swallowed. 'Shit.'

The room fell silent.

Schofield could hear Rebound's breathing. He was breathing fast, hyperventilating.

Everyone watched Schofield, waited for him to make the call.

Schofield took a deep breath, tried to evaluate the situation. The SAS – the British Special Air Service, the most dangerous special forces unit in the world, was on its way to Wilkes Ice Station right now.

And it was being led by Trevor Barnaby – the man who had *taught* Shane Schofield everything he knew about covert incursionary warfare. The man who, in the eighteen years he had been in command of the SAS, had never once failed in a mission.

On top of all that, Barnaby was also jamming Schofield's radio, stopping him from getting in contact with McMurdo. Stopping him from making contact with the only people in the world who were capable of taking out the French warship that was hovering off the coast, waiting to launch its missiles at Wilkes Ice Station.

Schofield checked his stopwatch. It read:

2:02:31

2:02:32

2:02:33

Shit, Schofield thought.

Less than an hour until they launched.

Shit. It was all happening too fast. It was as if the whole world was closing in around him.

Schofield looked at the rangefinder viewscreen again, looked at the swarm of dots approaching Wilkes Ice Station.

Twenty hovercrafts, he thought. Probably two or three men in each. That meant a minimum of fifty men.

Fifty men.

And what did Schofield have.

Three good men in the station proper. Three more down in the cave. Mother down in the storeroom and Snake handcuffed to a pole on E-deck.

The situation didn't just look bad.

It looked hopeless.

Either they stayed here and fought a suicidal battle with the SAS, or they ran – made a break for McMurdo in the hovercrafts – and brought back reinforcements later.

There really was no choice at all.

Schofield looked up at the small group gathered around him.

'All right,' he said. 'We get out of here.'

Schofield's feet clanged loudly as they landed hard on the cold metal floor of E-deck. Schofield strode quickly across the deck toward the south tunnel and Mother's storeroom.

'What's going on?' a voice called out from the other side of the deck. Snake. 'Trouble, Lieutenant?'

Schofield approached the handcuffed soldier. He saw the two French scientists kneeling on the floor on either side of him. They just stared resignedly at the floor.

'You made a mistake,' Schofield said to Snake. 'You started killing your own men too soon. You should have waited until you were sure we had this station secured. Now we've got twenty British hovercrafts speeding toward us and no reinforcements in sight. They're going to be here in twenty-three minutes.'

Snake's face remained impassive, cold.

'And you know what,' Schofield said. 'You're gonna be here when they arrive.' He began to walk away.

'You're going to *leave* me here?' Snake said in disbelief.

'Yes.'

'You can't do that. You *need* me,' Snake said.

Schofield looked at his watch as he walked.

Twenty-two minutes until the SAS arrived.

'Snake, you had your chance and you blew it. Now, you'd better pray that we break through their line and get to McMurdo. Because if we don't, this whole station – and whatever's buried down in the ice beneath it – is gonna be lost forever.'

Schofield stopped by the entrance to the south tunnel and turned around. 'And in the meantime, you can take your chances with Trevor Barnaby.'

With that, Schofield turned away from Snake and entered the south tunnel. He immediately swung right and entered Mother's storeroom. Mother was seated on the floor by the wall again. She looked up when Schofield came in.

'Trouble?' she said.

'As always,' Schofield said. 'Can you move?'

'What's happening?'

'Our favourite ally just sent their best troops in to take this station.'

'What do you mean?'

'The SAS are on their way and they don't sound friendly.'

'How many?'

'Twenty hovercrafts.'

'Shit,' Mother said.

'That's what I thought. Can you move?' Schofield was already probing around behind Mother's chair, to see if he could gather together all of her fluid bags and intravenous drips.

'How long till they get here?' Mother asked.

Schofield looked quickly at his watch. 'Twenty minutes.'

'Twenty minutes,' Mother said.

Behind her, Schofield quickly grabbed two fluid lines.

'Scarecrow . . .' Mother said.

'Just a second.'

'*Scarecrow.*'

Schofield stopped what he was doing and looked up at Mother.

'Stop,' Mother said gently.

Schofield looked at her.

Mother said, 'Scarecrow. Get out of here. Get out of here now. Even if we had a full squad of twelve swordsmen, we'd never be able to hold off an entire platoon of SAS commandos.' 'Swordsman' was Mother's term for a Marine, a reference to the sword of honour that every Marine wore when in full dress uniform.

'Mother . . .'

'Scarecrow, the SAS, they aren't regular troops like we are. They are killers, trained killers. They are *trained* to go into a hostile zone and kill everyone in sight. They don't take prisoners. They don't ask questions. They kill.' Mother paused. 'You have to evacuate the station.'

'I know.'

'And you can't do that with a one-legged old hag like me weighing you down. If you're gonna run that blockade, you're gonna need people who can move, people who can move fast.'

'I'm not going to leave you here – '

'Scarecrow. You *have* to get to McMurdo. You have to get reinforcements.'

'And then what?'

'And then what? And then you can come back here with a fucking *battalion* of swordsmen, you nuke these British sons-of-bitches, you rescue the girl and you save the fucking day. That's what.'

Schofield just stared at Mother. Mother returned his gaze, looked him squarely in the eye.

'Go,' she said softly. 'Go now. I'll be all right.'

Schofield didn't say anything, he just continued to stare at her.

Mother shrugged nonchalantly. 'I mean, hey, like I've said before, it's nothing one good kiss from a fine-looking man like you wouldn't – '

At that moment, without warning, Schofield leaned forward and kissed Mother quickly on the lips. It was only a short kiss – an innocent peck – but Mother's eyes went as wide as saucers.

Schofield stood up. Mother took a deep breath.

'Whoa, *mama*,' she said.

'Find a place to hide and stay there,' Schofield said. 'I'll be back. I promise.'

And then Schofield left the room.

The hovercraft's engine roared to life.

In the driver's seat, Rebound floored the accelerator. The needle on the tachometer bounced up to 6000 rpm's.

At that moment, the second Marine hovercraft came gliding across the hard-packed snow. Its engine revved loudly as it slid to a halt alongside Rebound's hovercraft.

Buck Riley's voice came over Rebound's radio. '*Fifteen minutes to go, Rebound. Let's get 'em over to the main building and load 'em up.*'

Schofield looked at his watch as he strode quickly round the outer tunnel of B-deck.

Fifteen minutes to go.

'Fox. Can you hear me?' he said into his helmet mike as he walked. While he waited for a reply, Schofield quickly put his hand over the microphone.

'Let's *go* people!' he yelled.

The remaining residents of Wilkes – Abby and the three male scientists, Llewellyn, Harris and Robinson – were hurrying in and out of their respective rooms.

Llewellyn and Robinson ran past Schofield. They were dressed in thick black windbreakers. They hurried off toward the central shaft of the station.

Suddenly Gant's voice came over Schofield's earpiece. *'Scarecrow, this is Fox, I read you. You're not gonna believe what's down here.'*

'Yeah, well, you're not gonna believe what's up here,' Schofield said. 'Sorry, Fox, but you're gonna have to tell me about it later. We're in big trouble up here. We've got a whole platoon of SAS commandos heading toward this station and they're gonna be here in about fourteen minutes.'

'Jesus. What are you going to do?'

'We're gonna pull out. We have to. There's just too many of them. Our only chance is to get back to McMurdo and bring back the cavalry.'

'What should we do down here?'

'Just stay where you are. Point your guns at that pool and shoot the first thing that pokes its head out of the water.'

Schofield looked around himself as he spoke. He couldn't see Kirsty anywhere.

'Listen, Fox, I have to go,' he said.

'Be careful, Scarecrow.'

'You, too. Scarecrow, out.'

Schofield spun instantly. 'Where's the girl!' he yelled.

He received no reply. Abby Sinclair and the scientist named Harris were busy grabbing their parkas and other valuable items from their rooms. Just then, Harris

381

emerged from his room and ran past Schofield with a bundle of papers in his arms.

Schofield saw Abby emerge from her room. She was hurriedly putting on a heavy, blue parka.

'Abby! Where's Kirsty?' Schofield called.

'I think she went back to her room!'

'Where is her room?'

'Down the tunnel! On the left,' Abby yelled, pointing down the tunnel behind Schofield.

Schofield ran down the outer tunnel of B-deck, looking for Kirsty.

Twelve minutes to go.

Schofield threw open every door he came to.

First door. A bedroom. Nothing.

Second door. Locked. A three-ringed biohazard sign on it. The Biotoxin Laboratory. Kirsty wouldn't be in there.

Third door. Schofield threw it open.

And suddenly he stopped.

Schofield hadn't seen this room before. It was a walk-in freezer of some sort, the kind used for storing food. *Not anymore*, Schofield thought. Now this freezer room stored something else.

There were three bodies in the room.

Samurai, Mitch Healy, and Hollywood. They all lay on their backs, face-up.

After the battle with the French, Schofield had ordered that the bodies of his fallen men be taken to a freezer of some sort, where they were to be kept until they could be returned home for a proper burial. This was obviously where the bodies had been taken.

There was, however, a fourth body in the freezer room. It lay on the floor next to Hollywood's body, and it had been covered over with a brown hessian sack.

Schofield frowned.

Another body?

It couldn't have been one of the French soldiers, because they had not been moved from where they lay –

And then suddenly Schofield remembered.

It was Bernard Olson.

Doctor Bernard Olson.

The scientist James Renshaw was said to have killed several days before Schofield and his team had arrived at Wilkes. The residents of Wilkes must have placed his body in here.

Schofield checked his watch.

Eleven minutes.

And then suddenly Schofield remembered something that Renshaw had said after Schofield had woken up inside his room, bound to the bed. When Renshaw had released Schofield he had asked him to do something odd. He had asked him – if he ever got the chance – to check Olson's body, in particular the tongue and the eyes.

Schofield didn't understand what the dead man's tongue and eyes had to do with anything. But Renshaw had insisted that they would prove his innocence.

Ten-and-a-half minutes.

Not enough time. Got to get out of here.

But then, Renshaw *had* saved his life . . .

All right.

Schofield hurried into the freezer room and fell to his knees beside the brown hessian sack. He swept it off the body.

Bernard Olson stared up at Schofield with cold, lifeless eyes. He was an ugly man – fat and bald, with a pudgy, wrinkled face. His skin was bone white in colour.

Schofield didn't waste any time. He checked the eyes first.

They were deeply red around the rims, inflamed. Horribly bloodshot.

Then he turned his attention to the dead man's mouth.

The mouth was shut. Schofield tried to open it, but the jaw was locked firmly in place. It wouldn't open an inch.

Schofield leaned closer and prized the dead man's lips apart so that he could examine the tongue.

The lips came apart.

'Urghhh,' Schofield winced as he saw it. He swallowed quickly, held back the nausea.

Bernie Olson had bitten his own tongue off.

For some reason, before he had died, Bernie Olson had bitten down hard with his teeth, clamping them shut. He had bitten down so hard that he had cut his own tongue in half.

Ten minutes.

That's enough, time to go.

Schofield ran for the door, and as he passed Mitch Healy's body on the way out, he grabbed the dead Marine's helmet from the floor.

Schofield emerged from the freezer room just as Kirsty came running down the outer tunnel of B-deck.

'I had to get a parka,' she said apologetically. 'My other one got wet – '

'Come on,' Schofield said, grabbing her hand and pulling her down the tunnel.

As they turned into the tunnel that led to the central shaft, Schofield heard someone shout, 'Wait for me!'

Schofield spun.

It was Renshaw. He was hurrying as fast as his little legs would carry him, racing around the curved outer tunnel toward Schofield and Kirsty. He was dressed in a heavy blue parka and he was carrying a thick book under his arm.

'What the hell were you doing?' Schofield said.

'I had to get this,' Renshaw said, indicating the book under his arm as he ran past Schofield and headed for the central well.

Schofield and Kirsty followed. 'What the hell is in there that's so important?' Schofield yelled.

Renshaw called back, 'My innocence!'

Outside the station, snow was flying horizontally.

It assaulted Schofield's face – bounced off his silver

glasses – as he emerged from the main entrance with Kirsty and Renshaw by his side.

Eight minutes to go.

Until the SAS arrived.

The two white Marine hovercrafts were already parked outside the main entrance to the station. Book and Rebound stood beside the two big vehicles, hustling the residents of Wilkes onto Rebound's white hovercraft.

Schofield's plan was simple.

Rebound's hovercraft would be the transport. It held six people, so it would be used to carry all of the residents of Wilkes – Abby, Llewellyn, Harris, Robinson and Kirsty – plus Rebound himself.

Book and Schofield would ride shotgun, defending the transport craft as it raced eastward and attempted to outrun the SAS hovercrafts speeding towards Wilkes Ice Station.

Book would drive the second Marine hovercraft, Schofield the French unit's orange hovercraft. James Renshaw, Schofield decided, would ride with him.

Schofield saw Rebound slam the sliding door of his hovercraft; saw Book leap up onto the skirt of his hovercraft and disappear inside the cabin. Book re-emerged a second later with a large, black Samsonite trunk in his hands. Book hurled the big black trunk across the snow towards Schofield. It landed with a loud thud.

'Pest control!' Book called.

Schofield hurried toward the trunk.

'Here,' he said to Renshaw as he ran. 'Put this on.'

Schofield handed Renshaw the Marine helmet that he had picked up on his way out of the freezer room. Then Schofield quickly picked up the big Samsonite trunk and headed for the French hovercraft.

The French hovercraft sat silently in the snow outside the main entrance to the station. Unlike the two white USMC hovercrafts, it was painted a bright, garish orange.

Seven minutes.

Schofield leapt up onto the skirt of the French hovercraft and yanked open the sliding door. He got Renshaw to pass the big Samsonite trunk up to him, and he threw it inside.

Schofield hurried into the cabin and made for the driver's chair. Renshaw jumped in behind him and pulled the sliding door shut.

Schofield keyed the ignition.

The engine roared to life.

The big seven-foot fan at the rear of the hovercraft began to rotate. It got faster and faster until, like the propeller on an old biplane, it suddenly snapped into overdrive and became a rapidly spinning blur.

Beneath the hovercraft's black rubber skirt, four smaller turbofans also kicked into action. The big hovercraft lifted slowly off the ground as the skirt inflated like a balloon.

Schofield brought the big orange vehicle around so

that it came alongside the two white Marine hovercrafts. They were all pointing outward, away from the station.

Looking out through the reinforced windscreen of his hovercraft, Schofield could see the horizon to the south-west. It glowed a haunting orange.

Superimposed upon it were a collection of dark shadows. Small, black boxes with fat, rounded bases that seemed to kick up a haze of dust behind them.

The British hovercrafts.

Closing in on Wilkes Ice Station.

'All right, people,' Schofield said into his helmet mike. 'Let's get out of here.'

The ground raced by beneath them.

The three American hovercrafts whipped across the ice plain at phenomenal speed, side-by-side. Book and Schofield were on the outside, Rebound's transport was in the middle.

They raced east, in the direction of McMurdo. The three hovercrafts kept to the coastline, skirting around the edge of a cliff that towered above an enormous bay-like expanse of water. From point to point, the bay was about one mile across, but to go *around* it by land required a trek of almost eight miles. The mountainous waves of the Southern Ocean crashed loudly against the base of the cliffs.

As his hovercraft sped across the ice plain, Schofield looked behind him. He saw the British hovercrafts approaching Wilkes Ice Station from the west and the south.

'They must have landed at one of the Australian stations,' he said over his helmet intercom. Casey Station, most likely, he thought. It was the nearest one, about 700 miles due west of Wilkes.

'*Fucking Australians,*' Rebound's voice said.

*

Five miles away, in the silent interior of an American-made Bell Textron SR.N7-S hovercraft, Brigadier-General Trevor J. Barnaby stared impassively out through the reinforced glass windshield of his hovercraft.

Trevor Barnaby was a tall, solid man, fifty-six years old, with a fully shaven head and a pointed, black goatee. He stared out through the windshield of his hovercraft with cold, hard eyes.

'You're running, Scarecrow,' he said aloud. 'My, my, you are a clever one.'

'They're heading east, sir,' a young SAS corporal manning the radio console next to Barnaby said. 'Out along the coast.'

'Send eight crafts after them,' Barnaby commanded. 'Kill them. Everyone else is to proceed to the station as planned.'

'Yes, sir.'

The speedometer on Schofield's hovercraft edged over eighty miles per hour. Snow pounded against the windshield.

'*Sir, they're coming!*' Rebound's voice shouted over Schofield's helmet intercom.

Schofield's head snapped right and he saw them.

Several British hovercrafts had broken away from the main group and were heading toward the three escaping American hovercrafts.

'*The others are going for the station,*' Book's voice said.

'I know,' Schofield said. 'I know.'

Schofield whirled around in the driver's seat. He saw Renshaw standing in the back section of the cabin, looking slightly ridiculous in Mitch Healy's oversized Marine helmet.

'Mr Renshaw,' Schofield said.

'Yes.'

'Time to make yourself useful. See if you can open that trunk on the floor there.'

Renshaw immediately dropped to his knees and flipped the latches on the black Samsonite trunk that lay on the floor in front of him.

Schofield drove, turning around every few seconds to see how Renshaw was faring with the trunk.

'Oh, *shit*,' Renshaw said as he opened the trunk and saw what lay inside it.

At that moment, there came a sudden, booming sound from outside and Schofield snapped around again.

He knew that sound . . .

And then he saw it.

'Oh, no . . .' Schofield groaned.

The first missile slammed into the snow-covered ground *right in front of* Schofield's speeding hovercraft.

It left a crater ten feet in diameter and a split second later, Schofield's hovercraft screamed over the edge of the crater, exploding through the dustcloud above it.

'*Incoming!*' Rebound's voice yelled.

'Get inland!' Schofield called back, as he caught sight

of the cliff edge about a hundred yards to his left. 'Get away from the edge!'

Schofield's head snapped around again as he spoke. He saw the cluster of British hovercrafts behind him.

He also saw the second missile.

It was white and round, cylindrical, and it cut through the driving snow in front of the lead British hovercraft, its spiralling smoke trail looping through the air behind it. A Milan anti-tank missile.

Renshaw saw it, too. '*Yikes!*'

Schofield floored it.

But the missile was closing in too quickly. It angled in toward Schofield's speeding hovercraft, fast.

Too fast.

And then suddenly at the last moment, Schofield yanked hard on the steering yoke of his hovercraft and the whole craft swerved dramatically to the left, *toward* the cliff edge.

The missile shot across the bow of the speeding hovercraft and Schofield instinctively swerved back right and the missile slammed into the snow off to his left, exploding in a spectacular shower of white.

Schofield immediately swung back left, just as a second missile slammed into the snow-covered earth right next to him.

'Keep swerving!' Schofield yelled into his helmet mike. 'Don't let them get a lock on you!'

The three American hovercrafts all began to swerve as one as they rocketed across the flat Antarctic landscape, the hailstorm of unguided British missiles slamming down into the snow all around them. Deafening explosions filled the air. Massive gouts of snow and earth erupted from the ground.

Schofield fought desperately with the steering yoke of his hovercraft. The hovercraft screamed across the ice plain, a juggernaut out of control, ducking and swerving as it avoided the missiles that rained down all around it.

'*The trunk!*' Schofield yelled to Renshaw. '*The trunk!*'

'Right!' Renshaw said. He lifted a compact, black tube out of the Samsonite trunk. It was about five feet long.

'All right,' Schofield said as he yanked hard on the steering yoke to avoid another screaming British missile. The hovercraft rocked sharply as it swung hard to the right. Renshaw lost his balance and fell against the wall of the cabin.

'Lock the tube onto the gripstock!' Schofield yelled.

Renshaw found the gripstock in the trunk. It looked like a gun without a barrel – just the grip and the trigger and a stock that you rested on your shoulder. The compact, cylindrical tube clicked firmly into place on top of the gripstock.

'All right, Mr Renshaw. You just made yourself a Stinger missile launcher! Now use it!'

'How?'

'Open the door! Put it on your shoulder! Point it at the bad guys, and when you hear the tone, pull the trigger! It'll do the rest!'

'Okay . . .' Renshaw said doubtfully.

Renshaw yanked open the right-hand sliding door of

the hovercraft. Screaming Antarctic wind instantly invaded the interior of the craft. Renshaw struggled against it, forced his way toward the open door.

He rested the Stinger on his shoulder, shuffled it so that his eyes settled into its sights. Through the night-sights, he saw the lead British hovercraft from head-on, caught between a pair of cross-hairs. The British hover-craft glowed green –

And then suddenly Renshaw heard a dull, buzzing sound.

'I hear the tone!' he yelled excitedly.

'Then pull the trigger!' Schofield called back.

Renshaw pulled the trigger.

The recoil of the Stinger sent Renshaw flying back onto the floor of the cabin.

The missile shot forward from its launcher. The backblast – the sudden, explosive burst of fire that shoots out the back of a rocket launcher when it is fired – shattered the windows behind Renshaw.

Schofield watched as the Stinger spiralled through the air towards the lead British hovercraft. Its smoke-trail looped gracefully through the air behind it, reveal-ing its flight path.

'Goodnight,' Schofield said.

The Stinger slammed into the lead British hovercraft and the hovercraft exploded instantly, shattered into a thousand pieces.

The other British hovercrafts continued relentlessly

forward, ignoring their fallen comrade. One of the rear ones just shot straight *through* the burning remains of the exploded lead hovercraft.

'Good shot, Mr Renshaw!' Schofield said, knowing full well that Renshaw really had nothing to do with the success of the shot.

Schofield had guessed – correctly – that the British were firing Milan anti-*tank* missiles at him. But as Schofield well knew, Milans are made to hit tanks and armoured vehicles. They are not made to hit vehicles travelling faster than forty miles per hour. That was why they were performing so badly against Schofield's speeding hovercrafts.

The Hughes MIM-92 Surface-to-Air 'Stinger' Missile, on the other hand, was a different story altogether. It was *made* to hit fighter jets. It was *made* to hit vehicles that travelled at supersonic speeds. As such, it was more than capable of hitting a hovercraft travelling at a mere eighty miles per hour.

What Schofield also knew was that the Stinger was potentially *the* most user-friendly shoulder-launched assault weapon ever made. You simply pointed the weapon, heard the tone and pulled the trigger. The missile did the rest.

In the cabin behind Schofield, Renshaw awkwardly got to his feet again. Once he had regained his balance, he looked out through the side door of the hovercraft and saw the fiery remains of the British hovercraft he had destroyed.

'Yikes,' he said softly.

The seven remaining British hovercrafts closed in.

'*Book!*' Rebound's voice yelled. '*I need help over here!*'

'Hang on! I'm coming over!' Book yelled as he yanked on the steering yoke of his LCAC.

The hovercraft swung right – around and behind Rebound's transport, cutting in between it and the approaching British hovercrafts.

Book looked out to his right just as a volley of bullets peppered his side windows. Scratch marks appeared, but the glass didn't crack. It was bullet-resistant Lexan glass.

The British hovercrafts were close now. Maybe twenty yards away. Whipping across the icy landscape.

They closed in on the three American hovercrafts like a pack of hungry sharks.

'*Book! Help me!*'

Book was travelling behind Rebound now.

Swarming in from their right, however, were four of the British hovercrafts.

Book pushed open one of his side windows with the barrel of his MP-5 and pulled the trigger. A line of bulletholes strafed the ice alongside the nearest, speeding British hovercraft.

And then all of a sudden the British hovercraft swung in hard, and rammed the side of Book's hovercraft and Book was thrown out of his chair by the impact.

'Scarecrow! Where are you!' Book yelled.

Book climbed back into his chair and looked out through his side window at the British hovercraft next to him. It was so close that Book could see the driver – a man, dressed completely in black, wearing the trademark black balaclava of the SAS. There were two other men in the back of the British hovercraft, also wearing black. Book saw one of them yank open the side door of their hovercraft.

They were going to board him –

And then suddenly the British hovercraft filled with light and its reinforced glass windows shattered as one and blew out of their frames.

Book watched in amazement as the hovercraft alongside him exploded into flames and fell away behind him. Then he looked over his shoulder and saw Schofield's orange hovercraft sweep around behind him. The smoke trail of a Stinger still lingered in the air in front of it.

'Thanks, Scare – '

'*Book! Watch your left!*' Schofield's voice shouted.

The impact knocked Book sideways through the air and the world tilted crazily as his hovercraft was lifted off the ground by the stunning impact, and then suddenly – *whump* – the big hovercraft thudded back down to earth without any loss of speed.

Book was totally disoriented. He was trying to climb back into the driver's seat when another smashing impact rocked his hovercraft again, this time from the right.

'*Scarecrow!*' Book yelled.

' – *I'm in a lot of trouble here!*'

'I see you, Book! I see you! I'm coming!' Schofield peered out through the snow-streaked windshield of his own speeding hovercraft.

He saw Book's hovercraft, racing forward across the ice plain in front of him. On either side of it were two of the black British hovercrafts, taking turns in ramming it hard.

'Renshaw! How's that new Stinger coming?'

'Almost there . . .' Renshaw said from behind Schofield. He was furiously trying to jam a new tube into the gripstock.

'Hold on, Book!' Schofield said.

Schofield gunned the engine of his LCAC and the hovercraft responded by increasing its speed. Gradually, it began to haul in the three hovercrafts in front of it – Book's and the two British ones.

Slowly, gradually, Schofield's orange hovercraft overtook the three hovercrafts on the left-hand side and then suddenly, swiftly, it swept across in front of them.

Schofield looked back through his rear windshield, through the blur of his rear turbofan and saw the three hovercrafts behind him. Schofield then snapped to look forward and he saw Rebound's transport hovercraft racing across the ice plain about twenty yards to his left.

'Rebound!' Schofield said.

'*Yeah!*'

'Get ready to go in and grab Book!'

'*What?*'

'Just get ready!'

'*What are you gonna do?*'

'A slingshot,' Schofield said as he drew his MP-5. He turned to Renshaw. 'Mr Renshaw . . .'

'What?'

'Hold on.'

And with that, Schofield slipped the hovercraft into neutral and yanked the steering yoke hard to the right.

Like a bizarre two-ton ballet dancer, Schofield's hover-craft did a complete, lateral, one-hundred-and-eighty-degree spin *right in front* of Book's hovercraft and the two British hovercrafts.

In the cabin, Schofield quickly jammed the big vehicle into reverse and engaged the turbofan again.

Now he was travelling backwards!

At eighty miles per hour.

In front of Book and the two British hovercrafts!

Schofield thrust his MP-5 out through the driver's side window and let rip with an extended burst of gunfire.

The front windshield of the left-hand British hover-craft exploded with bulletholes. Schofield could see the men behind the windshield convulse as they were hit by the barrage of gunfire.

The shot British hovercraft immediately peeled away from Book's hovercraft and faded back into the distance.

Book was still in hell.

The British hovercraft to his left was gone now, but the one on his right was ramming him with renewed intensity.

The two hovercrafts careered across the flat expanse of ice, side-by-side, their engines roaring.

And then suddenly Book saw the side door of the British hovercraft open. A thick black gun barrel protruded from it.

'Oh, *shit*,' Book said.

A puff of smoke appeared from the end of the gun barrel – it was an M-60 grenade launcher – and a second later the whole side door of Book's hovercraft suddenly exploded inwards.

Wind rushed into the cabin.

They'd blown open the side of his hovercraft!

At that moment, a small, black object flew in through the hole in the side of the hovercraft and clattered across the floor of the cabin.

Book saw it immediately.

It was a small, black, cylindrical object with blue numbers written along its side. As it rolled across the floor of the cabin, it looked like an ordinary grenade, but as Book knew it was a whole lot more than that.

It was a nitrogen charge.

The signature weapon of the SAS.

The most advanced grenade in the world. It even had a tamper mechanism so that you couldn't pick it up and throw it back at the person who threw it at you. Standard time delay: five seconds.

Get out of the hovercraft! Book's mind screamed.

Book dived for the left-hand side of the cabin – the side farthest away from the British hovercraft – and reached for the door. He slid it open fast.

Five . . .

Freezing Antarctic wind rushed at his face. Slicing horizontal snow lashed his eyes. Book didn't care. Snow wouldn't kill him; and a fall from the hovercraft might. But the nitrogen charge definitely would.

Four . . . Three . . .

Book dived out into the freezing wind and immediately jammed the sliding door shut behind him. He lay flat against the top of the black rubber skirt that ran around the base of the speeding hovercraft. His face was pressed awkwardly up against the outside of the windows of the cabin. The screaming, speeding wind assaulted his ears.

Two . . . One . . .

Book prayed to God that the reinforced Lexan glass windows of the hovercraft could withstand the –

The nitrogen charge went off inside the hovercraft.

Smack!

A wave of ice-blue, liquid nitrogen slapped hard against the glass right in front of Book's face. Book instinctively jerked his head back.

He stared in amazement at the interior of the

hovercraft's cabin. Supercooled liquid nitrogen had splattered itself against every exposed surface inside the cabin.

Every exposed surface.

The whole of the inside of the window in front of him was dripping with gooey blue poxy. Book sighed with relief. The reinforced glass had held, just.

And then suddenly . . . *craaaaack* – !

Book pulled his head back just as the window – snap-frozen by the liquid nitrogen and contracting rapidly – broke out into a thousand spiderwebs.

'*Book!*'

Book spun and saw Rebound's hovercraft pull up alongside his own. He could see Rebound through the windscreen, sitting in the driver's seat.

'*Get on!*'

Rebound's hovercraft nudged closer to Book's. The side door of Rebound's hovercraft slid open. The rubber skirts of the two hovercrafts touched briefly, then parted again.

'*Jump!*' Rebound said, his voice loud in Book's earpiece.

Book tried to get to his feet.

'*Come on!*' Rebound said urgently.

Book tried to keep his eyes focused on the black rubber skirt of Rebound's hovercraft. Tried not to look at the white streaks of snow racing by at eighty miles an hour beneath the two speeding hovercrafts.

And then out of the corner of his eye, Book saw it.

Saw the black hovercraft materialize in the background behind Rebound's hovercraft.

Suddenly Book heard Rebound yell, '*Get there, Scare-crow!*' and then he saw the side door of the British hovercraft open. Saw the Milan anti-tank missile launcher appear inside it.

And then Book saw the familiar puff of smoke and he saw the missile shoot out of its launcher and fly through the air toward him, its looping white smoke trail spiralling crazily behind it, and in that instant, in that moment, Book knew it was too –

'*Book! For God's sake, jump! Jump now! Shit!*'

Book jumped.

Book flew through the air.

As he flew, out of the corner of his eye, he saw the British hovercraft explode as it was hit by an American Stinger. But it had got its own missile off before it had been hit. Book saw the white-tipped missile roll through the air toward him.

And then suddenly Book's hands came down hard on the black rubber skirt of Rebound's hovercraft and Book forgot about the British missile as he scratched desperately for a handhold.

Just as his feet were about to hit the speeding ground, Book got a grip on a tie-down stud on the skirt of Rebound's hovercraft and he looked up just in time to see the British missile slam into the rear of his recently abandoned hovercraft and blow it to smithereens.

'Have you got him?' Schofield said into his helmet mike.

Schofield was still racing along in front of Rebound's hovercraft – still travelling backwards. He could see Rebound's transport speeding across the ice plain behind him.

'*We got him,*' Rebound replied. '*He's inside.*'

'Good,' Schofield said.

It was then that Schofield heard the gunfire.

His head immediately snapped left and he saw them.

It was the same British hovercraft that had blasted open the side of Book's hovercraft. Only now it had a fearsome-looking General Purpose Machine Gun – or 'Gimpy' as it is known – sticking out of its open side door. The large, heavy-duty machine-gun was mounted on a tripod and Schofield saw a three-foot tongue of fire flare out from its barrel as it emitted a deafening, ungodly roar.

Rebound's hovercraft took the brunt of the machine gun's fury. Sparks and bulletholes and cracks and puncture marks burst out all over it.

A thin line of black smoke began to rise up from the rear of Rebound's hovercraft. The hovercraft visibly began to slow.

'*Scarecrow!*' Rebound yelled. '*We've got a serious problem here!*'

'I'm coming!' Schofield said.

'*I'm hit bad and slowing down! I need to offload some weight so I can maintain my speed!*'

Schofield was thinking fast. He was still travelling backwards across the ice plain. Rebound's hovercraft was off to his right, the British hovercraft off to his left.

At last, Schofield said, 'Mr Renshaw . . .'

'What?'

'Take the wheel.'

'*What?*' Renshaw said.

'It's just like driving a car, only with a little less responsiveness,' Schofield said.

Renshaw stepped into the driver's seat, took hold of the steering yoke.

'Now, shut your eyes,' Schofield said.

'Huh?'

'Just do it.' Schofield said as he calmly raised his MP-5 . . .

. . . *and blasted the forward windshield of his own hovercraft!*

Renshaw covered his eyes as shards of glass exploded out all around him. When he opened his eyes again he had a completely clear view of the two hovercrafts speeding along the ice plain 'behind' him.

'Okay,' Schofield said, 'pull us over in front of the black one.'

Renshaw gently applied pressure to the steering yoke. The hovercraft slid smoothly over to the left, so that it was in front of the black British hovercraft that was blasting away at Rebound's hovercraft.

'All right,' Schofield said. 'Hold it here.'

Schofield wrapped the shoulder strap of his MP-5 around his neck, and pulled the slide on his Desert Eagle automatic pistol, cocking it.

'All right, Mr Renshaw. Hit the brakes.'

Renshaw looked up at Schofield in surprise. 'What?'

And then he realized what Schofield was doing.

'Oh, no. You can't be serious – '

'Just do it,' Schofield said.

'All right . . .'

Renshaw shook his head, and then, after taking a deep breath, he jammed both of his feet down as hard as he could on the brake pedal of the hovercraft.

Schofield's hovercraft lost all of its forward momentum in an instant and the British hovercraft behind it slammed into it at full speed and the two hovercrafts collided nose-to-nose.

Renshaw braced himself for the impact and when it came, it jolted him back into his seat. When he looked up, however, he couldn't believe his eyes. He saw Schofield climbing out through the shattered forward windshield of their hovercraft and up onto its hood.

The two hovercrafts made for an incredible sight. They were now joined at their noses, both travelling forward. The only thing was, one was pointed forward while the other was pointing *backwards*.

In three fluid steps the small figure of Schofield danced across the forward hood of the leading orange hovercraft and leapt across onto the hood of the pursuing black hovercraft.

Schofield's feet pounded against the forward hood of the British hovercraft. Horizontal snow pelted against his back as he blasted away at the forward windshield of the British hovercraft with his MP-5. The windshield shattered and Schofield saw the driver go down in a fountain of blood.

But there were still two more men inside the cabin who any second now would be turning their guns on Schofield.

Schofield ran forward and leapt onto the roof of the speeding hovercraft just as a volley of bullets shot out from inside the cabin.

Schofield slid feet first across the roof of the British hovercraft. The left-hand door of the hovercraft was still open and Schofield rolled onto his stomach and reached over the edge of the roof with his MP-5 and jammed it in through the open side door. He pulled the trigger and fired blindly at his unseen enemy.

His MP-5 went dry, and Schofield listened and waited. If either of the two SAS commandos had survived his barrage of gunfire, then they would be up any second now.

No one came out of the hovercraft.

The deafening machine-gun fire from the tripod-mounted machine-gun had ceased. The only sound that Schofield heard was the whistling of the wind as it sped past his ears.

Schofield swung himself down and in through the open side door of the British hovercraft.

None of the SAS commandos had survived his assault. The three men all lay on the floor of the cabin, covered in blood.

Schofield stepped over to the driver's chair.

'Mr Renshaw, can you hear me?' he said.

*

Inside the orange French hovercraft, James Renshaw was gripping the steering yoke so hard his fingers were turning white. His hovercraft was still travelling backwards at incredible speed.

'Yeah, I hear you,' Renshaw said into his oversized helmet's microphone.

'*You're gonna have to swing her around,*' Schofield's voice said. '*I need you to help Rebound. He needs to offload some of his people so he can maintain a decent speed. I need you to take a couple of people off his hovercraft.*'

'I can't do that!' Renshaw said. 'You do it.'

'*Mr Renshaw . . .*'

'All right. All right.'

Schofield's voice said, '*Now, do you want me to take you through it?*'

'No,' Renshaw said. 'I can do this.'

'*Then do it. I gotta go,*' Schofield's voice said quickly. And with that, Renshaw saw Schofield's newly acquired black British hovercraft peel off to the left, and head towards Rebound's wounded hovercraft.

'All right,' Renshaw said to himself as he gripped the steering yoke even more firmly in his hands. 'I can do this. I saw him do it before, it can't be that hard. Slingshot . . .'

Renshaw slipped the hovercraft into neutral and he felt the big vehicle lose a little bit of speed.

'Okay,' he said. 'Here we go . . .'

Renshaw yanked his steering yoke hard to the right.

The hovercraft immediately spun laterally on its axis

and Renshaw yelled 'Aaaahhhhh!!' as the whole vehicle snapped around in a sharp one-eighty and then all of a sudden it was facing forward again and Renshaw jammed the steering yoke back in the other direction and suddenly the vehicle was steady again and – good God – travelling forward.

Renshaw was stunned. He jammed the hovercraft back into high gear.

'Holy *shit*,' he said. 'I did it. I *did* it!'

'*Congratulations, Mr Renshaw*,' Schofield's voice said in Renshaw's ear. '*I've seen kids on snowbikes do better slingshots than that. Now, if you don't mind, would you kindly shut up and get your ass over here. Rebound needs our help.*'

Schofield's hovercraft came alongside Rebound's.

Both hovercrafts looked like hell. Rebound's was pockmarked all over with bulletholes. Schofield's had no front windshield.

The three remaining British hovercrafts circled all around them, cut across in front of them, swung in behind them.

Schofield brought his hovercraft closer to Rebound's, so that his open left-side door was directly opposite Rebound's open right-side door.

Schofield yelled, 'Okay! Send two of your passengers over to me! Renshaw'll be over in a second! He can take two more!'

'*Ten-four, Scarecrow*,' Rebound's voice replied.

Schofield hit the cruise control button on his dashboard and hurried back into the cabin of the hovercraft. He came to the open side door and looked across the gap between the two speeding hovercrafts. He saw Book standing in the doorway of the speeding white hovercraft, eight feet away. He had Kirsty with him.

'Okay!' Schofield yelled into his helmet mike as Rebound brought his hovercraft closer. 'Send her over!'

Book edged out onto the skirt of his hovercraft, gently bringing Kirsty with him. The little girl looked scared to death as she stepped out into the freezing, speeding wind.

Schofield ventured out onto his own skirt, his arms outstretched.

'Come on, honey!' he called. 'You can do it!'

Kirsty tentatively stepped forward.

The ground raced by beneath them.

'Reach out! Reach out! And jump now!' Schofield yelled. 'I'll catch you!'

Kirsty jumped.

A timid, little girl's jump.

Schofield lunged forward and clutched hold of her parka and pulled her inside the cabin of his speeding black hovercraft.

Once they were safely inside, he asked, 'Are you okay?'

As Kirsty opened her mouth to answer him, the whole hovercraft was rocked by a ferocious impact. Schofield and Kirsty were both thrown against the frame of the open doorway. Kirsty screamed as she fell out

411

through the doorway, but Schofield threw out his hand and snatched her gloved hand just in time.

They'd been rammed from the right. Schofield snapped round to see what had hit them.

Another British hovercraft.

Schofield pulled Kirsty back inside the cabin, and braced himself for the next impact.

It never came.

Instead, the whole right-hand side of his hovercraft's cabin simply exploded inwards.

Kirsty screamed and Schofield dived on top of her, shielding her from the flying debris. Schofield tried to peer out through the smoke to see where the British hovercraft was, to see what its owners were doing.

But Schofield couldn't see the hovercraft.

He just saw smoke and haze.

And then, after a moment, Schofield heard the thud of feet landing on the skirt of his hovercraft and he felt a knot tighten in his stomach as he saw two wraith-like figures emerge from the smoke and enter his cabin with their guns raised.

The two SAS commandos emerged from the smoky haze. Schofield was on the ground, covering Kirsty, totally exposed.

'*Scarecrow! Duck!*' Book's voice shouted loudly in Schofield's ear.

Schofield ducked and immediately heard the sharp *whoosh! whoosh!* of two bullets flying low over his head and the first SAS man dropped like a stone – shot by Book, from the other hovercraft.

The second SAS commando was momentarily startled and that was all Schofield needed. He sprang to his feet like a cat and tackled the SAS man and both men went flying against the dashboard of the hovercraft.

The ensuing hand-to-hand fight was all one-way traffic.

The SAS guy was all over Schofield. One hit to his injured throat and Schofield couldn't breathe, another to the ribcage and Schofield heard one of his ribs snap. Schofield doubled over and the SAS man grabbed him by his collar and his belt and hurled him out through the destroyed forward windscreen of the speeding hovercraft.

Schofield thudded against the forward hood of the hovercraft. His body ached, he couldn't breathe. He coughed up blood as he looked up –

– just in time to see the SAS commando reach for his holster and draw his service pistol.

At the sight of the gun, suddenly Schofield's breath came back to him and everything became clear.

Speeding hovercraft.

Man, gun.

Certain death.

His body aching, Schofield rolled forward, toward the rounded bow of the hovercraft. The black rubber skirt dropped away in front of him. The ground rushed by beneath it at seventy miles an hour.

You are going to die . . .

Schofield found a handhold and quickly lowered his feet over the bow of the speeding hovercraft. His feet touched the speeding earth and skipped up off the surface.

The SAS man in the cabin seemed to be amused by what Schofield was doing, and he paused for a fraction of a second as he levelled his automatic pistol at Schofield's head.

Schofield – his face bruised, his teeth bloody, his body bent over the inflated skirt at the bow of the hovercraft – looked up at the SAS commando and smiled. He saw the SAS commando smile back at him. And then he saw him raise his gun a little higher.

At that moment, Schofield ducked his head beneath the skirt of the hovercraft. He heard the gun go off, heard the bullet ping off the top of the skirt.

Schofield was hanging off the bow of the speeding hovercraft now, pressing his body against the inflated rubber skirt. His feet were dragging on the ground as it rushed by beneath him at incredible speed.

Suddenly, he heard a sound and he looked up and saw the SAS man standing above him, on the forward hood of the hovercraft, looking down at him, with his gun still in his hand.

And as the SAS commando raised his gun to fire, Shane Schofield knew there was only one thing he could do. He released his grip on the inflated rubber skirt and disappeared under the bow of the hovercraft.

The sound of the turbofans was absolutely ear-shattering.

Schofield's helmet slammed down against the ground and Schofield slid on his back underneath the hovercraft.

The rush of air and the deafening roar of the four turbofans above him was like being in a wind tunnel. Schofield saw the inflated insides of the skirt, saw the rapidly rotating blades of the turbofans –

And then he shot out from underneath the speeding hovercraft, and the deafening roar of the turbofans was gone as Schofield slid on his back across the flat, icy plain *behind* the hovercraft he had been standing on only moments before.

Schofield didn't waste any time.

He rolled onto his stomach as he aquaplaned across the ice and in one swift movement, he pulled his Maghook from his belt and looked up at the rear of the hovercraft as it sped away from him. He raised the Maghook and fired.

The bulbous magnetic head of the Maghook flew through the air, its tail of rope unspooling wildly behind it. The magnet thudded into the metal wall of the cabin just above the hovercraft's skirt and stuck, and Schofield was suddenly yanked forward behind the speeding hovercraft.

He was now being dragged across the ice plain behind the speeding hovercraft, like a flailing waterskier trying desperately to get back on his feet again.

And then abruptly the ground all around Schofield was raked with gunfire.

Schofield spun to look behind him.

A second British hovercraft was *right behind him*!

It was bearing down on him, as if it were about to trample him.

Schofield rolled onto his back – holding onto his Maghook's launcher with one hand – as he was dragged behind the first hovercraft. With his free hand, he drew his Desert Eagle and fired back at the pursuing hovercraft. The Desert Eagle boomed, ripped open several holes in the skirt of the speeding hovercraft.

But the hovercraft didn't slow down.

It was almost on him.

It only had to get over him and then slow down slightly and then the hovercraft would lower itself and he would be chopped to shreds by the turbofans underneath it.

The turbofans underneath it . . .

Schofield desperately searched his brain for something – anything – anything that he could use to –

His helmet.

Still being dragged behind the first hovercraft, Schofield quickly holstered his gun and yanked off his helmet.

He would have to get this just right. It would have

to be *bouncing*, bouncing high, so that it would get caught up in the fan blades of the pursuing hovercraft.

Schofield tossed his helmet behind him.

The helmet flew threw the air – it seemed to float for an eternity – and then it bounced on its dome and then the pursuing hovercraft roared over the top of it.

Schofield guessed that the helmet must have bounced up into the forward fan of the hovercraft, because in that moment, in that sudden, shocking instant, the whole hovercraft just snapped over on itself and did a complete seventy-mile-an-hour cartwheel – it just flipped over on itself and came slamming down hard on its own cabin. The battered hovercraft slid across the flat icy ground – on its roof, right behind Schofield – for about fifty yards before it ground to a halt and shrank into the distance behind him.

Schofield rolled back over onto his stomach. His body bounced roughly on the hard, icy ground as it was dragged along behind the first hovercraft at phenomenal speed. Tiny flecks of kicked-up ice assaulted his silver, anti-flash glasses.

Then Schofield hit the black button on his Maghook – the button that reeled in the hook without demagnetizing it – and the Maghook began to reel itself in, drawing Schofield forward, toward the rear of the speeding hovercraft, until at last he reached the black rubber skirt. The wind from the hovercraft's rear turbofan blasted his face, but Schofield didn't care. He grabbed hold of a tie-down stud on top of the black rubber skirt and hauled himself up onto the hovercraft.

Five seconds later, he was standing in the open left-hand side doorway of the hovercraft. He got there just in time to see the SAS commando slap Kirsty hard across the face and send her crashing to the floor.

'*Hey!*' Schofield called.

The SAS man turned and saw him, and a sneer formed around his mouth.

'Kirsty,' Schofield said, never once taking his eyes off the British commando. 'Cover your eyes, honey.'

Kirsty covered her eyes.

The SAS commando stared at Schofield for a long moment. They just stood there, in the cabin of the speeding hovercraft, like two gunfighters facing off against each other on a deserted western street.

And then in a sudden blur of movement, the SAS man went for his gun.

Schofield went for his.

Both guns came up fast but only one went off.

'You can open your eyes now,' Schofield said, as he stepped forward – over the body of the dead SAS commando – and bent down beside Kirsty.

Slowly, Kirsty opened her eyes.

Schofield saw the bruise forming around her left cheekbone. 'Are you all right?' he said kindly.

'No,' she said, tears welling in her eyes. She pulled her asthma puffer out from her pocket and took two deep, sobbing puffs on it.

'Me neither,' Schofield said, taking the asthma puffer from her and gulping down a couple of puffs himself before putting the puffer in his pocket.

Then he stood up and grabbed the steering vane of the British hovercraft. As he drove, he popped the clip of his Desert Eagle and jammed in a fresh magazine.

Kirsty stepped up alongside him. 'When you . . . when you went under the hovercraft,' she said, 'I thought . . . I thought you were dead.'

Schofield jammed his pistol back into its holster and looked down at Kirsty. He saw the tears in her eyes.

As he looked down at her, Schofield realized that he was still wearing his silver anti-flash glasses. He took the silver glasses off, and crouched down in front of Kirsty.

'Hey,' he said. 'It's okay. It's all right. I'm not going to die on you. *I am not going to die on you.*' Schofield smiled. 'I mean, hey, I can't die. I'm the hero of this story.'

Despite herself, Kirsty smiled. Schofield smiled, too.

And then, to his surprise, Kirsty stepped forward and hugged him. Schofield returned her hug.

As he held her, though, he heard a strange noise. A noise that he had not heard before.

It was a loud, rhythmic, crashing noise.

Boom.

Boom.

Boom.

It sounded to Schofield like –

Like waves crashing on a beach.

With a sickening rush, Schofield realized where they were. They were near the cliffs. Their evasive manoeuvres during the hovercraft chase had taken them out near the sheer, three-hundred-foot cliffs that towered over the bay. The loud, booming noise that he was hearing was the sound of the mountainous waves of the ocean smashing against the ice cliffs.

Schofield was still holding Kirsty in his arms. As he held her, though, something behind her caught his eye.

Attached to the side of the British hovercraft's dashboard was a small compartment, mounted on the wall. Its door hung ajar. Inside the compartment, Schofield could see two, silver canisters. They were each about a foot long, and cylindrical in shape. Each silver canister had a wide, green band painted across its mid-section. Schofield saw some lettering stencilled onto the side of one of the silver canisters:

TRITONAL 80/20

Tritonal 80/20? Schofield thought. *Why on earth would the British bring that to Wilkes?*

Tritonal 80/20 was a highly concentrated, explosive poxy – a highly combustible liquid filler that was used in air-launched drop bombs. Tritonal wasn't nuclear, but when it blew, it blew big and it blew hot. One kilogram of the stuff – the amount contained in each of the canisters Schofield was now looking at – could level a small building.

Schofield released Kirsty gently, put his glasses back on and moved toward the compartment near the dashboard. He pulled one of the silver-and-green canisters from it.

He came back to Kirsty. 'Are you all right, now?'

'Yeah,' Kirsty said.

'Good,' Schofield said, sliding the Tritonal charge into one of his long, thigh pockets. 'Because I really have to get back to – '

Schofield never saw it coming.

The impact threw him off his feet.

His whole hovercraft lurched suddenly to the left.

Schofield looked out through the gaping hole in the right-hand side of his speeding hovercraft and saw one of the two remaining British hovercrafts racing across the ice plain right alongside him!

It rammed them again.

Hard.

So hard, in fact, that Schofield felt his hovercraft slide sideways, to the left.

'What the – ' Schofield said aloud.

He looked left and in a sudden terrifying instant he realized what they were doing.

'Oh, no,' he said. 'Oh, *no* . . .'

The British hovercraft rammed them again, and once again Schofield and Kirsty's hovercraft was pushed to the left.

Schofield looked out through his destroyed forward windshield and saw the flat ice plain stretching endlessly away from him. But off to the left, he saw that the flat ice plain ended abruptly. In fact, it looked as if it just fell away . . .

The cliffs.

With every impact, the British hovercraft was pushing Schofield and Kirsty closer to the edge.

They were trying to ram them off the cliff.

Schofield began to wrestle with the steering vane of his hovercraft, but it was no use.

There was nowhere he could go.

With no room to move – no room to get a run-up – he just found himself shunting the speeding British hovercraft ineffectually.

Schofield snapped to look forward again, and he saw the cliff edge racing by less than ten yards off to his left.

He caught a glimpse of tiny white-crested waves beyond the cliff edge. They were a *long* way down.

Jesus . . .

Suddenly another impact hit them and Schofield's hovercraft jolted further to the left, slid closer to the cliff edge.

The edge was barely eight yards away.

A few more hits, Schofield thought, and that would be it.

Schofield instinctively reached for his helmet mike to call for help. But it wasn't there. It had been attached to his helmet and he wasn't wearing his helmet anymore.

Shit.

No helmet. He couldn't get in contact with the others.

Another impact. Harder this time.

The hovercraft slid sideways again.

Five yards from the edge.

Schofield looked out to his right, out through the hole in the side of his speeding hovercraft, and saw the black British hovercraft whipping across the ice plain beside him. He saw it widen the gap between the two hovercrafts and then suddenly rush back in at them.

The two hovercrafts collided again and Schofield felt his hovercraft jolt another couple of yards towards the edge.

Two yards to go.

The two hovercrafts raced along the edge of the clifftop, three hundred feet above the churning white waves of the Southern Ocean.

Schofield was still watching the British hovercraft alongside him.

As it widened the gap between the two hovercrafts once more – like a boxer pulling his arm back in preparation for the next blow – suddenly Schofield saw another hovercraft materialize in the distance beyond the black British hovercraft.

Schofield blinked.

It was the orange French hovercraft.

The orange hovercraft? Schofield thought.

But the only person in that hovercraft was . . .

Renshaw.

Schofield saw the gaudy orange hovercraft pull alongside the speeding British hovercraft. Now there were three hovercrafts travelling side-by-side along the edge of the ice cliff!

Suddenly, the British hovercraft rammed them again and the skirt of Schofield's hovercraft jutted out over the edge of the cliff. Large chunks of snow were thrown off the edge. They became tiny specks of white as they disappeared into the churning foam of the sea three hundred feet below.

'Come on,' Schofield suddenly grabbed Kirsty's hand.

'What are we – '

'We're leaving,' Schofield said.

Schofield pulled Kirsty over to the gaping hole in the right-hand side of his hovercraft.

He saw the British hovercraft pull away from them again, preparing itself for the killing blow.

Schofield swallowed. He would have to time this just right . . .

He drew his Desert Eagle pistol.

The British hovercraft rushed in toward them.

The two hovercrafts collided and in that instant, Schofield leapt across onto the skirt of the British hovercraft, pulling Kirsty with him.

They landed on the skirt of the speeding British hovercraft just as their own went careering off the edge of the cliff. The empty hovercraft rolled through the air for an instant before it plummeted three hundred feet straight down. It hit the water with a stunning impact and smashed into a thousand pieces.

Schofield and Kirsty never stopped moving.

They skipped across the roof of the British hovercraft and as they did so, Schofield pointed his pistol straight down and fired three quick shots into the roof beneath him and then suddenly they were on the *other* side of the hovercraft and Schofield could see Renshaw's hovercraft in front of them.

The orange hovercraft swung in closer just as Schofield and Kirsty leapt off the skirt of the British hovercraft. They landed safely on the skirt of Renshaw's hovercraft and it instantly peeled away from the black British hovercraft.

Schofield looked back at the British hovercraft – saw a star of blood on the forward windshield. Someone inside the hovercraft was still moving, clambering forward in an attempt to grab the steering vane.

Schofield figured that he must have hit the driver and

now whoever was still in there was desperately trying to regain control of the –

Too late.

The British hovercraft looked like a stunt car leaping off a ramp as it shot off the edge of the cliff. It sailed through the air for a moment – soaring high – before gravity took its course and the hovercraft began to arc downwards. Schofield caught a fleeting glimpse of the man inside it as the hovercraft dropped below the edge of the clifftop and disappeared forever.

Schofield turned to see the sliding side door of the orange hovercraft open in front of him and he saw Renshaw's smiling face appear.

'Can I drive this thing or what?' Renshaw said.

Now there was only one British hovercraft remaining. Outnumbered now by two-to-one it kept its distance.

Schofield grabbed Renshaw's Marine helmet and put it on. He keyed the helmet mike. 'Rebound, you still out there?'

'*Yeah.*'

'Is everyone okay?'

'*More or less.*'

'What about the hovercraft?' Schofield asked.

'*She's a bit beat up, but she's okay. We've got full power again,*' Rebound's voice said.

'Good,' Schofield said. 'Good. Listen, if we take care of this last guy, do you think you can get a head start and make it to McMurdo?'

'*We'll get there.*'

'All right, then,' Schofield said as he looked down at Kirsty. 'Stand by. You're about to get another passenger.'

Schofield got Renshaw to pull his hovercraft alongside Rebound's transport. He wanted to put Kirsty on the transport and then send it on its way to McMurdo, while he and Renshaw took care of the last British hovercraft.

428

The two speeding hovercrafts came together.

Both side doors slid open.

Book appeared in the side door of Rebound's transport craft. Schofield stood with Kirsty in the door of the orange French hovercraft opposite him.

The last British hovercraft hovered ominously behind them, two hundred yards astern.

'*Okay, let's go,*' Book's voice said in Schofield's earpiece.

Schofield said to Kirsty, 'You ready?'

'Uh-huh,' she said.

They stepped out onto the skirt together.

In the cabin of the transport craft, Rebound was keeping a wary eye on the British hovercraft.

It just seemed to sit there, watching them.

'What are you doing, you son of a bitch?' Rebound said aloud.

Book yelled, '*Okay, send her over!*'

Schofield and Kirsty edged forward, toward the edge of their hovercraft's skirt. The wind buffeted them relentlessly.

On the other skirt in front of them, Book reached out for Kirsty's outstretched hands. Schofield held her from behind. The transfer was almost complete –

And then suddenly Rebound's voice burst across their helmet intercoms, '*Oh, fuck! It just launched!*'

Schofield and Book both snapped around at the same time.

They saw the smoke trail first.

It spiralled through the air. A thin, white, vapour trail.

And in front of it – a missile.

Its source – the last British hovercraft.

It was another Milan anti-tank missile, and it stayed low, close to the ground. It rocketed through the air, covering the distance between them fast, and then suddenly, with shocking intensity, it slammed into the back of Schofield's orange hovercraft and detonated.

The hovercraft jolted ferociously with the impact and Schofield lost his grip on Kirsty and fell back into his hovercraft's cabin. As he fell backwards he looked up and the last thing he saw before he hit the floor of the cabin was a fleeting glimpse of Book – lunging forward, off balance – desperately trying to get hold of Kirsty's hands as she fell down in between the two speeding hovercrafts.

Book and Kirsty fell.

The black rubber skirt of one of the hovercrafts filled Book's field of vision as he tumbled down between the two hovercrafts.

He held Kirsty by the hand, and as they fell, he pulled her close to his body and rolled in the air so that when they hit the ground, he would take the brunt of the fall.

And then suddenly, concussively, they hit the speeding ground.

'Book is down! Book is down!' Rebound's voice yelled loudly in Schofield's earpiece. *'The little girl fell with him!'*

Schofield's hovercraft shot across the ice plain, totally out of control.

The missile's impact to the rear of the hovercraft had destroyed its rear fan and half its tail rudder, causing the hovercraft to fishtail wildly and shoot left – *and head straight for the cliff edge.*

Renshaw grappled desperately with the steering yoke, but with its tail rudder half-destroyed, the hovercraft would only turn *left*. Renshaw heaved on the steering yoke and gradually, the hovercraft began to turn in a slow, wide arc so that it was now careering across the clifftops *back* toward Wilkes Ice Station!

'Rebound!' Schofield yelled into his helmet mike, ignoring Renshaw's efforts to keep control of the hovercraft.

'*What?*'

'Get out of here!'

'*What!*'

Schofield said fiercely, 'We've been hit bad over here! We're fucked, our game's over. Go! Get to McMurdo! Get help! You're the only chance we've got!'

'*But what about –*'

'Go!'

'*Yes, sir.*'

At that moment, Renshaw said, 'Ah, Lieutenant . . .'

Schofield wasn't listening. He was watching Rebound's hovercraft as it sped away in the other direction, into the driving snow.

Then Schofield looked out through the side window of his destroyed hovercraft and saw in the distance, a small, dark lump on the ice plain.

Book and Kirsty.

'Lieutenant . . .'

Schofield saw the last British hovercraft approach Book and Kirsty, saw it slow to a halt beside Book's doubled-over body. Black-clad men got out of the hovercraft.

Schofield just stared. 'Damn.'

Beside him, Renshaw was wrestling with the steering yoke. 'Lieutenant! *Hold on!*'

At that moment, as Renshaw pulled on it, the steering yoke snapped and broke and suddenly the hovercraft spun laterally to the left and performed a slingshot, and in an instant Schofield and Renshaw were travelling backwards again.

'What the hell are you doing!' Schofield yelled.

'I was *trying* to avoid *that*!' Renshaw yelled as he pointed out through the destroyed rear end of the hovercraft – the end that was now their *leading* edge.

Schofield followed Renshaw's finger and his eyes widened.

They were hurtling – in reverse – towards the edge of the cliff.

'Why can't this *fucking* day just end,' Schofield said.

'I think it's about to,' Renshaw said flatly.

Schofield shoved Renshaw out of the driver's seat and slid into it. He began to pump the brake pedal.

No response.

The hovercraft continued to rush toward the edge.

'I *tried* that!' Renshaw said. 'No brakes!'

The hovercraft raced toward the cliff edge, travelling backwards, totally out of control.

Schofield grabbed the broken steering vane. No steering, either.

They would have to jump –

But the thought came too late.

The cliff edge rushed toward them, too fast.

And then all of a sudden they ran out of ground and Schofield felt his stomach lurch sickeningly as the hovercraft shot out from the clifftop and flew out at incredible speed into the clear, open sky.

SIXTH INCURSION

16 June 1635 hours

The hovercraft fell through the air, rear-end first.

Inside the cabin, Schofield snapped around in his chair to look out through the shattered forward windshield of the hovercraft. He saw the cliff edge high above him getting smaller and smaller as it got farther and farther away.

In the seat beside him, Renshaw was hyperventilating. 'We're gonna die. We are *really* gonna die.'

The hovercraft went vertical – its tail pointing down, its nose pointing up – and suddenly Schofield saw nothing but sky.

They were falling fast.

Through the side window of the hovercraft, Schofield saw the vertical cliff face streaking past them at phenomenal speed.

Schofield grabbed his Maghook and put his nose in Renshaw's face, silencing him. 'Grab my waist and don't let go.'

Renshaw stopped his whimpering and stared at Schofield for a second. Then he quickly wrapped his arms around Schofield's waist. Schofield raised his Maghook above his head and fired it up through the destroyed forward windshield of the falling hovercraft.

The Maghook shot through the air in a high arc – its steel grappling hook snapping open in mid-flight, its rope splaying out in a crazy, wobbling line behind it.

The hook came down hard on the edge of the cliff-top and then slid quickly backwards toward the edge, its claws digging into the snow.

The hovercraft continued to fall through the air, rear-end first. The grappling hook found a purchase on the clifftop and suddenly it snapped to a halt and held, and its rope went instantly taut –

– and Schofield and Renshaw – at the other end of the rope – suddenly shot up out of the falling hovercraft.

The hovercraft fell away beneath them – fell and fell – before it smashed loudly against the white-tipped waves, one hundred and fifty feet below them.

Schofield and Renshaw swung back in toward the cliff face. The hovercraft had launched itself a good distance from the cliff, so they had a long way to swing back, and when they hit the cliff face, they hit it hard.

The impact with the cliff jarred Renshaw's grip on Schofield's waist and he fell for an instant, grabbing Schofield's right foot at the very last moment.

The two men hung there for a full minute, halfway down the sheer vertical cliff face, neither one of them daring to move.

'You still there?' Schofield asked.

'Yeah,' Renshaw said, petrified.

'All right, I'm going to try and reel us up, now,' Schofield said, shifting his grip on his launcher slightly so that he could press down on the black button that reeled in the rope without collapsing the grappling hook.

Schofield looked up at the cliff edge high above them. It must have been at least a hundred and fifty feet away. Schofield figured he must be hanging at the full length of his Maghook's rope –

It was then that Schofield saw him.

A man. Standing up on the clifftop, peering out over the edge, looking down at Schofield and Renshaw.

Schofield froze.

The man was wearing a black balaclava.

And he was holding a machine-gun in his hand.

'Well?' Renshaw said from down near Schofield's feet. 'What are you waiting for?' From his position, Renshaw wasn't able to see the SAS commando up on the clifftop.

'We're not going up anymore,' Schofield said flatly, his eyes locked on the black-clad figure at the top of the cliff.

'We're not?' Renshaw said. 'What are you talking about?'

The SAS commando was looking directly down at Schofield now.

Schofield swallowed. Then he glanced down at the smashing waves a hundred and fifty feet below him. When he looked up again, the SAS commando was pulling a long, glistening knife from its sheath. The commando then bent down over the Maghook's rope at the top of the cliff.

'Oh, no,' Schofield said.

'Oh, no what?' Renshaw said.

'Are you ready to go for a ride?'

'No,' Renshaw said.

Schofield said, 'Breathe all the way down, and then at the last second, take a deep breath.' That was what they told you when you jumped out of a moving helicopter into water. Schofield figured the same principle applied here.

Schofield looked up again at the SAS commando at the top of the cliff. He was about to cut the rope.

'All right,' Schofield said. 'Let's cut the crap. I'll be damned if I'm gonna wait for *you* to cut my rope. Renshaw, are you ready? We're going.'

And at that moment, Schofield pressed down twice on the trigger of the Maghook.

At the top of the cliff the claws of the grappling hook responded immediately and collapsed inward, and in doing so, they lost their purchase on the snow. The hook slithered out over the edge of the cliff, past the bewildered SAS commando, and Schofield, Renshaw and the Maghook fell – together – down the cliff face and into the crashing waves of the Southern Ocean below.

In the silence of the ice cavern, Libby Gant just stared at the semi-eaten bodies that lay draped over the rocks in front of her.

Since they had arrived in the cavern about forty minutes ago, the others – Montana, Santa Cruz and Sarah Hensleigh – had barely even looked at the bodies. They were all totally engrossed in the big, black spacecraft on the other side of the underground cavern. They walked around it, under it, peered at its black metal wings, tried to look in through the smoked-glass canopy of its cockpit.

After Schofield had informed Gant of the impending arrival of the British troops and his own plan to flee, she had set up two MP-5s on tripods, facing the pool at the end of the cavern. If the SAS tried to enter the cavern, she would pick them off one-by-one as they broke the surface.

That had been half an hour ago.

Even if the SAS had arrived at Wilkes Ice Station by now, it would still take them another hour to lower someone down in the diving bell and a further hour to swim up the underwater ice tunnel to the cavern.

It was a waiting game now.

After Gant had set up the tripods, Montana and Sarah Hensleigh had gone back to examining the spacecraft. Santa Cruz had stayed with Gant a while longer, but soon he, too, went back over to look at the fantastic black ship.

Gant stayed with the guns.

As she sat there on the cold, icy floor of the cavern, she gazed at the dismembered bodies on the far side of the pool. The amount of damage that had been done to the bodies had stunned her. Heads and limbs missing; whole sections of flesh literally *chewed* to the bone; the whole scene itself soaked in blood.

What on earth could have done it? Gant thought.

As she thought about the bodies, Gant's gaze wandered over to the pool. She saw the round holes in the ice walls above it – the enormous, ten-foot holes. They were identical to the ones she had seen in the underwater ice tunnel on the way here.

Gant had a strange feeling about those holes, about the bodies, about the cave itself. It was almost as if the cave were some kind of –

'This is absolutely *incredible*,' Sarah Hensleigh said as she came over and stood beside Gant. Hensleigh hurriedly brushed a strand of long, dark hair from her face. She was practically brimming with excitement at the discovery of the spaceship.

'It has no markings on it whatsoever,' she said. 'The whole ship is completely and utterly *black*.'

Gant didn't care much for Sarah Hensleigh right

now. In fact, she didn't care much for the spaceship, either.

In fact, the more she thought about it – about the spaceship and the cavern and the half-eaten bodies and the SAS up in the station – Gant couldn't help but think that there was no way in the world that she would ever be leaving Wilkes Ice Station alive.

The SAS team's entry into Wilkes Ice Station was fast and fluid – professional.

Black-clad men charged into the station with their guns up. They fanned out quickly, moved in pairs. They opened every door, checked every room.

'A-deck, *clear*!' one voice yelled.

'B-deck, *clear*!' another voice yelled.

Trevor Barnaby strode out onto the A-deck catwalk and surveyed the abandoned station like a newly crowned king looking out over his domain. Barnaby looked down upon the station with a cold, even gaze. A thin smile creased his face.

The SAS troops made their way down to E-deck, where they found Snake and the two French scientists handcuffed to the pole. Two SAS commandos covered them while more black-clad troops poured down the rung-ladders and disappeared inside the tunnels of E-deck.

Four SAS commandos raced into the south tunnel. Two took the doors to the left. Two took the doors to the right.

The two on the right came to the first door, kicked it in, looked inside.

A storeroom. Battered wooden shelves. Some scuba-diving tanks on the floor.

But empty.

They moved down the corridor, guns up. It was then that one of them saw the dumb waiter, saw the two stainless steel doors glistening in the cold white light of the tunnel.

With a short whistle, the lead SAS man caught the attention of the other two commandos in the tunnel. He pointed with two fingers at the dumb waiter. The other two men understood instantly. They positioned themselves on either side of the dumb waiter while the leader and the fourth SAS commando aimed their guns at the stainless steel doors.

The leader nodded quickly and the two men on either side of the dumb waiter instantly yanked it open, and the leader let rip with a sudden burst of gunfire.

The bare walls of the empty dumb waiter were instantly ripped to shreds.

Mother squeezed her eyes shut as the SAS commando's gunfire roared loudly less than a foot above her head.

She was sitting in complete darkness, at the base of the dumb waiter's miniature elevator shaft, curled up in a tight ball, in the crawlspace *underneath* the dumb waiter.

The dumb waiter shuddered and shook under the

weight of the SAS commando's gunfire. Its walls blew out, and jagged, splintered holes appeared all over it. Dust and wood shavings showered down on Mother, but she just kept her eyes firmly shut.

And then at that moment, as the gunfire echoed loudly in her ears, a jarring thought hit Mother.

They could fire their guns safely inside the station again . . .

The amount of flammable gas in the station's atmosphere must have dissipated –

And then abruptly the gunfire ceased and the doors of the dumb waiter closed and all of a sudden there was silence again and for the first time in three whole minutes, Mother let out a breath.

Schofield and Renshaw plummeted down the face of the cliff and plunged into the ocean.

The cold hit them like an anvil, but Schofield didn't care. His adrenalin was pumping and his body heat was already high. Most experts would give you about eight minutes to live in the freezing Antarctic waters. But with his thermal wetsuit on and his adrenalin pumping, Schofield gave himself at least thirty.

He swam upward, searching for air and then suddenly he broke the surface and the first thing he saw was the largest wave he had ever seen in his life bearing down upon him. The wave crashed down against him and drove him – *slammed* him – back against the base of the ice cliff.

The impact knocked the wind out of him and Schofield's lungs clawed for air.

Suddenly the wave subsided and Schofield felt himself get sucked down into a trough between two waves. He let himself float in the water for a few seconds while he got his breath and his bearings.

The sea around him was absolutely mountainous. Forty-foot waves surrounded him. A mammoth wave smashed into the cliffs twenty yards to his right. Icebergs – some as tall and as wide as New York skyscrapers; others as long and flat as football fields – hovered a hundred yards off the coast, silent sentries guarding the ice cliffs.

Suddenly Renshaw burst up out of the water right next to Schofield. The short scientist immediately began gulping in air in hoarse, heaving breaths. For an instant, Schofield worried about how Renshaw would cope with the extreme cold of the water, but then he remembered Renshaw's neoprene bodysuit. Hell, Renshaw was probably warmer than he was.

At that moment Schofield saw another towering wave coming toward them.

'Go under!' he yelled.

Schofield took a deep breath and dived, and suddenly the world went eerily silent.

He swam downwards; saw Renshaw swimming alongside him, hovering in the water.

And then Schofield saw an explosion of white foam fan out above their heads as the wave on the surface crashed with all its might against the cliff.

Schofield and Renshaw surfaced again.

As he bobbed and swayed in the water, Schofield saw the entire side door of a hovercraft float past him in the water.

'We have to get further out,' Schofield said. 'If we stay here any longer, we're gonna get pulverized against these cliffs.'

'Where to?' Renshaw said.

'Okay,' Schofield said. 'See that iceberg out there?' He pointed at a large berg that looked like a grand piano on its side, about two hundred yards out from the cliffs.

'I see it.'

'That's where we're going,' Schofield said.

'All right.'

'Okay, then. On three. One. Two. Three.'

On three, both men drew deep breaths and went under. They kicked off the cliff and breaststroked their way through the clear Antarctic water. Explosions of white foam flared out above their heads as they made their way through the water.

Ten yards. Twenty.

Renshaw ran out of breath, surfaced, took a quick gulp of air and then went under again. Schofield did the same, clenching his teeth as he too ducked beneath the waves again. His newly broken rib burned with pain.

Fifty yards out and the two men broke the surface again. They were beyond the breaking waves now, so they stretched out into freestyle, powering over the vertiginous peaks of the towering forty-foot waves.

At last, they came to the base of the iceberg. It loomed above them, a wall of white, sheer in some places, beautifully curved and grooved in others. Magnificent, vaulted tunnels disappeared into the virgin ice.

The big berg levelled off at one point, descending to the ocean where it formed a kind of ledge. Schofield and Renshaw made for the ledge.

When they got there, they saw that the ledge was actually poised about three feet above the water.

'Push off my shoulder,' Schofield said.

Renshaw obeyed, and quickly hoisted his left foot onto Schofield's shoulder and pushed off it.

The little man's hands reached up and clasped the ice ledge and he awkwardly hauled himself up onto it. Then he lay flat on the edge of the ledge and reached back down for Schofield.

Schofield reached up and Renshaw began to haul him up out of the water. Schofield was almost on the ledge when suddenly, Renshaw's wet hands slipped off his wrist and Schofield fell clumsily back down into the water.

Schofield plunged underwater.

Silence. Total silence. Like the womb.

The blasting explosions of the waves crashing against the ice cliffs no longer assaulted his ears.

The massive white underbelly of the iceberg filled his vision. It stretched down and down until it disappeared into the cloudy depths of the ocean.

And then suddenly Schofield heard a sound and he snapped upright in the water. The sound travelled well in the water and he heard it clearly.

Vmmmmmm.

It was a low, droning, humming sound.

Vmmmmmm.

Schofield frowned. It sounded almost . . . *mechanical*. Like a motorized door opening somewhere. Somewhere close.

Somewhere . . . *behind* him.

Schofield spun around instantly.

And then he saw it.

It was so huge – so *monstrously* huge – that the mere sight of it sent Schofield's heart into overdrive.

It was just hovering there in the water.

Silent. *Huge*.

Looming over Schofield as he hovered in the water alongside the iceberg.

It must have been at least a hundred metres long, its hull black and round. Schofield saw the two horizontal stabilizing fins jutting out from either side of the conning tower, saw the cylindrical, snub nose of the bow and suddenly his heart was pumping very loudly inside his head.

Schofield couldn't believe his eyes.

He was looking at a submarine.

Schofield burst up out of the water.

'Are you all right?' Renshaw asked from up on the ledge.

'Not anymore,' Schofield said before he quickly took another breath and submerged again.

The world was silent again.

Schofield swam a little deeper and stared at the massive submarine in awe. It was about thirty yards away from him but he could see it clearly. The enormous submarine just sat there – completely submerged – hovering in the underwater silence like an enormous, patient leviathan.

Schofield looked it over, looked for the signature features.

He saw the narrow conning tower; saw the four torpedo ports on the bow. One of the torpedo ports, he saw, was in the process of opening. *Vmmmmm*.

And then Schofield saw the colours painted on the forward left-hand side of the bow – saw the three vertical shafts of colour – blue-white-red.

He was looking at the French flag.

*

Renshaw watched as Schofield burst up out of the water again.

'What *are* you doing down there?' he asked.

Schofield ignored him. Instead, he thrust his left arm out of the water and examined his watch.

The stopwatch read:

2:57:59

2:58:00

2:58:01

'Oh, Jesus,' Schofield said. 'Oh, *Jesus.*'

In the bedlam of the hovercraft chase, he had completely forgotten about the French warship hovering off the coast of Antarctica, waiting to fire its missiles at Wilkes Ice Station. Its codename, he recalled, was 'Shark'.

It was only now, though, that Schofield realized he had made a mistake. He had jumped to the wrong conclusion. 'Shark' wasn't a warship at all.

It was a submarine.

It was *this* submarine.

'Quickly,' Schofield said to Renshaw. 'Get me out.'

Renshaw thrust his hand down and Schofield clasped it firmly. Renshaw hauled Schofield up as quickly as he could. When he was high enough, Schofield grabbed hold of the ice ledge and hauled himself up onto it.

Renshaw had half-expected Schofield to drop down

onto the ice and catch his breath as he himself had done, but Schofield was up on his feet in an instant.

In fact, no sooner was he up on the ledge than he was running – no *sprinting* – out across the flat expanse of the iceberg.

Renshaw gave chase. He saw Schofield hurdle an ice-mound as he bounded for the edge of the iceberg about thirty metres away. There was a slight incline which Schofield ran up, toward the edge of the iceberg. On the other side of the incline, Renshaw saw, was a sheer ten-metre drop down to the water below.

As he ran, Schofield checked his stopwatch. The seconds continued to tick upward, toward the three-hour mark.

Toward firing time.

2:58:31

2:58:32

2:58:33

Schofield was thinking as he ran.

It's going to destroy the station. Destroy the station.

Going to kill my Marines. Kill the little girl . . .

Got to stop it.

But how? How does a man destroy a submarine?

And then suddenly he remembered something.

He unshouldered his Maghook as he ran. Then he quickly hit the button marked 'M' and saw the red light on the Maghook's magnetically charged head come to life.

Then he pulled a silver canister from his thigh pocket. It was the foot-long, silver canister with the green band painted around it that he had found inside the British hovercraft.

The Tritonal 80/20 high-powered explosive charge.

Schofield looked at the silver-and-green canister as he ran. It had a stainless-steel pneumatic lid on it. He turned the lid and heard a soft *hiss!* The lid popped open and he saw a familiar digital timing display next to an 'ARM-DISARM' switch. Since it was a demolition device, a Tritonal charge could be disarmed at any time.

Twenty seconds, he thought. *Just enough time to get clear.*

He set the timer on the Tritonal charge for twenty seconds and then held the silver canister out above the bulbous magnetic head of his Maghook. Immediately the steel cylinder thunked down hard against the powerful magnet, and stuck to it, caught in its vice-like magnetic grip.

Schofield was still running hard, sprinting across the rugged landscape of the iceberg.

Then he came to the edge of the iceberg and without so much as a second thought, he hit it at full speed and leapt off it, out into the air.

Schofield flew through the air in a long wide arc – hung there for a full three seconds – before he splashed down hard, feet first, into the freezing-cold water of the Southern Ocean one more time.

*

Bubbles flew up all around him and for a moment Schofield saw nothing. And then suddenly the bubbles cleared and Schofield found himself hovering in the water *right in front of* the gargantuan steel nose of the French submarine.

Schofield checked his watch.

2:58:59

2:59:00

2:59:01

One minute to go.

The outer doors of the torpedo tube were fully open now. Schofield swam toward it. The torpedo tube opened wide in front of him, ten yards away.

This had better work, Schofield thought as he raised his Maghook, with the Tritonal charge attached to its head. Schofield pressed the 'ARM-DISARM' switch on the Tritonal charge.

Twenty seconds.

Schofield fired the Maghook.

The Maghook shot out from its launcher, leaving a thin trail of white bubbles in its wake. It sliced through the water toward the open torpedo port . . .

. . . and hit the steel hull of the submarine just *below* the torpedo port with a loud, metallic *clunk*! The Maghook – with the live Tritonal charge attached to it – bounced off the thick steel hull of the sub and began to sink limply into the water.

Schofield couldn't believe it.

He'd missed!

Shit! his mind screamed. And then suddenly another thought hit him.

The people inside the sub would have heard it. Must have heard it.

Schofield quickly hit the black button on his grip that reeled the Maghook in, hoped to hell that it got back to him before twenty seconds expired.

Have to get another shot.

Have got to get another shot.

The Maghook began to reel itself in.

And then suddenly Schofield heard another noise.

Vmmmmmm.

Off to Schofield's left, on the other side of the bow, one of the other torpedo doors was opening!

This door was smaller than the one Schofield had tried to shoot his Maghook into.

Smaller torpedoes, Schofield thought. *Ones that are designed to kill other subs, not whole ice stations.*

And then with a sudden *whoooosh!* a compact white torpedo whizzed out from the newly opened torpedo port and rolled through the water toward Schofield.

Schofield couldn't believe it.

They had fired a torpedo at him!

The Maghook returned to its launcher and Schofield quickly pressed the 'ARM-DISARM' switch on the Tritonal charge – with four seconds to spare – just as the torpedo shot past his waist, its wash knocking him over in the water.

Schofield breathed with relief. He was too close. The torpedo hadn't had time to get a lock on him.

It was then that the torpedo slammed into the iceberg behind Schofield and detonated hard.

Renshaw was standing on the edge of the iceberg, looking down into the water when the torpedo hit, about twenty yards away.

In an instant, a whole segment of the iceberg exploded in a cloud of white and just fell away into the ocean like a landslide, cut clean from the rest of the massive berg.

'Yikes,' Renshaw breathed in awe.

And then suddenly he saw Schofield surface about twenty yards out, saw him gulp in a lungful of air, and then he saw the Lieutenant go under again.

With the sound of the torpedo's explosion still reverberating through the water all around him, and a large slice of the iceberg plunging into the water behind him, Schofield aimed his Maghook at the torpedo port a second time.

2:59:37

2:59:38

2:59:39

Once again, Schofield pressed the arm switch on the Tritonal charge – *twenty seconds* – and fired.

The Maghook shot through the water . . .

. . . hung there for a long time . . .

. . . and then disappeared inside the torpedo port.

Yes!

Schofield quickly pressed the button marked 'M' on his grip and inside the torpedo tube the magnetic head of the Maghook responded immediately by releasing its grip on the silver-and-green Tritonal charge.

Then Schofield reeled in the Maghook, leaving the Tritonal charge *inside* the torpedo tube.

And then Schofield swam.

Swam for all he was worth.

Inside the torpedo room of the French submarine, the world was deathly silent. A young ensign called the countdown.

'*Vingt secondes de premier lancer*,' he said. Twenty seconds to primary launch. Twenty seconds to the launch of the eraser, a nuclear-tipped, Neptune-class torpedo.

'*Dix-neuf . . . dix-huit . . . dix-sept . . .*'

From the iceberg Renshaw saw Schofield break the surface, saw him swimming frantically through the water, Maghook in hand.

The French ensign's count continued. '*Dix . . . neuf . . . huit . . . sept . . .*'

*

Schofield was swimming hard, trying to put as much distance between himself and the sub as he could, because if he was too close when the Tritonal charge went off, the implosion would suck him right in. He'd been ten yards away when he'd fired the Tritonal charge. Now he was twenty yards away. He figured twenty-five and he would be okay.

Renshaw was yelling at him, 'What the hell is happening!'

'Get away from the edge!' Schofield yelled as he swam. 'Move!'

'*Cinq . . . quatre . . . trois . . .*'

The French ensign's count never got beyond 'three'.

Because at that moment – at that terrible, stunning moment – the Tritonal charge inside the torpedo tube suddenly went off.

From where Renshaw stood, the underwater explosion was absolutely spectacular, and all the more so because it was unexpected.

It was instantaneous. The dark shadow under the surface that was the French submarine spontaneously erupted into an enormous cloud of white. An immense spray of water fifty feet high and two hundred feet long shot up out of the water and fell slowly back down to earth.

*

From water-level, Schofield saw a hoard of monstrous blue bubbles suddenly begin to billow out from a gaping hole in the bow of the submarine, like tentacles reaching out for him. And then just as suddenly they began to retrace their steps and, with terrifying force, the bubbles *shot back in toward the submarine* and Schofield suddenly felt himself getting sucked back toward the sub.

Implosion.

At that moment, the massive French sub collapsed in on itself like a great big aluminium can and the suction from the implosion ceased. Schofield felt the water's grip on him relax and he let himself float to the surface. The submarine was gone.

A few minutes later, Renshaw pulled Schofield out of the water and dragged him up onto the iceberg.

Schofield dropped down onto the ice – breathing hard, soaking wet, freezing cold. He was gasping for breath, his body overwhelmed with fatigue, and at that moment – with the French submarine destroyed, and himself and Renshaw hopelessly marooned on an iceberg – the only thing in the world that Shane Schofield wanted to do was sleep.

In the Capitol Building in Washington D.C., the NATO conference reconvened.

George Holmes, the US representative, leaned back in his chair as he watched Pierre Dufresne, the head of the French delegation stand to speak.

'My fellow delegates, ladies and gentlemen,' Dufresne began, 'the Republic of France would like to express its total and unconditional support for the North Atlantic Treaty Organization, this fine organization of nations that has served the West so well for almost fifty years . . .'

The speech dragged on, extolling the virtues of NATO and France's undying loyalty to it. George Holmes shook his head. All morning, the French delegation had been calling recesses, stalling the conference, and now, all of a sudden, they were pledging their undying loyalty to the Organization. It didn't make sense.

Dufresne finished speaking, sat down. Holmes was about to turn and say something to Phil Munro when suddenly the British delegate to the conference – a well-groomed statesman named Richard Royce – pushed his chair back and stood up.

'Ladies and gentlemen,' Royce said, in a very articulate, London accent, 'if I may beg your indulgence, the British delegation requests a recess.'

At that very same moment, directly across the road from the Capitol Building and the NATO conference, Alison Cameron was entering the atrium of the Library of Congress.

Comprised of three buildings, the Library of Congress is the largest library in the world. In fact, its goal upon its founding was to be the single largest repository of knowedge in the world. That is what it is.

Which was why Alison was not surprised to learn that the object of her search – the mysterious 1978 'Preliminary Survey' by C.M. Waitzkin – was to be found at the Library of Congress. If any library was going to have it, the Library of Congress would be it.

Alison waited at the Enquiries Desk as one of the library's attendants went down to the Stack to get the survey for her. The Library of Congress was a closed-stack library, which meant that the staff got the books for you. It was also a non-circulating library, which meant that you were not allowed to take books out of the building.

The attendant was taking a while, so Alison began to browse through another book she had bought on the way to the Library.

She looked at the cover. It read:

THE ICE CRUSADE:
REFLECTIONS ON A YEAR SPENT IN ANTARCTICA

DR BRIAN HENSLEIGH
Professor Emeritus in Geophysics. Harvard University

Alison scanned the introduction.

Brian Hensleigh, it appeared, was the head of Harvard University's Geophysics faculty. He was into ice core research – a study that involved extracting cylindrical ice cores from the continental ice shelves in Antarctica and then examining the air that had been trapped inside those ice cores thousands of years before.

Apparently, so the book said, ice core research could be used to explain global warming, the greenhouse effect and the depletion of the ozone layer.

In any case, it appeared that for the whole of 1994, this Hensleigh fellow had worked at a remote research station in Antarctica collecting ice core samples.

The name of that research station was Wilkes Ice Station.

And its location: Latitude minus 66.5 degrees, Longitude 115 degrees, 20 minutes and 12 seconds east.

At that moment, the attendant returned and Alison looked up from the book.

'It's not there,' the attendant said, shaking her head.

'What?'

'I checked it three times,' the attendant said. 'It's not

on the shelf. "Preliminary Survey" by C.M. Waitzkin, 1978. It's not there.'

Alison frowned. This was unexpected.

The attendant – her name badge said her name was Cindy – shrugged helplessly. 'I don't understand it. It's just . . . *gone*.'

Alison felt a sudden rush of excitement as something occurred to her.

'If it's not there, wouldn't that mean that someone is reading it *right now*?' she asked.

Cindy shook her head. 'No, the computer says that the last time it was loaned out to anybody was in November, 1979.'

'November, 1979,' Alison said.

'Yeah, spooky huh?' Cindy looked about twenty years old, a college student no doubt. 'I took down the name of the borrower if you're interested. Here,' she handed Alison a slip of paper.

It was a photocopy of a Request Form, similar to the one Alison herself had filled out to get the survey. The Library of Congress obviously kept every form on file – probably for exactly this situation.

On the Request Form, in the box marked 'Name of Person Requesting Item' was a name:

O. NIEMEYER.

'It happens,' Cindy the attendant was saying. 'This Niemeyer guy probably liked it so much that he just walked out with it. We didn't have magnetic tags on our books back then, so he probably just slipped out past the guards.'

Alison ignored her.

She just stood there, entranced by the Request Form in her hand, by this twenty-year-old piece of evidence that had been sitting in a filing cabinet somewhere in the depths of the Library of Congress, waiting for this day.

Alison's eyes glowed as they stared at the words:

O. NIEMEYER.

Brigadier-General Trevor Barnaby walked across the pool deck of Wilkes Ice Station. He'd been in control of Wilkes Ice Station for a little over an hour now and he was feeling confident.

Only twenty minutes ago he had sent a team of fully armed divers down in the station's diving bell. But it would be at least ninety minutes before they reached the underground cave. Indeed, the diving bell's cable was still plunging into the pool at the base of the station right now.

Barnaby himself was dressed in a black thermal wet-suit. He planned to go down to the underground cave with the second team – to see for himself what was really down there.

'Well, now,' Barnaby said as he saw Snake and the two French scientists handcuffed to the pole. 'What have we here? Why, if it isn't Sergeant Kaplan.' By the look on his face, Snake was obviously surprised that Barnaby knew who he was.

'Gunnery Sergeant Scott Michael Kaplan,' Barnaby said. 'Born: Dallas, 1953; enlisted in the United States Marine Corps at age eighteen in 1971; small arms expert; hand-to-hand combat expert; sniper. And as of 1992, under suspicion by British Intelligence as a member of the American spy agency known as the Intelligence Convergence Group.

'I'm sorry, what is it that they call you? *Snake*, isn't it. Tell me, Snake, is this a common occurrence for you? Does your commanding officer often chain you to poles, leaving you at the mercy of the incoming enemy?'

Snake didn't say anything.

Barnaby said, 'I would hardly have thought that Shane Schofield would be the kind of master to chain up his loyal squad members. Which means there must be some *other* reason why he chained you up, n'est-ce pas?' Barnaby smiled. 'Now, whatever could that reason be?'

Snake still said nothing. Every now and then, his eyes would steal a look at the diving bell's cable as it plunged into the pool behind Barnaby.

Barnaby turned his attention to the two French scientists. 'And who might you be?' he asked.

Luc Champion blurted out indignantly, 'We are French scientists from the research station Dumont d'Urville. We have been detained here against our will by American forces. We *demand* that we be released in accordance with international – '

'Mr Nero,' Barnaby said flatly.

A mountain of a man stepped out from behind Barnaby and stood next to him. He was at least six-foot-five, with broad shoulders and impassive eyes. He had a scar that ran down from the corner of his mouth to his chin.

Barnaby said, 'Mr Nero, if you please.'

At that moment, the big man named Nero calmly raised his pistol and fired at Champion from point-blank range.

Champion's head exploded. Blood and brains instantly splattered against the side of Snake's face.

Henri Rae, the second French scientist, began to whimper.

Barnaby turned to face him. 'Are you French, too?'

Rae began to sob.

Barnaby said, 'Mr Nero.'

Rae saw it coming and he screamed, '*No!*' just as Nero raised his gun again and a moment later the other side of Snake's face was splattered all over with blood.

In the pitch-darkness of the crawlspace at the base of the elevator shaft, Mother snapped up at the sound of the gunshots.

Damn it, she thought. She must have blacked out again.

Got to stay awake, she thought.

Got to stay awake . . .

Mother stared at the clear, plastic fluid bag she had brought with her. It was connected by a tube to an intravenous drip that was stuck into her arm.

The fluid bag was now empty.

Had been for the last twenty minutes.

Mother began to shiver. She felt cold, weak. Her eyelids began to close.

She bit her tongue, trying to force her eyes open with the jolt of pain.

It worked for the first few times. And then it didn't.

Alone at the base of the elevator shaft, Mother lapsed into unconsciousness.

Out on E-deck, Trevor Barnaby stepped forward, his eyes narrowing. 'Sergeant Kaplan. Snake. You've been a naughty boy, haven't you?'

Snake said nothing.

'*Are* you ICG, Snake? A turncoat? A traitor to your own unit? What did you do, did you blow your cover too soon, did you start killing your own men before you knew for sure that this station was secure? I bet the Scarecrow wasn't too pleased when he found out. Is that why he chained you to a pole and left you here for me?'

Snake swallowed.

Barnaby stared at him coldly. 'It's what I would have done.'

At that moment, a young SAS corporal came up behind Barnaby. 'Sir.'

'Yes, corporal.'

'Sir, the charges are being set around the perimeter.'

'At what range?'

'Five hundred yards, sir. In an arc, like you ordered.'

'Good,' Barnaby said. Soon after he had arrived at Wilkes, Barnaby had ordered that eighteen Tritonal charges be placed in a semi-circular arc on the landward side of the station. They were to have a special purpose. A very special purpose.

Barnaby said, 'Corporal, how long do you expect the laying of the charges to take?'

'Allowing for the drilling, sir, I'd say another hour.'

'Fine,' Barnaby said. 'When they're all set, bring me the detonation unit.'

'Yes, sir,' the corporal said. 'Oh, and sir, there's one other thing.'

'Yes.'

'Sir, the prisoners who fell from the American hover-craft have just arrived. What should we do with them?'

Barnaby had already been told via radio of the soldier and the little girl who had fallen from one of the escaping hovercrafts and been picked up by his men.

'Take the girl to her quarters. Keep her there,' Barnaby said. 'Bring the Marine to me.'

Libby Gant was standing in a dark corner of the underground cavern, alone. The beam of her flashlight illuminated a small, horizontal fissure in the ice wall.

The fissure was at ground level, at the point where the ice wall met the floor. It was about two feet high and stretched horizontally for about six feet.

Gant crouched down on her hands and knees and peered down into the horizontal fissure. She saw nothing but darkness. There did, however, appear to be empty space in there –

'*Hey!*'

Gant turned.

She saw Sarah Hensleigh standing underneath the spacecraft at the other end of the cavern, over by the pool, waving her arms.

'*Hey!*' Hensleigh called excitedly. 'Come and have a look at this.'

Gant walked over to the big, black spaceship. Montana was already there when she got there. Santa Cruz was standing guard over by the pool.

'What do you think of that?' Hensleigh pointed at somthing on the underbelly of the ship.

Gant saw it, frowned. It looked like a keypad of some sort.

Twelve buttons, arranged in three columns, four buttons per column, with what looked like a rectangular screen at the top of it.

But there was something very odd about this 'keypad'.

There were no symbols on any of the keys.

Like the rest of the ship, the keypad was completely and utterly black – black buttons on a black background.

And then Gant saw that there was one button which did have a marking on it. The second button in the middle column had a small red circle printed on it.

'What do you think it is?' Montana asked.

'Who knows,' Hensleigh said.

'It could be a way to open it up,' Gant suggested.

Hensleigh snorted. 'Not likely. Do you know any aliens that use keypads?'

'I don't know any aliens,' Gant said. 'Do you?'

Hensleigh ignored her. 'There's no telling what it is,' she said. 'It could be an ignition key, or a weapons system . . .'

'Or a self-destruct mechanism,' Gant said dryly.

'I say we just press it and find out,' Hensleigh said.

'But which button do we press?' Montana said.

'The one with the circle on it, I suppose.'

Montana pursed his lips in thought. He was the senior man down here. It was his call. He looked to Gant.

Gant shook her head. 'We're not here to see what it does. We're just here to hold it until the cavalry arrives.'

Montana looked to Santa Cruz, who had come over from the pool to look.

'Press it,' Cruz said. 'If I'm gonna buy it for this fuckin' thing, I wanna see what's inside it.'

Montana turned back to face Sarah Hensleigh. She nodded. 'Let's see what it does.'

At last, Montana said, 'Okay. Press it.'

Sarah Hensleigh nodded and took a deep breath. Then she stretched out with her hand and pressed the button with the red circle on it.

*

At first, nothing happened.

Sarah Hensleigh lifted her finger off the keypad and looked up at the spaceship above her, as if she expected it to take off or something.

Suddenly, there came a soft harmonic tone, and the screen above the keypad began to glow.

And then another second later, a sequence of symbols appeared across the screen.

'Oh, *shit*,' Montana said.

'What the . . .' Hensleigh said.

The screen read:

```
24157817 _ _ _ _ _ _ _ _ _ _ _ _ _ _ _ _ _


        ENTER AUTHORIZED ENTRY CODE
```

'Numbers?' Montana said.

'*English?*' Sarah Hensleigh said. 'What the hell is this thing?'

For her part, Gant just shook her head. And as she walked away from the 'spaceship' she began to laugh softly.

Schofield and Renshaw lay flat on their backs on the cold hard surface of the iceberg, listening to the rhythmic sound of the waves crashing against the ice cliffs two hundred yards away.

They just lay there for a while, catching their breath.

After a few minutes, Schofield reached around with his hand until he found a small, black unit attached to his waist. He pressed a button on the unit.

Beep!

'What are you doing?' Renshaw said, not looking up.

'Initializing my GPS unit,' Schofield said, still lying on his back. 'It's a satellite location system that uses the Navistar Global Positioning System. Every Marine has one, for use in emergencies. You know, so people can find us if we end up in a life raft out in the middle of the ocean. I figured this wasn't too much different.' Schofield sighed. 'In a dark room on a ship somewhere, a flashing red dot just appeared on someone's screen.'

'Does that mean they're gonna come for us?' Renshaw asked.

'We'll be long dead by the time anybody gets here. But they'll at least be able to find our bodies.'

Renshaw said, 'Oh, *great*. It's nice to see my tax dollars at work. You guys build a satellite location system so that they can *find my body*. Wow.'

Schofield turned to look at Renshaw. 'At least I can leave a note attached to our bodies telling whoever finds us exactly what happened at the station. At least then they'll know the truth. About the French, about Barnaby.'

Renshaw said, 'Well, that makes me feel better.'

Schofield propped himself up on his elbow and looked out toward the cliffs. He saw the mountainous waves of the Southern Ocean smash against them and explode in spectacular showers of white.

Then, for the first time, Schofield took in the iceberg around him.

It was *big*. In fact, it was so big it didn't even rock in the heavy seas. Above the surface, the whole thing must have been at least a mile long. Schofield couldn't even begin to guess how large it was *under* the surface.

It was roughly rectangular in shape with an enormous white peak at one end. The rest of the iceberg was uneven and cratered. It looked to Schofield like a ghostly, white moonscape.

Schofield stood up.

'Where are you going?' Renshaw said, not getting up. 'You gonna walk home?'

'We should keep moving,' Schofield said. 'Keep warm for as long as we can, and while we're at it, see if there's some way we can get back to the coast.'

Renshaw shook his head and reluctantly got to his

feet and followed Schofield out across the uneven surface of the iceberg.

They trudged for almost twenty minutes before they realized they were going in the wrong direction.

The iceberg stopped abruptly and they saw nothing but sea stretching away to the west. The nearest iceberg in that direction was three miles away. Schofield had hoped they might be able to 'iceberg-hop' back to the coast. It wouldn't happen in this direction.

They headed back the way they had come.

They made very slow going. Icicles began to form around Renshaw's eyebrows and lips.

'You know anything about icebergs?' Schofield asked as they walked.

'A little.'

'Educate me.'

Renshaw said, 'I read in a magazine once that the latest trend among assholes with too much money is "iceberg climbing". Apparently it's quite popular among mountaineer-types. The only problem is that eventually your mountain melts.'

'I was thinking about something a little more *scientific*,' Schofield said. 'Like, do they ever float back in toward the coast?'

'No,' Renshaw said. 'Ice in Antarctica moves from the middle *out*. Not the other way round. Icebergs like this one break off from coastal ice-shelves. That's why the cliffs are so sheer. The ice overhanging the ocean

gets too heavy and it just breaks off, becoming – '
Renshaw waved his hand at the iceberg around them
' – an iceberg.'

'Uh-huh,' Schofield said, as he trudged across the ice.

'You get some big ones, though. *Really* big ones.
Icebergs bigger than whole countries. I mean, hell, take
this baby. Look how big she is. Most large icebergs live
for about ten or twelve years before they ultimately melt
and die. But given the right weather conditions – and if
the iceberg were big enough to begin with – an iceberg
like this could float around the Antarctic for up to thirty
years.'

'Great,' Schofield said drily.

They came to the spot where Renshaw had hauled
Schofield out of the water after Schofield had destroyed
the French submarine.

'Nice,' Renshaw said. 'Forty minutes of walking and
we're back where we started.'

They started up a small incline and came to the spot
where the French submarine's torpedo had hit the
iceberg.

It looked like a giant had taken a huge bite out of the
side of the iceberg.

The large landslide of ice that had just fallen away
under the weight of the explosion had left a huge semi-
circular hole in the side of the iceberg. Sheer, vertical
walls stretched down to the water ten metres below.

Schofield looked down into the hole, saw the calm
water lapping up against the edge of the enormous
iceberg.

'We're gonna die out here, aren't we?' Renshaw said from behind him.

'I'm not.'

'You're not?'

'That's *my* station and I'm gonna get it back.'

'Uh-huh,' Renshaw looked out to sea. 'And do you have any idea as to exactly *how* you're gonna do that?'

Schofield didn't answer him.

Renshaw turned around. 'I *said*, how in God's name do you plan to get *your* station back when we're stuck out here!'

But Schofield wasn't listening.

He was crouched down on his haunches, looking down into the semi-circular hole the torpedo had carved into the iceberg.

Renshaw came over and stood behind him.

'What are you looking at?'

'Salvation,' Schofield said. 'Maybe.'

Renshaw followed Schofield's gaze down into the semi-circular hole in the iceberg and he saw it immediately.

There, embedded in the ice a couple of metres down the sheer, vertical cliff face, Renshaw saw the distinctive square outline of a frozen, glass window.

Schofield tied their two parkas together and using the two jackets as a rope, got Renshaw to lower him down to the window set into the ice cliff.

Schofield hung high above the water, in front of the frozen glass window. He looked at it closely.

It was definitely man-made.

And old, too. The wooden panes of the window were weathered and scarred, bleached to a pale grey. Schofield wondered how long the window – and whatever structure it was attached to – had been buried inside this massive iceberg.

The way Schofield figured it, the blast from the submarine's torpedo must have dislodged the ten metres or so of ice in front of the window, exposing it. The window and whatever it was attached to had been buried *deep* within the iceberg.

Schofield took a deep breath. Then he kicked hard, shattering the window.

He saw darkness beyond the now-open window, a small cave of some sort.

Schofield pulled a flashlight from his hip pocket and with a final look up at Renshaw, swung himself in through the window and into the belly of the iceberg.

The first thing Schofield saw through the beam of his flashlight were the upside-down words:

HAPPY NEW YEAR 1969!
WELCOME TO LITTLE AMERICA IV!

The words were written on a banner of some sort. It hung limply – upside-down – across the cave in which Schofield now stood.

Only it wasn't a cave.

It was a room of some sort – a small wooden-walled room, *completely* buried within the ice.

And everything was upside-down. The whole room was inverted.

It was a strange sensation, everything being upside-down. It took Schofield a second to realize that he was actually standing on the *ceiling* of the underground room.

He looked off to his right. There seemed to be several other rooms branching off from this one –

'*Hello down there!*' Renshaw's voice sailed in from outside.

Schofield poked his head out through the window in the ice cliff.

'Hey, what's happening? I'm freezing my nuts off out here,' Renshaw said.

'Have you ever heard of Little America IV?' Schofield asked.

'Yeah,' Renshaw said. 'It was one of our research stations back in the sixties. Floated out to sea in '69 when the Ross Ice Shelf calved an iceberg nine thousand square kilometres big. The Navy looked for it for three months but they never found it.'

'Well, guess what,' Schofield said. 'We just did.'

Cloaked in three, thick woollen blankets, James Renshaw sat down on the floor of the main room of Little America IV. He rubbed his hands together vigorously, blew on them with his warm breath, while Schofield – still dressed in his waterlogged fatigues – rummaged through the other rooms of the darkened, inverted station. Neither man dared to eat any of the thirty-year-old canned food that lay strewn about the floor.

'As I remember it, Little America IV was kind of like Wilkes,' Renshaw said. 'It was a resource exploration station, built into the coastal ice shelf. They were after off-shore oil deposits buried in the continental shelf. They used to lower collectors all the way to the bottom to see if the soil down there contained – '

'Why is everything upside-down?' Schofield asked from the next room.

'That's easy. When this iceberg calved, it must have flipped over.'

'The iceberg flipped over?'

'It's been known to happen,' Renshaw said. 'And if you think about it, it makes sense. An iceberg is top heavy when it breaks off the mainland, because all the ice that's been living *underwater* has been slowly eroded over the years by the warmer sea water. So unless your iceberg is perfectly balanced when it breaks free from the mainland, the whole thing tips over.'

In the next room, Schofield was negotiating his way through piles of rusty, overturned junk. He stepped around a large, cylindrical cable-spooler that lay awkwardly on its side. Then he saw something.

'How long did you say the Navy looked for this station?' Schofield asked.

'About three months.'

'Was that a long time to look for a lost station?'

In the main room, Renshaw shrugged. 'It was longer than usual. Why?'

Schofield came back in through the doorway. He was carrying some metal objects in his hands.

'I think our boys were doing some things down here that they weren't supposed to,' Schofield said, smiling.

He held up a piece of white cord. It looked to Renshaw like string that had been covered over with white powder.

'Detonator cord,' Schofield said, as he tied the white, powdery cord in a loop around his wrist. 'It's used as a fuse for close-quarter explosives. That powdery stuff you see on it, that's magnesium-sulphide. Magnesium-based detonator cords burn hot and fast – in fact, they burn so hot that they can cut clean through metal. It's good stuff, we sometimes use it today.

'And see this,' Schofield held up a rusted, pressurized canister. 'VX poison gas. And this – ' he held up another tube ' – sarin.'

'Sarin gas?' Renshaw said. Even he knew what that was. Sarin gas was a chemical weapon. Renshaw recalled an incident in Japan in 1995, when a terrorist group had detonated a canister of sarin gas inside the Tokyo sub-way. Panic ensued. Several people were killed. 'They had that stuff in the sixties?' he asked.

'Oh, yes.'

'So you think this station was a chemical weapons facility?' Renshaw asked.

'I think so, yes.'

'But why? Why test chemical weapons in Antarctica?'

'Two reasons,' Schofield said. 'One: back home, we keep nearly all of our poison gas weapons in freezer storage, because most poison gases lose their toxicity at higher temperatures. So it makes sense to do your testing in a place that's cold all year round.'

'And the second reason?'

'The second reason is a lot simpler,' Schofield said, smiling at Renshaw. 'Nobody's looking.'

Schofield headed back into the next room. 'In any case,' he said as he disappeared behind the doorway, 'none of that's really much use to us right now. But they do have something *else* back here that *might* be helpful. In fact, I think it might just get us back in the game.'

'What is it?'

'This,' Schofield said, as he reappeared in the doorway and pulled a dusty scuba tank out into view.

Schofield set to work calibrating the thirty-year-old scuba gear. Renshaw was tasked with cleaning out the breathing apparatus – the mouthpieces, the valves, the air hoses.

The compressed air was the main risk. After thirty years of storage, there was a risk that it had gone toxic.

There was only one way to find out.

Schofield tested it – he took a deep inhalation and looked at Renshaw. When he didn't drop dead, he declared the air okay.

The two men worked on the scuba gear for about twenty minutes. Then, as they were nearing readiness, Renshaw said quietly, 'Did you ever get to see Bernie Olson's body?'

Schofield looked over at Renshaw. The little scientist was bent over a pair of mouthpieces, washing them out with sea water.

'As a matter of fact, I did,' Schofield said softly.

'What did you see?' Renshaw said, interested.

Schofield hesitated. 'Mr Olson had bitten his own tongue off.'

'Hmmm.'

'His jaw was also locked rigidly in place and his eyes were heavily inflamed – red-rimmed, bloodshot.'

Renshaw nodded. 'And what were you told happened to him?'

'Sarah Hensleigh told me you stabbed him in the neck with a hypodermic needle and injected liquid drain cleaner into his bloodstream.'

Renshaw nodded sagely. 'I see. Lieutenant, could you have a look at this please?' Renshaw pulled a water-logged book from the breast pocket of his parka. It was the thick book that he had taken from his room when they had evacuated the station.

Renshaw handed it to Schofield. *Biotoxicology and Toxin-Related Illnesses*.

Renshaw said, 'Lieutenant, when someone poisons you with drain cleaner, the poison stops your heart, just like *that*. There's no struggle. There's no fight. You just die. Chapter 2.'

Schofield flipped the watersoaked pages to Chapter 2. He saw the heading: *Toxin-Related Instantaneous Physiological Death*.

He saw a list of what the author had called 'Known Poisons'. In the middle of the list, Schofield saw 'industrial cleaning fluids, insecticides'.

'The point is,' Renshaw said, 'there are no *outward* signs of death by such a poison. Your heart stops, your body *just stops*.' Renshaw held up his finger. 'But not so, certain *other* toxins,' he said. 'Like, for instance, sea snake venom.'

'Sea snake venom?' Schofield said.

485

'Chapter 9,' Renshaw said.

Schofield found it. *Naturally Occurring Toxins – Sea Fauna*.

'Look up sea snakes,' Renshaw said.

Schofield did. He found the heading: *Sea Snakes – Toxins, Symptoms and Treatment*.

'Read it,' Renshaw said.

Schofield did.

'Out loud,' Renshaw said.

Schofield read, 'The common sea snake (*Enhydrina schistosa*) has a venom with a toxicity level three times that of the king cobra, the most lethal land-based snake. One drop (0.03 ml) is enough to kill three men. Common symptoms of sea snake envenomation include aching and stiffness of muscles, thickening of the tongue, paralysis, visual loss, severe inflammation of the eye area and dilation of the pupils, and most notably of all, lockjaw. Indeed, so severe is lockjaw in such cases, that it is not unknown for victims of sea snake envenomation to – '

Schofield cut himself off.

'Read it,' Renshaw said softly.

' – to sever their own tongues with their teeth.' Schofield looked up at Renshaw.

Renshaw cocked his head. 'Do I look like a killer to you, Lieutenant?'

'Who's to say you didn't put sea snake venom inside that hypodermic syringe?' Schofield countered.

'Lieutenant,' Renshaw said, 'at Wilkes Ice Station, sea snake venoms are kept in the Biotoxins Lab, which is

486

always – *always* – locked. Only a few people have access to that room and I'm not one of them.'

Schofield remembered the Biotoxins Laboratory on B-deck, remembered the distinctive three-circled bio-hazard sign pasted across its door.

Strangely, though, Schofield also found himself remembering something else.

He remembered Sarah Hensleigh telling him earlier: 'Before all this happened, I was working with Ben Austin in the Bio Lab on B-deck. He was doing work on a new antivenom for *Enhydrina schistosa*.'

Schofield shook the thought away.

No. Not possible.

He turned to Renshaw, 'So who do *you* think killed Bernie Olson?'

'Why, someone who had access to the Biotoxins Lab, of course,' Renshaw said. 'That could mean only Ben Austin, Harry Cox, or Sarah Hensleigh.'

Sarah Hensleigh . . .

Schofield said, 'Why would any of them want to kill Olson?'

'I have no idea,' Renshaw said. 'No idea.'

'So as far as you know, not one of those people had a motive to kill Olson?'

'That's right.'

'But *you* had a motive,' Schofield said. 'Olson was stealing your research.'

'Which kind of makes me the ideal person to set up, doesn't it?' Renshaw said.

Schofield said, 'But if someone really wanted to set

you up, they would have actually used drain cleaner to kill Olson. Why go to the trouble of using sea snake venom?'

'Good point,' Renshaw said. 'Good point. But if you read that book, you'll find that drain cleaner has a 59% mortality rate. Sea snake venom has a 98% mortality rate. Whoever killed Olson wanted to *make sure* that he died. That's why they used the sea snake venom. They did not want him to be resuscitated.'

Schofield pursed his lips in thought.

Then he said, 'Tell me about Sarah Hensleigh.'

'What about her?'

'Do you two get along? Do you like her, does she like you?'

'No, no and no.'

Schofield said, 'Why don't you like her?'

'You *really* want to know?' Renshaw sighed deeply. He looked away. 'It's because she married my best friend – actually, he was also my boss – and she didn't love him.'

'Who was that?' Schofield asked.

'A guy named Brian Hensleigh. He was head of geophysics at Harvard before he died.'

Schofield remembered Kirsty telling him about her father before. How he had taught her advanced maths. And how he had died only recently.

'He died in a car accident, didn't he?'

'That's right,' Renshaw said. 'Drunk driver jumped the kerb and killed him.' Renshaw looked up at Schofield. 'How come you know that?'

'Kirsty told me.'

'Kirsty told you,' Renshaw nodded slowly. 'She's a good kid, Lieutenant. Did she tell you that she's my goddaughter?'

'No.'

'When she was born, Brian asked me to be her godfather, you know, in case anything ever happened to him. Her mother, Mary-Anne, died of cancer when Kirsty was seven.'

Schofield said, 'Wait a second. Kirsty's mother died when she was seven?'

'Yep.'

'So, Sarah Hensleigh *isn't* Kirsty's mother?'

'That's right,' Renshaw said. 'Sarah Hensleigh was Brian's *second* wife. Sarah Hensleigh is Kirsty's *step-*mother.'

Suddenly, things began to make sense to Schofield. The way Kirsty hardly ever spoke to Sarah. The way she withdrew into herself whenever she was near Sarah. The natural response of a child to a stepmother she didn't like.

'I don't know why Brian married her,' Renshaw said. 'I know he was lonely, and, well, Sarah *is* attractive and she *did* show him quite a bit of attention. But she was ambitious. Boy, was she ambitious. You could see it in her eyes. She just wanted his name, wanted to meet the people he worked with. She didn't want *him*. And the last thing she wanted was his kid.'

Renshaw laughed sadly. 'And then that drunk driver skipped the kerb and killed Brian and in one fell swoop, Sarah lost Brian *and* got the kid she never wanted.'

Schofield asked. 'So why doesn't she like *you*?'

Renshaw laughed again. 'Because I told Brian not to marry her.'

Schofield shook his head. Obviously there had been a lot more going on at Wilkes Ice Station before he and his Marines had arrived than initially met the eye.

'You ready with those mouthpieces?' Schofield asked.

'All set.'

'This conversation is to be continued,' Schofield said, as he got to his feet and began to shoulder into one of the scuba tanks.

'Wait a second,' Renshaw said, standing. 'You're going back in there *now*? What if you get killed going back in? Then there'll be nobody left who believes my story.'

'Who said *I* believed your story?' Schofield said.

'You believed it. I know you believed it.'

'Then it looks like you'd better come with me. Make sure I don't get killed,' Schofield said as he walked over to the window set into the iceberg and looked out through it.

Renshaw paled. 'Okay, okay, let's just slow down for a second here. Have you given any thought to the fact that there is a pod of *killer whales* out there. Not to mention some kind of seal that *kills* killer whales – '

But Schofield wasn't listening. He was just staring out through the window set in the ice. In the distance to the south-west – at the top of one of the nearby ice cliffs – he saw a faint, intermittent, green flash. Flash-flash. Flash-flash. It was the green beacon light mounted on top of Wilkes Ice Station's radio antenna.

'Mr Renshaw, I'm going back in there . . . with or without you, whatever might be in the way.' Schofield turned to face him.

'Come on. It's time to retake Wilkes Ice Station.'

Wrapped in two layers of oversized, 1960s-era wetsuits, Schofield and Renshaw swam through the icy silence, breathing with the aid of their thirty-year-old scuba gear.

They both had the same length of steel cable tied around their waists – cable that stretched all the way back to the large cylindrical spooler inside Little America IV, about a mile to the north-east of Wilkes Ice Station. It was a precaution, in case either of them got lost or separated and had to get back to the station.

Schofield held a harpoon gun that he had found inside the Little America station out in front of him.

The water around them became crystal clear as they swam underneath the coastal ice shelf and into a forest of jagged stalactites of ice.

Schofield's plan was that they would swim *under* the ice shelf – depending on how deep it went – and come up inside Wilkes Ice Station. Outside, he had taken his bearings from the position of the green beacon light atop the station's radio antenna. Schofield figured that if he and Renshaw could keep swimming in the general direction of the beacon, once they went under the ice shelf, they would eventually be able to spot the pool at the base of the station.

Schofield and Renshaw were in a world of white. Ghostly-white ice formations – like mountain peaks turned upside-down – stretched downward for nearly four hundred feet.

Schofield frowned inside his diving mask. They would have to go quite a way down before they could come up again inside the station.

Schofield and Renshaw swam down the side of one of the enormous ice formations. Through his mask, the only thing Schofield could see was a wall of solid, white ice.

After a while, they came to the bottom of the ice formation – the pointed 'peak' of the inverted mountain. Schofield slowly swam underneath the peak, and the wall of white glided out of his view –

– and he saw it.

Schofield's heart nearly skipped a beat.

It was just hanging there in the water in front of him, suspended from its winch cable, making its slow journey back up toward the station.

The diving bell.

Heading back up toward the station.

And then Schofield realized what that meant.

The British had already sent a team down to investigate the cavern.

Schofield hoped to hell that his Marines down in the cavern were ready.

As for him and Renshaw, they had to get to that

diving bell. It was a free ride up to Wilkes Ice Station that Schofield did not want to miss.

Schofield spun in the water to signal Renshaw. He saw the short scientist behind him, swimming underneath the inverted mountain peak. He signalled for Renshaw to pick up the pace and the two men hurried through the water toward the diving bell.

'How many are down there?' Barnaby asked softly.

Book Riley didn't say a word.

Book was on his knees, with his hands cuffed behind his back. He was down on E-deck, by the pool. Blood poured out from his mouth. His left eye was half-closed, puffy and swollen. After falling from the speeding hovercraft with Kirsty, Book had been brought back to Wilkes. As soon as he had arrived back at the station, he had been brought down to E-deck to face Barnaby.

'Mr Nero,' Barnaby said.

The big SAS man named Nero punched Book hard in the face. Book hit the ground.

'How many?' Barnaby said. He was holding Book's Maghook in his hand.

'*None!*' Book yelled through bloody teeth. 'There's no one down there. We never got a chance to send anyone down there.'

'Oh, really,' Barnaby said. He looked at the Maghook in his hands thoughtfully. 'Mr Riley, I find it very difficult to believe that a commander of the calibre of the Scarecrow would neglect to make the task of sending a squad down to that cave *the very first thing that he did once he got here.*'

'Then why don't you ask him.'

'Tell me the truth, Mr Riley, or very soon I am going to lose my temper and feed you to the lions.'

'There's no one down there,' Book said.

'Okay,' Barnaby said, turning abruptly to face Snake. 'Mr Kaplan,' he said. 'Is Mr Riley telling me the truth?'

Book looked up sharply at Snake.

Barnaby said to Snake, 'Mr Kaplan, if Mr Riley is lying to me, I will kill him. If *you* lie to me, I will kill *you.*'

Book looked up at Snake with wide, pleading eyes.

Snake spoke. 'He's lying. There are four people down there. Three Marines, one civilian.'

'You *son of a bitch*!' Book said to Snake.

'Mr Nero,' Barnaby said, tossing Book's Maghook to Nero. 'String him up.'

Schofield and Renshaw surfaced together inside the slow-moving diving bell.

They climbed up out of the water, and stood on the metal deck that surrounded the small pool of water at the base of the spherical diving bell.

Renshaw removed his mouthpiece, gasped for breath. Schofield scanned the interior of the empty diving bell, looking for weapons, looking for anything.

He saw a digital depth counter on the far wall. It was ticking downwards as the diving bell ascended: 360 feet. 359 feet. 358 feet.

'Ah-ha,' Renshaw said from the other side of the bell.

Schofield turned. Renshaw was standing in front of a small TV monitor that was attached to the wall high up near the ceiling. Renshaw clicked it on. 'I forgot about this,' he said.

'What is it?' Schofield asked.

'It's another of old Carmine Yaeger's toys. You remember the old guy I told you about before, the guy who used to watch the whales all the time. Do you remember I told you he used to watch them sometimes from inside the diving bell? Well this monitor is another one of his video feeds of the station's pool. Yaeger had it installed so he could watch the surface of the pool while he was underwater in the bell.'

Schofield looked up at the small black and white monitor.

On the screen, he saw the same view of E-deck that he had seen when he was in Renshaw's room earlier. The view from the camera on the underside of the retractable bridge on C-deck, looking straight down on E-deck.

Schofield froze.

He saw people on the screen.

SAS troops with guns. Snake still cuffed to the pole. And Trevor Barnaby, pacing slowly around E-deck.

And there was one other person.

There on the deck, down at Barnaby's feet, having his feet tied up, was Book Riley.

'All right, hoist him up,' Barnaby said, once Nero had finished tying the Maghook's cable around Book's ankles.

Somebody else had already splayed out the Maghook's rope and tossed its launcher over the retractable bridge on C-deck, creating a pulley-like mechanism.

Nero took the launcher from one of the other British commandos and wedged its grip between two rungs of the rung-ladder between E-deck and D-deck. Then he pressed the black button on the launcher that reeled in the rope.

As a result of the pulley mechanism – the rope being stretched taut over the bridge on C-deck – Book was suddenly lifted off the deck by his ankles. His hands were still cuffed behind his back. He swung out over the pool and dangled helplessly – head-down – in the air above the water.

'What the hell are they doing?' Renshaw asked as he and Schofield stared at the black and white monitor.

On the monitor they could see Book dangling directly beneath them, hanging from his own Maghook out over the water.

At that moment, the diving bell rocked slightly, and Schofield grabbed the wall to steady himself.

'What was that?' Renshaw said quickly.

Schofield didn't have to answer him.

The answer lay right outside the windows of the slow-moving bell.

Several large, dark shapes rose through the water all around the diving bell, their distinctive black and white outlines all too familiar.

The pod of killer whales.

They were heading up toward the station.

The first dorsal fin pierced the surface of the water and a murmur went up among the twenty or so SAS troops gathered around the pool on E-deck.

Book was still dangling upside-down above the pool. He saw it, too: the enormous black outline of a killer whale gliding slowly through the water beneath him. Book began to wriggle, but it was no use – his hands were firmly cuffed, his feet firmly bound.

His dogtags began to slip over his head. A couple of seconds later they dropped off his chin and plonked down into the water and sank fast.

Barnaby watched the killer whales from the poolside deck. 'This should make things very interesting.'

At that moment, one of his corporals came up to him. It was the same corporal who had reported to him before. 'Sir, the Tritonal charges are all set.'

The corporal offered Barnaby a small black unit the size of a thick calculator. It had a numbered keypad on it. 'The detonation unit, sir.'

Barnaby took it. 'How are the outer markers looking?'

'We have five men stationed along the outer perimeter monitoring the horizon with laser rangefinders, sir. Last check, there was no one within fifty miles of this place, sir.'

'Good,' Barnaby said. 'Good.'

He turned his attention back to the pool and the American Marine hanging helplessly above it.

'Gives us a little time for some R&R,' Barnaby said.

'Jesus, can't this thing go any faster,' Schofield said as he stared at the depth counter. It ticked slowly downward as they rose through the water. They were still 190 feet from the surface. Still at least seven minutes away.

Schofield watched the image of Book on the screen.

'Shit!' Schofield said. '*Shit!*'

'Mr Nero,' Barnaby said.

Nero pressed a button on the Maghook's launcher and suddenly, the Maghook began to play out its rope and Book began to *descend* toward the pool, head-first.

The water beneath him was choppy. Killer whales sliced through it in every direction. Suddenly, one of them rose above the surface beneath Book and blew a spray of water out of its blowhole.

Book's head descended toward the water. He was one foot above it when he jolted to a sudden halt.

'Mr Riley!' Barnaby called from the safety of the deck.

'What?'

'Rule Britannia, Mr Riley!'

Nero hit the button again and Book's head and upper body plunged underwater.

No sooner was Book underwater than a line of sharp, white teeth whooshed past his face.

Book's eyes went wide.

There were so many of them! Killer whales all around him. A slow-moving forest of black and white. The whales seemed to *prowl* around the water.

And then suddenly Book saw one of them spot him, saw it turn suddenly in the water and come at him – at speed.

Book hung there, upside-down in the water, totally exposed, unable to move.

The killer charged at him.

The SAS commandos cheered when they saw the enormous dorsal fin of the killer make a beeline for the submerged Marine.

*

In the diving bell, Schofield was glued to the monitor.

'Come on, Book,' he said. 'Tell me you've got something up your sleeve.'

Book shook his hands behind his back. The cuffs wouldn't budge.

The killer came at him.

Fast.

It opened its jaws and rolled onto its side and –

– slid past him, brushing roughly against the side of Book's body.

The SAS commandos booed.

In the diving bell, Schofield breathed a sighed of relief.

Behind him, Renshaw said softly, 'It's over.'

'What do you mean, it's over?'

'Remember what I told you before. They stake their claim with the first pass. Then they eat you.'

Book screamed with frustration under the water.

He couldn't get his hands free.

Couldn't . . . get . . . his . . . hands . . . free . . .

And then he saw the killer whale again.

It was coming at him a second time. The *same* whale.

The killer whale powered through the water, faster

this time, moving with purpose, its high dorsal fin cutting hard through the chop.

Book saw its jaws open again, and this time he saw the white teeth and the pink tongue and as it came closer and closer his terror became extreme.

The killer whale didn't roll sideways this time.

It didn't brush past him this time.

No, this time, the seven-ton killer whale *ploughed* into Book with pulverizing force and before Book even knew what had hit him, the big whale's jaws came crashing down around his head.

Inside the diving bell, Schofield stared at the monitor in silence.

'Holy *Christ*,' Renshaw breathed from behind him.

The image on the screen was absolutely horrifying.

A fountain of blood spewed out from the water. The whale had crunched into Book's suspended body and consumed his entire upper half. Now it was shaking the corpse violently, trying to wrench it free from the rope – like a great white shark grappling with a piece of meat hung out over the side of a boat.

Schofield didn't say anything.

He swallowed back the vomit welling in his throat.

Down in the cavern, Montana and Sarah Hensleigh stared at the screen above the keypad. Gant had left them. She had gone back over to the fissure she had found at the other end of the cavern.

Sarah Hensleigh stared at the screen.

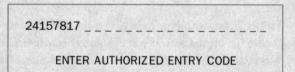

```
24157817 _ _ _ _ _ _ _ _ _ _ _ _ _ _ _ _

       ENTER AUTHORIZED ENTRY CODE
```

'It's a way in,' she said.

Eight digits were already displayed on the screen. 24157817. Then there were sixteen blank spaces to be filled in with the entry code.

'Sixteen gaps to fill,' Montana said. 'But what's the entry code?'

'More numbers,' Hensleigh said thoughtfully. 'It's got to be some kind of numerical code, a code that follows on from the eight numbers already on the screen.'

'But even if we could figure out the code, how do we insert it into the spaces?' Montana said.

Sarah Hensleigh leaned forward and pressed the first black button on the keypad.

A number '1' appeared instantly on the screen – in the first blank space.

Montana frowned. 'How did you know that?'

Hensleigh shrugged. 'If this thing has instructions written in English, then it's man-made. Which means this keypad is also man-made. Which means it's probably just a regular keypad, with numbers set out on it like on a calculator or a telephone. Who knows, maybe the guys who built it just didn't get round to putting numbers on it.'

Hensleigh hit the second button.

A '2' sprang up in the next blank space. Hensleigh smiled, vindicated.

Then she began to whisper to herself. 'Sixteen digit code, ten digits to choose from. Shit. We're talking *trillions* of possible combinations.'

'Do you think you can crack it?' Montana said.

'I don't know,' Hensleigh said. 'It depends on what the first eight digits are supposed to mean, and whether I can figure that out.'

At that moment, Montana leaned forward and pressed the first button fourteen times. On the screen, the blank spaces filled up quickly.

The screen beeped suddenly. And then a new prompt appeared at the bottom:

```
24157817 1 2 1 1 1 1 1 1 1 1 1 1 1 1 1 1

INCORRECT CODE ENTERED – ENTRY DENIED
ENTER AUTHORIZED ENTRY CODE
```

The screen then reverted back to the original screen, with the original eight numbers and the sixteen blank spaces.

Hensleigh looked at Montana, perplexed. 'How did you know that?'

Montana smiled. 'It gives you a second chance if you enter the wrong code. Like most military entry-code systems.'

At the other end of the cavern, Gant was crouched down on the ground over by the fissure she had found at the base of the ice wall. She pointed her flashlight inside the horizontal fissure.

Gant wanted to know more about this cavern. There was something about the cavern itself and the man-made 'spaceship' they had found in it that made her wonder . . .

Gant peered in through the fissure. In the beam of her flashlight, she saw a cave. A round, ice-walled cave that seemed to stretch away to the right. The floor of the cave was about five feet beneath her.

Gant lay down on her back and shimmied herself through the fissure. She began to lower herself down to the floor of this new cave.

And then suddenly, without warning, the ice beneath her gave way and Gant fell clumsily to the floor of the cave.

Clanggggg – !

The sound of her landing on the floor of the cave reverberated all around her. It had sounded like someone hitting a piece of steel with a sledgehammer.

Gant froze.

Steel?

And then slowly – very slowly – she gazed down at the floor beneath her.

The floor was covered with a thin layer of frost, but Gant saw it clearly. Her eyes widened.

She saw the rivets first – small round domes on a dark grey background.

It was metal.

Thick, reinforced metal.

Gant panned her flashlight around the small cave. It was cylindrical in shape – like a train tunnel – with a high, round ceiling that rose above the horizontal fissure through which she had come. The horizontal fissure was about halfway up the wall. In fact, Gant could almost see *through* the thick ice wall above the fissure, as if it were translucent glass.

Gant swung her flashlight around and pointed it at the tunnel leading away from her.

And then she saw it.

It looked like a door of some sort, made of heavy, grey steel. It was set into the ice, and was completely covered in frost and icicles. It looked like a door on a naval vessel or submarine – solid-looking, hinged on a sturdy metal bulkhead.

'Jesus Christ,' Gant breathed.

Pete Cameron called the *Post*'s office in Washington D.C. for the third time. He was sitting in Andrew Trent's living room.

At last, Alison picked up.

Cameron said, 'Where have you been? I've been calling all afternoon.'

'You're not gonna believe what I found,' Alison said.

She recounted for him what she had found on the All-States Libraries Database: how the references to latitude and longitude that Cameron had picked up at SETI referred to the location of an ice station in Antarctica – Wilkes Ice Station.

Cameron pulled out his original notes from his visit to SETI, looked at them as Alison spoke.

Then Alison told him about the academics who lived down at the ice station and the papers and books they had written. She also told him about the Library of Congress and the 'Preliminary Survey' by C.M. Waitzkin.

'It was signed out to an O. Niemeyer in 1979,' Alison said.

Cameron frowned. 'Niemeyer? *Otto* Niemeyer? Wasn't he on the Joint Chiefs of Staff under Nixon?'

'Under Carter, too,' Alison said.

Andrew Trent came into the living room. 'Did someone say Niemeyer?'

'Yeah,' Cameron said. 'Otto Niemeyer. Know him?'

'Know *of* him,' Trent said. 'He was Air Force. Full colonel. Got on a plane in '79 and never came back.'

'That's the one,' Alison said, over the phone. 'Hey, who is that?'

'Andrew Wilcox,' Cameron said, looking at Trent.

'Oh, hey, Andrew, nice to meet you,' Alison said. 'And yes, you're right. Niemeyer got on a silver Air Force Boeing 727 at Andrews Air Force base on the night of 30 December 1979, heading for destination *unknown*. He never returned.'

'Aren't there any records about where he went?' Pete asked.

'That's classified, baby,' Alison said. 'Classified. I *was* able to get a history on him, though. Niemeyer flew Phantoms in Vietnam. Got shot down over the Mekong Delta in '65. POW for a year. Both legs broken. Rescued in '66. Drove a desk at the Pentagon after that. Headed the USAF's Procurement Division for six years from '68 to '74. Appointed to the Joint Chiefs of Staff in 1972 by Nixon, continued there under Carter.

'Apparently, Niemeyer was a player on the stealth project in '77. He was on the Air Force selection committee that chose the B-2 stealth bomber, made by

Northrop-Boeing. The official record, however, shows that Niemeyer voted for the *loser* in the tender, a consortium made up of General Aeronautics and a small electronics company from California called Entertech Ltd.'

Pete Cameron said, 'So why would he steal a preliminary land survey about some university research station in Antarctica?'

'See, that's the thing,' Alison said. 'I don't think it's the same station.'

'What?'

Alison said, 'Listen, I was looking in this book I bought by one of those Antarctic guys, a guy named Brian Hensleigh. According to him, Wilkes Ice Station was built in 1991.'

'Uh-huh.'

'But Niemeyer disappeared in 1979.'

'So what are you saying?' Pete said.

'What I'm saying is that Niemeyer was looking up a station at that location twelve years *before* Wilkes Ice Station was ever even thought of.'

Alison paused. 'Pete, I think there were *two* stations. Two stations built on the *same piece of land*. One in 1978 – the one for which a land survey by C.M. Waitzkin was drawn up – and another in 1991.'

Pete Cameron leaned forward, spoke into the phone. 'What do you mean, you think they built the second station *on top of* the first one?'

'I don't think the people who built the second station – Wilkes Ice Station – even *knew* about the first one,' Alison said. 'Brian Hensleigh doesn't mention it *at all* in his book.'

'So what was it?' Pete said. 'Niemeyer's station, I mean.'

'Who knows,' Alison said.

At that moment, Andrew Trent saw the sheet of notepaper in Pete's hand, took it, and began examining it.

Alison said, 'So, what about you? Get anything news-worthy on your travels?'

'You could say that,' Cameron said, as he recalled in his mind everything Trent had told him about his unit's slaughter, his official 'death' and the Intelligence Convergence Group.

'*Hey,*' Trent said suddenly from across the room. He held up Cameron's SETI notes. 'Where did you get these?'

Pete broke off from Alison and looked at the notes he had made at SETI.

COPY 134625
CONTACT LOST – > IONOSPHERIC DISTURB.
FORWARD TEAM
SCARECROW
– 66.5
SOLAR FLARE DISRUPT. RADIO
115, 20 MINS, 12 SECS EAST
HOW GET THERE SO – SECONDARY TEAM EN ROUTE

512

Pete told Trent about his visit to SETI, told him that those notes were his record of what had been caught on the airwaves by SETI's radio telescopes.

'And these co-ordinates,' Trent said, pointing to the words ' – 66.5' and '115, 20 MINS, 12 SECS EAST' they refer to a research station in Antarctica?'

'That's right,' Pete said.

Trent looked hard at Pete Cameron. 'Do you know anything about Marine Force Reconnaissance Units, Mr Cameron?'

'Only what you've told me.'

'They're a forward team,' Trent said.

'Okay,' Pete said, seeing the words 'FORWARD TEAM' on his notes.

'Scarecrow . . .' Trent said, staring down at the notes.

Pete looked from the notes to Trent. 'What's a Scarecrow? An operation?'

'No,' Trent said a little too suddenly. 'Scarecrow's a man. A Marine lieutenant. A friend of mine.'

Pete Cameron waited for Trent to say something more, but he didn't. And then suddenly, Trent looked up into Cameron's eyes.

'*Son of a bitch*,' Trent said. 'Scarecrow's down there.'

'What do you mean?' Alison said a few minutes later. 'You think there are *Marines* down at that station?'

'We think so, yes,' Cameron said, excited.

'Jesus, there's a secondary team en route, too,' Trent said, looking down at the notes again. 'Shit.'

Trent turned to Cameron. 'Hang up for a second. I have to make a phone call.'

Cameron told Alison he'd call her back.

Trent quickly dialled a number. Cameron just watched him.

'Yes, hi, Personnel, please,' Trent said into the phone. He waited a second, then said, 'Yes, hi, I was wondering if you could tell me where I could find Lieutenant Shane Schofield, please. It's a family emergency. Yes, I'll hold.'

Trent waited a full minute before someone returned to the line.

'Yes, hi,' Trent said. 'What – oh, I'm his brother-in-law, Michael.' There was a pause. 'Oh, no,' Trent said softly. 'Oh my God. Yes, thank you. Goodbye.'

Trent practically slammed the phone down. He turned to Cameron. 'Holy shit.'

'What?'

'According to the United States Marine Corps Personnel Department, First Lieutenant Shane M. Schofield *died* in a training accident in the South Pacific at 0930 hours yesterday morning. Arrangements are being made to contact his family right now.'

Cameron frowned. 'He's dead?'

'According to them he is,' Trent said softly. 'But that doesn't necessarily mean it's true, now does it.' Trent paused. 'The secondary team . . .'

'What about it?'

'There's a secondary team on its way to Wilkes Ice Station right now, right?'

'Yeah . . .'

'And according to the United States Marine Corps, Shane Schofield is already dead, right?'

'Yeah . . .'

Trent thought about that for a long moment. Then he looked up suddenly. 'Schofield's found something. They're gonna kill him.'

Cameron got Alison back on the phone.

'Quick, send it through now,' he said.

'All right. All right. Just hold on a second, honey buns,' Alison said. Cameron heard the clicking of computer keys at the other end of the line.

'Okay, I'm sending it through now,' Alison said.

On the far side of the living room, Trent flicked on his computer. He clicked through several screens, came to his e-mail screen.

A small information bar at the bottom of the screen blinked:

YOU HAVE NEW MAIL.

Trent clicked on the 'Open' icon.

A list appeared immediately on the screen:

ALL-STATES LIBRARY DATABASE
SEARCH BY KEYWORD
SEARCH STRING USED: LATITUDE – 66.5°
                          LONGITUDE 115° 20′ 12″

NO. OF ENTRIES FOUND: 6

TITLE	AUTHOR	LOCATION	YEAR
DOCTORAL THESIS	LLEWELLYN, D.K.	STANFORD, CT	1998
DOCTORAL THESIS	AUSTIN, B.E.	STANFORD, CT	1997
POST-DOCTORAL THESIS	HENSLEIGH, S.T.	USC, CA	1997
FELLOWSHIP GRANT RESEARCH PAPER	HENSLEIGH, B.M.	HARVARD, MA	1996
'THE ICE CRUSADE – REFLECTIONS ON A YEAR SPENT IN ANTARCTICA'	HENSLEIGH, B.M.	HARVARD, MA AVAIL: AML	1995
PRELIMINARY SURVEY	WAITZKIN, C.M.	LIBCONG	1978

It was the list Alison had got from the All-States Database. The list of every work that referred to Latitude −66.5° and Longitude 115° 20′ 12″.

'All right,' Pete said.

'What are you going to do with it?' Alison's voice said over the speaker phone.

'We're gonna use this list to find their addresses,' Trent said, typing quickly at the keyboard. 'The e-mail addresses of the academics down in Antarctica, so we can send a message to Schofield.'

'We figure that most university professors have e-mail,' Pete said, 'and we're hoping that Wilkes Ice Station is patched in to a satellite phone so that the message can get through.'

Suddenly Trent said, 'All right, I got one! Hensleigh, Sarah T. The e-mail address is at USC in California, but it's been routed to an external address: sarahhensleigh @wilkes.edu.us. That's it!'

Trent typed some more.

'All *right*,' he said a minute later. 'Excellent. They've got a universal address down there: allwilkes@wilkes .edu.us. *Excellent*. Now, we can send an e-mail to *anyone* who has a computer at that station.'

'Do it,' Cameron said.

Trent typed a message, then did a quick cut-and-paste. When he was finished he practically slammed his finger down on the 'SEND' button.

Libby Gant stood in front of the heavy steel door set into the small ice tunnel.

It had a rusty pressure-wheel attached to it. With some difficulty, Gant turned it. She rotated it three times.

And then suddenly, Gant heard a loud clunking noise from within the great steel door, and the door creaked opened a fraction.

Gant pulled the door wide and shone her flashlight beyond it.

'Whoa,' she said.

It looked like an aeroplane hangar. It was so big, Gant's flashlight wasn't even strong enough to see the far end. But she could see enough.

She could see walls.

Man-made walls.

Steel walls, with heavy reinforcing girders holding up a high aluminium ceiling. Huge, yellow, robotic arms stood silently in the gloom, covered in frost. Halogen lights lined the ceiling. Some metal girders lay at awkward angles on the ground in front of her. Gant saw that several of them had jagged marks at their ends –

they had been broken clean in two. Everything was covered in a layer of ice.

Gant saw a piece of paper at her feet. She picked it up. It was frozen solid, but she could still read the letterhead. It read:

ENTERTECH LTD.

Gant walked back to the small tunnel that led back to the main cavern. She called to Montana and Hensleigh.

A few minutes later, Montana rolled through the horizontal fissure and walked with Gant into the giant subterranean hangar.

'What the hell is going on here?' he said.

They entered the hangar, their flashlights creating beams of light. Montana went left. Gant went right.

Gant came to an office-type structure which seemed to be overgrown with ice. The door to the office opened with a loud creak, and slowly, very slowly, Gant stepped inside.

A body was lying on the floor of the office.

A man.

His eyes were closed, and he was naked. His skin had turned blue. He looked like he was asleep.

Gant saw a desk on the far side of the office, saw something on it. Moving toward the desk, she saw that it was a book of some kind, a leatherbound book.

It just sat there on the desk all by itself. The rest of the desk was bare. It was almost, Gant thought, as if someone had left it there *deliberately*, so that it would be the first thing a visitor found.

Gant picked up the book. It was covered in a layer of frost and the pages were hard, like cardboard.

Gant opened it.

It appeared to be a diary of some sort.

Gant read an entry near the beginning:

2 June, 1978
Things are going well. But it's so cold!! I can't believe they brought us all the way down here to build a fucking attack plane! The weather outside is terrible. Blizzard conditions. Thankfully, our hangar is built below the surface, so we stay out of the weather. The sad irony is, we *need* the cold. The system's plutonium core maintains its grade for longer in the colder temperatures . . .

Gant jumped ahead to a page not far from the end of the diary.

15 February, 1980
No one's coming. I'm sure of it now. Bill Holden died yesterday and we had to cut Pat Anderson's hands off they were so frostbitten.

It's been two months now since the quake hit and I've given up all hope of rescue. Someone said Old Man Niemeyer was supposed to be coming down here in December, but he hasn't showed.

When I go to sleep at night, I wonder if anyone but Niemeyer knows we're here.

Gant flipped back some pages, looking for something. She found what she was looking for around the middle of the diary.

20 December, 1979
I don't know where I am. We were hit by an earthquake yesterday, the biggest motherfucking earthquake you have ever seen. It was as if the earth opened up and just swallowed us whole.

I was down in the hangar when it happened, working on the bird. First, the ground began to shake and then suddenly this massive wall of ice just thrust up out of the ground and ripped the hangar in half. And then we just seemed to fall. Fall and fall. Massive chunks of the ice shelf (each one the size of a building, I estimated) called in on either side of us as we were sucked down into the earth – I saw them make enormous dents in the roof of the hangar. BOOM! BOOM! BOOM! The quake must have ripped an enormous hole underneath the station and we just fell down into it.

We just kept going down. Down and down. Shaking and falling. One of the big robot arms fell on Doug Myers, crushed him to death . . .

Gant was stunned.

This 'hangar' had been an ice station.

An ice station that had been set up in the utmost secrecy to build a plane of some sort – a plane, Gant noticed, that used plutonium. But this station, it seemed, had originally been up on the surface – or rather, buried just underneath the surface like Wilkes Ice

Station – until an earthquake had hit it and sucked it underground.

Gant flicked to the very last page of the diary.

17 March, 1980
I am the last one alive. All of my colleagues are dead. It has been almost three months now since the quake hit and I know no one is coming. My left hand is frostbitten and gangrenous. I cannot feel my feet anymore.

I cannot go on. I am going to strip myself naked and lie down in the ice. It should only take a few minutes. If anyone should read this in the future, know that my name was Simon Wayne Daniels. I was an aviation electronics specialist for Entertech Ltd. My wife, Lily, lives in Palmdale, although I don't know if she'll be there when you read this. Please find her and tell her that I loved her and tell her that I'm so sorry I couldn't tell her where I went.

It is so very cold.

Gant looked at the naked body on the floor at her feet.

Simon Wayne Daniels.

Gant felt a pang of sadness for him. He had died here, alone. Buried alive in this cold, icy tomb.

And then all of a sudden, Santa Cruz's voice exploded across her helmet intercom, shattering her thoughts: *'Montana! Fox! Get out here! Get out here now! I have a visual on enemy divers! I repeat! Enemy divers are about to come up inside the cavern!'*

The team of SAS divers made their way up the under-water ice tunnel with the aid of sea sleds. There were eight of them, and by virtue of their twin-propeller sea sleds, they moved quickly through the water. All of them wore black.

'Base. This is Dive Team. Come in,' the lead diver said into his helmet communicator.

'*Dive Team, this is Base*,' Barnaby's voice came in over the intercom. '*Report.*'

'Base, time is now 1956 hours. Dive time since leaving the diving bell is fifty-four minutes. We have a visual on the surface. We are coming up to the cavern.'

'*Dive Team, be aware. We have intel that there are four hostile agents inside that cavern waiting for you. I repeat, there are four hostile agents inside the cavern waiting for you. Use appropriate action.*'

'Copy Base. We will. Dive Team out.'

Gant and Montana came sprinting back into the main cavern.

They came up alongside Santa Cruz, who was manning the tripod-mounted MP-5s. He pointed down into the pool.

Several ominous black shadows could be seen rising up through the clear, aqua-coloured water.

The three Marines took up positions behind various boulders, MP-5s in their hands. Montana told Sarah Hensleigh to stay behind him and stay down.

'*Don't be impatient,*' Montana's voice said over their helmet intercoms. '*Wait for them to breach the surface. It's no use firing into the water.*'

'Got it,' Gant said as she saw the first shadow rise steadily through the water toward the surface.

A diver. On a sea sled.

He came closer and closer, up and up, until strangely, just below the surface, he stopped.

Gant frowned.

The diver had just stopped there, about a foot below the surface.

What was he doing –

And then suddenly the diver's hand shot up out of the water and Gant saw the object in his hand instantly.

'Nitrogen charge!' Gant yelled. 'Take cover!'

The diver tossed the nitrogen charge and it bounced onto the hard, icy floor of the cavern. Gant and the other Marines all ducked behind their boulders.

The nitrogen charge exploded.

Supercooled liquid nitrogen splattered everything in sight. The gooey, blue poxy smacked against the boulders the Marines were hiding behind, splattered against the walls of the cavern. Some of it even hit the big, black ship standing in the middle of the enormous cave.

It was the perfect diversion.

Because no sooner had the nitrogen charge gone off than the first SAS commando was charging out of the water with his gun pressed to his shoulder and his finger jamming down on the trigger.

The diving bell was almost at the surface now. It continued its slow rise upward.

An angry commander, acting under the influence of rage or frustration will almost certainly get his unit killed.

Trevor Barnaby's words echoed inside Shane Schofield's head. Schofield ignored them.

After he had seen Barnaby feed Book Riley to the killer whales, his anger had become intense. He wanted to kill Barnaby. He wanted to rip his heart out and serve it up to him on a –

Schofield untied the length of cable wrapped around his waist and ripped the two bulky sixties wetsuits off his body. Then he grabbed his MP-5 and chambered a round. If he didn't kill Barnaby, then he was damn well going to take out as many of them as he could.

As he readied his gun, Schofield saw a small Samsonite carry case on one of the shelves of the diving bell. He opened it. And saw a row of blue nitrogen charges sitting in a cushioned interior, like eggs in an egg-box.

The SAS must have left them here when they went down

to the cave, Schofield thought as he grabbed one of the nitrogen charges and put it in his pocket.

Schofield looked outside. The killer whales, it seemed, had disappeared for the moment. For a brief instant, Schofield wondered where they had gone.

'What are you doing?' Renshaw said.

'You'll see,' Schofield said as he stepped around the circular pool at the base of the diving bell.

'You're going *out there*?' Renshaw said in disbelief. 'You're leaving me *here*?'

'You'll be okay.' Schofield tossed Renshaw his Desert Eagle pistol. 'If they come for you, use that.'

Renshaw caught the gun. Schofield didn't even notice. He just turned around, and without even a second glance back at Renshaw, stepped off the metal deck of the diving bell and dropped into the water.

The water was near-freezing but Schofield didn't care.

He kept hold of the diving bell and climbed up one of its exterior pipes, pulled himself up onto its spherical roof.

They were almost up at the station now.

And as soon as they got there, Schofield thought, as soon as they broke the surface, he was going to let rip with the most devastating burst of gunfire the SAS had ever seen – aimed first and foremost at Trevor J. Barnaby.

The diving bell rose through the water, approaching the surface.

Any second now, Schofield thought as he gripped his MP-5.

Any second . . .

The diving bell broke the surface with a loud splash.

And there, standing on top of it, holding onto its winch cable, dripping with water, was Lieutenant Shane Schofield, with his MP-5 raised.

But Schofield didn't fire.

He blanched.

The whole of E-deck was lined with at least twenty SAS troopers. They stood in a ring around the pool, surrounding the diving bell.

And they all had their guns trained on Shane Schofield.

Barnaby stepped out from the southern tunnel, smiling. Schofield turned and saw him, and as he did so, he cursed himself, cursed his anger, cursed his impulsiveness, for he knew now that in the heat of the moment, in the pure anger that he had felt following Book's death, he had just made the biggest mistake of his life.

Shane Schofield tossed his MP-5 over to the deck. It clattered against the metal decking. The SAS commandos caught hold of the diving bell with a long hook and pulled it through the water toward the deck.

Schofield's mind was working again, and with crystal clarity. In the moment that he had broken the surface and seen the SAS troops with their guns pointed at him, his senses had returned with all their force.

He hoped to hell that Renshaw was keeping himself hidden inside the diving bell.

Schofield jumped down off the diving bell and landed with a loud clang on E-deck. He breathed a hidden sigh of relief when the SAS commandos released the diving bell and let it float back out into the centre of the pool. They hadn't seen Renshaw.

Then two big SAS commandos grabbed Schofield roughly, pinned his arms behind his back and slapped a pair of handcuffs around his wrists. Another SAS soldier frisked Schofield thoroughly and pulled the nitrogen charge out of his pocket. He also took Schofield's Maghook.

Trevor Barnaby came over. 'So, Scarecrow. At last we meet. It's good to see you again.'

Schofield said nothing. He noticed that Barnaby was wearing a black thermal wetsuit.

He's planning on sending another team down to the cave, Schofield thought, *with himself included*.

'You've been watching us from the diving bell, haven't you,' Barnaby said, grinning. 'But so, too, have we been watching *you*.' Barnaby smiled as he indicated a small grey unit mounted on the edge of the pool. It looked like a camera of some sort, pointed down into the water.

'One never leaves *any* flank unguarded,' Barnaby said. 'You of all people should know that.'

Schofield said nothing.

Barnaby began to pace. 'You know, when I was told that you were leading the American protective force on this mission, I'd hoped that we might get a chance to meet. But then, when I arrived, *you* flew the coop.' Barnaby stopped his pacing. 'And then I heard that you were last seen flying off a cliff in a hovercraft and suddenly I was sure we wouldn't be meeting.'

Schofield said nothing.

'But now, well,' Barnaby shook his head, 'I'm so glad I was wrong. What a pleasure it is to see you again. It's really quite a shame that we have to meet in these circumstances.'

'Why is that?' Schofield said, speaking for the first time.

'Because it means that one of us has to die.'

'My sympathies to your family,' Schofield said.

'Aha!' Barnaby said. 'Some fight. I like that. That's

what I always liked about you, Scarecrow. You've got *fight* in you. You may not be the greatest strategic commander in the world, but you're a damned determined son of a bitch. If you don't pick up something right away, you knuckle down and learn it. And if you find yourself on the back foot, you never give up. You can't *buy* that sort of courage these days.'

Schofield said nothing.

'Take heart, Scarecrow. Truth be told, you *never* could have won this crusade. You were hobbled from the start. Your own men weren't even loyal to you.'

Barnaby turned to look at Snake Kaplan on the far side of the pool. Schofield turned to look, too.

'You'd like to kill him, wouldn't you?' Barnaby said, staring at Snake.

Schofield said nothing.

Barnaby turned, his eyes narrowing. 'You *would*, wouldn't you?'

Schofield remained silent.

Barnaby seemed to think about something for a moment. When he turned back to face Schofield, he had a glint in his eye.

'You know what,' he said. 'I'm going to give you the chance to do exactly that. A sporting chance, of course, but a chance nonetheless.'

'What do you mean?'

'Well, since I'm going to kill you both anyway, I figure I might as well leave it up to the two of you to decide who gets fed to the lions and who dies on his feet.'

531

Schofield frowned for a second, not understanding, and then he looked back at the pool. He saw the high, black dorsal fin of one of the killer whales cut through the water toward him.

The killers were back.

'Unlock him,' Barnaby called to the SAS soldiers guarding Snake. 'Gentlemen, to the drilling room.'

With his hands cuffed firmly behind his back, Schofield was led down the southern tunnel of E-deck. As he walked past the storeroom, he stole a quick glance inside it.

The storeroom was empty.

Mother was gone.

But Barnaby hadn't said anything about Mother before . . .

They hadn't found her.

The SAS men marched Schofield down the long narrow corridor and shoved him into the drilling room. Schofield stumbled inside and spun around.

Snake was shoved into the drilling room a couple of seconds later. His handcuffs had been removed.

Schofield looked at the drilling room around him. In the centre of the room stood the large black core-drilling apparatus. It looked like a miniature oil well, with a long, cylindrical plunger suspended in the middle of a black skeletal rig. The plunger, Schofield guessed, was the part of the machine that drilled down into the ice and obtained the ice cores.

On the far side of the core-drilling machine, however, Schofield saw something else.

A body.

Lying on the floor.

It was the crumpled, blood-smeared body of Jean Petard, untouched since Petard had been shredded by the hailstorm of shrapnel from his own Claymore mines several hours earli –

'Gentlemen,' Barnaby said suddenly from the doorway. It was the only way in or out of the room. 'You are about to fight for the privilege of living. I will return in five minutes. When I return, I expect one of you to be dead. If, after that time, *both* of you are still alive, I will shoot you both myself. If, on the other hand, one of you is dead, the winner will get to live for a short while and die in a more noble fashion. Any questions?'

Schofield said, 'What about these cuffs?' His hands were still handcuffed behind his back. Snake's were free.

'What about them?' Barnaby said. 'Any more questions?'

There were none.

'Then, do as you will,' Barnaby said, before he left the room and closed the door behind him, locking it.

Schofield immediately turned to Snake. 'All right, listen, we have to figure out a way to – '

Snake slammed into Schofield hard.

Schofield was lifted clean off the ground and rammed with stunning force into the wall behind him. He doubled over, gasped for breath, and looked up just in time to see Snake's open palm rushing at his face. He ducked quickly and Snake's hand hit the wall.

Schofield's mind went into overdrive. Snake had just come at him with a standard hand-to-hand combat move – an open-palmed punch that was designed to send the other guy's nose back into his brain, killing him with one hit.

Snake was out to kill him.

In five minutes.

The two men were still close so Schofield thrust up hard with his knee and caught Snake in the groin. Schofield leapt clear of the wall. Once he was clear of Snake and the wall, Schofield jumped up quickly and brought his cuffed hands forward – under his feet – so that they were now in front of his body.

Snake came at him with a flurry of kicks and punches. Schofield parried each blow with his cuffed hands and the two men parted and began to circle each other like a pair of big cats.

Schofield's mind raced. Snake would want to get him onto the ground. While he remained on his feet, he would be okay – because even with his hands cuffed, he could still parry any blow Snake threw at him. But if they both went to the ground, it would be all over. Snake would have him in no time.

Got to stay off the ground . . .

Got to stay off the ground . . .

The two Marines circled each other – on either side of the black drilling apparatus in the centre of the room.

Suddenly Snake grabbed a length of steel from the floor and swung it hard at Schofield. Schofield ducked, too late, and took a glancing blow to the left side of his head. He saw stars for a second and lost his balance.

Snake was on him in a second, launching himself across the room, tackling Schofield hard, slamming him back against the wall.

Schofield's back slammed into a power switch on the wall and instantly, across the room, the vertical plunger on the drilling machine suddenly whirred to life and began to spin rapidly. It emitted a shrill, roaring sound like that of a buzzsaw.

Snake threw Schofield to the ground.

No!

Schofield hit the ground hard and rolled immediately –

– only to find himself lying face-to-face with Jean Petard.

Or, at least, what was left of Petard's face after it had been ripped to shreds by the blast of the Claymore mines.

And then at that moment – in that fleeting moment – Schofield caught a glimpse of something inside Petard's jacket.

A crossbow.

Schofield reached desperately for the crossbow with his cuffed hands. He got his hands around the grip, got a hold of it and –

– then Snake crash-tackled into him, and both men slid across the floor and slammed into the drilling machine in the centre of the room. The sound of the spinning plunger roared in their ears.

Schofield lay on his back, on the ground. Snake knelt astride him.

And in a sudden instant, Schofield saw that he still had the crossbow in his hands. He blinked. He must have kept hold of it when Snake had crash-tackled him.

It was then that Snake hit Schofield with a pulverizing blow.

Schofield heard his nose crack and saw the blood explode outwards from his face. His head slammed back against the floor. Hard.

The world spun and for a fleeting instant Schofield blacked out. Suddenly Schofield felt a wave of panic – if he blacked out completely, that would be the end of it. Snake would kill him where he lay.

Schofield opened his eyes again and the first thing he saw was the spinning plunger of the drilling machine hovering three feet above his head!

It was right over the top of him!

Schofield saw the leading edge of the spinning cylinder – the sharply serrated leading edge – the edge that was designed to cut down through solid ice.

And then suddenly Schofield saw Snake move in front of the plunger, his face contorted with anger, and then Schofield saw Snake's fist come rushing down at his face.

Schofield tried to raise his hands in his defence but they were still cuffed together, pinned underneath Snake's body. Schofield couldn't get them up –

The blow hit home.

The world became a blur. Schofield struggled desperately to see through the haze.

He saw Snake draw his hand back again, preparing for what would no doubt be the final blow.

And then Schofield saw something off to the right.

The switch on the wall that had started the drilling machine. Schofield saw three big round buttons on the switch panel.

Black, red and green.

And then, with startling clarity, the words on the black button suddenly came into focus.

'LOWER DRILL.'

Schofield looked up at Snake, saw the rapidly spinning plunger right above his head.

There was no way Schofield could shoot Snake with the crossbow, but if he could just angle his hands slightly, he might be able to . . .

'Snake, you know what?'

'*What?*'

'I never liked you.'

And with that Schofield raised his cuffed hands slightly, aimed his crossbow at the big black button on the wall, and fired.

The arrow covered the distance in a millisecond and . . .

. . . hit the big black button right in its centre – *pinning* it to the wall behind it – just as Schofield thrust his head clear of the drilling machine and the plunger, spinning at phenomenal speed, came rushing down into the back of Snake's head.

Schofield heard the sickening crunch of breaking bone as Snake's whole body was yanked violently downwards – head first – by the weight of the plunger and then suddenly, grotesquely, the plunger – its shrill buzzing filling the room – carved *right through* Snake's head and a flood of thick red-and-grey ooze poured out from his skull and then with a final *sprack!* the plunger popped out through the other side of Snake's head and continued on its way down into the ice hole beneath it.

Still somewhat dazed from the fight, Schofield rose to his knees. He turned away from the hideous sight of Snake's body pinned underneath the blood-spattered drilling machine and quickly put the crossbow in his thigh pocket. Then he spun and quickly began looking about himself for any kind of weapon he could use –

Schofield's eyes fell instantly on the body of Jean Petard, lying on the floor nearby.

Still breathing hard, Schofield crawled over to it, knelt beside it. He began rifling through the dead Frenchman's pockets.

After a few seconds, Schofield pulled a grenade out from one of Petard's pockets. It had writing on it: M8A3-STN.

Schofield knew what it was instantly.

A stun grenade. A flasher.

Like the one the French commandos had used earlier that morning. Schofield put the stun grenade into his breast pocket.

The door to the drilling room burst open. Schofield instantly fell back to the floor, tried to look tired, wounded.

Two SAS commandos stormed into the drilling room with their guns up. Trevor Barnaby strode in behind them.

Barnaby winced when he saw Snake's body lying flat on the floor, face down, with its head positioned underneath the large black drilling apparatus – complete with a gaping red hole right through the middle of it.

'Oh, Scarecrow,' Barnaby said. 'Did you have to do *that* to him?'

Schofield was still breathing hard, and he had tiny flecks of blood splattered all over his face. He didn't say anything.

Barnaby shook his head. He almost seemed disappointed that Schofield hadn't been killed by Snake.

'Get him out of here,' Barnaby said quietly to the two SAS men behind him. 'Mr Nero.'

'Yes, sir.'

'String him up.'

Down in the cave, another battle was underway.

No sooner had the first SAS diver stepped out of the water, than a second SAS diver was up and standing in the shallows behind him.

The first SAS commando stormed out of the water, firing hard. The second man followed him up, sloshing through the knee-deep water with his gun up when suddenly – *whump!* – he was violently yanked beneath the surface of the water.

The first commando – up on dry land and oblivious to the fate that had befallen his partner – snapped to his right and drew a bead on Montana, just as Gant bobbed up from behind her boulder and took him out from the left.

Gant turned, saw more SAS commandos surfacing in the pool with their sea sleds.

Then suddenly something else caught her eye.

Movement.

A large, black object just slid out from one of the wide, ten-foot holes in the ice wall above the pool and dropped smoothly into the water.

Gant's jaw dropped.

It was an animal of some sort.

But it was so *huge*. It looked like . . . like a *seal*. A great, big, enormous seal.

At that moment, another massive seal emerged from a second hole in the ice wall. And then another. And another. They just slid out from their holes and splashed down into the pool, raining down on the team of SAS divers from every side.

Gant just watched them with her mouth wide open.

The pool was a broiling froth now, choppy and frothy. Suddenly, another SAS diver went under, replaced by a slick of his own blood. And then abruptly the man next to him fell forward in the water as one of the enormous seals ploughed into him from behind and drove him under. Gant saw the animal's glistening wet back rise above the water for an instant before it submerged on top of the British soldier.

A couple of SAS divers made it to land. But the seals just followed them right out of the water. One diver was on his hands and knees, clawing his way across the ice, trying desperately to get away from the water's edge when a giant, seven-ton seal launched itself out of the pool right behind him.

The massive creature landed on the ice a bare two feet behind him and the earth shook beneath its weight. The big seal then lumbered forward and clamped its jaws shut around the SAS man's legs. Bones crunched. The man screamed.

And then before he even knew what was happening, the big seal began to eat him.

Roughly, with great, slashing bites. The high-pitched tearing sound of flesh being ripped from bone filled the cavern.

Gant stared at the scene in silent awe.

The SAS men were screaming. The seals were barking. Several of them began eating their victims *while they were still alive*.

Gant just stared at the seals. They were huge. At least as big as killer whales. And they had bulbous round snouts that she had seen in a book once.

Elephant seals.

Gant noticed that there were two smaller seals in the group. These two smaller animals had peculiar teeth – strange, elongated lower canines that rose up from their lower jaws and *over* their upper lips, like a pair of inverted tusks. The larger seals, Gant saw, did not have these tusks.

Gant tried to recall everything she knew about elephant seals. Like killer whales, elephant seals lived in large groups made up of one dominant male, known as the bull or beachmaster, and a harem of eight or nine females, or cows, which were all smaller than the bull.

Gant felt a chill as she saw the sex of one of the big seals in front of her.

These were the females of the group.

The two smaller seals that she saw were their pups. *Male* pups, Gant noticed.

Gant wondered where the bull was. He would almost certainly be larger than these females. But if the females were this big, how big would he be?

More questions flitted through Gant's mind.

Why did they attack? Elephant seals, Gant knew, could be exceptionally aggressive, especially when their territory was under threat.

And why now? Why had Gant and her team been allowed to pass safely through the ice tunnel only several hours before, while the SAS had been subjected to so violent an attack now?

There came a sudden, final scream from the pool followed by a splash and Gant looked out from behind her boulder.

There was a long, cold silence. The only sound was that of waves lapping against the edge of the pool.

All of the SAS divers were dead. Most of the seals were up inside the cavern now, bent over the spoils of their victory – the bodies of the dead SAS commandos. It was then that Gant heard a nauseating crunch and she turned round to see that the elephant seals had begun to feed en masse.

This battle was well and truly over.

Schofield stood on the pool deck of Wilkes Ice Station with his hands cuffed in front of him. One of the SAS commandos was busy tying the grappling hook of Book's Maghook around his ankles. Schofield looked off to his left and saw the high black fin of a killer whale slice through the murky red water of the pool.

'Dive Team, report,' an SAS radio operator said into his portable unit nearby. 'I repeat. Dive Team, come in.'

'Any word?' Barnaby said.

'There's no response, sir. The last thing they said was that they were about to surface inside the cavern.'

Barnaby gave Schofield a look. 'Keep trying,' he said to the radio operator. Then he turned to Schofield. 'Your men down in that cave must have put up quite a fight.'

'They do that,' Schofield said.

'So,' Barnaby said. 'Any last requests from the condemned man? A blindfold? Cigarette? Shot of brandy?'

At first, Schofield said nothing, he just looked down at his handcuffed wrists in front of him.

And then he saw it.

Suddenly Schofield looked up.

'A cigarette,' he said quickly, swallowing. 'Please.'

'Mr Nero. A cigarette for the lieutenant.'

Nero stepped forward, offered a pack of cigarettes to Schofield. Schofield took one with his cuffed hands, raised it to his mouth. Nero lit it. Schofield took a deep draw and hoped to hell that nobody saw his face turn green. Schofield had never smoked in his life.

'All right,' Barnaby said. 'That's enough. Gentlemen, hoist him up. Scarecrow, it was a pleasure knowing you.'

Schofield swung, upside down, out over the pool. His dogtags hung loosely off his chin, glistening silver in the white artificial light of the station. The water beneath him was stained an ugly shade of red.

Book's blood.

Schofield looked up at the diving bell in the centre of the pool, saw Renshaw's face in one of the portholes – saw a single terrified eye peering out at Schofield.

Schofield just hung there, three feet above the hideous red water. He calmly held the cigarette to his mouth, took another puff.

The SAS soldiers must have thought it a vain act of bravado – but while the cigarette dangled from Schofield's mouth, they never saw what he was doing with his hands.

Barnaby offered Schofield a salute. 'Rule Britannia, Scarecrow.'

'Fuck Britannia,' Schofield replied.

'Mr Nero,' Barnaby said. 'Lower away.'

Over by the rung-ladder, Nero pressed a button on the Maghook's launcher. The launcher itself was still wedged in between two rungs of the ladder while its rope was stretched taut over the retractable bridge up on C-deck, creating the same pulley-like mechanism that had been used to lower Book into the water.

The Maghook's rope began to play out.

Schofield began to descend toward the water.

His hands were still cuffed in front of him. He held the cigarette between the fingers of his right hand.

His head entered the murky red water first. Then his shoulders. Then his chest, his stomach, his elbows . . .

But then, just as Schofield's wrists were about to go under, Schofield quickly twisted the cigarette in his fingers and pointed it toward the loop of magnesium detonator cord that he had now looped around the chain-link of his handcuffs.

Schofield had seen the detonator cord when he had been standing on the deck only moments before. He had forgotten that he'd tied a loop of it around his wrist back in Little America IV. The SAS, when they had frisked him and relieved him of all his weapons earlier, must have missed it, too.

The burning tip of the cigarette touched the detonator cord a split second before Schofield's wrists disappeared below the surface.

The detonator cord ignited instantly, just as Schofield's wrists disappeared into the inky, red water.

It burned bright white, even under the water, and cut through the chain-link of Schofield's handcuffs like a knife through butter. Suddenly Schofield's hands broke apart, free.

At that moment, a pair of jaws burst through the red haze around Schofield's head and Schofield saw the enormous eye of a killer whale looking right at him. And then suddenly, it disappeared back into the haze and was gone.

Schofield's heart was racing. He couldn't see a thing. The water around him was impenetrable. Just a murky cloud of red.

And then suddenly a series of bizarre-sounding clicks began to echo through the water around him.

Click-click.

Click-click.

Schofield frowned. What was it? The killers?

And then it hit him.

Sonar.

Shit!

The killer whales were using sonar clicks to find him in the murky water. Many whales were known to use sonar – sperm whales, blue whales, killers. The principle was simple: the whale made a loud *click* with its tongue, the click travelled through the water, bounced off any object in the water, and returned to the whale – revealing to it the object's location. Sonar units on man-made submarines operated on the same principle.

Schofield was desperately searching the cloudy red haze around him – searching for the whales – when suddenly one of them exploded out of the haze and rushed toward him.

Schofield screamed underwater, but the whale slid past him, brushing roughly against the side of his body.

It was then that Schofield remembered what Renshaw had told him earlier about the killer whales' hunting behaviour.

They brush past you to establish ownership.

Then they eat you.

Schofield did a vertical sit-up, broke the surface. He heard the SAS commandos on E-deck cheer. He ignored them, gulped in air, went under again.

He didn't have much time. The killer whale that had just staked its claim on him would be coming back any second now.

Loud clicks echoed through the red water around him.

And then suddenly, a thought struck Schofield.

Sonar . . .

Shit, Schofield thought, patting his pockets, do I still have it?

He did.

Schofield pulled Kirsty Hensleigh's plastic asthma puffer from his pocket. He pressed the releasing button and a short line of fat bubbles rushed out from the puffer.

Okay, need a weight.

Need something to weigh it down . . .

Schofield saw them instantly.

Quickly, he pulled his stainless steel dogtags from around his neck and looped their neckchain around the puffer's releasing button so that it held it down.

A continuous stream of fat bubbles began to rush out from the puffer.

Schofield felt the body of water around him rock and sway. Somewhere out in the red murk of the pool, that killer whale was coming back for him.

Schofield quickly released the small asthma puffer, now weighed down by his steel dogtags.

The puffer sank instantly, leaving a trail of fat bubbles shooting up through the water behind it. After a second, the puffer sank into the murky red haze and Schofield lost sight of it.

A moment later, the killer whale roared out of the haze, coming right at Schofield, its jaws bared wide.

Schofield just stared at the massive black and white beast and prayed to God that he had remembered it right.

But the killer just kept coming. It came at him fast – frighteningly fast – and soon Schofield could see nothing but its teeth and its tongue and the closing yawn of its jaws and then –

Without warning, the killer whale banked sharply in the water and veered downward, chasing after the asthma puffer and its trail of bubbles.

Schofield sighed with relief.

In a dark corner of his mind, Schofield thought about sonar detection systems. Although it is widely stated that sonar bounces off an *object* in water, this is not entirely true. Rather, sonar reflects off the microscopic layer of *air* that lies in *between* an object in water and the water itself.

So when Schofield sank the asthma puffer – spewing out a trail of nice, fat air bubbles behind it – he had, at least insofar as the sonar-using killer was concerned, created a whole new target. The whale must have detected the stream of bubbles with its clicking and assumed that it was *Schofield* trying to get away. And so it had chased after it.

Schofield didn't think about it any more.

He had other things to do now.

He reached into his breast pocket and pulled out Jean Petard's stun grenade. Schofield pulled the pin, counted to three and then did a quick sit-up in the water and broke the surface. He then tossed the stun grenade vertically into the air and let himself fall back underwater squeezing his eyes shut.

Five feet above the surface of the pool, the stun grenade reached the zenith of its arc and hung in the air for a fraction of a second.

Then it went off.

Trevor Barnaby saw the grenade pop up out of the water. It took him an extra second to realize what it was, but by then it was too late.

Along with every one of his men, Barnaby did the most natural thing in the world when he saw a foreign object pop up out of a pool of water.

He looked at it.

The stun grenade exploded like an enormous flash-bulb, blinding all of them. The SAS men on E-deck recoiled as one, as a galaxy of stars and sunspots came to life on the insides of their eyes.

Schofield did another sit-up in the water. Only this time, when he broke the surface, he had Petard's crossbow gripped in his hands, reloaded and ready to go.

Schofield took his aim quickly and fired.

The crossbow's arrow shot across the expanse of E-deck and found its target. It slammed into the Mag-hook's launcher, wedged as it was between the rungs of the rung-ladder.

The launcher jolted out of its position, and swung free from the rung-ladder, swung toward the pool. When it had been wedged in between the rungs of the rung-ladder, the Maghook's rope had been stretched up toward the retractable bridge on C-deck at a 45° angle. Now that it was released from the rung-ladder – and since Schofield was floating in the water and, therefore, not putting any weight on it at the other end – the launcher swung back like a pendulum, out over the pool and smacked into the middle of Schofield's waiting hand.

All right!

Schofield looked up at the bridge on C-deck. The Maghook's rope was now stretched over the bridge like a block-and-tackle – with the length of rope going *up* parallel to the length of rope going *down*.

Schofield gripped the launcher tightly as he hit the black button on the grip of the Maghook. Instantly, he felt himself fly up out of the bloodstained water as the reeling mechanism of the Maghook hoisted him up toward the bridge on C-deck, its rope speeding over the bridge itself, using it as a block-and-tackle.

Schofield came to the bridge and hauled himself up onto it just as the first SAS men down on E-deck reached for their machine-guns.

Schofield didn't even look at them. He was already running off the bridge when they started firing.

*

Schofield climbed the rung-ladder up to B-deck two rungs at a time.

When he got up onto what was left of the B-deck catwalk, he reloaded his crossbow. Then he dashed toward the east tunnel and headed for the living quarters. He had to find Kirsty and then somehow he had to figure out a way to get out of here.

Suddenly, an SAS commando rounded the corner in front of him. Schofield whipped his crossbow up and fired. The SAS commando's head snapped backwards as the arrow lodged in his forehead and his feet went out from under him.

Schofield quickly went over to the body, crouched down over it.

The SAS commando had an MP-5, a Glock-7 pistol, and two blue grenades that Schofield recognized as nitrogen charges. Schofield took them all. The SAS man also had a lightweight radio headset. Schofield took that, too, wrapped it around his head, and ran off down the tunnel.

Kirsty. Kirsty.

Where were they keeping her? Schofield didn't know. He presumed somewhere on B-deck, but only because that was where the living quarters were.

Schofield entered the circular outer tunnel of B-deck just in time to see two SAS commandos racing toward him. They raised their machine-guns just as Schofield brought *both* of his guns up and fired them simultaneously. The two SAS men went down in an instant.

Schofield didn't miss a step as he strode over their bodies.

He moved swiftly round the circular corridor, looking left, looking right.

Suddenly a door to Schofield's left opened and another SAS commando emerged, gun up. He managed to get a shot off before Schofield's guns blasted to life and sent the commando flying back into the room from whence he had come.

Schofield entered the room after him. It was the common room.

He saw Kirsty instantly. He also saw two more SAS commandos who were in the process of shoving the little girl toward the door.

Schofield entered the common room warily, with both of his guns up.

When Kirsty saw Schofield step inside the common room with his two guns raised, she thought she had seen a ghost.

He looked awful.

He was soaked to the skin; his nose was broken; his face was bruised and his body armour was battered all over.

One of the SAS soldiers behind Kirsty stopped dead in his tracks when he saw Schofield step into the room. He held Kirsty out in front of him, put a gun to her head, used her as a shield.

'I'll kill her, mate,' the commando said calmly. 'I

swear to fucking Christ, I'll paint the walls of this room with her brains.'

'Kirsty,' Schofield said as he calmly levelled his pistol at the SAS man's forehead, while at the same time aiming his MP-5 at the other SAS commando's brain.

'Yeah,' Kirsty said meekly.

Schofield said evenly, 'Shut your eyes, honey.'

Kirsty shut her eyes and the world went black.

And then suddenly she heard the double *boom! boom!* of guns being fired and she didn't know whose guns had fired and then suddenly she was falling backwards, still in the grip of the SAS man who had grabbed hold of her to use as a shield. They hit the ground hard and Kirsty felt the SAS commando's grip loosen.

Kirsty opened her eyes.

The two British soldiers were lying on the floor beside her. Kirsty saw their feet, their waists, their chests –

'Don't look at them, honey,' Schofield said, moving to her. 'You don't want to see that.'

Kirsty turned around and looked up at Schofield. He picked her up and held her in his arms. Then Kirsty buried her head in Schofield's shoulderplate and cried.

'Come on. It's time to get out of here,' Schofield said gently.

Schofield quickly reloaded his weapons and grabbed Kirsty's hand and the two of them left the common room.

They raced around the curved outer tunnel, heading for the east passageway. They turned the corner.

And suddenly Schofield stopped.

Mounted on the wall to his left he saw a large, rectangular black compartment. Written across it were the words: FUSE BOX.

The fuse box, Schofield thought. This must have been where the French cut the lights earlier . . .

Schofield got an idea.

He spun where he stood and saw the door leading to the Biotoxin Lab behind him. Next to it, he saw a door marked 'STORAGE CLOSET'.

Yes.

Schofield wrenched open the door to the storage closet. Inside it, he saw mops and buckets, and old wooden shelves loaded with cleaning agents. Schofield quickly reached up and grabbed a plastic bottle of ammonia from one of the shelves.

Schofield emerged from the closet and hurried over to the fuse box. He yanked open the door and saw a series of wires, wheels and power units inside.

Kirsty was standing further down the east tunnel, looking out into the central shaft of the station.

'Hurry *up*,' she whispered. 'They're coming!'

Schofield heard voices over his newly acquired headset:

' – *Hopkins, report* –'

' – *going after the girl* –'

' – *perimeter team, return to the station at once. We have a problem here* –'

At the fuse box, Schofield quickly found the wire he was looking for. He pulled back the sheath, exposed the copper wire. Then he punched a hole in the plastic ammonia bottle with the butt of his gun and positioned it above the exposed strand of wire. A small trickle of ammonia fluid began to drip slowly out of the bottle, *down onto the exposed wire.*

The drops of ammonia smacked rhythmically against the wire.

Smack-smack. Smack-smack.

At that moment, in time with the rhythm of the ammonia drops hitting the exposed wire, every light in the tunnel – indeed, every light in the whole station – began to flicker on and off, like a strobe. On. Off. On. Off.

In the flickering light of the tunnel, Schofield grabbed Kirsty's hand and took off toward the central shaft. Once they got to the catwalk, they hurried up the nearest rung-ladder to A-deck.

Schofield strode around the A-deck catwalk, heading toward the main entrance to the station. The station around him flickered black and white. Darkness, light, darkness, light.

If he could just get to the British hovercrafts, he thought, he might be able to get away and get back to McMurdo.

There was movement everywhere. Shouts echoed through the station as the shadows of SAS commandos raced around the catwalks in the flickering light, searching for Schofield.

Schofield saw that some of the British commandos had tried to put on night-vision goggles.

But night vision would be useless now. With the station's lights flickering on and off, anyone wearing night-vision goggles would be blinded every time the lights came *on* – which was every couple of seconds.

Schofield reached the main entrance passageway, just as an SAS soldier came bursting out of it onto the catwalk. The SAS man collided with Schofield, and Schofield was almost bowled over the catwalk's railing.

The SAS man hit the ground, rose to his knees, raised his gun to fire but Schofield let fly with a powerful kick that connected with the SAS soldier's jaw and sent him crashing down to the catwalk.

Schofield was about to step over the downed soldier's body when suddenly he saw a large, black satchel stretched over the man's shoulder. Schofield grabbed it, opened it.

He saw two silver canisters inside the satchel. Two silver canisters with green bands painted around them.

Tritonal 80/20 charges.

Schofield frowned.

He had wondered earlier why the British would bring Tritonal charges to Wilkes Ice Station. Tritonal was an extremely powerful explosive, usually used for demolition purposes. Why would Barnaby have it here?

Schofield grabbed the satchel off the unconscious man's shoulder.

As he did so, however, he heard shouts coming from inside the entrance passageway. Then he heard footsteps, then the click of safeties being removed from MP-5s.

The SAS commandos outside, the perimeter team . . .

They were coming back inside!

'Kirsty! Get down!' Schofield yelled. He spun quickly and brought both of his guns up just as the first SAS commando charged in through the main entrance of Wilkes Ice Station.

The first man went down in a hail of blood and bullets.

The second and the third learned from his error and they entered the station firing.

'Back inside!' Schofield yelled to Kirsty. 'We can't go this way!'

Schofield slid down the nearest rung-ladder with Kirsty on his back.

They hit B-deck. A bullet pinged off the steel ladder next to Schofield's eyes.

Schofield heard more voices over his British headset:

' – *the fuck did he go* –'

' – *took the girl! Killed Maurice, Hoddle and Hopkins* –'

' – *saw him on A-deck* –'

And then Schofield heard Barnaby's voice. '*Nero! The lights! Either get them on or get them off! Find that fucking fuse box!*'

The station was in chaos, absolute chaos. There was no steady light, just the terrible, incessant flickering.

Schofield saw shadows on the other side of B-deck.

Can't go there.

Schofield looked out over the central shaft, and in a flickering instant, his eyes fell on the retractable bridge on C-deck.

The bridge on C-deck . . .

Schofield quickly checked his inventory.

One Glock pistol. One MP-5. Neither of which would be enough to take out twenty SAS commandos.

Schofield still had the satchel he had stolen from the SAS man who had come in from outside. Two Tritonal charges were in the satchel. He also had the two nitrogen charges he had liberated from the very first SAS commando he had killed after flying up out of the water

'All right,' Schofield said, looking down at the narrow on the Maghook.

retractable bridge on the deck beneath him. 'It's time to end this.'

In the ghostly flickering light of the station, Schofield and Kirsty stepped out onto the retractable bridge on C-deck.

If anybody had seen them, they would have seen them walk right out onto the middle of the bridge; would then have seen Schofield crouch down on one knee and do something to the bridge for several minutes.

And then, when he was done, they would have seen Schofield just crouch down next to Kirsty and wait.

A few minutes later, the British found the fuse box and the flickering stopped and the lights to the station came on again. The station glowed white under its bright fluorescent lights.

It didn't take the SAS long to spot Schofield and Kirsty.

Schofield stood up on the bridge as the remainder of the SAS unit – about twenty men – adopted positions on the C-deck catwalk, surrounding him. It was a strange sight – Schofield and Kirsty out in the middle of the shaft, standing in the centre of the retractable bridge, while the SAS took up positions on the circular catwalk all around them.

The SAS raised their guns . . .

. . . just as Schofield held one of the Tritonal charges high above his head.

Good strategy is like magic. Make your enemy look at one hand while you're doing something with the other . . .

'*Hold your fire,*' Barnaby's voice came over Schofield's headset. '*Hold your fire.*'

Schofield saw Barnaby step out onto the pool deck fifty feet below him, alone. All of the SAS platoon except for Barnaby were up on C-deck, surrounding Schofield.

Schofield glanced at the pool next to Barnaby. The killer whales were nowhere to be seen. Good.

'I've armed the Tritonal charge!' Schofield shouted. 'And my finger is holding the "ARM" button down! The timer is set for two seconds! If you shoot me, I'll drop the charge and we all die!'

Schofield stood with his feet spread apart out in the middle of the retractable bridge. Kirsty was kneeling at his feet, huddled beneath him. Schofield hoped that the SAS didn't see his hands shaking. He hoped they didn't see that his shoelaces were missing.

'And if you shoot the girl,' Schofield said, seeing one of the SAS men lower his sights at Kirsty, 'I'll *definitely* drop the charge.'

As he spoke, Schofield cast a worried glance over at the alcove on the catwalk.

If they retracted the bridge . . .

Barnaby shouted up to Schofield, 'Lieutenant, this is

very unpleasant. You have killed no less than six of my men. Have no doubt, we *will* kill you.'

'I want safe passage out of here.'

'You're not going to get it,' Barnaby said.

'Then we all go up in flames.'

Barnaby shook his head. 'Lieutenant Schofield, this is not you. You would sacrifice your own life, I know that. Because I *know* you. But I also know that you could never sacrifice the girl.'

Schofield felt his blood chill.

Barnaby was right. Schofield could never kill Kirsty. Barnaby was calling his bluff. Schofield glanced again at the alcove over on the catwalk. The alcove that housed the bridge controls.

Nero caught him looking.

Schofield watched intently as Nero looked from Schofield to the alcove and then back at Schofield again.

'*This is Nero,*' Schofield heard Nero's voice whisper over the headset. '*Subject is looking at the bridge controls over here. He looks pretty nervous about it.*'

Make your enemy look at one hand . . .

Barnaby's voice: '*The bridge. He doesn't want us to open the bridge. Mr Nero. Retract the bridge.*'

'*Yes, sir.*'

Schofield then saw Nero walk slowly toward the alcove and reach for the button that retracted the bridge. He made a point of watching Nero all the way – for this to work he needed the British to *think* that he was worried about them retracting the bridge . . .

'*Watson*,' Barnaby's voice said.

'*Yes, sir.*'

'*When the bridge opens, kill him. Take him out with a head shot.*'

'*Yes sir.*'

'*Houghton. Take the girl.*'

'*Yes, sir.*'

Schofield felt his knees begin to shake. This was going to be close. Very, very close.

. . . while you're doing something with the other . . .

'Are you ready?' Schofield said to Kirsty.

'Uh-huh.'

In the alcove, Nero hit the large rectangular button marked 'BRIDGE'.

There came a loud mechanical clanking sound from somewhere within the walls of the alcove and then suddenly the bridge underneath Schofield's feet jolted as it came apart at the centre and began to retract.

As soon as the bridge began to retract, two of the SAS soldiers fired at Schofield and Kirsty, but they had already dropped out of sight and the bullets whizzed over their heads.

Schofield and Kirsty let themselves fall down into the shaft.

They fell fast.

Down and down, until they splashed into the pool at the bottom of the station.

It had happened so fast that the SAS men up on C-deck didn't know what was going on.

It didn't matter.

For it was then that the two nitrogen charges that Schofield had tied to the ends of the retractable portions of the bridge suddenly and explosively went off.

It was the *way* that Schofield had tied the nitrogen charges to the bridge with his shoelaces that did it.

He had tied them down in such a way that each nitrogen charge lay on *either* side of the *join* between the two platforms that extended out to form the bridge.

What Schofield had also done, however, was tie the *pins* of each nitrogen charge to the *opposite* platform, so that when the bridge parted, the retraction of the two platforms would pull *both* pins from their grenades. What he had needed, however, was for the SAS to retract the bridge.

And right up until they exploded, the SAS soldiers never saw the nitrogen charges. They had been too busy looking at Schofield, first, as he held the (unarmed) Tritonal charge above his head, and secondly, as he and Kirsty fell down into the pool.

Make your enemy look at one hand while you're doing something with the other.

As he hit the freezing water, Schofield almost smiled. Trevor Barnaby had taught him that.

*

The two nitrogen charges on the bridge went off.

Supercooled liquid nitrogen blasted out in every direction on C-deck, splattering every SAS commando on the surrounding catwalk.

The results were horrifying.

Nitrogen charges are like no other grenade – for the simple fact that they do not have to *penetrate* the skin of their victims in order to kill them.

The theory behind their effectiveness is based on the special qualities of *water* – water is the only naturally occurring substance on earth that *expands* when it is cooled. When a human body is hit by a burst of supercooled liquid nitrogen, that body becomes very cold, *very* fast. Blood cells freeze instantly and, *being made up of approximately 70% water*, they begin to *expand* rapidly. The result: total body haemorrhage.

And when every single blood cell in a human body explodes it makes for a horrifying sight.

The SAS men on C-deck had their faces exposed – and that was where the liquid nitrogen hit them. So it was in their faces that the supercooled liquid nitrogen took its most devastating effect. The blood vessels under their facial skin – veins, arteries, capillaries – instantly began to rupture and then suddenly, *spontaneously*, they began to explode.

Black lesions instantly appeared all over their faces as the blood vessels under their skin exploded. Their eyes filled with blood and the soldiers could no longer see. Blood exploded out from the pores of their skin.

The SAS commandos fell to their knees, screaming.

But they wouldn't scream for long. Brain death would occur within the next thirty seconds as the blood vessels in their brains froze over and themselves began to haemorrhage.

They would all be dead soon, and it would be agony every second of the way.

From down on E-deck, Trevor Barnaby just stared up at the scene above him.

His whole unit had just been cut down by the blast of the two nitrogen charges. In fact, nearly the whole of the interior of the station was covered in blue, liquid goo. Hand railings began to crack as the nitrogen froze them. Even the cable that held up the diving bell was covered with a layer of ice – it, too, began to crack as the supercooled liquid nitrogen made it contract in on itself at an alarming rate. Even the portholes of the diving bell down in the pool were covered over with the blue poxy.

Barnaby couldn't believe it.

Schofield had just killed twenty of his men with one stone . . .

And now he was the only one left.

Barnaby's mind raced.

All right. Think. What is the objective? The spacecraft is the objective. Must control the spacecraft. How do I control the spacecraft? Wait –

I have men down there with it.

Get to the cavern.

Barnaby's eyes fell on the diving bell.

Yes . . .

At that moment, on the far side of the diving bell, Barnaby saw Schofield and the little girl break through the thin layer of ice that had formed on the surface of the pool when it had been hit by the spray of liquid nitrogen; saw them start swimming for the far deck.

Barnaby ignored them. He just grabbed a scuba tank from the ground next to him and dived into the pool, heading for the diving bell.

Schofield lifted Kirsty out of the water and up onto the deck.

'Are you okay?' he said.

'I got wet again,' Kirsty replied sourly.

'So did I,' Schofield said as he spun around and saw Trevor Barnaby swimming frantically for the diving bell.

Schofield looked up at the ice station above him. It was silent. There were no more SAS commandos left. It was only Barnaby now. *And* whoever Barnaby had already sent down to the cavern.

'Get a blanket and stay warm,' Schofield said to Kirsty. 'And don't go upstairs until I come back.'

'Where are you going?'

'After *him*,' Schofield said, pointing at Barnaby.

*

Trevor Barnaby surfaced inside the diving bell, where he was greeted by the barrel of Schofield's .45 calibre Desert Eagle automatic pistol.

James Renshaw gripped the pistol with both hands, pointed it at Barnaby's head. He was holding the gun so tightly, his knuckles were turning white.

'Don't fucking *move*, mister,' Renshaw said.

Barnaby just looked up at the little man standing inside the diving bell. The little man was wearing some really old kind of scuba gear, and he was clearly nervous. Barnaby looked at the gun in Renshaw's hand and he laughed.

Then he brought his own gun up from under the water.

Renshaw pulled the trigger on his Desert Eagle.

Click!

'Huh?' Renshaw said.

'You have to chamber a round first,' Barnaby said as he raised his own pistol at Renshaw.

Renshaw saw what was coming and, with a short squeal, he jumped down into the water next to Barnaby – scuba gear and all – and disappeared underwater.

Barnaby climbed up into the diving bell and made straight for the dive controls. He didn't waste any time. He blew the ballast tanks immediately. The diving bell began to descend.

Up on E-deck, Schofield saw the ballast tanks blow.

Shit, he's going down already, Schofield thought as he

came to a halt next to one of the rung-ladders. He had planned to go up to the winch controls on C-deck and stop the diving bell from there –

And then at that moment, there came a monstrous noise from somewhere up above him.

Snap-twanggggg!

Schofield looked up just in time to see the cable that held up the diving bell – frozen solid by the liquid nitrogen – contract and crack for the final time.

The frozen cable snapped.

The diving bell submerged.

Schofield blanched. Then he ran.

Ran as fast as he could. Toward the pool. Because now this would be the *last* trip the diving bell would be making to the underwater tunnel and it was the only way to get to the cavern and if Barnaby were to get there and the Marines down there were already dead, then the British would have the spaceship and the battle would be lost and Schofield had come too fucking far to lose everything now –

Schofield hit the edge of the deck running and dived high into the air, just as the diving bell disappeared under the surface.

After penetrating the water, Schofield shot downwards.

And then he swam. Hard. With strong, powerful strokes, chasing the descending diving bell.

Now free of its winch cable, the diving bell began to sink fast and Schofield had to use all of his strength to catch it. He came close, reached out and . . . grabbed the piping that ran around the exterior of the diving bell.

Inside the diving bell, Barnaby holstered his gun and pulled out his detonation unit.

He checked the time. 8:37 p.m.

Then he set the timer on the detonation unit. He gave himself two hours, enough time to get to the underground cavern. It was crucial that he be down there when the ring of Tritonal charges surrounding Wilkes Ice Station went off.

Barnaby then pulled his Navistar Global Positioning System transponder from his pocket and hit the 'TRANS-MIT' button.

Barnaby smiled as he put the GPS transponder back into his pocket. Despite the loss of his men up in the station, his plan – his *original* plan – was still on track.

When the eighteen Tritonal charges went off, Wilkes Ice Station would float out to sea on a newly formed iceberg. Then, thanks to Barnaby's GPS receiver, British rescue forces – and British rescue forces alone – would know *exactly* where to find the iceberg, the station, Barnaby himself, and, most importantly of all, the spaceship.

The diving bell fell downwards through the water – *fast* – with Shane Schofield clutching onto the piping on top of it.

Slowly, hand-over-hand, Schofield made his way down the side of the falling diving bell. The big bell rocked and swayed as it careered downward through the water, but Schofield held on.

And then, at last, Schofield came to the base of the bell and swung himself under it.

Schofield burst up inside the diving bell.

He saw Barnaby right away, saw the detonation unit in his hand.

Barnaby whirled around and drew his gun, but Schofield was already launching himself out of the water. Schofield's fist shot up out of the water and slammed into Barnaby's wrist. Barnaby's gun hand popped open in a reflex and the gun flew out of it and clattered to the deck.

Schofield's feet found the deck of the diving bell just as Barnaby crash-tackled him. The two men slammed into the curved interior wall of the bell. Schofield tried to kick Barnaby away from him, but Barnaby was too skilled a fighter. Barnaby crunched Schofield against the wall, and let fly with a powerful kick. His steel-capped boot connected with Schofield's cheek, and Schofield flailed backwards and felt his face slam up against the cold glass of one of the portholes of the diving bell.

At that moment – and for just a split second – Schofield saw the glass of the porthole in front of him; saw a thin crack begin to form in the glass right in front of his eyes.

Schofield didn't have time to ponder that. Barnaby kicked him again. And again. And again. Schofield fell to the floor.

'You never give up, do you,' Barnaby said as he lay the boot into Schofield. 'You never give up.'

'This is my station,' Schofield said through clenched teeth.

Another kick. The steel cap of Barnaby's boot slammed into the rib that Schofield had broken during his fight with the SAS commando in the hovercraft earlier. Schofield roared in agony.

'It's not your station anymore, Scarecrow.'

Barnaby kicked at Schofield again, but this time Schofield rolled out of the way and Barnaby's boot hit the steel wall of the diving bell.

Schofield kept rolling until he came up against the metal rim of the pool at the base of the diving bell.

And then suddenly he saw it.

The harpoon gun.

The harpoon gun that he had taken from Little America IV. It was just lying there on the deck, right in front of his eyes.

Off-balance, Schofield reached for the harpoon gun just as Barnaby leapt down onto the deck in front of him and let fly with a brutal side-kick.

The kick connected and Schofield fell – harpoon gun and all – off the deck and into the small pool of water at the base of the diving bell, and suddenly he found himself *outside* the falling diving bell!

The diving bell plummeted past him and Schofield reached out with his left hand and caught hold of a pipe on the side of it as it rushed past him and suddenly he was yanked downwards.

Schofield kept a hold of the harpoon gun as he wrapped one of his legs around the exterior piping of the falling diving bell. He could only guess how deep they had fallen.

A hundred feet? Two hundred feet?

Schofield peered in through one of the small, round portholes of the diving bell. This porthole also had a thin, white crack running across it.

Schofield saw the crack and suddenly he realized what it was. The liquid nitrogen that had splattered against the diving bell up in the station was *contracting* the porthole's glass, *weakening* it, causing it to crack.

Schofield saw Barnaby inside the diving bell, saw him standing on the small metal deck, saluting at Schofield, waving his detonation unit at him, as if it were all over.

But it wasn't over.

Schofield stared at Barnaby through the porthole.

And then, as he looked at Barnaby from outside the diving bell, Schofield did a strange thing, and in an instant, the smile vanished from Barnaby's face.

Schofield had raised his harpoon gun –

– and pointed it at the cracked porthole.

Barnaby saw it a second too late and Schofield saw the British General step across the diving bell and scream, '*No!*' just as Schofield pulled the trigger on the harpoon gun and the harpoon shot straight *through* the cracked glass of the diving bell's porthole.

The result was instantaneous.

The harpoon shot through the cracked glass of the porthole, puncturing the high pressure atmosphere of the diving bell. With the integrity of the diving bell lost, the immense weight of the ocean pressing in all around it suddenly became overwhelming.

The diving bell imploded.

Its spherical walls came rushing inwards at phenomenal speed as the colossal pressure of the ocean crushed it like a paper cup. Trevor Barnaby – Brigadier-General Trevor J. Barnaby of Her Majesty's SAS – was crushed to death in a single, pulverizing instant.

Shane Schofield just hung there in the water as he watched the remains of the diving bell sink into the darkness.

Barnaby was dead. The SAS were all dead.

He had the station back.

And then Schofield had another thought and a wave of panic swept over him. He was still a hundred feet below the surface. He would never be able to hold his breath long enough to get back up.

Oh Jesus, no.

No . . .

At that moment, Schofield saw a hand appear in front

of his face and he almost jumped out of his skin because he thought it must have been Barnaby, that Barnaby had somehow managed to escape from the diving bell a second before it had –

But it wasn't Trevor Barnaby.

It was James Renshaw.

Hovering in the water above Schofield, breathing through his thirty-year-old scuba gear.

He was offering Schofield his mouthpiece.

It was 9:00 p.m. when Schofield stepped back up onto E-deck.

It was 9:40 by the time he had searched the station from top to bottom, searching for any SAS commandos who might still have been alive. There weren't any. Schofield picked up various weapons as he went – an MP , a couple of nitrogen charges. He also got his Desert Eagle back from Renshaw.

Schofield also looked for Mother but there was no sign of her.

No sign at all.

Schofield even looked inside the dumb waiter that ran between the different decks, but Mother wasn't inside it either.

Mother was nowhere to be found.

Schofield sat down on the edge of the pool on E-deck, exhausted. It had now been more than twenty-four hours since he had last slept and he was beginning to feel it.

Beside him, Renshaw's scuba gear from Little America IV lay dumped on the deck, dripping. It still had the long length of steel cable tied to it – the cable that stretched back down through the water, down under the ice shelf and out to sea, back to the abandoned station in the iceberg about a mile off the coast. Schofield shook his head as he looked at the ancient scuba gear. Behind him on the deck sat one of the British team's sea sleds – a sleek, ultra-modern unit. The exact opposite of Little America IV's primitive scuba gear.

Renshaw was upstairs in his room on B-deck, getting some bandages, scissors and disinfectant to use on Schofield's wounds.

Kirsty was standing on the deck behind Schofield, watching him, concerned. Schofield took a deep breath and shut his eyes. Then he grabbed his nose and – *craaaack* – his broken nose went back into place.

Kirsty winced. 'Doesn't that hurt?'

Schofield grimaced and nodded. 'A lot.'

Just then, there came a loud splash and Schofield spun around just in time to see Wendy burst up out of the water and land on the metal deck. She loped over to him and Schofield patted her on the head. Wendy immediately rolled over onto her back and got him to pat her on the belly. Schofield did so. Behind him, Kirsty smiled.

Schofield looked down at his watch.

9:44 p.m.

He thought about the breaks in the solar flare that Abby Sinclair had told him about earlier.

Abby had said that breaks in the flare would be

passing over Wilkes Ice Station at 7:30 p.m. and 10:00 p.m.

Well, he'd missed the 7:30 break.

But there were still sixteen minutes until the last break passed over the station at 10:00 p.m. He'd try to get on a radio then and call McMurdo.

Schofield sighed, turned around. He had some things to do before then, though.

He saw a Marine helmet on the deck. Snake's, he guessed. Schofield reached over and grabbed it, put it on his head.

He then positioned the helmet's microphone in front of his mouth. 'Marines, this is Scarecrow. Montana. Fox. Santa Cruz. Do you copy?'

At first there was no reply, then suddenly Schofield heard: '*Scarecrow? Is that you?*'

It was Gant. '*Where are you?*' she said.

'I'm up in the station.'

'*What about the SAS?*'

'Killed 'em. Got my station back. What about you? I saw that Barnaby sent a team down there.'

'*We had a little help, but we took care of them without any losses. Everyone's accounted for. Scarecrow, we have got a lot to talk about.*'

Down in the ice cavern, Libby Gant looked out from behind the horizontal fissure.

After the short-lived battle with the British dive team, she and the others had retreated to the fissure, not to get away from the SAS commandos – they were all dead – but rather to get away from the giant elephant seals that had begun to prowl around the cavern after gorging themselves on the SAS troops. Right now, Gant saw, the seals were clustered around the big black ship, like campers gathered around a campfire.

'*Like what?*' Schofield's voice said.

'Like a spaceship that isn't a spaceship,' Gant said.

'Tell me about it,' Schofield said wearily.

Gant quickly told Schofield about what she had found. About the 'spaceship' itself and the keypad on it, about the hangar and the diary and the earthquake that had buried the whole station deep within the earth. It looked like a top secret military project of some sort – the secret construction by the US Air Force of some special kind of attack plane. Gant also mentioned the reference in the diary to a plutonium core inside the plane.

Then she told Schofield about the elephant seals and the bodies inside the cave and how the seals had cut down the SAS troops as they had emerged from the water. Their viciousness, Gant said, was shocking.

Schofield took it all in silently.

He then told Gant of the elephant seal that he had seen earlier on the monitor inside Renshaw's room; told her about the abnormally large lower canines that pro-truded up from its lower jaw like a pair of inverted fangs. As he spoke, an image formed in his mind – an image of the dead killer whale they had seen surface earlier; it had had two, long, tearing gashes going all the way down its belly.

'We saw a couple of seals with teeth like that, too,' Gant said. 'Smaller ones, though. Juvenile males. The one you saw must have been the bull. From what you're saying, though, it seems like only the males have large lower canines.'

Schofield paused at that. 'Yes.'

And then at that moment, something clicked inside his head. Something about why only the *male* elephant seals had abnormally large lower teeth.

If the spaceship really had a plutonium core inside it, then it was a good bet that that core was slowly emitting passive radiation. Not a leak. Just passive, ambient radiation, which occurred with *any* nuclear device. If the elephant seals had set up a nest near the ship, then over time the passive radiation from the plutonium might have had an effect on the male seals.

Schofield remembered seeing the infamous Rodriguez Report about passive radiation near an old nuclear weapons facility in the desert in New Mexico. In nearby towns, there were found to be unusually high instances of genetic abnormality. There were also found to be strikingly higher instances of such abnormalities in *men* than in women. Elongated fingers was a common mutation. Elongated dentures was another. *Teeth*. The writers of the report had linked the higher incidence of genetic abnormalities in men to testosterone, the male hormone.

Perhaps, Schofield thought, that was what had happened here.

And then suddenly, Schofield had another thought. A more disturbing thought.

'Gant, when did the SAS team arrive in the cave?'

'I'm not sure, somewhere around eight o'clock, I think.'

'And when did *you* arrive in the cave?'

'We left the diving bell at 1410 hours. Then it took us another hour or so to swim up the tunnel. So I'd say about three o'clock.'

Eight o'clock. Three o'clock.

Schofield wondered when the original team of divers from Wilkes Ice Station had gone down to the cave. There was something there, something that he couldn't quite put his finger on just yet. But it might have been able to explain . . .

Schofield looked at his watch.

9:50 p.m.

Shit, time to go.

'Gant, listen, I have to go. There's a window in the solar flare coming over the station in ten minutes and I have to use it. If you and the others are safe down there, do me a favour and look around that hangar. Find out everything you can about that plane, okay?'

'*You bet.*'

Schofield clicked off. But no sooner had he done so, than he heard a voice from somewhere high up in the station.

'*Lieutenant!*'

Schofield looked up. It was Renshaw. He was up on B-deck. '*Hey!* Lieutenant!' Renshaw shouted.

'What?'

'I think you better see this!'

Schofield and Kirsty entered Renshaw's room through the square-shaped hole in the door.

Renshaw was standing over by his computer.

'It's been on all day,' Renshaw said to Schofield, 'but I only looked at it just now. It said I had new mail, so I brought up my e-mail screen and had a look. It came in at 7:32 p.m. and it's from some guy in New Mexico named Andrew Wilcox.'

'What's it got to do with me?' Schofield said. He didn't even know anyone named Andrew Wilcox.

'Well, that's the thing, Lieutenant. It's addressed to you.'

Schofield frowned.

Renshaw nodded at the screen. On it was a list of some sort, with a message written above it.

Schofield read the message. After a moment, his jaw dropped. The e-mail read:

SCARECROW,

THIS IS HAWK. BE ADVISED:

AWARE OF YOUR LOCATION.

USMC PERSONNEL DEPARTMENT HAS YOU LISTED AS DEAD.
SECONDARY TEAM IS EN ROUTE TO YOUR LOCATION.

SUSPECT THAT YOUR MISSION HAS BEEN TARGETED FOR TERMINATION
BY ICG.
FEAR THAT THIS SECONDARY UNIT WILL BE HOSTILE TO YOUR INTERESTS.
WOULD HATE FOR THE SAME FATE TO BEFALL YOU AS BEFELL ME IN
PERU.

WITH THIS IN MIND, SCAN THE FOLLOWING LIST OF KNOWN ICG
INFORMERS. MY UNIT IN PERU HAD BEEN INFILTRATED LONG BEFORE I
GOT THERE. YOURS MIGHT BE, TOO.

TRANSMIT NO. 767–9808–09001
REF NO. KOS-4622
SUBJECT: THE FOLLOWING IS AN ALPHABETICAL LIST OF PERSONNEL
           AUTHORIZED TO RECEIVE SECURE TRANSMISSIONS.

NAME	LOCATION	FIELD/RANK
ADAMS, WALTER K.	LVRMRE LAB	NCLR PHYSICS
ATKINS, SAMANTHA, E	GSTETNR	CMPTR SFTWRE
BAILEY, KEITH, H.	BRKLY	AERONTL ENGNR
BARNES, SEAN M.	N. SEALS	ENSGN
BROOKES, ARLIN F.	A.RNGRS	CPTN
CARVER, ELIZABETH R.	CLMBIA	CMPTR SCI
CHRISTIE, MARGARET V.	HRVRD	IDSTRL CHMST
DAWSON, RICHARD K.	MCROSFT	CMPTR SFTWRE
DELANEY, MARK M.	IBM	CMPTR HRDWRE
DOUGLAS, KENNETH A.	CRAY	CMPTR HRDWRE
DOWD, ROGER F.	USMC	CPRL
EDWARDS, STEPHEN R.	BOEING	AERONTL ENGNR
FAULKNER, DAVID G.	JPL	AERONTL ENGNR
FROST, KAREN S.	USC	GNTC ENGNR
GIANNI, ENRICO R.	LCKHEED	AERONTL ENGNR
GRANGER, RAYMOND K	A. RANGERS	SNR SGT
HARRIS, TERENCE X.	YALE	NCLR PHYSCS
JOHNSON, NORMA E.	U.ARIZ	BIOTOXNS
KAPLAN, SCOTT M.	USMC	GNNY SGT
KASCYNSKI, THERESA E.	3M CORP	PHSPHTES

KEMPER, PAULENE J.	JHNS HPKNS	DRMTLGY
KOZLOWSKI, CHARLES R.	USMC	SGT MJR
LAMB, MARK I.	ARMALTE	BLLSTCS
LAWSON, JANE R.	U.TEX	INSCTCIDES
LEE, MORGAN T.	USMC	SNR SGT
MAKIN, DENISE, E.	U.CLRDO	CHMCL AGNTS
MCDONALD, SIMON K.	LVRMRE LAB	NCLR PHYSICS
NORTON, PAUL G.	PRNCTN	AMNO ACD CHNS
OLIVER, JENNIFER F.	SLCN STRS	CMPTR SFTWRE
PARKES, SARAH T.	USC	PLNTLGST
REICHART, JOHN R.	USMC	SNR SGT
RIGGS, WAYLON J.	N.SEALS	CMMDR
SHORT, GREGORY, J.	CCA CLA	LQD SCE
TURNER, JENNIFER, C.	UCLA	GNTC ENGNR
WILLIAMS, VICTORIA D.	U.WSHGTN	GEOPHYS
YATES, JOHN F.	USAF	CMMDR

P.S. SCARECROW, IF AND WHEN YOU GET BACK TO THE STATES, CALL A MAN NAMED PETER CAMERON AT THE WASHINGTON POST IN D.C. HE WILL KNOW WHERE TO FIND ME.

GOOD HUNTING,
HAWK

Schofield stared at the e-mail for a moment, stunned. 'Hawk' was Andrew Trent's call-sign.

Andrew Trent, who – Schofield had been told – had died in an 'accident' during that operation in Peru in 1997.

Andrew Trent was *alive* . . .

Renshaw printed off a copy of the e-mail and handed it to Schofield. Schofield scanned the e-mail again, thunderstruck.

Somehow, Trent had discovered that Schofield was down in Antarctica. He had also discovered that a secondary team was on its way to Wilkes. Most disturbing of all, however, he had discovered that the United States Marine Corps had already listed Schofield as officially dead.

And so Trent had sent Schofield this e-mail, complete with a list of known ICG informers, in case Schofield had any traitors in his unit.

Schofield looked at the time of the e-mail. 7:32 p.m. It must have been transmitted via satellite during the 7:30 p.m. break in the solar flare.

Schofield scanned the list. A couple of names leapt out at him.

KAPLAN, SCOTT M.   USMC   GNNY SGT

Snake. As if Schofield needed to know that Snake was a traitor. And then:

KOZLOWSKI, CHARLES R.   USMC   SGT MJR

Oh, God, Schofield thought.

Chuck Kozlowski. The Sergeant-Major of the Marine Corps, the highest-ranking enlisted soldier in the Corps, was a member of the ICG.

And then Schofield saw another name that made him freeze in horror.

LEE, MORGAN, T.   USMC   SNR SGT

'Oh, no,' Schofield said aloud.
'What?' Renshaw said. 'What is it?'

Montana, Schofield thought. Montana's real name was Morgan Lee. Morgan T. Lee.

Schofield looked up in horror.

Montana was ICG.

Down in the hangar, Gant and the others were searching for information about the black plane.

In a small workshop, Santa Cruz was looking at some schematics. Sarah Hensleigh was sitting at a desk behind him, with a pencil and paper out.

'Nice name,' Cruz said, breaking the silence.

'What?' Sarah said.

'The name of the plane. Says here that they called it "The Silhouette",' Santa Cruz said. 'Not bad.'

Sarah nodded. 'Hmmm.'

'Any luck with that code?' Santa Cruz asked.

'I think I'm getting closer,' Hensleigh said. 'The number that we were given, 24157817, seems to be a series of prime numbers: 2, 41, 5, 7, until you get to 817. But 817 is divisible by 19 and 43, which are also prime numbers. But then, again, 817 could be two numbers, 81 and 7, or maybe even three numbers. That's the hard part, figuring out just how many numbers 24157817 is supposed to represent.'

Santa Cruz smiled. 'Better you than me, ma'am.'

'Thanks.'

At that moment, Montana came into the workshop. 'Doctor Hensleigh?' he said.

'Yes.'

MATTHEW REILLY

'Fox said to tell you that you might like to have a look at something she's found over in the office. She said it was a codebook or something.'

'All *right*.' Hensleigh got up and left the workshop.

Montana and Santa Cruz were alone.

Santa Cruz resumed his examination of the ship's schematics.

Santa Cruz said, 'You know, sir, this plane is something else. It's got a standard turbofan powerplant with supercruise capability. And it's got eight small, retro jets on its underbelly for vertical take off and landing. But the strange thing is, *both* of these power plants run on regular jet fuel.'

'So?' Montana said from the doorway.

'So . . . what does the plutonium core do?' Santa Cruz said, turning to face Montana.

Before Montana could reply, Cruz turned back around to face his schematics. He pulled some handwritten notes out from under them.

'But I think I figured it out,' Santa Cruz said. 'I was telling Fox about this before. These notes I found say that the engineers at this hangar were working on some new kind of electronically generated stealth mechanism for the Silhouette, some kind of electromagnetic field that surrounded the plane. But to generate this electromagnetic field they needed a *shitload* of power, something in the neighbourhood of 2.71 gigawatts. But the only thing capable of generating that kind of power is a controlled nuclear reaction. Hence, the plutonium.' Santa Cruz nodded to himself, pleased.

He never noticed Montana stepping up quickly behind him.

'I tell ya,' Santa Cruz went on, 'this has been one seriously fucked up mission. Spaceships, French troops, British troops, secret bases, plutonium cores ICG traitors. Fuck. It's just – '

Montana's knife entered Santa Cruz's ear. It went in hard, and penetrated Santa Cruz's brain in an instant.

The young private's eyes went wide, then he fell forward and slammed down face-first on the desk in front of him. Dead.

Montana extracted his bloody knife from Santa Cruz's skull and turned around –

– and saw Libby Gant standing in the doorway to the workshop, with a bundle of papers in her hands, staring at him in apoplectic horror.

Schofield keyed his helmet mike. 'Gant! Gant! Come in!'

There was no reply.

Schofield glanced at his watch.

9:58 p.m.

Shit. The break in the solar flare would be here in two minutes.

'Gant, I don't know if you can hear me, but if you can, listen up. *Montana is ICG!* I repeat, *Montana is ICG!* Don't turn your back on him! Neutralize him if you have to. I repeat, neutralize him if you have to. I've gotta go.'

And with that, Schofield raced upstairs and headed for the radio room.

Gant ran across the cavernous hangar with Montana in hot pursuit. She sprinted past an ice wall just as a line of bulletholes erupted across it.

Gant unslung her MP-5 as she raced through the bulkhead doorway that led back to the fissure and the main cavern. She fired wildly behind her. Then she dived into the horizontal fissure and rolled through it just as Montana appeared in the bulkhead doorway behind her and let off another burst of gunfire.

Another line of bulletholes raked across the ice wall around Gant, only this time, the line of bulletholes cut across the middle of her body.

Two bullets lodged in her breast-plate. One opened up a jagged, red hole in her side.

Gant stifled a scream as she rolled through the fissure, clutching her side. She clenched her teeth, saw the trickle of blood seep between her fingers. The pain was excruciating.

As she rolled out of the fissure and into the main cavern, Gant saw the elephant seals over by the space-ship, and indeed, no sooner was she out of the fissure than she saw one of the seals lift its head and look over in her direction.

It was the male. The big, bull male, with its fearsome lower fangs. He must have returned sometime in the last half hour, Gant thought.

The male barked at her. Then it began to move its massive body toward her, its bulging layers of fat rippling with every lumbering stride.

The bullet wound in Gant's side burned.

She crawled on her backside away from the fissure, keeping one eye on the approaching elephant seal and the other on the fissure itself. A snail-trail of her blood stained the frosty floor behind her, betraying her path.

*

Montana emerged from the horizontal fissure, gun first.

Gant was nowhere to be seen.

Montana saw the trail of blood on the floor, leading off to the right, around and behind a large boulder of ice.

Montana followed the trail of blood. He quickly came round the ice boulder and let rip with a burst of gunfire. He hit nothing. Gant wasn't there. Her MP-5 just lay there on the floor behind the ice boulder.

Montana spun.

Where the hell was she?

Gant saw Montana come back round the ice boulder and catch sight of her.

She was now sitting on the floor in front of the horizontal fissure, clutching at her side with both hands. It had taken all of her strength – and both of her hands – to get to her feet and run back to the *left*-hand side of the fissure without spilling any more blood before Montana had emerged from the hole. She had actually intended to go back in through the fissure, but she had only managed to get this far.

Montana smiled, walked slowly over to her. He stood in front of her, with his back to the main part of the cavern.

'You're a complete son of a bitch, you know that,' Gant said.

Montana shrugged.

'It's not even an alien fucking spaceship, and you're

still killing us,' Gant said, looking out into the cavern behind Montana.

'It's not just the ship anymore, Gant. It's what you know about the ICG. That's why you can't be allowed to go back.'

Gant looked Montana right in the eye. 'Do your fucking worst.'

Montana raised his gun to fire, but at that moment, a blood-curdling roar echoed across the cavern.

Montana spun just in time to see the big, bull elephant seal come charging across the cavern toward him, roaring loudly. The floor shook with every booming stride.

Gant took the opportunity and rolled quickly back through the horizontal fissure behind her. She fell in a clumsy heap to the floor of the tunnel behind the fissure.

The big seal loped across the cavern at incredible speed, covering the distance between the ship and the fissure in seconds.

Montana raised his gun, fired.

But the animal was too big, too close.

From inside the tunnel, Gant looked up and saw Montana's outline on the other side of the translucent ice wall above her.

And then suddenly – *whump!* – she saw Montana's body get slammed up against the other side of the translucent ice wall. A grotesque, star-shaped explosion of blood flared out from Montana's body as the big seal slammed him against the ice wall with thunderous force.

Slowly, painfully, Gant got to her feet and peered out through the horizontal fissure into the main cavern.

She saw the elephant seal extract its fangs from Montana's belly. The long, blood-slicked teeth came clear of his wetsuit and Montana just dropped to the floor. The elephant seal stood over his prone body in triumph.

And then suddenly Gant heard Montana groan.

He was still alive.

Just barely, but – yes – definitely alive.

Gant then watched as the big seal bent down over Montana and ripped a large chunk of flesh from his ribcage.

Schofield strode into the radio room on A-deck on the tick of ten o'clock. Renshaw and Kirsty came in behind him. Schofield sat down in front of the radio console, keyed the microphone.

'Attention, McMurdo. Attention, McMurdo. This is the Scarecrow. Do you copy?'

There was no reply.

Schofield repeated his message.

No reply.

And then suddenly: '*Scarecrow, this is Romeo, I read you. Give me a Sit-Rep.*'

Romeo, Schofield thought. 'Romeo' was the call-sign of Captain Harley Roach, the commanding officer of Marine Force Reconnaissance Unit Five. Schofield had met Romeo Roach on a couple of occasions before. He was six years older than Schofield, a good soldier, and a legend with the ladies – hence his call-sign, Romeo.

What was more, he was a *Marine*. Schofield smiled. He had a Marine on the line.

'Romeo,' Schofield said, relief sweeping over him. 'Situation is as follows: we are in control of the target objective. I repeat, we are in control of the target objective. Heavy losses have been sustained, but the target objective is ours.' The target objective, of course, was Wilkes Ice Station. Schofield sighed. 'What about you, Romeo, where are you?'

'*Scarecrow, we are currently in hovercrafts, in a holding pattern approximately one mile from the target objective –*'

Schofield's head jerked up.

One mile . . .

But that was right outside the front door . . .

' *– and we are under orders to hold here until further instructed. We have strict instructions not to enter the station.*'

Schofield couldn't believe it.

There were Marines outside Wilkes Ice Station, *right outside* Wilkes Ice Station. Only one mile out. The first thing Schofield wanted to know was –

'Romeo, how long have you been out there?'

'*Ah, about thirty-eight minutes now, Scarecrow,*' Romeo's voice said.

Thirty-eight minutes, Schofield thought with disbelief. A squad of Recon Marines had been sitting on their asses outside Wilkes for the last half hour.

Suddenly, a voice came over Schofield's helmet intercom – *not* over the radio room's speakers. It was Romeo.

'*Scarecrow, I gotta talk to you privately.*'

Schofield clicked off the station's radio and spoke into his helmet mike. Romeo was using the closed-circuit Marine channel.

'Romeo, what the *fuck* are you doing?' Schofield said.

He couldn't believe it. While he had been inside the station doing battle with Trevor Barnaby, a whole unit of Marines had been arriving at Wilkes Ice Station, and waiting outside.

'*Scarecrow, it's a fucking circus out here. Marines. Green Berets. Hell, there's a whole goddam platoon of Army Rangers out here patrolling the one-mile perimeter. National Command and the Joint Chiefs sent every unit they could find to cover this station. But the thing is, once we got here, they ordered us to wait until a Navy SEAL team arrived. Scarecrow, my orders are very clear: if any one of my men moves toward that station before that SEAL team arrives, they are to be fired upon.*'

Schofield was stunned. For a moment, he didn't say anything.

Suddenly, the situation became clear to him.

He was in exactly the same position that Andrew Trent had been in in Peru. He had got to the station first. He had found something inside it. And now they were sending a SEAL team – the most ruthless, most deadly, special forces unit the United States possesses – into the station.

A line from Andrew Trent's e-mail suddenly popped into Schofield's head:

USMC Personnel Department has you listed as dead.

Schofield swallowed deeply as the horror of the realization hit him.

They were sending in the SEALs.

They were sending in the SEALs to kill him.

SEVENTH INCURSION

Tuesday 16 June 2200 hours

SEVENTH INCURSION

'Romeo, listen to me,' Schofield said quickly. 'The ICG planted men in my unit. One of my own men began killing my wounded. That SEAL team they're sending in is going to come in here and kill me. You have to do something.'

Schofield felt a chill run down his spine when he realized that he was saying to Romeo *exactly* the same thing that Andrew Trent had said to him from that temple in Peru.

'*What do you want me to do?*' Romeo said.

'Tell them that there's nothing in here,' Schofield said. 'Tell them there's no spaceship buried in the ice. Tell them it's just an old Air Force black project that got left down here for some reason.'

'*Uh, Scarecrow, I have no information on what's inside that station. I don't know anything about spaceships buried in the ice or Air Force black projects.*'

'Well, that's what this is all about, Romeo. Listen to me. I have fought French paratroopers for this station. I have fought Trevor Barnaby and a platoon of SAS commandos for this station. *I do not* want to be killed by a bunch of my own psycho countrymen after all I've been through, you hear me!'

'*Just hold on a second, Scarecrow.*'

There was silence on the other end of the line.

After a minute, Romeo said, '*Scarecrow, I just consulted with the Army Ranger captain out here — guy named Brookes, Arlin Brookes — and he said that he will shoot any of my men who attempt to enter the station before the SEAL team arrives.*'

Schofield pulled out his printed copy of Andrew Trent's e-mail, the list of ICG informers.

His eyes fell on one entry.

BROOKES, ARLIN F.   A RNGRS   CPTN

Son of a bitch, Schofield thought. It was the *same* guy he had run into outside the temple in Peru. Arlin F. Brookes. ICG cocksucker.

Romeo said, '*Okay, Scarecrow. Listen up. I may not be able to come in, but I'll tell you something I heard about thirty minutes ago. The* Wasp *is sailing about 300 nautical miles off the coast, out in the open sea. After we got here, I got a call from Jack Walsh on the* Wasp*. About thirty minutes ago, a patrol of four Marine Harriers shot down a British VC-10 tanker plane about 250 nautical miles off the coast after the tanker tried to make a run for it.*'

Schofield was silent.

He knew what Romeo was getting at.

Tanker airplanes exist for one reason and one reason

only: to top up the fuel on *attack* planes on long-distance missions.

If a British tanker airplane had been shot down 250 miles off the coast, then it was a good bet that somewhere out there, there was *another* British plane, an *attack* plane – a bomber or a fighter – that had been getting its fuel from the tanker. And it probably had orders to –

Oh, no, Schofield thought, realizing. *It was Barnaby's eraser.*

Like the French team's eraser, that British fighter probably had orders to fire upon Wilkes Ice Station if Trevor Barnaby didn't call in within a certain time.

Romeo said, '*The Air Force has been called in. They're sweeping the air over the ocean with AWACS birds and F-22 fighters. They're looking for a rogue British fighter and they have orders to shoot on sight.*'

Schofield fell back into his chair.

He frowned, rubbed his forehead. The world was closing in around him.

He was trapped. Totally and utterly trapped. The SEALs would be coming in soon – whether or not they realized there was nothing to be gained from this station. And even if Schofield managed to evade them after they stormed the station, there remained the possibility that Wilkes would be destroyed by an air-to-ground missile from a rogue British fighter off the coast.

There was *one* option, though, Schofield thought.

Go outside and surrender to Romeo before the SEALs arrived. At least that way, they would stay alive.

And if Schofield had learned nothing from this whole day, it was that if you stayed alive, you still had a chance.

Schofield keyed his helmet mike, 'Romeo, listen – '

'*Oh, shit, Scarecrow. They're here.*'

'What?'

'*The SEALs. They're here. They just let them through the outer perimeter. Four hovercrafts. They're coming toward the station complex now.*'

One mile out from Wilkes Ice Station an armada of hovercrafts formed a long, unbroken line. They were arrayed in a semi-circle on the landward side of the station and they were all pointed inwards – pointing in toward the station.

At that moment, however, four navy-blue hovercrafts broke through the line and glided across the ice plain toward the station. They wended their way through the outer buildings of the station complex, in no apparent hurry.

They were the SEAL hovercrafts.

Inside the lead hovercraft, the SEAL commander keyed his radio. 'Air Control, this is SEAL team, report,' he said. 'I confirm previous instructions. We *will not* enter the station until we are sure you have the bogey.'

'*SEAL team, this is Air Control. Stand by,*' a voice on the radio said. '*We are standing by for a report from our birds right now.*'

*

At that very same moment, at a point 242 nautical miles out from Wilkes Ice Station, six F-22 USAF fighters rocketed over the Southern Ocean.

The F-22 is the most advanced air superiority fighter in the world, the heir to the throne of the old F-15 Eagle. But while the F-22 looks a little like the old F-15 Eagle, the F-22 has one thing the F-15 never had – stealth.

In the lead F-22, the squadron leader was listening to his helmet radio. When the voice at the other end finished speaking, the squadron leader said, 'Thanks Bigbird, I see him.'

On his computerized display screen, the squadron leader saw a small blip heading west. A readout on the screen read:

TARGET ACQUIRED: 103 nm WNW

AIRCRAFT DESIGNATED: E-2000.

An E-2000, the squadron leader noted. The Eurofighter 2000. A twin-engined, highly manoeuvrable, pocket fighter, the E-2000 was a joint project of the British, German, Spanish and Italian Air Forces.

On the squadron leader's screen, the blip appeared to be flying casually, completely unaware of the stealthy American fighters a hundred miles behind it.

'All right, people, target has been acquired,' the F-22 pilot said. 'I repeat, target has been acquired. It's time to rock and roll.'

Inside Wilkes Ice Station, Shane Schofield didn't know what the hell to do.

He knew he couldn't surrender to the SEALs. The SEALs were almost certainly ICG. If they got him, they would kill him.

He considered going down to the cave and hiding down there – and if necessary holding the spaceship for ransom – but then he realized that it was no longer possible to get down to the cave since the diving bell had been destroyed.

Schofield led Kirsty and Renshaw out of the radio room on A-deck and down the rung-ladder to the lower decks.

'What's going on?' Renshaw said.

'We just got screwed,' Schofield said. His mind was racing. Their only option now, he figured, was to hide somewhere inside the station and hold out until the SEALs and everyone else were gone . . .

And then what are you gonna do, Schofield asked himself. *Walk home?*

If you stay alive, you still have a chance.

Schofield slid down the rung-ladder, looked down at the pool on E-deck.

And then he saw something.

He saw Wendy, lying on the deck, happily dozing off to sleep.

Wendy, he thought.

Something about Wendy . . .

The F-22 squadron leader spoke into his helmet mike, 'Bigbird, this is Blue Leader. Maintaining stealth mode.

Estimate target will be in missile range in . . . twenty minutes.'

Suddenly it hit Schofield.

He spun to face Kirsty. 'Kirsty, how long can Wendy hold her breath for?'

Kirsty shrugged. 'Most male fur seals can hold their breath for about an hour. But Wendy's a girl, and a lot smaller, so she can only hold her breath for about forty minutes.'

'Forty minutes . . .' Schofield said, doing the calculations in his head.

'What are you thinking?' Renshaw asked.

Schofield said, 'It takes us roughly two hours to get from the station to the cave, right. One hour to go *down* three thousand feet in the diving bell and then another hour or so to go *up* through the ice tunnel.'

'Yeah, so . . .' Renshaw said.

Schofield turned to face Renshaw. 'When Gant and the others were approaching the ice cavern, Gant said the strangest thing. She said that they had a visitor. Wendy. Gant said that Wendy was swimming with them as they made their way up the ice tunnel.'

'Uh-huh.'

Schofield said, 'So, even if Wendy could swim *twice* as fast as we can, if she swam all the way down and then all the way back up the ice tunnel, *she'd run out of breath before she got to the cavern.*'

Renshaw was silent.

Schofield said, 'I mean, it'd be suicide for her not to turn back after she'd swum for *twenty minutes* because she'd have to know she could get back to an air source – '

Schofield looked from Renshaw to Kirsty.

'There's another way into that ice tunnel,' he said. 'A short cut.'

'*SEAL team, this is Blue Leader. We are closing in on the target. Estimate target will be in missile range in fifteen minutes,*' the voice of the squadron leader said over the radio of the SEAL team's hovercraft.

The SEALs sat rigidly in their places in the cabin of their hovercraft. Not a trace of emotion crossed any of their faces.

Down on E-deck now, Schofield tossed the low-audibility breathing tanks onto the deck. Kirsty was already putting on a thermal-electric wetsuit. It was so hopelessly big for her that she had to roll up the sleeves and ankles to make it fit. Renshaw – already dressed in his neoprene bodysuit – just went straight for the LABA gear.

'Here, swallow these,' Schofield said as he handed a blue capsule to each of them. They were N-67D anti-nitrogen capsules. The same pills that Schofield had given to Gant and the others when they had gone down to the cavern earlier. They all quickly swallowed the pills.

Schofield discarded his fatigues and put his body

armour and gunbelt back on over his wetsuit. As he went through the pockets of his fatigues he found, among other things, a nitrogen charge and Sarah Hensleigh's silver locket. Schofield transferred both items to pockets in his wetsuit. Then he quickly began to put on one of the scuba tanks.

There were three tanks in all, all of them filled with four hours' worth of a saturated helium-oxygen mix: 98% helium, 2% oxygen. They were the auxiliary tanks that Schofield had got Gant to prepare before she had gone down to the cave earlier.

As he put his own LABA gear on, Renshaw helped Kirsty get into hers.

Schofield got his tanks on first. When he was ready, he immediately began searching the deck around him for something heavy – something *very* heavy – since they would need a good weight to take them down fast.

He found what he was looking for.

A length of the B-deck catwalk that had fallen down to E-deck back when the whole of B-deck had gone up in flames earlier. The length of metal catwalk was about ten feet long, and made of solid steel. It even had a section of its handrail still attached to it.

When Renshaw was also ready, Schofield got him to help drag it to the edge of the pool. The big length of metal catwalk screeched loudly as they dragged it across the deck.

As they worked, Wendy hopped up and down beside them, like a dog begging to go for a walk.

'Is Wendy coming with us?' Kirsty asked.

Schofield said, 'I hope so. I was hoping she would show us the way.'

At that, Kirsty leapt to her feet and hurried over to the wall by the side of the pool. She grabbed a harness from a hook and brought it back to the edge of the pool. Then she began to strap the harness around Wendy's mid-section.

'What's that?' Schofield asked.

'Don't worry. It'll help.'

'Fine, whatever. Just stay close,' Schofield said as he and Renshaw positioned the length of catwalk on the edge of the deck, so that it was all-but-ready to fall off.

'All right,' Schofield said. 'Everybody in the water.'

The three of them jumped into the water and swam back underneath the length of catwalk. Wendy happily leapt into the water after them.

'All right, get a grip on the catwalk,' Schofield's voice said over their underwater headsets.

They all grabbed hold of the length of catwalk. They looked like a set of Olympic swimmers preparing to swim a backstroke race.

Schofield placed his hand over Kirsty's, to make sure she didn't lose her hold on the catwalk as it sank through the water.

'Okay, Mr Renshaw,' Schofield said. '*Pull!*'

At that moment, Schofield and Renshaw heaved on the catwalk, and suddenly the length of heavy catwalk tipped off the edge of the deck and fell into the water with a massive splash.

The metal catwalk sank through the water fast.

The three small figures of Schofield, Renshaw and Kirsty clung grimly to it as it fell. They were all pointing downwards, their feet flailing *above* them. Wendy swam quickly down through the water behind them.

Schofield looked at the depth gauge on his wrist.

Ten feet.

Twenty feet.

Thirty feet.

Down they went, falling fast, through the magnificent white underwater world.

As they fell, Schofield tried to keep one eye on the white ice wall to his left. He searched for a hole in it, searched for the entrance to the short-cut tunnel that led to the underwater ice tunnel.

They hit a hundred feet. Without the pills, the nitrogen in their blood would have killed them by now.

Two hundred feet.

Three hundred.

They flew downwards through the water. It became darker, harder to see.

Four hundred, five hundred.

They were falling so quickly.

Six hundred. Seven hundred.

Eight –

And then suddenly Schofield saw it.

'All right, let go!' he yelled.

The others immediately let go of the falling metal catwalk. They hovered in the water as the catwalk disappeared into the gloom beneath them.

Schofield swam over to the ice wall.

A large, round hole had been burrowed into it. It looked like a tunnel of some sort, a tunnel that descended into inky darkness.

Wendy swam up alongside Schofield and disappeared inside the dark tunnel. She popped out again several seconds later.

Schofield hesitated.

Renshaw must have seen the doubt in his eyes. 'What choice do we have?' he said.

'Right,' Schofield said, pulling out his flashlight. He clicked it on. Then he kicked with his feet and swam into the tunnel.

The tunnel was narrow, and it meandered steeply downwards. Schofield swam in the lead, with Kirsty behind him and Renshaw bringing up the rear. Since they were swimming downwards, they made swift progress. They just allowed the lead weights on their weight-belts to pull them down.

Schofield swam cautiously. It was quiet here, like a tomb . . .

And then suddenly, Wendy whipped past him from behind and darted off down the tunnel in front of him.

Schofield looked at his depth gauge.

They had reached a thousand feet.

Dive time was twelve minutes.

'Bigbird, this is Blue Leader. Target is now in missile range. I repeat. Target is now in missile range. Preparing to launch AMRAAM missiles.'

'*You may fire when ready, Blue Leader.*'

'Thank you, Bigbird. All right, people. I have missile lock. Missile bay is open. Target appears to be unaware of our presence. Okay. This is Blue Leader, Fox One . . . *fire!*'

The squadron leader jammed down on his trigger.

At that moment, a long, sleek AIM-120 AMRAAM missile slid out from the missile bay of the F-22 and shot forward after its prey.

The British fighter saw the missile on its scopes straight away.

The greatest problem for stealth aircraft is that although an aircraft itself may be invisible to radar, any missiles hanging from its wings will not be invisible. Hence, all stealth aircraft like the F-22, the F-117A stealth fighter and the B-2A stealth bomber, carry their missiles internally.

Unfortunately, however, as soon as a missile is fired, it will be seen instantly on radar. Which meant that the moment the F-22 launched its AMRAAM missile at the

E-2000 over the horizon, the British plane saw the missile on its scopes.

The British pilot gave himself one minute at the most.

'General Barnaby! General Barnaby! Report!'

There was no reply.

Which was strange, because Brigadier-General Barnaby knew that this time – 2200 hours to 2225 hours – was a designated contact time, one of only two times a break in the solar flare would permit radio contact. Barnaby had reported in at 1930, another designated contact time, right on schedule.

The British pilot tried the secondary frequency. Still no luck. He tried to hail Nero, Barnaby's second in command.

Still no luck.

'General Barnaby! This is Backstop. *I am under attack!* I repeat, *I am under attack!* If you do not answer me in the next thirty seconds, I will have to assume that you are dead and pursuant to your orders, I will have no choice but to fire upon the station.'

The British pilot looked at his missile light – it was blinking. He had already preset the co-ordinates of Wilkes Ice Station into the guidance computer of his AGM-88/HLN cruise missile.

The designator letters on the missile said it all.

'AGM' stood for air-to-ground missile; 'H' for high speed; and 'L' for long range. 'N' however, had a special meaning.

It stood for *nuclear*.

Thirty seconds expired. Still no word from Barnaby.

'General Barnaby! This is Backstop! I am launching the eraser . . . *now*!' The British pilot hit his trigger and a split-second later, the nuclear-tipped cruise missile attached to the end of his wing streaked away from his plane.

The missile only just got away, for a bare two seconds later – just as the British pilot was reaching for his ejection lever – the American AMRAAM missile slammed into the back of the E-2000 and blew it and its pilot out of the sky.

The American pilots saw the bright orange explosion on the night horizon, saw the blip on their scopes disappear.

A couple of them cheered.

The squadron leader smiled as he looked at the orange fireball on the horizon. 'SEAL team this is Blue Leader. The bogey has been eliminated. I repeat, the bogey has been eliminated. You are free to enter the station. You are free to enter the station.'

Inside the SEAL hovercraft, the squadron leader's voice echoed through the speaker: '*You are free to enter the station. You are free to enter the station.*'

The SEAL commander said, 'Thank you, Blue Leader. All units, be aware. SEAL team is switching over to closed circuit channels for the assault on the station.'

He clicked off his radio, turned to his men.

'All right, people. Let's go fuck somebody up.'

Out over the Southern Ocean, the F-22 squadron leader continued to look out through his canopy at the remains of the British E-2000. Thin, orange firetrails descended slowly down to earth like cheap fireworks.

Consumed as he was with this sight, the squadron leader didn't notice a new, *smaller* blip appear on his radar screen – a blip heading south, toward Antarctica – until almost thirty seconds later.

'What the hell is that?' he said.

'*Oh, Jesus,*' someone else said. '*It must have got a missile off before it was hit!*'

The squadron leader tried to raise the SEAL team again, but this time he couldn't get through. They'd already switched over to closed circuit channels for their assault on Wilkes Ice Station.

The main doors to the station exploded inwards and the SEAL team stormed inside with their guns blazing.

It was a textbook-perfect entrance. The only problem was, the station was empty.

Schofield looked at his depth gauge: 1470 feet.

He pushed on and a few minutes later, he emerged from the narrow short-cut tunnel and found himself inside a wider, ice-walled tunnel.

Schofield knew where he was instantly, even though he had never been here before.

On the far side of the underwater ice tunnel he saw a series of round, ten-foot holes carved into the tunnel walls. Sarah Hensleigh had told him about them before. And Gant had mentioned them as well, when she had approached the cave. The elephant seals' caves. He was inside the underwater ice tunnel that led up to the spacecraft's cavern.

Schofield breathed a sigh of relief. *Yes!*

Schofield and the others swam out into the underwater ice tunnel. Then they swam quickly upward, watching the holes in the ice walls around them with more than a little trepidation.

Although the sight of the holes in the walls made him uneasy, Schofield felt fairly certain that the elephant seals would not attack them. He had a theory about that. So far, the only group of divers to have approached the underwater ice cave unharmed had been Gant's group – and they had all been wearing LABA tanks, low audibility breathing gear. The other groups to have gone down – the scientists from Wilkes and the British – hadn't. And they had been attacked. The way Schofield figured it, the elephant seals hadn't been able to *hear* Gant and her team when they had approached the cavern. And so they hadn't been attacked.

At that moment, Schofield caught sight of the surface and his thoughts about the elephant seals were forgotten.

He looked at his depth gauge. 1490 feet.

Then he looked at his watch. It had taken them all of eighteen minutes to get here. Very quick time.

And then suddenly, a low whistle cut through the water.

Schofield heard it, tensed. He saw Kirsty holding onto Wendy in the water beside him. Wendy had sensed it, too.

Suddenly, a second whistle answered the first and Schofield felt his heart sink.

The seals knew they were there . . .

'Go!' Schofield said to Renshaw and Kirsty. '*Go!*'

Schofield and Renshaw broke out into swift strokes, heading for the surface. Kirsty just slapped Wendy's flank and Wendy shot forward through the water.

Schofield looked at the surface above him. It looked beautiful, glassy, calm. Like a smooth, glass lens.

The whistles around them became more intense, and

then suddenly Schofield heard a hoarse bark cut across the underwater spectrum. Schofield spun in the water, looked about himself, then he snapped up to look at the lens-like surface again.

And at that moment, the lens shattered.

Elephant seals plunged into the water from every side. Others roared out of the submerged holes in the walls and charged at Schofield and the others. Their shrieks and barks and whistles filled the water.

Wendy raced for the surface, with Kirsty clutching onto her harness. It was like a rollercoaster ride as Wendy ducked and weaved and banked and turned to avoid the biting teeth of the elephant seals charging at her and Kirsty from every side.

And then suddenly Wendy spotted a gap and caught a glimpse of the surface. With Kirsty clutching onto her harness, she went for it.

Elephant seals lunged and snapped at them from every side but Wendy was too quick. She hit the surface and exploded out of the water.

Kirsty hit the solid ice floor of the cavern with a hard thump. She looked up and saw Wendy moving quickly away from the edge of the pool. Kirsty leapt to her feet just as the earth shook behind her.

Kirsty turned. One of the elephant seals had launched itself out of the water behind her, and now it was loping across the flat floor of the cavern, chasing after her!

Kirsty ran, then stumbled, then fell.

The elephant seal continued its charge. Kirsty was on the floor of the cavern, totally exposed –

– and then suddenly *boom!* the elephant seal's face exploded with blood and the big seal went sprawling headfirst to the ground.

The elephant seal dropped to the floor, revealing behind it: Schofield, hovering in the pool thirty feet away, with his pistol extended. *He had just shot the seal through the back of the head.* Kirsty almost fainted.

Renshaw broke the surface on the other side of the pool and found himself right next to the edge when all of a sudden he felt a sharp pain around his right ankle and *whump!* he was yanked under.

Underwater, Renshaw looked down and saw that one of the elephant seals had its mouth around his right foot. This seal looked smaller than the others and it had those distinctive lower fangs that he had seen on the larger male before.

Renshaw used his spare foot to kick the small seal in the snout. The seal squealed with pain as it released him and Renshaw swam again for the surface.

Renshaw burst up out of the water, and saw the edge of the pool right in front of him. Then he grabbed the nearest rock and hauled himself out of the water just as another, larger seal swept through the water behind him and narrowly missed biting his feet clean off.

*

Schofield was swimming madly for the edge of the pool.

As he swam, he caught fleeting glimpses of the cave around him – Kirsty over on one side of the pool, Renshaw over on the other. And then he saw the ship, the big black ship, standing like an enormous, silent bird of prey in the middle of the massive subterranean cavern.

And then suddenly the open jaws of the big bull seal rose up out of the water in front of him, obliterating his view of the big, black ship.

The big seal was already moving fast and it *ploughed* into Schofield at phenomenal speed and Schofield gasped as he felt the wind get knocked out of him and he went under.

The bull seal had rammed into his chest with its long lower fangs. Ordinarily, Schofield guessed, this would have been enough to kill any would-be victim, since the big seal's fangs would pierce the victim's chest.

But not with Schofield. He was still wearing his body armour over his wetsuit, and the bull seal's fangs had lodged in his kevlar breast-plate.

The elephant seal drove him downward through the water, pushing against his chest. Schofield struggled, but it was no use. By virtue of his breast-plate, he was practically *impaled* on the big animal's fangs.

Down and down Schofield went, on the end of the giant seal's nose. Bubbles shot out from the big animal's heaving mouth as it expelled vast quantities of air in its exertion.

Schofield had to do something. He reached into his pocket, searched for whatever lay in there.

He pulled out a British nitrogen charge, looked at it for a second.

Oh, what the hell, he thought.

Schofield quickly pulled the pin on the nitrogen charge and jammed the live grenade into the open jaws of the big elephant seal.

Then he pushed himself off the big animal's fangs and the seal shot past him in the water. It quickly realized that it had lost him, and when it did, the big seal began to turn around.

It was then that the nitrogen charge went off.

The bull seal's head exploded. Then it *imploded*. And then the most shocking thing of all happened.

A wave of *ice* shot out from the dead seal's body.

At first Schofield didn't know what it was, and then suddenly he realized. It was the liquid nitrogen from the charge, expanding through the water, *freezing* the water as it went!

The wall of ice shot through the water towards Schofield, constantly expanding, like a living, breathing ice formation *growing* through the water.

Schofield watched it with wide eyes. If it enveloped him, he would be dead in an instant.

Get out of here!

And then suddenly, Schofield felt something nudge against his shoulder and he turned.

It was Wendy!

Schofield grabbed her harness and Wendy immediately sped off.

The wall of ice behind them gave chase, expanding through the water at phenomenal speed, building upon itself at an exponential rate.

Wendy swam hard, pulling Schofield with her. But he was heavier than Kirsty and she swam more slowly than she had before.

The ice wall closed in on them.

Another elephant seal swung in behind them, spying an easy meal, but the ice wall caught the big seal, enveloped it within its expanding mass and swallowed it whole, froze it within its icy belly.

Wendy swam toward the surface, deftly avoiding any elephant seals that tried to cut across her path.

She saw the surface, hauled Schofield toward it.

Behind them, the wall of ice had lost its momentum. The nitrogen from the charge had ceased expanding. The ice wall fell away behind them.

Wendy shot out from the water, with Schofield holding onto her harness. They both hit the icy floor of the cavern with a clumsy thud and Schofield found himself lying on his belly. He rolled over onto his back –

– only to see another elephant seal leap out of the water and come rushing down toward him!

Schofield rolled. The elephant seal slammed down onto the ground right next to him. Schofield leapt to his feet, spun around, looked for the others.

'*Lieutenant! Over here! Over here!*' Sarah Hensleigh's voice yelled.

Schofield snapped around and saw Sarah Hensleigh waving from inside a small, horizontal hole in the wall about fifty yards away.

Renshaw, Kirsty – and Wendy, too – were already running toward the horizontal fissure. Schofield took off after them. As he ran across the cavern, he saw Kirsty roll in through the horizontal hole, then he saw Wendy go in after her, then Renshaw.

Suddenly a wash of static cut across Schofield's consciousness and a voice yelled loudly in his ear.

' – *you out there? Scarecrow, are you out there? Please respond!*' It was Romeo.

'What is it, Romeo?'

'*Jesus! Where have you been? I've been trying to get you for the last ten minutes.*'

'I've been busy. What is it?'

'*Get out of the station. Get out of the station now.*'

'I can't do that now, Romeo,' Schofield said as he ran.

'*Scarecrow, you don't understand. Air Force just called us. A group of F-22s just shot down a British fighter about 250 nautical miles out, but the bogey got a shot off before it was hit.*' Romeo paused. '*Scarecrow, it's heading right for Wilkes Ice Station. Satellite scans of radiation emissions from the missile indicate that it is nuclear.*'

Schofield felt a chill run down his spine as he ran. He came to the fissure in the wall and dropped to the ground, baseball-style, and slid through the horizontal fissure.

'How long?' he asked when he landed inside the

small tunnel. He ignored the others standing around him.

'*243 miles at 400 miles per hour. That gives you thirty-seven minutes until detonation. But that was nine minutes ago, Scarecrow. I've been trying to get through to you, but you haven't been responding. You have twenty-eight minutes until a live nuke hits that ice station. Twenty-eight minutes.*'

'Swell,' Schofield said, looking at his watch.

'*Scarecrow. I'm sorry, but I can't stay here. I've got to get my men to a safe distance. I'm sorry but you're on your own now, buddy.*'

Schofield looked at his watch.

It was 10:32 p.m.

Twenty-eight minutes. The nuclear missile would hit Wilkes Ice Station at 11:00 p.m.

Schofield looked up at the group around him. Sarah Hensleigh, Renshaw, Kirsty and Wendy. And Gant. It was only then that Schofield realized that Gant was in the tunnel, too, sitting down on the icy floor. He saw the ugly red stain in her side and rushed over to her.

'Montana?' he said.

Gant nodded.

'Where is he?' Schofield asked.

'He's dead. The seals got him. But he killed Santa Cruz and he winged me.'

'Are you okay?'

'No,' Gant winced.

It was then that Schofield saw the wound. It was a gut shot, to the side of Gant's stomach. The bullet must have sneaked past the clasp on the side of her body armour. It wasn't a nice wound to have – a gut-shot was a slow and painful way to die.

'Hold on,' Schofield said. 'We'll get you outta here – '

He began to move Gant, but as he did so, Gant brushed roughly against his leg and dislodged something from his ankle pocket.

It was a silver locket.

Sarah Hensleigh's silver locket. The locket that she had given to Schofield before she had gone down to the cave.

The locket landed face-down on the icy ground and in a fleeting instant, Schofield saw the writing engraved on the back of it:

To Our Daughter,
Sarah Therese Parkes
On Your Twenty-First Birthday.

Schofield froze when he saw the engraving. He quickly pulled out his printed copy of Andrew Trent's e-mail.

He scanned the list of ICG informers.

And he found it.

PARKES, SARAH T.   USC   PLNTGST

Schofield snapped up to look at Sarah Hensleigh.

'What's your maiden name, Sarah?' he asked.

Snick-snick.

Schofield heard the sound of the gun cocking before he saw it emerge from behind Sarah Hensleigh's back.

*

Sarah Hensleigh held the pistol out at arm's length, pointed it at Schofield's head. With her spare hand, she pulled Santa Cruz's helmet headset out from behind her and adjusted the channel dial on the belt clip. She spoke into the headset.

'SEAL team, this is Hensleigh. Come in.'

There was no reply. Hensleigh frowned.

'SEAL team, this is Hensleigh. Come in.'

'There's no one up there, Sarah,' Schofield said, cradling Gant in his arms. 'They've evacuated the station. They're gone. There's a cruise missile on its way here right now and it's nuclear, Sarah. Those SEALs are long gone. We have to get out of here, too.'

Suddenly, Schofield heard a voice come over Sarah's headset. *'Hensleigh, this is SEAL Commander Riggs. Report.'*

Schofield cringed, looked at his watch.

10:35 p.m. Twenty-five minutes to go.

He wasn't to know that the SEALs up in the station had switched over to a closed-circuit channel to launch their attack on Wilkes. He wasn't to know that they didn't know about the nuclear missile coming toward the station.

Hensleigh said, 'SEAL commander. I have the Marine leader down here with me in the cavern. I have him under forced arrest.'

'We'll be down there soon, Hensleigh. You have authority to kill him if you have to. SEAL team out.'

'Sarah, what are you doing?' Renshaw said.

'Shut up,' Hensleigh said, swinging the gun round so that its cold barrel touched Renshaw's nose. 'Get over there,' she said, waving Renshaw and Kirsty to Schofield's side of the tunnel. Schofield noticed that Sarah Hensleigh held the gun with confidence and authority. She had used guns before.

Schofield said, 'Where are you from, Sarah? Army or Navy?'

Sarah looked at him for a moment. Then she said, 'Army.'

'What section?'

'I was at the CDC in Atlanta for a while. Then I did some work for the Chem Weapons Division. And then, wouldn't you know it, I suddenly felt the urge to teach.'

'Were you ICG before or after you went to teach at the university?'

'Before,' Hensleigh said. 'Long before. Hell, Lieutenant, the ICG *sent* me to teach at USC. They *asked* me to retire from the Army, gave me a lifetime pension, and sent me off to the university.'

'Why?'

'They wanted to know what was going on there. In particular, they wanted to know about ice core research – they wanted to know about the chemical gases people like Brian Hensleigh were finding buried in the ice. Gases from highly toxic environments that disappeared hundreds of millions of years ago. Carbon monoxide variants, *pure* chlorine gas molecules. The ICG wanted to know about it – they can find uses for that sort of thing. So I got into the field, and I got to know Brian Hensleigh.'

Renshaw said, 'You married him to get *information* out of him?'

Over in the corner of the tunnel, Kirsty watched this conversation with almost stunned interest.

'I got what *I* wanted,' Sarah Hensleigh said. 'So did Brian.'

'Did you kill him?' Renshaw asked. 'The car accident?'

'No,' Hensleigh said. 'I didn't. ICG wasn't involved in that at all. It was exactly that, an accident. Call it whatever you want, destiny, fate. It just happened.'

'Did you kill Bernie Olson?' Schofield asked quickly.

Sarah paused before she answered that.

'Yes,' she said. 'I did.'

'Oh, you *fucking* bitch,' Renshaw said.

'Bernie Olson was a liar and a thief,' Hensleigh said. 'He was going to publish Renshaw's findings before Renshaw did. I didn't really care about that. But *then* when Renshaw struck *metal* fifteen hundred feet down, Olson told me he was going to publish *that*, too. And I just couldn't allow that to happen. Not without the ICG knowing about it, first.'

'Not without the ICG knowing about it first,' Schofield repeated bitterly.

'It's our job to know everything first.'

'So you killed him,' Schofield said. 'With sea

snake venom. And you made it look like Renshaw did it.'

Sarah Hensleigh looked at Renshaw. 'I'm sorry, James, but you were far too easy a target. You and Bernie fought all the time. And when you fought that night, it was just too good an opportunity to miss.'

Schofield looked at his watch. 'Sarah, listen. I know you don't believe me, but we have to get out of here. There is a nuclear missile – '

'There is no missile,' Hensleigh snapped. 'If there were, the SEALs wouldn't be here.'

Schofield glanced at his watch again.

10:36 p.m.

Shit, he thought. It was so frustrating. They were stuck here, at the mercy of Sarah Hensleigh. And she was just going to wait here until the nuke arrived and killed them all.

It was at that moment that Schofield's watch flicked over to 10:37 p.m.

Schofield hadn't known about the eighteen Tritonal 80/20 charges that Trevor Barnaby had lain in a semi-circle around Wilkes Ice Station with the intention of creating an iceberg.

Hadn't known that exactly two hours ago – at 8:37 p.m. – when Barnaby had been inside the diving bell alone, that Barnaby had set a timer to detonate the Tritonal charges in two hours' time.

The eighteen Tritonal charges exploded as one and the blast was absolutely devastating.

Three hundred foot geysers of snow shot up into the air. A deafeningly loud groan echoed out across the landscape as a deep, semi-circular chasm formed in the ice shelf. And then suddenly, with a loud, ominous *crack*, that part of the ice shelf containing Wilkes Ice Station and everything below it – a whole three cubic kilometres of ice – suddenly dropped away and began to fall into the sea.

Down in the ice tunnel in the cavern, the world tilted crazily. Chunks of ice rained down on everyone inside the tunnel. The collective boom of the eighteen Tritonal charges going off sounded like an enormous thunderclap.

At first, Schofield thought it was the nuclear missile. Thought that Romeo had made a terrible mistake and that the nuke had arrived half an hour earlier than expected. But then Schofield realized that it had to be something else – if it had been the nuke, they would all have been dead by now.

The tunnel lurched suddenly and Sarah Hensleigh was thrown off balance. Renshaw seized the opportunity and dived forward, tackling her. The two of them hit the ice wall hard, but Hensleigh threw Renshaw clear of her.

Schofield was still holding Gant. He put Gant down and made to stand up but Sarah Hensleigh whirled around and pointed her gun right at his face.

'I'm sorry, Lieutenant. I kind of liked you,' she said.

Despite the cacophony of sound all around them, the sound of the gun going off inside the small ice tunnel was deafening.

Schofield saw Sarah Hensleigh's chest explode with blood.

Then he saw her eyes bulge and her knees buckle as she dropped to the floor, dead.

Schofield's Desert Eagle was still smoking when Gant put it back in Schofield's thigh holster. Schofield had never had a chance to draw it, but Gant, down by his knees, had.

Kirsty just stared at the scene with her mouth open. Schofield rushed over to her.

'Jesus, are you okay,' he said. 'Your mother . . .'

'She wasn't my mother,' Kirsty said quietly.

'Would it be all right if we talked about this later?' Schofield asked. 'In about twenty-two minutes this place is gonna be water vapour.'

Kirsty nodded.

'Mr Renshaw,' Schofield said, looking at the shuddering walls all around him. 'What's happening?'

Renshaw said, 'I don't know – '

At that moment, the whole tunnel lurched suddenly and dropped about ten inches.

'It feels like the ice shelf has been dislodged from the mainland,' Renshaw said. 'It's becoming an iceberg.'

'An iceberg . . .' Schofield said, his mind turning. All of a sudden, his head snapped up and he looked at Renshaw. 'Are those elephant seals still out in that cave?'

Renshaw looked out through the fissure.

'No,' Renshaw said. 'They're gone.'

Schofield crossed the tunnel and picked up Gant in his arms, carried her toward the fissure. 'I thought that might happen,' he said. 'I killed the bull. They're probably out looking for him, now.'

'How are we going to get out of here?' Renshaw said.

Schofield hoisted Gant up into the fissure and pushed her through. Then he turned to face Renshaw, his eyes gleaming.

'We're gonna fly out of here.'

The big, black fighter stood magnificently in the middle of the underground cavern – its sharply pointed nose tilted downwards and its sleek black wings swept low. Large chunks of ice rained down from the cavern's high ceiling and exploded against its fuselage.

Schofield and the others raced across the shaking floor of the cavern and took shelter underneath the belly of the big, black plane.

As Schofield held her in his arms, Gant showed him the keypad and the entry code screen.

The entry code screen glowed green.

```
 24157817 _ _ _ _ _ _ _ _ _ _ _ _ _ _ _ _ _ _

    ENTER AUTHORIZED ENTRY CODE
```

'Did anybody figure out the code?' Schofield said.

'Hensleigh was working on it, but I don't think she ever figured it out.'

'So we don't know the code,' Schofield said.

'No, we don't,' Gant said.

'Great.'

At that moment, Kirsty stepped up alongside Schofield and peered at the screen.

'Hey,' she said, 'Fibonacci number.'

'*What?*' Schofield and Gant said at the same time.

Kirsty shrugged self-consciously. '24157817. It's a Fibonacci number.'

'What's a Fibonacci number?' Schofield said.

'Fibonacci numbers are a kind of number sequence,' Kirsty said. 'It's a sequence where each number is the sum of the two numbers before it.' She saw the amazed looks around her. 'My dad showed it to me. Does anybody have a pen and a piece of paper?'

Gant had the diary she had found earlier in her pocket. Renshaw had a pen. At first it dribbled with ink-coloured water, but then it worked. Kirsty began to scribble some numbers in the diary.

Kirsty said, 'The sequence goes like this: 0, 1, 1, 2, 3,

5, 8, 13 and so on. You just add the first two numbers to get the third. Then you add the *second* and the *third* to get the *fourth*. If you just give me a minute . . .' Kirsty said as she began to scribble frantically.

Schofield looked at his watch.

10:40 p.m.

Twenty minutes to go.

As Kirsty scribbled in the diary, Renshaw said to Schofield, 'Lieutenant, exactly *how* do you plan to fly out of here?'

'Through there,' Schofield said absently, pointing at the pool of water over on the other side of the cavern.

'*What?*' Renshaw said, but Schofield wasn't listening. He was busy looking down at the diary as Kirsty wrote in it.

After two minutes, she had five rows of numbers written out. Schofield wondered how long this was going to take. He looked at the numbers as she wrote them:

0, 1, 1, 2, 3, 5, 8, 13, 21, 34, 55, 89, 144, 233, 377, 610, 987, 1597, 2584, 4181, 6765, 10,946, 17,711, 28,657, 46,368, 75,025, 121,393, 196,418, 317,811, 514,229, 832,040, 1,346,269, 3,524,578, 5,702,887, 9,227,465, 14,930,352, 24.157.817

'And see that,' Kirsty said. 'There's your number. 24157817.'

'Holy shit,' Schofield said. 'Okay, then. What are the next two numbers in the sequence.'

Kirsty scribbled some more.

39,088,169, 63,245,986

'That's them,' Kirsty said, showing the diary to Schofield.

Schofield took it and looked at it. Sixteen digits. Sixteen blank spaces to fill. Amazing. Schofield punched the keys on the keypad.

The screen beeped.

24157817 3 9 0 8 8 1 6 9 6 3 2 4 5 9 8 6

ENTRY CODE ACCEPTED. OPENING SILHOUETTE

There came an ominous droning sound from within the big black ship and then suddenly Schofield saw a narrow flight of steps fold down slowly from ship's black underbelly.

He gave Kirsty a kiss on the forehead. 'I never thought math would save my life. Come on.'

And with that, Schofield and the others entered the big black ship.

They came into a missile bay of some sort. Schofield saw six missiles locked into place on two, triangular racks, three missiles per rack.

Schofield carried Gant across the missile bay and lay her on the floor just as Renshaw and Kirsty stepped up into the belly of the plane. Wendy hopped clumsily up the steps behind them. Once the little seal was safely inside, Renshaw pulled the stairs up behind her.

Schofield headed forward, into the cockpit. 'Talk to me, Gant!'

Gant called forward, the pain evident in her voice: 'They called it "The Silhouette". It's got some kind of stealth feature that we couldn't figure out. Something to do with the plutonium.'

Schofield stepped into the cockpit.

'*Whoa.*'

The cockpit looked amazing – futuristic – especially for a plane that was built in 1979. There were two seats: one forward and to the right, the other – the radar operator/gunner's chair – behind it and to the left. The steepness of the cockpit – it pointed sharply downwards

– meant that the pilot in the front seat sat well *below* the gunner in the back seat.

Schofield jumped into the pilot's seat just as – *bang!* – a large chunk of ice exploded against the outside of the canopy.

Schofield stared at the console in front of him: four computer screens, standard control stick, buttons and dials and indicators everywhere. It looked like an amazing, hi-tech jigsaw puzzle. Schofield felt a sudden panic sweep over him. He would never be able to figure out how to fly this plane. Not in eighteen minutes.

But then, as he looked at the console more closely, Schofield began to see that it *wasn't* actually that much different from the consoles on the Harriers he had flown in Bosnia. This was a man-made aircraft, after all – why should it be different?

Schofield found the ignition switch, keyed it.

Nothing happened.

Fuel feed, he thought. *Got to pump the fuel feed.*

Schofield searched for the fuel feed button. Found it, pumped it. Then he hit the ignition switch again.

Nothing hap –

VRRRROOOOM!

The twin turbines of the Silhouette's jet engines roared to life and Schofield felt his blood rush. The sound of the engines blasting to life was like nothing he had ever heard.

He revved the engines. He had to warm her up fast.

Time, Schofield thought.

10:45 p.m.

Fifteen minutes to go.

He kept revving the engines. Usually such a warm-up routine would take upwards of twenty minutes. Schofield gave himself ten.

God, this was going to be close.

As Schofield revved the engines whole sections of the cavern's ice walls began to collapse around the big, black plane. After five minutes of revving, Schofield looked for the vertical take-off switch.

'Gant! Where's the vectored thrust?' On modern vertical-take-off-and-landing-capable fighters like the Harrier, vertical lift-off is achieved through directable, or 'vectored', thrusters.

'There aren't any,' Gant called from the missile bay. 'It has retro-firing jets instead! Look for the button that starts the retros!'

Schofield searched for it. As he did so, however, he came across another button. It was marked: 'CLOAK MODE'. Schofield frowned.

What the hell –

And then suddenly he saw the button he was looking for: 'RETROS'.

Schofield hit it.

The Silhouette responded immediately and began to rise into the air. But then abruptly, it jolted to a sudden halt. There came a loud grinding noise from behind it.

'Huh?' Schofield said.

He looked out through the back of the cockpit canopy and he saw that the two tail fins of the Silhouette were still firmly embedded within the ice wall behind it.

Schofield found the button marked 'AFTERBURNER'. Punched it.

Immediately, a white-hot spray of pure heat burst out from the twin thrusters at the back of the Silhouette and began to *melt* the ice holding the rear of the plane captive.

The ice melted quickly, the tail fins soon came free.

Schofield checked his watch.

10:53 p.m.

The entire cavern lurched downwards again.

Come on, now, don't go yet. I just need a couple more minutes. Just a couple more minutes . . .

Schofield kept warming the engine. He looked down at his watch as it ticked over to 10:54. Then 10:55.

All right, time's up. Time to go.

Schofield hit the button marked 'RETROS' again and the eight retro jets on the underside of the big black ship fired as one, shot out long, white puffs of gas.

This time, the Silhouette rose off the icy ground, and began to hover inside the enormous underground cavern. The cavern around it rumbled and shuddered. Chunks of ice rained down from the ceiling, banged down on the back of the big black plane.

Chaos. Absolute chaos.

10:56 p.m.

Schofield looked out through the tinted-glass canopy of the Silhouette. The whole cavern was tilting crazily. It was almost as if the whole ice shelf was lurching forward, *moving* into the ocean . . .

It's falling off the mainland, Schofield thought.

'What are you doing!' Renshaw called from the missile bay.

'I'm waiting for it to flip over!' Schofield called back.

Suddenly, Schofield heard Gant groan with pain. '*Renshaw!* Help her! Fix that wound! *Kirsty!* Get up here! I need you!'

Kirsty came forward into the cockpit and climbed up into the high, rear chair. 'What do you want me to do?'

'See that stick there,' Schofield said. 'The one with the trigger on it.'

Kirsty saw a control stick in front of her. 'Yeah.'

'Pull that trigger for me, will you.'

Kirsty pulled the trigger.

As soon as she did so, two dazzling-white pulses of light shot out from *both* wings of the big black fighter plane.

The two tracer bullets slammed into the ice wall in front of the Silhouette and exploded in twin clouds of white. When the two clouds dissipated, Schofield saw a large hole in the ice wall.

'Nice shootin', Tex,' he said.

Schofield pulled back on his stick and the Silhouette rose higher in the middle of the collapsing ice cavern.

'All right, everybody, hold on, this thing is gonna go any second now,' Schofield said. 'Kirsty, when I say so, I want you to press down on that trigger and hold it down, okay.'

'Okay.'

Schofield peered out through the canopy, looked out at the crumbling ceiling of the ice cavern, looked out at the pool of water through which they had all entered the cavern – the water in the pool was sloshing madly against the ice walls.

'And then at that moment, it happened. The whole cavern just *dropped* – straight down – and then tilted dramatically. In that instant, Schofield knew that the whole of the ice shelf containing Wilkes Ice Station had come completely free of the mainland.

It had become an iceberg.

Wait for it, Schofield told himself. *Wait for it. . .*

And then, abruptly, the whole cavern tilted again.

Only this time, the tilting was *much* more dramatic. This time the whole cavern *rotated* a full 180 degrees, right *around* the hovering Silhouette!

The iceberg had flipped over!

The whole cavern was now *upside-down*!

Suddenly, a torrent of water came rushing out of a wide hole in the 'ceiling' of the cavern – the hole that only moments before had been the mouth of the under-water ice tunnel that had led up into the cavern.

The underwater ice tunnel no longer led to the depths of the ocean. Now it led *upwards*. Now it led to the surface.

Schofield manoeuvred the Silhouette so as to avoid the cascade of water pouring out of the ice tunnel. After a good twenty seconds, the rush of water abated and Schofield pulled back on his stick. The Silhouette responded by rocking backwards in the air and pointing itself up at the wide hole in the ceiling.

'All right, Kirsty, *now*!'

Kirsty jammed down on her trigger.

Immediately, the Silhouette's wings spewed forth a devastating burst of tracer fire. The relentless wave of bullets disappeared inside the hole in the ceiling and assaulted any icy crags or outcroppings that dared to jut out of the walls of the ice tunnel.

At that moment, Schofield hit the thrusters and the Silhouette shot up into the tunnel, just as, behind it, the ceiling of the enormous cavern spectacularly collapsed in on itself.

The wing-mounted guns of the Silhouette blazed away, blasting at any imperfections in the ice tunnel as the big, black plane flew upwards through what had once been the underwater ice tunnel.

Schofield guided the sleek black plane up through the tunnel, shooting through puffs of white cloud, rolling the big plane onto its side when the tunnel narrowed, praying to God that the tracer bullets were clearing the way.

Up and up the Silhouette went, blasting away at the tunnel in front of it. Explosions boomed out all around the big, black plane. The sound of its wing-mounted guns firing away was deafening.

And then suddenly the tunnel *behind* the Silhouette began to collapse at a phenomenal rate.

Boom! Boom! Boom!

Massive chunks of ice began to rain down from the ceiling of the tunnel behind the speeding plane. The

Silhouette raced upwards through the tunnel, blasting away at the walls of the tunnel in front of it while at the same time outrunning the collapsing tunnel behind it.

Through the cockpit canopy it looked like some kind of video-game thrill ride. The tunnel swept past Schofield at phenomenal speed, and occasionally the world flipped upside down as he rolled the big plane to avoid falling chunks of ice.

Schofield watched as the barrage of tracer bullets decimated the walls of the tunnel in front of him, widening it, smoothing it, and then suddenly – *voom!* – the walls of the ice tunnel vanished and in a single, glorious instant, Schofield saw the sky open up in front of him.

The Silhouette burst out of the iceberg and flew up into the clear open sky.

The Silhouette shot up into the air, almost vertical, and Schofield looked back over his shoulder and saw that the ice shelf that had held Wilkes Ice Station within it was indeed no longer an ice shelf. It was now an iceberg.

An absolutely *massive* iceberg.

It had flipped over and Schofield saw the eroded underbelly of what had once been the ice shelf – the thin, icy stalactites; the glistening-wet mountain peaks – rising like spires above the new berg. He also saw the jagged, black hole through which the Silhouette had blasted out of the berg.

And then suddenly movement caught Schofield's eye:

a thin, white object racing over the ocean, heading toward the newly formed iceberg.

The missile.

And as the Silhouette roared into the sky, Schofield watched in silent awe as the nuclear-tipped missile slammed into the iceberg and *burrowed* into it. There was about a three-second delay . . .

And then the nuclear device detonated.

Armageddon.

The white-hot flash of the nuclear explosion – directly beneath the Silhouette as it shot up into the sky – was absolutely blinding.

Solid cliffs of ice were turned instantly to powder as every side of the iceberg containing Wilkes Ice Station and the underground cavern blew out with the blast wave.

The blast wave shot underwater, vaporizing everything in its path, creating huge waves of water that expanded out from the coast, *rocking* the massive icebergs that lined the cliffs as if they were a child's bath toys. Truth be told, it wasn't a large nuclear blast – three kilotons with a blast radius of half a kilometre. But then again, there really was no such thing as a small nuclear explosion.

But it wasn't over yet.

Suddenly, a monstrous black mushroom cloud began to form, shooting up into the air at incredible speed, *chasing after* the Silhouette as it shot skyward.

Schofield went vertical, tried to outrun the burgeoning mushroom cloud. The mushroom cloud rushed upward. The Silhouette screamed into the sky, its engines roaring, and just as the mushroom cloud began to engulf it, the cloud peaked and the Silhouette shot up and away to safety.

Schofield banked the plane sharply and headed out to sea.

The Silhouette shot across the ocean, heading north. It was dark, eternal twilight. The gargantuan mushroom cloud had just dipped below the horizon to the south of the big, black plane.

Schofield found the autopilot, engaged it, then he went back into the missile bay to check on Gant.

'How is she?' he asked Renshaw. Gant was lying on the floor of the missile bay, looking seriously pale. Her skin was clammy, her eyes were closed.

'She's lost a lot of blood,' Renshaw said. 'We have to get her to a hospital fast.'

At that moment, Gant's eyes popped open. 'Did we win?' she asked.

Schofield and Renshaw both looked down at her. Schofield smiled. 'Yes, Libby, we won. How are you feeling?'

'Terrible.' She lay back, shut her eyes again.

Schofield sighed. Where could he take her? A ship would be the best option but which –

The *Wasp*. Romeo had said that the USS *Wasp* was out here somewhere. It was Jack Walsh's ship. A *Marine* ship. It would be safe.

Schofield was about to hurry back to the cockpit when suddenly he saw the diary sticking out of Gant's breast pocket.

He grabbed it and headed forward into the cockpit.

Once he was seated in the pilot's chair, Schofield keyed the Silhouette's radio. 'USS *Wasp*. USS *Wasp*. This is Scarecrow. I repeat, this is Scarecrow. Do you copy?'

There was no reply.

Schofield tried again. No reply. He looked down at the diary in his hands. It had some looseleaf sheets of paper folded inside it. Gant must have found some documents and put them in the diary.

Schofield grabbed one of the loose sheets. It read:

DESIGN PARAMETERS FOR THE B-7A SILHOUETTE
The Principal desires an attack aircraft with total electronic and conventional invisibility, STOVL capabilities through a retrograde thruster system, and multiple-launch BVR medium-to-long-range (200 nm) air-to-air/ air-to-ground missile launch capabilities as expressed in the tender lodged by General Aeronautics Inc and Entertech Ltd in response to the Principal's Invitation to Tender No. 456–771–7A, dated 2 January 1977.

Schofield translated the jargon: 'STOVL' was Short Take-Off/Vertical-Landing; 'BVR' stood for Beyond Visual Range, which meant missiles that could be fired at targets – and be expected to hit those targets – at extremely long range. 'Electronic invisibility' meant invisibility to radar, or stealth. But what the hell was *'conventional* invisibility'?

Schofield flicked to the next sheet. It looked like a page out of Entertech Ltd's tender. It read:

THE ENTERTECH EDGE
The B-7A Silhouette benefits from Entertech Ltd's experience in the field of electronic countermeasures. Invisibility to radar – or 'stealth' – is accomplished in many ways: with radar absorbent paint, minimal radar cross-sections, or with a sharply angled fuselage design as was done with the F-117A stealth fighter. But conventional invisibility is more difficult to accomplish, and so far, it has remained unattainable. Until now.

Entertech Ltd has developed a system whereby an electromagnetic field is created around a given aircraft creating conventional invisibility. The electromagnetic field distorts the molecular structure of the air around the aircraft, creating an artificial refraction of light that renders that aircraft totally invisible to radar and even –

Schofield's jaw dropped. His eyes scanned the lines ahead and he found the word he was looking for:

We call it a cloaking device . . .

Jesus, Schofield thought.
A cloaking device.
A system which rendered an aircraft not only invisible to radar, but to the naked eye as well. Every aviator

knew that even if you were invisible to your enemy's radar, you could never escape someone seeing you directly. A billion-dollar stealth bomber can be *seen* by a spotter out the window of an AWACS plane forty miles away.

Schofield's mind buzzed. This was revolutionary. A cloaking device that distorted the air around an airplane, thus creating an artificial refraction of the light around the plane, making it invisible to the naked eye. The crazy thing was, it just might work.

Schofield knew about refraction. It was most commonly observed when one looked into a fishbowl. Light outside the fishbowl strikes the water – which has a greater *density* than the air above it. The greater density of the water causes the light to *refract* at an angle, distorting the size and position of the fish inside the bowl.

But this was refraction of *air*, Schofield thought. *This is artificially altering the density of air with electricity.*

There had to be a catch. And there was.

The plutonium.

This revolutionary new system – this system that could alter the refractive density of air – was *nuclear*.

Schofield searched for the relevant paragraph, found it. As one would expect from someone trying to win a government tender, it was carefully worded:

It must be appreciated that to effect the Silhouette's cloaking system requires an enormous amount of self-generated power. According to tests run by Entertech

Ltd and General Aeronautics Inc, to disrupt the molecular and electromagnetic structure of the ambient air
around a moving aircraft requires a total of 2.71 gigawatts of electromagnetic energy. The only known source
of such a quantity of energy is a controlled nuclear
reaction –

Schofield whistled softly to himself. General Aeronautics and Entertech had offered the US Air Force a plane
with a nuclear reactor on board. No wonder they built
it in Antarctica.

Schofield put the documentation down, tried the
radio again.

'USS *Wasp*. USS *Wasp*. This is Scarecrow. I repeat,
USS *Wasp*, this is Scarecrow. Please re – '

'*Unidentified aircraft using the name Scarecrow, this
is US Air Force fighter, Blue Leader. Identify yourself,*' a
voice said suddenly over Schofield's cockpit radio.

Schofield looked at his radar screen. He was now
almost two hundred nautical miles from the coast of
Antarctica, safely out over the sea. On his radar screen,
he saw nothing.

Damn it, Schofield thought. *Whoever this is, he's
operating under stealth.*

Schofield said, 'Blue Leader, this is Lieutenant Shane
Schofield, United States Marines Corps. I am flying an
unmarked US Air Force prototype fighter-bomber. I
mean you no harm.'

Schofield looked out the canopy to his left.

He saw six tiny dots on the horizon.

'*Unidentified Aircraft. You are to follow us under escort back to the US Navy carrier,* Enterprise, *where you will be debriefed.*'

Schofield said, 'Blue Leader, I do not wish to be taken under escort – '

'*Then you will be fired upon, Unidentified Aircraft.*'

Schofield bit his tongue. 'Blue Leader, identify yourself.'

'*What?*'

'What is your name, Blue Leader?'

'*My name is Commander John F. Yates, United States Air Force, and I want you to surrender to escort formation now!*'

Yates, Schofield thought, grabbing another sheet of paper from his own pocket. There it was.

YATES, JOHN F.   USAF   CMMDR

'What is this, an ICG convention?' Schofield said to himself.

At that moment, six F-22s swooped into place around Schofield's plane. Two in front. Two on the sides. Two behind. They all kept their distance, approximately two hundred yards. Their presence never registered on Schofield's radar even though he could see them.

Suddenly, a shrill buzzing sound droned out from Schofield's cockpit speakers.

The F-22s had missile lock on him.

Schofield said, 'What are your intentions, Commander Yates?'

'*Our intention is to get you back to the United States carrier* Enterprise *and debrief you.*'

'Do you intend to fire on me?'

'*Let's not make this harder than it's already going to be.*'

'Do you intend to fire on me!'

'*Goodbye, Scarecrow.*'

Oh, fuck!

They were going to fire. Schofield looked frantically around the cockpit for something to –

Schofield's eyes fell on a button on his display.

'CLOAK MODE'.

What the hell, you've got nothing to lose . . .

Schofield hit the cloak button just as, two hundred yards behind him, the lead F-22 launched one of its missiles.

What happened next was nothing short of incredible.

Commander John Yates – Blue Leader – looked out through the canopy of his F-22. In the dull orange twilight over the ocean, Yates saw the black aircraft hovering in the air in front of him, saw the luminescent red glow of its tail thrusters.

Then he saw the white vapour-trail of his own missile as it streaked away from his wing and headed in toward the black fighter's thrusters.

As the missile raced toward the black fighter's thrusters, a shimmering haze suddenly descended upon the black fighter. The sight was absolutely amazing. It looked like a shimmering, rippling, heat haze – like the kind that hangs over a highway on a hot summer's day – and it just descended over the black fighter as if someone were lowering a curtain over it.

Suddenly, the black plane was gone.

Yates's missile went berserk.

With its initial target lost, the missile immediately began searching for another target.

659

It found it in one of the F-22s flying in *front* of Schofield's Silhouette. The missile shot into the tailpipe of the forward F-22 and the stealth fighter exploded bright orange in the dark, twilight sky.

Yates was stunned. Voices shouted over his headset.

' – *just disappeared* –'

' – *fucking thing just vanished!* –'

Yates checked his scopes. The black fighter didn't appear on his radar. He searched the sky for the black plane with his eyes. He couldn't see it, couldn't see it anywhe –

And then he saw it.

Or at least he *thought* he saw it.

Overlaid on the orange horizon, Yates saw a shimmering body of air. It looked like a warped glass lens, a lens that had been superimposed on the flat horizon, causing one short section of that horizon to ripple continuously.

Yates couldn't believe his eyes.

Inside the Silhouette, Schofield was already flicking switches.

The missile had missed him and he could hear the comments of the F-22 pilots over his own radio. The F-22s couldn't see him. It was time to fight back.

'Renshaw! Bring Gant up here! Wendy, too!'

Renshaw brought Gant forward, into the back section of the cockpit. Wendy loped into the cockpit behind him.

'Shut the cockpit door,' Schofield said.

Renshaw shut the door. They were now cut off from the missile bay in the belly of the Silhouette.

Schofield flicked a final switch and saw a red warning light appear on his computer screen.

'MISSILES ARMED. TARGETING . . .'

The screen began to flash.

'5 TARGETS ACQUIRED. READY TO FIRE.'

Schofield jammed down on his thumb trigger.

At that moment, the missile bay door of the Silhouette opened and the two racks in the missile bay began to rotate.

One after the other, five missiles dropped through the missile bay doors and out into the sky. Schofield watched as the missiles streaked away from him and began searching for their targets like bloodhounds.

The first F-22 exploded in a giant fireball. When it went up in flames, the other F-22 pilots shouted as one.

' – *missile just came out of the fucking sky!*'

' – *can't see him anywhere –*'

'.– *bastard's using some sort of cloaking device –*'

A couple of the F-22 pilots hit their afterburners, but it was no use.

More missiles shot out from the shimmering body of air that was the Silhouette. Three hit their targets right away, blasted them to smithereens.

The sixth and final F-22 tried to make a run for it. It managed to get a mile away before the missile that had acquired it – the last missile to drop from the rotating missile racks inside the Silhouette – slammed into its tailpipe and blew it to hell.

Inside the Silhouette, Schofield breathed a sigh of relief.

As he turned north, he keyed his radio again.

'USS *Wasp*. Come in. USS *Wasp*. Please. Come in.'

After several tries, there finally came a reply.

'*Unidentified Aircraft, this is* Wasp. *Identify yourself.*'

Schofield gave his name and service number.

The person at the other end checked it and then said, '*Lieutenant Schofield, it's good to hear from you. The flight deck has been cleared. You have clearance to land. I am sending you our co-ordinates now.*'

The Silhouette flew into the night.

The USS *Wasp*, the Marine Corps' aircraft carrier-like vessel, was about eighty nautical miles from Schofield. It would take about fifteen minutes to cruise there.

In the luminescent green glow of his indicator dials, Schofield stared out at the orange horizon. He had lifted the cloaking device and was allowing the plane to go on autopilot for a while.

The previous twenty-four hours flitted through his mind.

The French. The British. The ICG. His own men who had died on a mission that was never meant to succeed. Faces flashed across his mind. Hollywood. Samurai. Book. Mother. Soldiers who had died so that their country could lay its greedy hands on some extra-terrestrial technology that never was.

A deep sadness fell over Schofield.

He leaned forward and began flicking some switches. The screen in front of him flashed:

MISSILE ARMED. TARGETING . . .

Schofield quickly hit another switch.

'MANUAL TARGETING SELECTED.'

Schofield manoeuvred the target selector on the screen until he found the target he was looking for. He pressed the 'SELECT' button on his stick.

Several other option screens appeared and Schofield calmly chose the options he wanted.

Then he hit his thumb trigger.

At that moment, the sixth and final missile inside his missile bay rotated on its rack and dropped down into the sky. Its thrusters kicked in and the missile shot off into the distance, climbing high into the deep, black sky.

The USS *Wasp* lay at rest in the middle of the Southern Ocean.

It was a big ship. With a length of 844 feet, it was as long as two-and-a-half football fields. The enormous five-storey superstructure in the middle of the ship – the operations centre of the ship known as 'the island' – looked down on the flight deck. On a normal day, the flight deck would have been dotted with choppers, Harriers, gunships and people, but not today.

Today the flight deck was deserted. There was no movement on it at all, no aircraft, no people.

It looked like a ghost town.

The Silhouette slowed perfectly in the air above the non-skid deck of the *Wasp*, its retros firing thin streams of gas down onto the deck beneath it. The ominous black fighter plane landed softly on the flight deck, near the stern of the ship.

Schofield peered out through the canopy of the Silhouette.

The flight deck in front of him was eerily empty, Schofield sighed. He had expected that.

'All right, everyone, let's get out of here,' he said.

Renshaw and Kirsty left the cockpit. Wendy went with them. Schofield said he would take care of Gant.

Before he left the cockpit, however, Schofield pulled a long, thin silver canister from the satchel that he had stretched over his shoulder.

Schofield set the timer on the Tritonal charge for ten minutes and then left it on the pilot's chair. Then he picked up Gant and carried her out of the cockpit and into the missile bay. Then he carried her down the steps and out of the Silhouette.

The flight deck was deserted.

In the orange twilight, Schofield and his motley collection of survivors stood in front of the ominous black plane. The big black Silhouette, with its sharply pointed, downturned nose and its sleek, low-swept wings looked like a gigantic bird of prey as it sat there on the deserted flight deck of the *Wasp* in the cold Antarctic twilight.

Schofield led the others across the empty flight deck, toward the five-storey superstructure in the middle of the ship. It was a strange sight – Schofield with Gant in his arms, Renshaw and Kirsty, and last of all, loping across the flight deck behind them, staring in awe at the massive metal vessel all around her, Wendy.

As they approached the island, a door opened at the base of the massive structure and a white light glowed from inside it.

Suddenly, a man's shadow appeared in the doorway,

silhouetted by the light behind him. Schofield came closer and he recognized the owner of the shadow, recognized the weathered features of a man Schofield knew well.

It was Jack Walsh.

The captain of the *Wasp*. The man who, three years ago, had defied the White House and sent a team of his Marines into Bosnia to get Shane Schofield out.

Walsh smiled at Schofield, his blue eyes shining.

'You've been getting a lot of noses out of joint today, Scarecrow,' Walsh said evenly. 'Lot of people talking about you.'

Schofield frowned. He had kind of expected a warmer reception from Jack Walsh.

'Why have you cleared the deck, sir?' Schofield said.

'I didn't – ' Walsh began, cutting himself off as suddenly another man brushed rudely past Walsh and stepped out onto the flight deck and just stood there in front of Schofield.

Schofield had never seen this man before. He had carefully groomed white hair, a white moustache, and a barrel-like torso. And he wore a blue uniform. Navy. The amount of medals on his breast pocket was staggering. Schofield guessed he must have been about sixty.

'So this is the Scarecrow,' the man said, looking Schofield up and down. Schofield just stood there on the flight deck, holding Gant in his arms.

'Scarecrow,' Jack Walsh said tightly, 'this is Rear-Admiral Thomas Clayton, the Navy's representative to the Joint Chiefs of Staff. He assumed command of the *Wasp* about four hours ago.'

Schofield sighed inwardly.

An *Admiral* from the Joint Chiefs of Staff. *Jesus.*

If what he had heard about the ICG was correct, the Joint Chiefs was its head, its brain. Schofield was looking at one of the *heads* of the ICG.

'*All right!*' Admiral Clayton yelled loudly to someone standing in the doorway behind Walsh. '*Get out there!*'

At that moment, a stream of men – all of them dressed in blue coveralls – poured out of the doorway in front of Schofield and headed across the deck toward the Silhouette.

Admiral Clayton turned to Schofield. 'Seems this mission is not going to be a complete waste of time after all. We heard the commentary of your dogfight with the F-22s. A cloaking device, huh? Who would have thought it.'

Schofield looked back out at the deck, saw the men in blue coveralls reach the stern-end of the flight deck, saw them begin to swarm all over the Silhouette. A couple of them went up the steps and inside the big, black plane.

'Captain Walsh,' Schofield said, indicating Gant. 'This Marine needs medical attention.'

Walsh nodded. 'Let's get her to the infirmary. Deckhand!'

A deckhand appeared, took Gant from Schofield, carried her inside.

Schofield turned to Kirsty and Renshaw, 'Go with her. Take Wendy, too.' Kirsty and Renshaw obeyed, went inside the island. Wendy hopped in through the doorway after them. Schofield made to follow them, but as he did, there came a shout from over by the Silhouette.

'*Admiral!*' One of the men in blue coveralls called out from underneath the pointed nose of the Silhouette.

'What is it?' Admiral Clayton said, walking over to the plane.

The man held up the Tritonal 80/20 charge that Schofield had left inside the cockpit. Clayton saw it. He didn't seem at all perturbed by its presence.

Admiral Clayton turned to Schofield from fifty yards away. 'Attempting to destroy the evidence, Lieutenant?'

The Admiral took the charge from the man, turned the pressurized lid and calmly flicked the 'DISARM' switch.

Clayton smiled at Schofield. 'Really, Scarecrow,' he called. 'You'll have to do better than that to beat me.'

Schofield just stared at Clayton, standing over by the Silhouette. 'I'm sorry about the deck, sir,' Schofield said quietly.

Behind him, Jack Walsh said, 'What?'

'I said, I'm sorry about the deck, sir,' Schofield repeated.

At that moment, there came a sudden, high-pitched whining sound. And then before anyone knew what was happening, the whine became a scream and then, like a thunderbolt sent from God himself, the sixth and final missile from the Silhouette came shooting down out of the sky and slammed into the Silhouette at nearly three hundred miles per hour.

The big, black fighter plane shattered in an instant, exploded into a thousand pieces. Every man inside or near it was killed instantly. Thee fuel tanks of the big, black plane exploded next, causing a red hot fireball of liquid fire to flare out from the destroyed plane. The fireball billowed out across the deck and engulfed Admiral Clayton. It was so hot, it wiped the skin from his face.

Admiral Thomas Clayton was dead before he hit the ground.

Shane Schofield stood on the bridge of the *Wasp* as it sailed east across the Southern Ocean, into the morning sun. He took a sip from a coffee mug with the words 'CAPTAIN'S MUG' written on it. The coffee was hot.

Jack Walsh came out onto the bridge and offered him a new pair of silver, anti-flash glasses. Schofield took them, put them on.

It had been three hours now since the Silhouette had been destroyed by one of its own missiles.

Gant had been taken to the infirmary, where her condition had worsened. Her blood loss had been severe. She had lapsed into a coma about half an hour ago.

Renshaw and Kirsty were in Walsh's stateroom, sleeping soundly. Wendy was playing in a dive preparation pool belowdecks.

Schofield himself had had a hot shower and changed into a tracksuit. A corpsman had attended to his wounds, reset his broken rib. He had said that Schofield would need further treatment when he got back home, but with a few painkillers, he would be okay for now.

When the corpsman had finished, Schofield had returned to Gant's bedside. He had only come up to the bridge when Walsh had called for him.

When he'd got there, Walsh had told him that the *Wasp* had just received a call from McMurdo Station. Apparently, a battered Marine hovercraft had just arrived at McMurdo. In it were five people – one Marine and four scientists – claiming that they had come from Wilkes Ice Station.

Schofield shook his head and smiled. Rebound had made it to McMurdo.

It was then that Walsh demanded a rundown of the events of the preceding twenty-four hours. Schofield told him everything – about the French and the British, the ICG and the Silhouette. He even told Walsh about the help he had received from a dead Marine named Andrew Trent.

When Schofield had finished recounting his story, Walsh just stood there for a moment in stunned silence. Schofield took another sip from his mug and looked aft, through the slanted panoramic windows of the bridge. He saw the gaping hole at the stern end of the flight deck where the missile had hit the Silhouette. Jagged lengths of metal stuck out into the hole, wires and cables hung loosely from it.

Of course, Walsh had accepted Schofield's apology for the damage to the deck. He hadn't much liked Admiral Clayton anyway, the asshole had assumed command of Walsh's ship and no skipper appreciated that. And then when Walsh heard about Schofield's experiences with the ICG down at Wilkes Ice Station, he had no pity for Clayton and his ICG men at all.

As he stood there gazing down at the hole in the flight deck, Schofield began to think about the mission again, in particular, about the Marines he had lost, the *friends* he had lost on this foolish crusade.

'Uh, Captain,' a young ensign said. Walsh and Schofield turned together. The young ensign was sitting at an illuminated table inside the communications room which adjoined the bridge. 'I'm picking up something very peculiar here . . .'

'What is it?' Walsh said. He and Schofield came over.

The ensign said, 'It appears to be some kind of GPS transponder signal, coming from just off the coast of Antartica. It's emitting a valid Marine code signal.'

Schofield peered at the illuminated table in front of the ensign. It had a computer-generated map drawn on it. Down on the coast of Antarctica – just off the coast, actually – there was a small, blinking red dot, with a blinking red number alongside it: **05**.

Schofield frowned. He remembered pressing his own Navistar Global Positioning System transponder when he and Renshaw had been marooned on the iceberg. His GPS transponder code was '01' since he was the unit commander. Snake was 02, Book was 03. The numbers then ascended in order of seniority.

Schofield tried to remember who '05' was.

'Holy shit,' he said, realizing. 'It's Mother!'

*

The *Wasp* sailed toward the rising sun.

As soon as Schofield realized who the GPS signal represented, Jack Walsh had sent a call to McMurdo. The Marines there – trusted Marines – sent a patrol boat out along the coast to pick up Mother.

A whole day later, as the *Wasp* entered the Pacific Ocean, Schofield got a call from the patrol boat. It had found Mother, on an iceberg just off the destroyed coastline. Apparently, the crew of the patrol boat – all of them dressed in airtight, radiation suits – had found her inside an old station of some sort, a station *buried within the iceberg*.

The skipper of the patrol boat said that Mother was suffering from severe hypothermia and radiation sickness from the fallout and that they were about to put her under sedation.

It was then that Schofield heard a voice at the other end of the line. A woman's voice, shouting wildly, 'Is that him? Is that Scarecrow?'

Mother came on the line.

After some obscene pleasantries, she told Schofield how she had hidden inside the elevator shaft, and how she had lapsed into unconsciousness. Then she told him how she had been woken by the sound of the Navy SEALs' gunfire as they had entered Wilkes Ice Station. Minutes later, she had heard every word of Schofield's conversation with Romeo, heard about the nuclear-tipped cruise missile heading towards Wilkes.

And so she had crawled out of the dumb waiter shaft – while the SEALs were still in the station – and headed for the pool deck, grabbing a couple of fluid bags from the storeroom on the way. When she got to the pool deck, she saw Renshaw's thirty-year-old scuba gear, lying on the deck, *with a cable attached to it.*

A steel cable that had led – with the help of the last remaining British sea sled – all the way back to Little America IV, one mile off the coast.

Schofield was amazed. He congratulated Mother and said his goodbyes, said he would see her back at Pearl. And as they took Mother away at the other end to sedate her, Schofield heard her shout, '*And I remember you kissed me!* You *hot* dog!'

Schofield just laughed.

Five days later, the USS *Wasp* sailed into Pearl Harbor in Hawaii.

A cluster of TV cameras was waiting on the dock when it arrived. Two days earlier, a charter plane flying over the south Pacific had spotted the *Wasp* and seen its damaged flight deck. One of the pilots had captured the damage on video camera. The TV news stations had eaten it up and now they were keen to find out what had happened to the great ship.

At the top of the gangway, Schofield watched as two midshipmen carried Gant off the ship on a stretcher. She was still in a coma. They were taking her to the nearby military hospital.

Renshaw and Kirsty met Schofield at the top of the gangway.

'Hey there,' Schofield said.

'Hi,' Kirsty said. She was holding onto Renshaw's hand.

Renshaw put on a bad Marlon Brando accent. 'Who'd have thought it? I'm the Godfather.'

Schofield laughed.

Kirsty spun around. 'Say, where's – '

At that moment, Wendy slid out from a nearby doorway. She loped straight up to Schofield and began nuzzling his hand. From tip to tail, the little fur seal was dripping wet.

'She's, ah, taken a bit of a liking to the ship's dive preparation pool,' Renshaw said.

'So I see,' Schofield said, as he gave Wendy a gentle pat behind the ears. Wendy preened, then she dropped to the deck and rolled onto her back. Schofield shook his head as he dropped to his haunches and gave her a quick pat on her belly.

'The captain even said she could stay here until we found somewhere else for her to live,' Kirsty said.

'Good,' Schofield said. 'I think it's the least we can do.' He gave Wendy a final pat and the little seal leapt to her feet and dashed away, heading back downstairs toward her favourite pool.

Schofield stood up again and turned to face Renshaw. 'Mr Renshaw, I have a question for you.'

'What?'

'What time did the people from your station dive down to the cave?'

'What *time*?'

'Yes, the time,' Schofield said. 'Was it day or night?'

'Uh,' Renshaw said. 'Night, I believe. I think it was somewhere around nine o'clock.'

Schofield began to nod to himself.

'Why?' Renshaw said.

'I think I know why the elephant seals attacked us.'

'Why?'

'Remember I said that the only group of divers to have approached that cave unharmed was Gant's group.'

'Yeah.'

'And I said that it was because her group had used low-audibility breathing gear.'

Renshaw said, 'Yeah. So did we. And as I recall it, the seals attacked us anyway.'

Schofield smiled a crooked smile. 'Yeah. I know. But I think I figure out why. We dived at night.'

'At night?'

'Yes. And so did your people, and so did Barnaby's men. Your people dived at nine o'clock. Barnaby's at around 8:00 p.m. *Gant's team*, however, went down at two in the afternoon. They were the only dive team to go down to that cavern in the *daytime*.'

Renshaw picked up what Schofield was saying. 'You think those elephant seals are diurnal?'

'I think that's a good possibility,' Schofield said.

Renshaw nodded slowly. It was quite common among unusually aggressive or poisonous animals to operate on what is known as a diurnal cycle. A diurnal cycle is essentially a twelve-hour passive-aggressive cycle – the animal is passive by day, aggressive by night.

'I glad you figured that out,' Renshaw said. 'I'll keep it in mind for the next time I stumble onto a nest of radiation-infected elephant seals who want to defend their territory.'

Schofield smiled. The three of them descended the gangway. At the bottom, they were met by a middle-aged Marine sergeant.

'Lieutenant Schofield,' the sergeant saluted Schofield. 'There's a car waiting for you, sir.'

'Sergeant. I'm going nowhere but the hospital, to check on Lance-Corporal Gant. If anybody wants me to go anywhere else, I ain't going.'

'That's okay with me, sir,' the sergeant smiled. 'My orders are to take you, Mr Renshaw and Miss Hensleigh to wherever you want to go.'

Schofield nodded, looked to Renshaw and Kirsty. They shrugged, sure.

'Sounds good to me,' Schofield said. 'Lead the way.'

The sergeant led them to a navy-blue Buick with dark, tinted windows. He held the car door open and Schofield got in.

A man was already sitting in the back seat when Schofield sat down.

Schofield froze when he saw the gun in the man's hand.

'Have a seat, Scarecrow,' Sergeant-Major Charles 'Chuck' Kozlowski said as Schofield sat down in the back seat of the Buick. Renshaw and Kirsty got in behind Schofield. Kirsty let out a gasp when she saw Kozlowski's gun.

Kozlowski was a short man, with a clean-shaven face and thick, black eyebrows. He was wearing a khaki Marine day uniform.

The sergeant got into the driver's seat and started the car.

'I'm terribly sorry, Scarecrow,' the highest-ranking non-commissioned officer in the Marine Corps said. 'But you and your friends here represent a loose end that cannot be allowed to stand.'

'And what's that?' Schofield said, exasperated.

'You know about the ICG.'

Schofield said, 'I told Jack Walsh about the ICG. Are you going to kill him, too.'

'Maybe not immediately,' Kozlowski said. 'But in good time, yes. You, on the other hand, represent a more immediate threat. We wouldn't want you going to the press, now, would we? No doubt, they will find out

678

about what went on down at Wilkes Ice Station, but the media will get what the ICG tells them, not what *you* tell them.'

'How can you kill your own men?' Schofield said.

Kozlowski said, 'You still don't get it, do you, Scarecrow.'

'I don't *get* how you can kill your own men and think you're doing the country a favour.'

'Jesus, Scarecrow, *you weren't even supposed to be there in the first place.*'

That stopped Schofield. 'What?'

'Think about it,' Kozlowski said. 'How did you come to get to Wilkes Ice Station before anybody else?'

Schofield thought back, right to the very beginning. He had been on the *Shreveport*, in Sydney. The rest of the fleet had gone back to Pearl, but the *Shreveport* had stayed down there for repairs. It was then that the distress signal had come through.

'That's right,' Kozlowski said, reading Schofield's thoughts. 'You were in for repairs in Sydney when the *Shreveport* received the distress signal from Wilkes. And then some dumb-fuck *civilian* sent you down there right away.'

Schofield remembered the voice of the Undersecretary of Defence coming in over the speakers of the briefing room on board the *Shreveport*, instructing him to go down to Wilkes and protect the spacecraft.

Kozlowski said, 'Scarecrow, the Intelligence Convergence Group doesn't set out to kill American units. It exists to *protect* Americans –'

'From what? The truth?' Schofield retorted.

'We could have had an Army Ranger unit *filled* with ICG men down at that station six hours after you got there. They could have taken that station – *even if* the French had already got there – and held it and no American soldiers would have had to have been killed.'

Kozlowski shook his head. 'But no, you just happened to be in the area. And that's why we stack units like yours with ICG men – for this very eventuality. In a perfect world, the ICG would get there first every time. But if the ICG can't get there first, then we make sure that reconnaissance units like yours are properly constituted so as to ensure that whatever information is found at the site *stays* at the site. For the sake of national security, of course.'

'You kill your own countrymen,' Schofield said.

'Scarecrow. This didn't have to happen. You were just in the wrong place at the wrong time. If anything, you got to Wilkes Ice Station too fast. If this had all been done as it should have been done, I wouldn't have to kill you now.'

The Buick came to the guard station at the outer fence of the dockyard. A boom gate was lowered in front of it. The driver wound down his window and had a short conversation with the boom gate guard.

And then suddenly, the door next to Kozlowski was yanked open from the outside and an armed Naval Policeman appeared in the open doorway with his gun aimed squarely at Kozlowski's head.

'Sir, would you please get out of the car.'

Kozlowski's face darkened. 'Son, do you have *any* idea who you are talking to?' He growled.

'No, he doesn't,' a voice said from outside the car. 'But I do,' Jack Walsh said as he appeared outside the open car door.

Schofield, Kirsty and Renshaw all got out of the car, totally confused. The navy-blue Buick was surrounded by a swarm of Naval Police, all with their guns out.

Schofield turned to Walsh. 'What's going on? How did you know?'

Walsh nodded over Schofield's shoulder. 'Looks to me like you got yourself a guardian angel.'

Schofield spun, looked for a familiar face amid the crowd. At first he didn't see a single face that he knew.

And then suddenly, he did. But it wasn't a face he expected to see.

There, standing ten yards behind the ring of Naval Police surrounding the Buick, with his hands in his pockets, was Andrew Trent.

As Kozlowski and his driver were taken away in handcuffs, Schofield walked over to Trent.

Standing with Trent were a man and a woman whom Schofield had never met before. Trent introduced them as Pete and Alison Cameron. They were reporters with *The Washington Post*.

Schofield asked Trent what had happened. How had

the Naval Police – backed up by Jack Walsh – known to stop Kozlowski's car?

Trent explained. A couple of days ago, he had seen the amateur footage of the *Wasp*'s damaged flight deck on TV. Trent knew missile damage when he saw it. Then, when he learned that the *Wasp* was heading back to Pearl – 'from a training exercise *in the Southern Ocean*' – he jumped on a plane to Hawaii.

The Camerons had come along with him. For, if by some chance, Shane Schofield, or indeed, *any* survivors from Wilkes Ice Station were on board the *Wasp* then it would be the story – and the scoop – of a lifetime. Other reporters saw a damaged flight deck. The Camerons saw the inside running on the Wilkes Ice Station story.

But when they had got to the dockyard at Pearl, Trent had seen Chuck Kozlowski standing next to a navy-blue Buick, waiting for the *Wasp* to dock.

Trent had felt a sudden chill. Why was Kozlowski here? Had the ICG won – as it had in Peru – and was Kozlowski here to congratulate the traitors. Or was he here for some other reason? For if Schofield had *survived*, then the ICG would almost certainly want to eliminate him.

And so Trent and the two reporters had just watched and waited. And then, when they saw Schofield emerge from the ship and get escorted to Kozlowski's Buick, Trent had called the only person he could think of who could – and would – pull rank on Chuck Kozlowski.

Jack Walsh.

'Who'd have thought it?' Welsh said, coming over. 'There I am, on the bridge of my wrecked boat, minding my own business, when my comtech comes running in and says he's got some guy on the external switch who says he *has* to talk to me. Says it's an emergency regarding Lieutenant Schofield. *Says his name is Andrew Trent.*' Walsh smiled. 'I figured I oughta take the call.'

Schofield just shook his head, amazed.

'You've been through a lot,' Trent said, putting his arm around Schofield's shoulder.

'You should talk,' Schofield said. 'I'd like to hear about Peru sometime.'

'You will, Shane, you will. But first, I have a proposition for you. How would you like to be on the front page of *The Washington Post*?'

Schofield just smiled.

On June 23 – two days after Schofield and the *Wasp* docked at Pearl – *The Washington Post* ran a front-page story containing a photo of Shane Schofield and Andrew Trent holding a copy of the previous day's *Post* between them. Beneath the photo were displayed copies of their official United States Marine Corps death certificates. Schofield's death certificate was three days old. Trent's was over a year old.

The headline read:

ACCORDING TO THE US MILITARY,
THESE TWO MEN ARE OFFICIALLY DEAD.

The accompanying story about the events that transpired at Wilkes Ice Station – a feature that ran for three pages – was written by Peter and Alison Cameron.

Later stories that ran about the events at Wilkes Ice Station told of the ICG and the systematic infiltration by it of elite military units, universities and private corporations. Flashbulbs popped across the country for the next six weeks as ICG moles were expunged from various regiments, institutions and companies and charged under various statutes with espionage.

No mention, however, was made in *any* of the newspaper and TV reports about the presence of French and British troops at Wilkes Ice Station.

Rumours abounded in the tabloids about which other countries had sent troops to Wilkes Ice Station. Iraq. China. Even Brazil had rated a mention.

It was claimed in some quarters that *The Washington Post* knew exactly who else had been down there. One rival newspaper even went so far as to say that the President himself had paid a surprise visit to Katharine Graham – the legendary owner of the *Post* – and asked her, in the name of America's diplomatic relations, not to publish the names of the countries who had been present at Wilkes Ice Station. This rumour was never confirmed.

The *Post*, however, never mentioned Britain or France.

It reported that a battle had taken place down in Antartica, but it steadfastly maintained that it did not know the identity of the opposing force or forces. Every article that appeared in the *Post* simply said that the conflict had been against 'enemies unknown'.

In any case, the Wilkes Ice Station story ran for six whole weeks before it was forgotten.

A few days after the *Wasp* returned, the NATO conference in Washington D.C. concluded.

Every TV and newspaper article on the event showed the smiling faces of the American, British and French delegates standing on the steps of the Capitol Building, shaking hands in front of their interwoven flags, smiling for the cameras, and proclaiming that the NATO alliance would continue for another twenty years.

The French representative, Monsieur Pierre Dufresne was quoted as saying, 'This is the strongest treaty on earth.' When asked where this strength emanated from, Dufresne said, 'Our *genuine friendship* is our bond.'

In a private room at the Naval Hospital at Pearl Harbor, Libby Gant lay in a bed with her eyes closed. A soft beam of sunlight filtered in through the room's window and draped itself across her bed. Gant was still in a coma.

'Libby? Libby?' A woman's voice said, invading her consciousness.

Slowly, Gant's eyes opened, and she saw her sister, Denise, standing above her.

Denise smiled. 'Well, hey there, sleepy head.'

Gant struggled to open her eyes. When she did, she just said, 'Hey.'

Denise offered Gant a crooked smile. 'You have a visitor.'

'What?' Gant said.

Denise cocked her head to the left. Gant looked over that way and saw Schofield, slumped in the guest's chair over by the window, fast asleep.

He had a pair of silver Oakley sunglasses perched on top of his head. His eyes – and the two scars that cut down across them – were there for all the world to see.

Denise whispered, 'He's been here ever since they fixed his rib. Wouldn't leave until you woke up. He gave one interview to *The Washington Post* and told the rest of them to come back after you woke up.'

Gant just looked at Schofield, asleep under the window. And she smiled.

EPILOGUE

Near Isla Santa Ines, Chile
30 November

It was a small island, one of the many hundreds to the south of the Straits of Magellan, at the bottom of Chile, at the bottom of South America, at the bottom of the world.

Barely five hundred miles south of the island, lay the South Shetland islands and Antarctica. This small island was the closest one got to Antarctica without actually being there.

The boy's name was José and he lived in a small fishing village on the west coast of the island. The village lay on the edge of the bay that the old women called *La Bahía de la Aguila Plata*, 'The Bay of the Silver Eagle'.

Local lore said that many years ago, a great big silver bird, with a tail of fire trailing behind it, flew into the sea just outside the bay. The bird, the women said, had offended God with its speed and its beauty, and so God had set it alight and cast it into the sea.

José didn't believe such stories. He was ten now, and as far as he was concerned, it was just another ghost story that the old women told to frighten small children.

Today was diving day and José planned to dive for oysters, and hopefully sell them to his father for pocket money.

The small boy dived into the sea and swam downwards. At this time of the afternoon, the ocean currents were coming in toward the island. José hoped they would bring the oysters with them.

He came to the bottom and quickly found his first oyster of the day, but he also found something else.

A small piece of plastic.

José grabbed the piece of plastic and headed back up to the surface. When he broke the surface, he peered at the strange object in his hand. It was rectangular in shape, and quite small. It was heavily faded, but José could read the name engraved on it:

NIEMEYER.

José frowned at the name badge. Then he threw the worthless piece of plastic away, and resumed his search for oysters.

HAMMOND INNES

Delta Connection

Pan Books £5.99

His latest spellbinding international adventure

A desperate escape from Romania in turmoil . . . a violent
introduction to new rules of warfare on the Afghan borders
. . . an icy struggle for survival amongst the world's highest
mountains. Death follows all who seek beyond the 'Delta
Connection' . . .

For Paul Cartwright, a young English mining engineer, the
quest begins at the huge Black Sea port of Constantza.
After the killing of a member of the secret police, he is
forced to escape by way of the Danube Delta, in the
company of a strange young woman.

The horror of her past life is poured out as they lie side-by-
side through a night of storm on an island of reeds. There
also gradually emerges a picture of Vikki, her mysterious,
domineering sister – known as 'the Little Sultana'. Years
previously, Cartwright had first encountered Vikki as a little
girl dancing alone in front of a captivated restaurant. His
own feet responding to the beat, the two of them had met
occasionally over the years – dancing their way into a hidden
world now about to prove most deadly dangerous.

Is Vikki really the daughter of a sultan? Where is the realm
she claims for her own? Above all, what is the hidden wealth
that now draws the Russian Mafia into the search? Mystery
will continue to dog Cartwright's footsteps through the
Khyber Pass and up into the 'lost' fastnesses of the Pamirs.
And, though the way ahead seems suicidal, somewhere in
those towering mountains must lie the answers.

JAY R. BONANSINGA

Head Case

Pan Books £5.99

Sheer suspense . . . breakneck pace . . . horrifying surprises

Following an appalling highway accident, the mystery patient nicknamed 'John Doe' wakes up in hospital suffering total amnesia. His very first visitor, supposedly, seems hell-bent on killing him. After a narrow escape, the bewildered amnesiac goes on the run – plunging ever deeper into a hideous walking nightmare where the whole world seems his enemy.

His sole ally is Jessie Bales, a small-town private investigator who agrees to help trace his former identity. But her initial discoveries are downright terrifying – a hotel room littered with grotesque 'snuff' photographs, the diary of a psychotic madman . . . and a trail of mutilated corpses. Is Jessie's new client responsible for this carnage? Or merely the victim of a diabolic frame-up?

And meanwhile dark presences continue to stalk them, as they close in on a truth more sinister than they could dare imagine.

'Enjoyable psychological thriller . . . Bonansinga maintains a reader's interest as he unravels the disturbing mystery'
Publishers Weekly

JOHN J. NANCE

The Last Hostage

Pan Books £5.99

Bestselling author of Pandora's Clock *and* Medusa's Child

High above the Rocky Mountains, crisis engulfs an inter-city flight as its 130 passengers listen in horror to the demands of an unseen hijacker. Unless a child murderer is hunted down, arrested and indicted within only eight hours, the aircraft will be blown out of the sky.

With the airline company in total confusion, the media in a frenzy, and the mystery hijacker forcing the 737 into increasingly dangerous midair manoeuvres, the FBI reluc-tantly calls in its nearest available hostage negotiator: a rookie female agent and psychologist named Katherine Bronsky.

She is immediately hurled into an impossible contest of wills between the desperate man fingering the trigger of a bomb and stonewalling Justice Department officials with no real intention of meeting his demands. When Bronsky's desper-ate attempts to negotiate backfire, she too becomes a hos-tage on the plane flying to hell.

Now Bronsky's only hope of saving her fellow passengers is to solve the shocking mystery that surrounds the killing of an eleven-year-old girl in a dark Connecticut forest two years earlier. And to achieve that she has only a laptop computer . . . and the few precious hours still remaining to them.

'A champ at dreaming up spellbinding premises'
Publishers Weekly

'A thrilling ride . . . doesn't let a reader go until the last page'
People

STEPHEN RHODES

The Velocity of Money

Pan Books £5.99

Is this the scenario for the next great crash?

In an age of electronic trading and speculative frenzies, fortunes can be made and lost within seconds. So, when lawyer Rick Hansen lands a job at a blue-chip global investment firm, he thinks he's entered the fast lane. Then suspicion arises that his predecessor's suicide was really murder . . .

Layer by layer, Hansen uncovers evidence that someone nearby is involved in the biggest potential swindle in history. For a shadowy cabal of financiers has found a way of precipitating the most devastating crash since October 1929. And, as disaster day approaches, time is running out to avert worldwide chaos – and for Hansen to save his own life.

A terrifying portrait of a market beholden to computers, electronic money, and split-second technology – in a market ripe for cataclysmic manipulation.

'Rhodes is an insider who uses his knowledge in a way that couldn't be more frightening. So real and believable, it's hard to put down'
Washington Times

'An impressive first novel – crisp dialogue, vivid description and financial jargon make this novel a smart read. A-rating'
Entertainment Weekly

'A bestseller collage of Clancy and Grisham'
Euromoney